T0121981

EX-COMMUNICATION

EX-COMMUNICATION

A NOVEL

Peter Clines

B\D\W\Y
BROADWAY BOOKS
NEW YORK

Copyright © 2013 by Peter Clines

Published in the United States by Broadway Books, an imprint of the Crown Publishing Group, a division of Random House, Inc., New York.
www.crownpublishing.com

BROADWAY BOOKS and its logo B \ D \ W \ Y, are trademarks of Random House, Inc.

Library of Congress Cataloging-in-Publication Data
Clines, Peter, 1969–
  Ex-communication : a novel / Peter Clines.—First edition
      pages   cm
  1. Zombies—Fiction. 2. Superheroes—Fiction. 3. Los Angeles (Calif.)—Fiction. I. Title.
PS3603.L563E93 2013
813'.6—dc23
2013007786

ISBN 978-0-385-34682-5
eISBN 978-0-385-34683-2

Cover illustration: Jonathan Bartlett
Cover design: Christopher Brand

First Edition

146122990

Prologue
NOW

"THIS IS THE northwest corner," shouted a man on the radio. A gunshot blasted over the open channel. "Twenty . . . something. We're under attack! Two maybe three hundred of them. We need help!" The call was punctuated by another shot.

Captain John Carter Freedom of the 456th Unbreakables, considered temporarily on leave from his post at Project Krypton, was only a few blocks from the northwest corner of the Big Wall. He heard two more sharp pops echo between the buildings. Rifles, but unfamiliar to his ears. Civilian weapons. That lined up with the voice's confusion at radio protocol. Freedom was pretty sure it had been the wall guard who went by the name Makana.

He looked down at the kids in front of him. Two boys and a girl, barely into their teens. All three of them sat on the curb with their hands zip-tied together behind their backs. They'd been trying to steal a car for a quick joyride when he found them. They'd been cowed by his appearance and surrendered without a fuss.

Most people were cowed by Freedom's appearance. He was a bald giant of a man, almost seven feet tall and over three hundred pounds of solid muscle. A leather duster hung open across his broad chest, and a silver sheriff's star sat on one lapel. Underneath the duster he wore a tan T-shirt and pants checkered with digital camouflage. Strapped to his thigh was a holster the size of a loaf of bread. He rarely had to draw the pistol it held.

A third and fourth shot rang in the air. The kids' heads swiveled back and forth from Freedom's face to the direction of the sound. One of the boys had gone wide-eyed with terror. They knew what the shots meant. They were aware of how vulnerable they were, tied up on the ground.

"You'll be fine," Freedom told them. "There's a deputy on the way to take charge of you."

Three more gunshots. And between the rounds he could hear a growing noise. The *click-click-click* that made life near the Big Wall so rough for some. The sound of teeth.

The girl opened her mouth to say something, but it vanished under the snap of his leather duster as he spun and bolted for the northeast corner. The captain had been quick for his size before joining the Army's super-soldier project. Now he could run a three-minute mile without breaking a sweat, do five of them before he even started to feel winded.

The gunfire was near constant by the time he reached the northeast corner. It made Los Angeles sound like Iraq. He could see the half-dozen guards on top of the wall. Four of them were shooting down into the area beyond the barrier. The other two were pushing back the figures climbing onto the upper deck.

Freedom never broke stride. His legs flexed and hurled him twenty feet into the air. His duster flapped around him, and he steeled himself for combat.

The top of the Big Wall was a continuous platform made from old pallets and plywood. A double line of rope served as a railing. It was a temporary fix until a more permanent bastion could be built. Freedom hit the wood surface just south of the large square that was the northwest corner and took in the situation as he straightened up.

This corner of the Big Wall sat at the intersection of Sunset and Vine in downtown Hollywood, right at the center of the road. A Borders bookstore and a vandalized Chase bank stood just outside the barrier.

Almost a thousand exes stood outside the wall, too. Thirty months since the world ended and people still called them exes rather than zombies. "Ex-humans" was just easier to deal with somehow. Even the military had used the term.

Back when there had been a functioning military, the captain reminded himself.

The former citizens of Los Angeles crowded the intersection beyond the wall, filling the air with the endless sound of chattering teeth. Even when there was nothing in their mouths, their jaws gnashed open and closed like machines. Some of those mouths were lined with gray teeth. Others held a mess of jagged stumps that splintered even more as they banged together. Most of them were coated with blood and gore. Their flesh was the color of old chalk, spotted with dark bruises where blood had pooled inside the skin. Most of their eyes were dusty and dull, but more than a few had empty sockets gaping in their faces. Many of the exes had deep cuts or punctures that would never heal but also didn't stop them. Some were missing fingers, hands, or whole limbs.

Something was different about the horde, though, and Freedom couldn't put his finger on what.

The wall guards fired into the crowd with their motley collection of weapons. Rifles scavenged from personal collections or motion-picture armories. A dreadlocked man he recognized as Makana was trying to keep them organized, but there was an air of desperation around the guards. One of them swung his rifle like a baseball bat and clubbed a thin figure off the platform. The guard turned and swung again. The blow was wild, but it caught his next target in the side of the head and tipped it back off the wall.

The guard was scared. Now that Freedom was on top of the wall, he could see that *all* the guards were scared. He wasn't sure what had them so spooked. He drew his massive sidearm, a modified AA-12 shotgun that had been cut down to a pistol for his huge hands. The armorer had nicknamed it Lady Liberty. His gaze went down to the horde again.

Some of the exes were moving quicker than the others. They ran at the Big Wall and lunged up. They grabbed handholds and kicked with their feet, pulling themselves up the barrier. A handful of exes had turned their attention to Freedom as he landed. Behind their dead eyes, Legion glared out at the giant officer.

Over the years, the people of Los Angeles had developed methods and procedures for dealing with the undead. The mindless exes were still a threat, but it was a contained threat. One they had lots of practice with.

Legion had changed everything. The exes were pawns for him to control. He could slip from zombie to zombie, using them as his puppets. They could be his eyes and ears. Or his hands and teeth. He made them smart. He made them unpredictable.

Freedom pulled back his boot and kicked a climbing ex just as its head rose above the top of the wall. The dead man flew back into the crowd. It took Freedom's mind a moment to register what he'd just seen, and then he realized what had caused the panic.

Most of the exes storming the Big Wall were wearing helmets.

Several of them wore motorcycle helmets with Lexan visors. A few looked like SWAT or National Guard issue. Freedom saw a few football helmets and hard hats. Even a few gleaming bicycle helmets, useless as they were.

Killing exes had always been a numbers game. Legion had shifted the numbers more in his favor and shaken the guards in the process. Their practiced methods and procedures were crumbling. They were hesitating and second-guessing shots.

Freedom had to restore morale and get their fire focused

before things fell apart. The Big Wall was on the edge of being overwhelmed. The attack was spread across a section almost forty feet long and, from the look of it, another twenty or thirty around the corner. Legion had at least four hundred exes under his control. Half a dozen civilians to defend seventy feet of ground against a few hundred opponents.

Not great odds.

A dead man wearing a red construction helmet climbed onto the platform. Its fingernails clawed at the wooden platform. Freedom stomped on one of the hands and took the ex's head off with another kick.

Makana and another noticed him and he saw their shoulders relax. The sheriff's star and his Army uniform still had that effect on people.

"Take your time," ordered Freedom. His voice bellowed out of his barrel chest, louder than the sound of teeth and rifle reports. He stabbed a thick finger at the horde. "Make them count." To accent his words, Lady Liberty roared and threw two more dead things back from the wall. At close range a twelve-gauge round packed enough raw force to shatter a Kevlar helmet and the skull inside it.

The panicked shooting slowed. A dead man with a biker helmet staggered back and fell. One in National Guard headgear stumbled from a shot, then threw itself back at the wall. A figure in a football helmet dropped with a bullet in its eye.

More of the exes fell, but more of them reached the wall. A dead woman made it to the platform, but a guard smashed her off with a baseball bat. Another withered hand slapped onto the platform. Captain Freedom grabbed it by the wrist and pushed it away. The ex, a dead man in an Oxford shirt, fell back into the horde and was crushed under dozens of feet. Freedom turned and cracked Lady Liberty's muzzle across the jaw of a teenage boy with a batting helmet and a bloody Atari T-shirt. The dead thing staggered back from the blow and vanished over the edge.

Captain Freedom shouted a few quick orders and got the guards spaced out to cover more area. "All units," he called over the radio, "this is Six. We have a major incursion at the northwest corner of the Big Wall. Request immediate assistance."

At least two people replied, but their words were drowned out by another burst from Lady Liberty. One of the rounds shattered a bicycle helmet and pulped the skull beneath it. The ex dropped and vanished into the tide of dead things below. Two of the others he hit struggled back to their feet.

The guard closest to him, a rail-thin woman with gray-streaked hair, paused to reload her rifle. It was an old M1, and Freedom was impressed by how fast she loaded the magazine without pinching her thumb. She brought it back up just in time to shoot a chalk-skinned man in the face. The round took a chunk out of the Lexan visor of the ex's helmet and knocked it back off the Big Wall.

A dead body threw itself up onto the platform a few feet away and struggled to its feet. Freedom took four quick steps and clotheslined it with a sweep of his massive arm. The ex pinwheeled back off the wall.

Another guard near the far end stopped to reload, but an ex crawled over the edge of the platform just as he pulled the magazine. He slammed the rifle stock into the zombie's face, right below the brim of its yellow hard hat, then smashed it again when the dead woman grabbed at his knee. The ex trembled and fell limp across the plywood.

The guard with the baseball bat, a wiry man with Asian features, swung a line drive that knocked one of Legion's puppets into the air. There was too much force behind the swing, though, and the man stumbled forward on the follow-through. His body bent over the ropes and the lines flexed. He dropped the bat, flailed for the lines, and added to his own momentum. An ex grabbed one of the waving hands and threw itself off the wall, dragging the man with it.

Freedom leaped to help the man, soaring two dozen feet

along the top of the wall, but it was too late. The exes closest to the wall passed the guard back over their heads, carrying him away from safety. He had time to look back at his friends before the dead things dropped him on the ground and fell on him. Then he started screaming.

The captain clenched his jaw. He fired three bursts into the swarm of exes before his pistol ran dry. Half of the exes dropped and the guard stopped screaming. Freedom half hoped he'd put the man out of his misery.

He kicked away another ex, loaded a new drum onto Lady Liberty, and sized up the situation. The line was too thin. It was down to himself and five guards. It wasn't even five minutes into the assault, but he knew which way it was going to go if something didn't change.

Movement caught the corner of his eye as his pistol spat out three-round bursts at the undead. Back at his position another ex had made it onto the platform, a gaunt figure with a bare chest and a black SWAT helmet. It crawled across the platform and rolled over the far edge.

Legion was inside.

Freedom tensed for a moment as the dead thing crawled to its feet. One ex compromising the security of the Wall could mean the end of everything. But it was too far away for a kill shot from here, and he couldn't risk leaving the Wall.

Then he realized what the ex had landed next to. Huge armored fingers wrapped around the zombie's helmet and lifted it into the air. Legion batted at the steel digits and swore in Spanish. Its voice was a dry rasp that barely carried over the sounds of gunfire and teeth.

The blue and silver titan stood just shy of nine feet tall and six feet wide. Flags decorated its shoulders, and each of its metal arms ended in a three-fingered fist a little bigger than a football. The battlesuit swung an arm and hurled the undead creature back over the wall. It sailed through the air and hit the pavement outside.

"Situation?" barked Danielle Morris from inside the armor. She had the suit in public-address mode and her voice echoed across the corner.

Freedom fired three more bursts into the horde. The Cerberus Battlesuit wouldn't've been his first choice for backup. It was powerful, but it no longer had ranged weapons. It was also too big and heavy for the platform on top of the Big Wall.

"You're the second line," he told her. "If anything gets past us, it's yours."

Legion took that moment to send another ex scampering over the wall. Cerberus took two steps, scooped up the dead teenager, and threw it over the barrier. "Got it," she said.

The huge officer turned and found himself face-to-face with a dead woman in a football helmet. The ex lunged at him, but its gnashing jaws were blocked by the face mask. Freedom gut-punched the creature and it flew back down into the chattering horde. He moved along the wall back to his starting position, blasting exes wherever he could. They'd put down close to a hundred since he arrived on the scene, and the dead were still coming.

Two more guards, a man and a woman, ran along the Big Wall from the east. They added their fire and helped hold everything beyond the corner of the barrier. It meant somewhere else had thinner defenses now. Freedom hoped they'd hold.

He heard Cerberus move behind him, the muffled clomp of metal toes and the hiss of servos, and another ex came sailing back over the wall. He hadn't even seen that one get past them. Not a good sign.

The thin woman with the gray streaks reloaded her M1 again. She shot him a nervous look he'd seen in other firefights. It was the last of her ammunition. He fired two bursts to cover her and Lady Liberty's slide clanged empty again.

The guard heard it and looked up. As she did, an ex in a gold CHP helmet wrapped its pale fingers around her ankle and yanked. She screamed and slid toward the edge as the dead man pulled itself up onto the platform. She kicked it once in the head with her free leg. It snarled at her.

Freedom took two steps and slammed his boot into the ex's chin. The head whipped back and its neck snapped with a sharp crack. It tumbled off the platform and knocked another one off the wall on its way down.

The woman scampered back and grabbed her rifle. Freedom grabbed another drum from his belt. He had one more after this.

He turned his attention to the horde and something fluttered in the corner of his eye. His weapon came up. And then he realized they might have a chance.

A woman stood a yard to his left. She was dressed head to toe in skintight black, crisscrossed with charcoal straps and belts. Holsters rode low on her thighs, like the ones on a Special Forces soldier or an old-time gunslinger. A wide hood hid her face in shadows, and her cloak settled around her like a parachute.

"Took you long enough," snarled Cerberus from somewhere behind him.

Stealth's Glock 18C pistols were already out and firing. The rounds came so fast Freedom thought the weapons were on full automatic. Then he saw her aim twitch and realized she was firing single shots, each one finding a new target.

More than a dozen of Legion's puppets dropped, their strings cut. Stealth took a step forward and her cloak swirled in the night breezes. The pistols never stopped. Every round found the open space in a helmet.

Within thirty seconds she'd dropped as many exes. Maybe more. She spun on her heel and kicked another as its head cleared the platform. The hard hat it wore cracked under her boot.

The pistols spun in her hands, came in close to her waist, and her fingers whirled. The Glocks came back up with fresh magazines and continued to fire. Freedom knew decorated marksmen and snipers who would've been in awe of the woman's accuracy.

He fired off another burst from his own weapon and saw an ex in a military helmet drop, its face an unrecognizable mess. A zombie slipped over the wall closer to the corner and flew back out a moment later. A second form followed it. The ex hit the ground hard. The second figure hovered in the air on the far side of the intersection.

St. George, the hero once known as the Mighty Dragon, was a solid six feet tall, and the muscles of his wiry body were visible even under his stitch-covered jacket. His golden brown hair gleamed in the spotlights from the Big Wall. It brushed his shoulders and matched the leather of the jacket.

Freedom felt his own shoulders relax a bit.

* * *

St. George settled in the air above the crowd of exes. Even with a quick sweep across the horde, he could pick out unique features on each of them. They'd been people once, after all. Before they'd died.

A gore-faced girl with a bright green tank top and charred-black hands. A Hasidic man whose beard was caked with blood. A dark-skinned woman with a quartet of bloody bullet holes in her chest. A little boy missing his lower jaw. A knife-thin man in a leather trench coat. About half of them wore some kind of protective helmet. One large, bald ex glared at him through a hockey mask before it gave him the finger with both hands.

He took in a deep breath, felt the tickle of mixing chemicals in the back of his throat, and sent a wave of fire washing down over the swarm. It lit up the intersection with golden light. He swung his head and washed the flames across the back line of the horde.

Half of the exes stared at the flying hero even as their hair and clothes caught fire, their teeth still clicking away. The others, the ones wearing helmets and hard hats, flinched. They moved in perfect synchronization, all turning their heads away to the right as they raised their left arms to shield their faces. A handful of them glared up at him.

St. George drifted down into the crowd, grabbed a few exes by their necks, and hurled them back away from the wall. He moved through the horde like a man weeding a garden, plucking one dead plant after another. Over a dozen of them crashed against the buildings and pavement before all of them shifted their attention to him. The horde took in a rasping breath and spoke with one voice.

"Next time, *pinche*," they growled.

A shift rippled through the crowd of exes as Legion's guidance vanished. Their expressions sagged and their teeth started clicking again. The ones closest to St. George stumbled toward him on unsteady legs.

He drifted into the air, away from the grasping hands, and back to the platform. A few more gunshots rang out, but he could see the horde was settling down. There were still a few dozen exes pawing at the wall, but without Legion controlling them it was a mindless action that would never get their feet off the ground. Climbing was too complicated for them.

"I think he's gone," St. George called out. Wisps of smoke drifted out of his mouth and nose, like an idling engine. His boots thudded against the platform across from Stealth. "Everyone okay here?"

Makana shook his head. "We lost Daniel."

Another guard raised a trembling hand. There was blood on his fingers. "I . . . I think I got bit," he said.

The thin woman eyed the man and raised her rifle a few inches. "You think?"

"It was all so fast," he said, his eyes locked on the rifle's muzzle. "I mighta just cut myself on something. That's probably all it is."

"Get over to the hospital," said St. George. "Get checked out. Cerberus, can you go with him?"

The battlesuit tipped its head and focused on the man. He walked down a wooden staircase and headed down the street. Cerberus followed a few steps behind him.

"Thanks for the assist, boss," Makana said to St. George, and then added a nod to Freedom that made his dreadlocks swing. "Bosses. Didn't think he'd have so many bodies ready to move that fast."

Captain Freedom gazed down at the exes. "Helmets," he said. "This is new."

Stealth looked at the guards, then turned her head to Freedom. "How much ammunition was expended in this assault?"

"Most of it," said Makana. He glanced at the other guards. They added shrugs and nods. "I've only got one mag left after this."

"I'm almost out," said the thin woman.

"I think I've got a couple rounds," said another man, "and two clips after that."

Twin streamers of smoke curled up and out of St. George's nostrils. "I guess we got here just in time. Let's get a resupply," he said, "and some relief guards. Captain, can you stay with them until everything gets here?"

"Of course, sir," said the giant officer.

"And somebody find out if Daniel has . . . had a family."

"I think he had a boyfriend," said Makana.

St. George nodded. "Let's get word to him then."

"It is unlikely Legion will make another attempt tonight," said Stealth. She holstered her weapons and focused on the crowd of exes below. "His demonstrated impatience and the mix of headgear imply this was the majority of his scavenged armor, possibly all of it."

St. George raised a skeptical brow. "Are you sure?"

"He has never returned in less than five hours once he has

been driven back. It is more likely he may strike at another part of the Wall, but I would say the odds are against that as well."

"So, is this what things are going to be like now?" asked the thin woman. "Because this sucked."

Stealth's expression was hidden beneath the blank fabric of her mask. Her body language was another story. St. George had known her long enough to see the subtle signs.

"Okay," he said, "if you've got this in hand, Captain, we'll leave you guys to it and get back to our patrol."

Freedom gave them a quick salute. St. George held out his hand and Stealth grabbed his wrist without a word. He focused on a spot between his shoulder blades and rose into the air. He lifted the woman and they shot into the sky, her cloak billowing behind them.

St. George sailed up to the top of the half-finished building at this corner of the Big Wall. If the world hadn't ended it would've been an office building or apartments by now. Instead, it was a framework of rusted girders and sheetrock. It gave them a good view of the north and west sides of the Wall.

Stealth lowered herself onto one of the beams. She held onto his hand even though her balance was perfect. She had a firm grip. St. George hung in the air near her, his fingers threaded between hers. "You've been expecting something like this, haven't you?"

"I have," she said. "It was only a matter of time before Legion realized he could use the resources of the city to outfit the exes. This will complicate matters for a time. Our ammunition stores are strained as it is."

"But you've already planned for it?"

"I have."

"So what's bothering you?"

"Before the assault, Captain Freedom detained three teenagers attempting to steal a car."

"So?"

"Petty crime has risen almost ten percent in the past few months since the Big Wall was completed. It is a distraction we do not need now that Legion has discovered these new assets."

"Yeah, but it's a good sign, in a way," said St. George. "If we're getting big enough to start having a crime problem, it means we've got a pretty sizable population. Things are getting better overall."

All around the Big Wall, and as far as they could see, figures shuffled and stumbled in the streets. The sound of their teeth popped and cracked in the night like a hundred distant bonfires. Even at night, St. George could see thousands of them, and he knew there were thousands more out there in the darkness. Stealth said there were just over five million exes in Los Angeles. In three years he hadn't seen anything to make him think otherwise.

At the best, every one of them was a mindless machine with no purpose past killing and feeding. A pack of ten could strip a person to bones in less than half an hour. At the worst, the undead were harboring Legion.

Stealth shook her head inside her hood. "As always," she said, "you are an optimist."

"Well, what is it they say?" St. George shrugged. " 'Better the devil you know . . .' "

Location , Location , Location
THEN

THE ARROW ON my GPS was starting to turn, but the road looked like it was turning with it. We'd been driving for about an hour at that point. Neither of us said much. We didn't speak the same language, so it wasn't that surprising.

My driver, Nikita (named after Khrushchev, his manager had told me), was an inch taller than me, maybe twice as wide, and with a permanent scowl cutting across his stubble. Picture every stereotypical Russian you've ever seen. The reason it's the stereotype is because so many of them look like that. Nikita's one of them. The scent of cloves hung on him like cologne, but he had the good manners not to light one up while we were in the car together.

To be honest, we tried to talk a couple times. I think that's just human nature. We've got another person next to us, so we feel obligated to say something. Every now and then I'd ask about our progress or part of the landscape or offer to show him the GPS so he could get his bearings. Once I tried asking about the weather. "It's a lot warmer than I expected," I said. "Is it always this warm here in the summer or is this a global warming thing?"

Half the time he'd ignore me. The other half he'd turn and reply with a few sentences. Or maybe one sentence with some really long words. I can't even speak a few words of Russian on my own, so it was hard to tell. Once, he delivered a long, impassioned speech about . . . something. Maybe a tree we passed that he grew up with or something. I have no idea.

It wouldn't've taken much to speak Russian, granted. There's a tattoo on my Adam's apple for just that sort of thing, and one behind each earlobe. But a lot of the stuff we were carrying was very sensitive and I couldn't risk it getting tainted by other energies.

So, anyway, when I'd tried to hire a guide, I hadn't thought to ask for someone who spoke English. It'd been hard enough explaining the location I wanted to the guy at the agency.

"Here," I told him, pointing at the map. "That's where I want to go."

The tour guide manager was a skinny man who reeked of cigarettes. His fingers were yellow. I got the sense they'd been a regular part of his diet for years. He looked at the map spread across the counter. "Cherepanovo?"

I shook my head and tapped the map again.

"Iskitim?" He shook his head. "Bad place for tourists."

"No," I said, shaking my head again. I double-checked my notes—as if I didn't have the exact location memorized—grabbed a pencil, and made a small X on the map. "There," I told him. "I want to go right there."

He frowned at the mark on his map, then peered at it. "Sixty kilometers away," he said. "Nothing out there but a few *poselok*—little villages."

"I just need to be there in two and a half hours," I told him. "Me and my equipment." I gestured at the bags and pulled a few bills from my wallet. This trip was costing me three months' pay, but if I pulled this off, it'd be worth it.

Granted, if I messed it up, there was a solid chance I was going to be very dead. Along with everyone in a forty-mile radius or so. Give or take a mile.

He shrugged, took the money, and picked up the phone. After a quick conversation in Russian he told me my driver would be here in twenty minutes. He explained Nikita's name as we killed time.

I expected to get two or three people and a truck. Instead I got Nikita. The man was an ox. He threw one bag onto his back and picked up one under each arm. He and the manager tossed a few quick words back and forth and then he marched over to a battered BMW sedan. He fit all three bags in the big trunk—you can't help but think of the Russian Mafia when you see a trunk that big—and waved me to the passenger side of the car.

For almost an hour now we'd been driving along a paved road that could've been in Kansas or Oklahoma or some fly-over, grain-belt state. You hear *Siberia* and you picture some nightmare arctic wasteland, but it's kind of beautiful. If you're into that sort of thing.

The arrow on the GPS began to swing again, but this time the road didn't swing with it. I looked ahead but didn't see any turnoffs. Nikita drove along at a steady fifty miles an hour or so. The arrow was pointing at the steering wheel, then him, and then it was aimed at the backseat.

"Stop," I told him. "We missed it."

He grunted, shook his head, and gestured at the road ahead of us.

"No," I said, shaking my own head. "Back there." I held up the GPS.

Nikita slowed the car to look at the little digital arrow, then glanced back over his shoulder. He sighed and turned the car around in a wide three-point turn.

We backtracked three-quarters of a mile until the arrow was perpendicular to the road. He watched it with me and brought the car to a smooth stop. I hopped out.

It looked like we were on the edge of someone's field, one that'd grown wild for a season or two. Just flat land for miles, broken by a couple small clumps of trees. For some reason I'd imagined this spot would be in some remote forest or something. Maybe a mountain plateau.

We were still half a mile away. I looked back at Nikita. He'd opened his door and looked over the car at me. "Come on," I told him. I pointed at the trunk. "Bring the bags."

He threw his hands up and looked around with a bewildered expression. He threw a few words at me and gestured at the road again.

I pointed out at the field with the GPS and tapped my watch. "The bags," I said again.

He sighed, slammed his door shut, and stomped over to the trunk.

I stumbled out into the field. The grass was just high and thick enough that I couldn't see the ground, so it was awkward. I made myself go slow. It would suck to get this close, after all this time, and break my ankle a few hundred yards from the site.

Nikita cleared his throat behind me. "We drive out here to see field?"

I stopped and looked back at him. "You can speak English?"

He snorted. "Of course I speak English. You think this is United States where people speak only one language? Russians much smarter."

"We were in the car for an hour."

"You very boring," he told me. "Talk of trees and weather. Is women-talk." He shook his head.

The GPS led us past the first cluster of trees, across a muddy line that might be a stream at a different part of the year, and over a small stretch of rock. Eleven minutes after we left the car, it beeped three times. A small target flashed on its screen. I walked in a circle, checking every direction. The GPS beeped again. The target kept flashing.

This was it.

I gestured for Nikita to set the bags down and kept circling, stomping the grass down. I needed room to work. Forty-six minutes till showtime. A little tighter than I'd hoped, but still more than I needed.

I pulled open the first bag. It had the three bracket sections, each one wrapped in a padded blanket to keep them safe. I double-checked the GPS one last time and started setting them up.

The first bracket popped open and I spread the legs. They were made out of iron. Weaker and heavier than steel, but they weren't conductive. At least, not conductive for what I was dealing with. I set the GPS down on the ground, shuffled it a few inches to the left, and then centered the bracket's arms over it. Once I felt comfortable with it I unwrapped the second blanket and started to unfold its legs.

Nikolai stood by the bags and cleared his throat again. "This is . . . how you say . . ." He dug around in his head for words. "This is science equipments?"

I locked the last leg into place. "Well," I told him, "it's a kind of science."

"You could not do this in Novosibirsk?"

"Not really," I said. "It's not just about the path of the Moon. It's also about what that path crosses. Have you ever heard of ley lines?"

"Lay lines?" Nikita echoed. "Is like . . . sex lines, yes? Pickup lines." He nodded.

I laughed and shook my head. "Different type of ley," I said. "The popular interpretations are all bullshit, of course. They're just an excuse for 'witches' and 'druids' to dance around in a field with their junk hanging out. But the general idea has some truth behind it."

I adjusted the legs and set the bracket in place across from the first one. "The Earth's just a big magnet, and there are lines of electromagnetic force circling the whole planet like a spiderweb. It's easier to work with the lines than against them. Spots where two lines intersect are very potent if you want to harness some of that energy."

Nikita nodded and tapped a clove cigarette out of his pack. I could tell I'd lost him and he was just feigning interest. He fumbled in his pocket for his lighter. I kept talking. It's not like he'd believe me, even if he understood everything I was saying.

"Now, if you can find one of those intersections," I told him, "and if it happens to be the site of another big cosmological event, you can work some serious mojo. Especially if you're knowledgeable about such things. Which I happen to be."

He nodded again and blew out a cloud of smoke. "Right," he said. "Cosmic event." He glanced at his watch.

I reached for the third bracket. "To be honest, I half expected to find another dozen or so folks out here, all fighting for the spot. This really is a once-in-a-lifetime thing. Although some of those guys are on their second or third lifetime at this point."

Nikita took another drag on his cigarette. He wasn't even feigning interest anymore.

Bag two was some tools and the Century stands. Big steel things they use on movie sets. Each one's like a tripod on steroids, with adjustable feet and height and an arm with a pivoting holder—a knuckle—at the end. They call them Century stands—C-stands—because they've got a hundred positions. I set them three and a half feet apart next to the assembled brackets.

Bag three was the convex lens. Thirty-nine inches across. Damn thing weighed over a hundred pounds. It was wrapped in foam and a padded blanket and two canvas tarps. Two pins on either end of its brass frame locked into the knuckles on the C-stands. Nikita had to help me get it into place. We locked it into position and then shuffled the stands until the big lens was over the brackets. I had a laser level that did measurements. It took me another fifteen minutes to make sure the lens was level and centered over the locked arms of the brackets.

Eighteen minutes to go. I grabbed a prybar from bag two and tossed it to Nikita. "I need you to make a line in the dirt around this," I told him. "One and a half meters out. Make it about two inches—six centimeters deep."

He looked at the bar. "What for?"

"Insulation. It'll help keep things stable."

He let out a mouthful of smoke. "I am just supposed to be driver."

"Fifty bucks," I told him. "Just get it done in the next ten minutes."

He grinned and bent down to start chopping at the ground with the hooked end of the prybar.

I pulled a pair of latex gloves from my pocket and my travel wallet out from under my coat. It rode on a sling around my neck and shoulder. It had two small bundles in it. I opened the smaller one—the one triple-wrapped in soft leather—first.

It was a two-inch lens I'd spent months carving. Obsidian is brittle, and there's a trick to working it with bone tools. It took me three blatant practices and six attempts to make the damned thing. I blew some dust off it. Any imperfection—even some oil or sweat from my fingertips—would ruin all this work. I set it in the top ring of the brackets. Another few minutes of fudging with the level made sure it was straight.

Then I pulled out the second bundle. The medallion. It went in the lower ring, and I spent another five minutes checking and double-checking that it was level. I had to resist the urge to fidget with the equipment. In and of itself, it was pretty simple. Big lens on the C-stands focuses on small lens in the brackets. Small lens focuses on the center point of the medallion.

Nikita grunted. He'd finished his circle and was tapping out another cigarette. I pulled two packages of salt from bag one. "Fill the circle with this," I told him. "The whole thing. There can't be any breaks. When it's done you can step over it but not on it."

He sighed and pushed the cigarette back into the pack. He tore open the first package, folded it into a rough spout, and started to pour the salt. "So what is?" he asked as he shuffled along the miniature trench. His eyes darted to the medallion. "Is more equipment?"

"That's what all this is about, yeah," I told him. I saw a glint in his eyes and shook my head. "It's not worth as much as it looks like, believe me. But if I've got all this right, in ten minutes it's going to be priceless."

He smirked. He was halfway around the circle now. I followed the line of salt with my eyes. He was doing a good job. Not a single break anywhere. He tore open the next bag of salt.

"Of course, I'm not going to let everything ride on one medallion," I told him. "Even if it comes out perfect, I still need to set up a couple of fail-safes before I can use it."

He finished the circle. Six minutes to go. Up above us, the glare of the sun started to vanish behind the moon.

"You might want to go back to the car," I told him. "This is probably going to be a little disturbing if you're not ready for it. To be honest, I've been working toward this for almost three years and I'm not sure I'm ready for it."

He glanced up at the forming eclipse and shook his head. "No big deal," he said. He knocked his sunglasses down over his eyes, slid out another cigarette, and fumbled with his lighter again. "I big boy. Not scared of the dark."

"Yeah," I said with a nod. "That's what everyone says their first time."

Two
NOW

ST. GEORGE WATCHED Jennifer pound one last nail into place before she saluted the sky with her hammer. "That's it," she said. "Done." She gave one of the shingles a glance and whacked its nail. "Now it's done," she said.

There was some scattered applause from the crowd. Not much.

The guard post wasn't impressive. The one-story structure wasn't much more than a shack. They'd found enough lumber to give it solid walls. It had two windows and a skylight. A roll of tar paper and a bundle of shingles gave it—in theory—a waterproof roof. They'd built it in the corner between the west gate of the Big Wall and the wooden staircase that led up to the walkway on top of the barrier.

The Big Wall stood fifteen feet high on average, and in places it was almost a dozen feet thick. They'd built it by pushing cars together and stacking them one on top of another. It had been long, tedious work, with dozens of men and women holding off the exes while dozens more pushed vehicle after vehicle into line. Most of them had flat tires, and it was like forcing the cars through thick mud to move them. Even with help from the heroes, and then later from the super-soldiers of Project Krypton, it had taken just short of a year to build. When they'd finished, an industrious little boy had informed St. George the Big Wall had exactly six thousand seven hundred and eighty-one cars in it. Stealth had told the boy he was off by two.

There wasn't anything near the wall the guards could use for shelter, though. It took only one rainy night in late February for them to realize that. The shack at the intersection of Melrose and Vine was for whoever was posted at the West Gate. There were still three more to build, one at each gate.

St. George beamed at the structure as Jennifer climbed down her ladder. He glanced over his shoulder at the crowd. "Oh, come on." He nodded at the shack. "You people know what this is? This is the first new building in Los Angeles in three years."

There was a quiet moment as they all stared at the little structure.

Hiram Jarvis cleared his throat. The lanky man had a dark beard streaked with premature white and gray. "Thank God," he said. "The housing market's finally bounced back."

They all smiled. A chuckle danced through the crowd. "Time to invest," called out Makana. The chuckles broke into applause. They all clapped this time. A few people hugged each other.

It was good to see a crowd of people smiling, thought St. George. It didn't happen often enough. He pounded his own hands together.

The applause grew for a moment and then stumbled. A few people kept clapping, but the sound was off. St. George followed the dull thwack through the shifting crowd to the gate.

The East Gate was two big arrays of vertical steel pipes just inches apart. It was strong enough to stop a speeding car. The goal was to eventually get both sides of it covered with chain-link fencing to keep the undead from reaching through. A double set of bars stretched across the panels to hold them in place, one at chest height and the other two feet off the ground.

On the other side of the gate, a baker's dozen of exes slapped their hands together. They all wore the same expression, wide eyes and a grin that was close to a sneer. As St. George got closer he could see the unhealing wounds marking all of the undead. One of the men was missing an eye. Another one slapped his hand against the ragged stump of his other wrist. There was a woman with gorgeous features who only had a few scrapes and bruises, and another who was little more than bones wrapped in papery skin. All of them had pale flesh and dull eyes. They kept clapping.

"Things are lookin' good in there, *esse*," one of them said to St. George. It was the dead man with the missing hand. The ex beat the stump against its palm. "Lookin' really good."

Twin trailers of smoke rose out of St. George's nose. "You want something, Rodney?"

The applause stopped. "I told you," said the dead man before the other exes joined it in one voice, "DON'T CALL ME RODNEY. IT'S LEGION, DAMNIT!"

"Whatever."

Half of the exes wandered away from the gate and milled about like the rest of the undead. Their jaws moved up and down, banging their teeth together. The ones left glared at St. George. The one-handed man tapped his knuckles against one of the pipes, and the other exes mirrored the gesture along the gate. "Someday soon, dragon man, I'm gonna get in there. You know it's coming. You won't be acting so smart then."

"Someday isn't today," said St. George. He spat out a burst of flame through the fence.

The exes took a step back, then held their ground. It wasn't enough fire to do more than singe them, but the one-handed man lost his eyebrows. They all glared at the hero and bared their teeth. Then their expressions went slack and their teeth started clacking against each other. They pushed their arms between the pipes and tried to reach St. George with slow, clumsy grabs.

A couple people gave halfhearted laughs and cheers, but the mood was dead. The crowd scattered. Guards turned to watch the streets outside the Big Wall while others walked up the wooden staircase to join them.

St. George turned away from the gate and saw that two people had stayed behind to speak with him. The first was Billie Carter, the nominal head of the scavengers, the people who headed out once or twice a week to search the city for whatever supplies they could find. From a distance, the Marine sergeant sometimes got mistaken for a teenage boy with a buzz cut. Up close, it was clear she was a woman who shouldn't be messed with.

The second was Jarvis. No one was quite sure where Jarvis fit into the scheme of things. He went out with the scavengers, but it wasn't uncommon to find him walking the Wall. He pulled shifts as a hospital guard and even spent time weeding in the gardens. His willingness to do whatever needed to be done meant everyone liked him, so they all tended to listen to him when he spoke. St. George found the man to be an endless source of cheerfulness and common sense without ever crossing the line that made cheerful people annoying.

"So," said the hero, "are we still on for tomorrow?"

Billie nodded. "Assuming Legion hasn't messed up the roads too bad, we should be able to make Sherman Oaks in an hour. There's lots of little shops out there that might be worth checking out. If we can make it all the way to Sepulveda there's a ton of apartment complexes."

"Probably too many to hit on the same day," said Jarvis, "but we can get a sense of how things are looking out that way."

"There better be something," said Billie. "We're getting close to the point this isn't worth it."

St. George glanced at her. "Meaning what?"

She shrugged. "Basic logistics. If we burn ten gallons of fuel to bring ten back, we're pretty much right back where we started. There's still a lot of gas stations out there, but we're getting near the point it's going to cost us more to go looking than we're going to get out of it. Especially with Legion making us fight for every mile we travel."

"Always nice to get out, though," said Jarvis.

"I'm serious," Billie said. "Every time we head out we're tied to the Mount, and we're running out of rope." She crossed her arms. "I think we need to think about setting up a forward base or two farther out. Something out in the valley, or over in Burbank. Maybe just a dozen or two people in a secure area. Someplace we can scavenge from without trucking what we find all the way back here."

St. George bit back a smile. "Stealth suggested something similar a few weeks ago," he said. "I wasn't sure how the idea would go over."

"You could've asked us," said Billie.

"She said if I waited you'd probably come up with the idea yourself. You specifically, Billie."

"'Course she did," smirked Jarvis.

"What if we try this? I can do a few scouting runs out into Van Nuys or maybe out toward Glendale. Maybe there's another small studio out there we could use, or a school."

"There's a National Guard armory out in Van Nuys," said Billie. "We had you check it out once. You said it still looked secure. We could definitely use whatever ammo's there."

The hero nodded. "We'd need to check it again. It only had one fence, right?"

She nodded.

"There's also downtown," said Jarvis. "We've avoided it till now, but maybe it's time to think about heading that way."

The hero shook his head. "Downtown's still a death trap," he said. "Stealth figures there's still at least six or seven hundred thousand exes down there. Plus it's wall-to-wall cars and tons of barricades the National Guard left behind. We wouldn't get five blocks before we were overrun, even if we had Cerberus and all of Freedom's soldiers with us."

"You could do some advance scouting and pave the way," Billie said. "You've made it down to the toy district three years now for Christmas."

He nodded. "That's why I know downtown's a bad idea. It's hell to grab a few trash bags full of Barbies and knockoff Transformers all on my own."

"One other issue," said Jarvis, "if y'all don't mind me bringing it up."

"Depends," said St. George. He gestured up the street and the three of them walked north along the Big Wall.

"Elections," said the bearded man. "We still shooting for six weeks from tomorrow?"

"Last I heard," said the hero. "Why?"

Jarvis shrugged. "Still time for someone to throw their name in the hat for mayor."

St. George shook his head. "I told you, not me."

"You should," said Billie. "You're the natural choice."

Jarvis nodded in agreement. "Everybody knows you," he said. "Pretty much everyone likes you. Only ones who don't still have to admit you've saved us all a dozen times over. You're a natural, boss."

"Same holds for you and Billie," the hero said.

She snorted.

"I'm serious," he said. "Jarvis, you'd make a great mayor. Why aren't you running?"

"To tell the truth," said the salt-and-pepper man, "I couldn't stand the cut in pay. Got me a pretty extravagant lifestyle to keep up." He raised his chin and straightened the lapel of his threadbare coat. "All kinda besides the point, though. If someone else don't step up, it's going to come down to Christian and Richard. And Richard just ain't mean enough for politics here in the big city."

"What are you getting at?"

"I'm just saying, if nothing changes in the race there's a good chance six weeks from now things are going to be real different around here. Might be best to get stuff done earlier than later, know what I mean?"

St. George shook his head. "We can't start making this an us-and-them thing," he said. "It took us over a year to get the Seventeens integrated. Last thing we need is to start making up political parties and dividing everyone that way."

"People are already divided, boss," Jarvis said. "Just the nature of the beast. Some folks want to go forward, some folks want to try to go back. There's all the religious nuts, too."

"Hey," said St. George. "Tolerance."

"Sorry, boss," said Jarvis. "Seriously, though, have you listened to some of this A.D. stuff?"

"It's all classic Book of Revelation," said Billie. She tipped her head at the Big Wall. "It's not that out there, all things considered. Pretty easy to think we're living in the end of days."

"I never knew you were religious," said St. George.

"I'm a Marine and I was in Afghanistan for a year and a half," she said. "I'm religious enough, I just don't push it on anyone. You know they all back Christian, right?"

"The A.D. folks?" asked the hero. "Not too surprising. She's been with them from the start, hasn't she?"

Billie nodded. "Someone told me she lost a niece when everything went to hell."

"I think I heard that once."

"Still," said Jarvis, "y'all get my point. Still a lot of work to do and we ain't quite the unified front we were a couple years ago."

"Yeah," said St. George. "I was saying something about this the other night. Is it a good thing or a bad thing that we've gotten big enough for people to start splitting apart?"

"What'd you decide?"

"That we'd have to wait and see." He shrugged. "Anything else?"

Billie shook her head. "I was going to put together a weapons detail tonight, make sure everything's good for tomorrow's mission."

"Did that yesterday with Taylor," said Jarvis. "Double-checked everything."

Billie shrugged. "So I'll have them triple-check it. What else is there to do?"

St. George shoved his hands into the pockets of his coat. "Maybe we should just relax."

"Sorry," said Billie, "you used some word I don't know."

"I'm serious," St. George said. He gestured at the Big Wall and let his hand swing back to the gate. "Things are tight, but we're at the point that we have to start living again. All of us. We can't make every minute of every day about survival."

"Legion's still out there," Billie said.

"Out there," said St. George. "Not in here."

Jarvis shrugged. "Okay."

Billie looked at him, then at St. George. "That's it?" she asked. "We're just supposed to do . . . nothing?"

"Not nothing," he said. "Just take a night off. Have a beer with some friends, play a game, watch a movie, hook up with someone. Go . . . I don't know, do whatever you used to do on your nights off."

Her lip twisted toward a frown, but he saw her force it back into a flat line. "What if I go work on some ideas for that forward base? Some basic supplies and requirements?"

St. George sighed. "If it's what you want to do, fine, but you don't have to. You can just take the night off. It won't be the end of the world."

"Yeah," agreed Jarvis. "End of the world happened years ago."

Three

NOW

IT WAS A little over a block from the West Gate down to the church, maybe two blocks from where St. George left Billie and Jarvis. He knew flying there was silly, but it was always good for people to see one of the heroes during the day.

Plus, it just felt cool to fly. Breathing fire and bending steel bars were great, but pushing himself away from the ground and hanging in the sky was just amazing. He'd never felt so free in his life.

He soared up a good thirty feet above the trees and spun once in the air. Far to the north, up in the hills, stood the letters of the Hollywood sign. It was getting gray after years of neglect. The thought crossed his mind of going up there with a few gallons of water and washing it. It'd be a big boost for everyone to see the whole thing bright and white up above them.

Two blocks west were the walls of the Mount, their original fortress. From here he could see the huge globe of the Earth balanced on one corner of the studio wall. Just past the globe and the stages there, he could see the top floor of the Hart Building. He knew he had to head over there soon, but wanted to make another stop first.

To the south, just inside the Big Wall, was the church. It wasn't the only church inside the barriers. They'd found a dozen of different sizes, denominations, and languages—but not one synagogue or mosque, which had caused a fair amount of grumbling. The one at Rossmore and Arden was the one St. George always thought of as *the* church, though. It was a large, Gothic building, with arched facades in the front and back and a cross on the high rooftop above the doors. He wasn't a particularly religious person, but he understood the need for symbols.

He landed on the steps. The big square doors were open to let in the breeze. He walked inside.

The church was lit by windows and a few candles. A dozen people were scattered through the pews. Two men stood near the back of the church, right by the door, speaking in hushed tones. One of them glanced at St. George and gave a faint tip of his head in acknowledgment.

Andy Shepard, former scavenger, was now Father Shepard, although he'd at least gotten most everyone to go with Father Andy. He tried to argue that he'd never been ordained, but eventually he broke down under the realization it was him or nothing for the practicing Catholics left in Los Angeles. They'd even found him a collar.

And the number of practicing churchgoers had gone up since the Zombocalypse. There'd been prayer and spiritual guidance inside the Mount, but it was a huge thing for many people to set foot in a church again once the Big Wall was finished. Especially if it had been their church before the end of the world. St. George had noticed how many people headed to the different services each Sunday morning. Not surprising, all things considered.

Father Andy exchanged a last few words with the other man and they shook hands. Then he stepped over to St. George and extended the hand again. "A bit weird to see you here," he said. "What's up?"

"Just checking in," said the hero. "I was flying by, realized I hadn't talked to you in a while. How are things going?"

Andy shrugged. "Not bad. The confessional's been busy.

There's a lot of people who've been burdened by things they've done, stuff they want to get off their chests."

"Anything I should know about?"

Andy shook his head. "It's survivor's guilt more than anything else. That's why all the churches are so popular. Hell, my last sermon was standing room only. Can't tell you the last time I saw that in a church."

"Are you allowed to say 'hell' now that you're a priest?"

"I have to say 'hell.' It's part of the job description. Although, technically, if I'm the last one left I think it makes me the Pope."

"Pope Andy the First does have a ring to it," said St. George.

The priest shook his head. "I've got to be honest. After all we've seen, I'd be tempted to take the name Thomas."

St. George smiled.

"Nothing else?" asked Father Andy.

The hero looked up at the big cross above the altar. "What can you tell me about the A.D. folks?"

Andy let out a noise somewhere between a chuckle and a snort. Then he shrugged. "Well, they're following general Christianity, for the most part," he said. "More of an oversized prayer circle or Bible study group than an actual religious sect. I mean, in the big scheme of things, they're like all of us. They're trying to understand God's plan and establish a set—"

"No," said St. George. "I'm not looking for a polite religious comparison. I want to know what you think about them."

The priest took in a slow breath, leaned against the back of a pew, and lowered his voice. "Look, I know every religion thinks every other religion's got it wrong, so anything I say they could probably say against me, but still . . . these people are grasping."

"How so?"

"How well do you know your Bible?"

St. George shook his head. "Not at all really. I mean, I know a couple of the stories, but . . ."

"Don't worry about it." Andy crossed his arms. "The After Death folks go through the Bible and cherry-pick verses that fit what they want to believe. Thessalonians, a fair amount of Revelation, one of them even spouted a few verses of Ezekiel at me once. They just pull stuff from anywhere without considering context. Have you ever heard the phrase 'When there is no room in Hell, the dead shall walk the Earth,' or some variation on it?"

"A few times, yeah." He took an educated guess. "Is it from Revelations?"

"Revelation, singular," said Father Andy. "And no, it isn't. It's just the tagline from an old zombie movie."

"It's not even based on one?"

Andy shook his head. "But they're still treating it like the word of God. They just clutch onto anything that lets them cope with what's happened to the world. More to the point, they try to spin all of it their way, no matter what the context or classical interpretation is. These days, I'm pretty damned liberal in interpreting the word of God, but I still can't see any way to resolve their beliefs with what the book actually says."

"You can say 'damn,' too?"

"Yep. Seriously, we all need to cope in our own way, but their whole mind-set is just a little too zealous for my liking. And I'm saying that as a Catholic priest."

"Yeah."

Father Andy uncrossed his arms and set them down on the back of the pew. It was a very relaxed pose. "I would've thought Stealth would've had all this down in a file somewhere already. With much more precise references."

"She probably does," the hero said with a shrug. "I was just flying by and saw the church, and their church a little farther down. Figured I'd stop by and talk to you about them."

"That's all?"

"Yeah. Why?"

Father Andy met his eyes for another few seconds and then nodded. "Okay," he said. "But you know, if you ever want to talk about anything . . ."

"I know where to find you." They shook hands again. "Do you miss going out on scavenging runs?"

The priest smiled. "Going out to fight with zombies over cans of beans? Not as much as you'd think."

* * *

St. George sailed back into the air. He flew in a lazy circle and swung down by the southwest corner of the Big Wall. The After Death church was below him, a newer building that looked more like a meeting hall than a place of worship.

There were three people he didn't recognize standing in the parking lot, each with a book tucked under their arm. One of them caught a glimpse of him and they all shielded their eyes to look up. They smiled and waved. The man who'd first seen him looked more familiar when he smiled.

It occurred to St. George, not for the first time, that there were enough people living in Los Angeles now that he couldn't recognize them all on sight.

The people went back to their discussion. St. George widened his flight circle to take him out over Larchmont and back across the South Wall. A few sentries waved or saluted as he flew past. He returned the gestures.

He passed over rows of houses that once had prices in the high six figures, maybe even seven. Most of them were first come, first serve now. Many of them had solar panels on their roofs, scavenged from across Los Angeles. It had only taken the end of the world to make the city embrace green technology.

He flew north and passed over the Melrose Gate. It was still strange to see the gates standing open and the streets mostly empty.

Cerberus was outside on the edge of the cobblestones, just where the road turned back to sun-cracked pavement. The armored battlesuit looked up at him with tennis ball–size lenses. He waved, and the metal skull returned it with a casual nod before turning and heading down the street. It had been in front of Gorgon's cross, a memorial to another hero who'd died defending the Mount over a year ago. That meant it was Danielle in the suit.

Danielle Morris had created the Cerberus Battle Armor System for the U.S. military just before the ex-humans appeared. There wasn't time to train anyone else, so she'd become the suit's de facto pilot and spent most of the past two and a half years inside it. Like most of the heroes, she'd just come to accept it.

But then they'd discovered another superhuman inside the Mount, a reformed Seventeen named Cesar Mendoza who tried desperately to get people to call him "the Driver." Cesar could project himself into machinery and possess it, which meant he could use the Cerberus suit just as well as Danielle. And with the fall of Project Krypton the year before, there was even a lieutenant living at the Mount now who'd spent months training to use the battlesuit.

The catch was, Danielle still didn't trust either of them with it.

St. George considered flying after the titan and talking to her, but he knew they both had other things to do. He turned in the air and looked across the parking lot to the Hart Building. He could see most of it. The guards there were probably waiting for him.

Then he spun and flew to the other side of the Mount.

He landed outside a large, warehouse-like building called Stage Four. The air prickled and St. George felt his hair rise off his scalp. Three years back, when the Mount had been a film studio, they'd shot television shows in Four. Now it was the hub of the new Los Angeles power grid.

Inside Four smelled like a welding shop. At the center of the huge space was a trio of interlocking rings—each wrapped with copper wire—that formed a rough sphere. The whole array resembled a seven-foot gyroscope, but everyone still used the nickname that had come up when it was being built. It was the electric chair.

The brilliant outline of a man, the negative image of a shadow, hovered at the center of the sphere. Arcs of crackling power shot from the gleaming figure to the copper-wrapped rings. St. George had known the other hero long enough to see his friend was staring over at a table dominated by a large flatscreen and a pile of DVDs.

Zzzap didn't notice St. George's entrance. He was busy arguing with the television.

Because it's dumb, that's why, said Zzzap. The buzz of his voice echoed in the large room. He paused for a moment and then shook his head. *Look, being able to run implies a certain degree of physical coordination, which means a specific level of brain activity and consciousness. You can't be mindless* and *have brain activity.* He waited a few moments, then shook his head again. *Well, then just look around. Have you ever seen one run in real life?*

The television, St. George noticed, wasn't turned on.

No, Legion doesn't count because he's only sort of mindless—what? The wraith spun inside the circle. *Hey,* he said to St. George. *I didn't hear you come in.*

"Yeah, you seemed kind of busy."

What? What do you mean?

The hero stared at his friend for a moment, then nodded at the television. "What's with all that?"

All what?

He gestured at the blank television.

Oh. Nothing. It's cartoon withdrawal, that's all.

"Cartoon withdrawal?"

I have a Yu-Gi-Oh! *addiction, okay? It's not pretty, but there it is. I just love the way he talks when he's the King of Games.*

"No, I'm serious."

Addiction is a serious thing, George. Don't mock it.

"You're really determined not to talk about this, aren't you?"

I'm fine. What's up?

He drummed his fingers on his thigh. "Are you sure?"

Yeah. Why wouldn't I be?

He shrugged.

So what's up?

The hero rocked back and forth on his heels. "I'm cooking dinner tonight. You want to come over?"

You're cooking?

"Yeah."

Cooking food?

"Is this hard for you to understand or hard to believe?"

A little of both. The brilliant wraith crossed his arms and leaned back. *This isn't some cheesy superhero thing where you're going to throw hot dogs in the air and try to cook them with your fire-breath, right?*

"If I had hot dogs, I wouldn't waste them like that."

Good.

"I've pulled in a couple favors. I've got two loaves of almost-French bread, a bunch of tomatoes and onions, and some of that homemade pasta the Ashmores are making over at Ren-Mar."

The stuff that's like thick fettuccine?

"They've gotten better since that first batch. I figure I can make something that passes for Italian food. So take the night off and come over."

Zzzap looked at him. *What's the occasion?*

St. George shrugged. "I just felt like doing something nice with my friends. Is that so wrong?"

Who else is coming?

"You, me, hopefully Danielle."

Danielle's coming?

"If I can get her to come out without the armor on, yeah."

The wraith's head tilted back to look at the copper-wrapped rings above him. *I don't know,* he said. *Do you think Stealth'll be okay with it? With me just taking a night off?*

"I already cleared it with her," said St. George.

Okay, then, yeah, I guess so.

"I really didn't think I'd have to talk you into eating a meal."

No, no, I'm in, said Zzzap. *Sorry. I've been kind of distracted.*

"I've noticed. You sure everything's okay?"

Zzzap's head twitched. *Yeah, of course. Stop trying to put your problems off on me.*

The hero frowned. "What's that supposed to mean?"

You think I don't know what all this care and concern is really about? You're putting off going to see him, aren't you?

"Maybe," he sighed.

You don't have to go, you know.

"I told him I would," said St. George. "Hell, I'm the only person he ever sees."

We're the only ones who know. Would you want him talking to anyone else?

* * *

The room's proper name—the one taped under one of Stealth's countless security monitors—was Cell Nine.

The Mount had six solitary cells for prisoners, but none of them got much use since the original South Seventeens gang had collapsed and been absorbed into the general population. There were also two large cells that served as drunk tanks and cooling-off rooms. Everyone knew where those cells were.

And then there was Cell Nine.

Cell Nine was in the basement of the Hart Building, one of several office spaces that had been converted into small apartments when the survivors moved into the Mount. When they'd been there for a little over a year, Stealth had ordered Hart cleaned out. The residents were all moved to other locations with many loud complaints and even one sit-in demonstration.

As for the Hart Building, a team was brought in to build a spacious cell in the basement storage area, twelve feet on a side. It was steel bars lined with heavy chain-link fence on both sides. When the cell was done, all the windows were boarded up on all floors, inside and out. All the doors were chained shut, including the fire door on the roof, and the locks welded solid. The only entrance was the front door on 3rd Street, and it had four padlocks on it. Two were keyed, two had combinations. Two guards stood there at all times. Each of them had one key and one combination.

Whispered stories went back and forth through the survivors of Los Angeles about what was down in the building's basement. Officially it was just high-security storage, but everyone knew you didn't put objects in a cell, you put living things. Which is how Cell Nine came to be known as the Cellar. And the Cellar was where they kept the Thing.

One of the more popular theories said the Cellar was a prison for infected citizens, or a dumping ground for people who'd been reanimated by the ex-virus. Some people thought the Thing was a reanimated superhero whose powers made him or her too dangerous to let wander through Los Angeles. A few folks who'd been part of the film industry back when the Mount was a studio told stories about how the Hart Building had always been a nexus of supernatural incidents, and had once been considered one of the most haunted places in Hollywood.

Even the guards didn't know what was in the Cellar. All they knew was that they had strict orders. If the Thing—whatever it was—tried to get out of the building, they weren't supposed to hesitate or ask questions. They were just supposed to shoot until they were out of ammunition.

It didn't help the rumors that only one person was allowed into the Hart Building. Once a month he would descend into the basement and the guards would lock the door behind him. He'd stay down there for an hour or two and then come out looking grim.

St. George landed on 3rd Street in front of the Hart Building. Today it was Mike Meryl and Katie O'Hare on guard. Mike walked with a limp from an old injury, so a static guard post was perfect for him. Katie liked any position where she didn't have to talk to people.

They each gave him a polite nod and bent to the locks. There was only one reason for him to come here, and they'd been expecting him for a day or two now. They set the padlocks on the steps and unwrapped the chain. It ran through four big eyebolts in the door frame.

The Hart Building didn't have a lobby. The doorway opened up onto a staircase landing. St. George stepped through and Katie closed the door behind him. He stood there while the chains rattled back into place. The padlocks thumped against the door and he headed down.

There was a short hallway that ended at another padlocked door. This one was more solid, and had rubber bumpers around the edge to help seal the inside from moisture and air. They'd stored videotapes and files down here once, years ago. George dug a key out of his pocket and the lock popped open. A wisp of smoke curled up out of his nose and he opened the door.

Cell Nine was in the middle of the room. A pair of mattresses were stacked in the far corner of the cell, decorated by a mess of sheets and blankets. A few dozen books were piled in the opposite corner. They were all battered paperbacks, or hardbacks that had been torn out of their cover. Nothing hard.

There was no toilet. Not even a bucket. The occupant never needed one, which made sense. He hadn't eaten anything in almost a year.

The prisoner didn't look up when St. George entered. He had a book in one hand. He made a show of turning the page and reading another paragraph before his eyes flitted up to meet the hero's.

"Hello, George," he said. "It's been a while. I thought you might've finally given up on me."

Four

NOW

"DO YOU BELIEVE him?"

St. George shrugged and set another tomato on the cutting board. "Not really. I mean, he was doing it again when I walked in."

Stealth gave a faint nod. "I have seen him go through the motions of conversations three times this past week alone. There was no evidence of another speaker."

"Did you check to see if he was talking to someone on the radio?"

"I did," she said. She carried a stack of plates and bowls to the table. She balanced them on one hand and held the silverware in the other. "I checked five months ago when his behavior patterns could no longer be denied."

"What?" The knife slipped to the side and grated against his finger. It ruined the edge of the blade. He glanced from the knife to Stealth and back. "Why didn't you say something?"

"I knew the answer would upset you. And there is currently nothing we can do about it."

He pulled another knife from the block on the counter and attacked the last tomato again. "And the answer is . . . ?"

Stealth did something quick with her left arm and a single plate slid onto the table in front of a chair. "He is not talking to anyone, George. I monitor all broadcast communications within the Mount, and many beyond it. There have been no radio conversations that match up with the ones he is having. I have checked during sixteen separate incidents since then. He is not communicating with anyone."

St. George stopped dicing. "What does that mean?"

She didn't meet his eyes. "It means he is talking to himself. Under normal circumstances, this would be seen as a sign of several possible personality disorders. Chronic anxiety. Dementia. Schizophrenia."

His eyes fell to the cutting board and he was quiet for a moment. Then he looked at her again. "Under normal circumstances?"

Another plate slid onto the table from the stack in her hand. She framed it with silverware. "It is worth noting that Zzzap speaks to himself," she said, setting down a spoon. "Barry does not."

"Are you sure?"

"I cannot say conclusively. The majority of his time is spent as Zzzap, and most of his time in his human form is spent sleeping. However, in five months of observation I have never seen Barry speak to himself."

"So it's something about being Zzzap that's doing this to him."

"Perhaps. Or something he is only susceptible to in his energy form."

St. George glanced at the door. He lifted the cutting board and used the knife to sweep the diced tomatoes into the pot. "So what do we do?"

She assembled the final place setting. "I do not know," she admitted. "We have converted many buildings to solar power, but Zzzap still supplies half the electricity within the Big Wall. It would be a major setback if we decided he was unable to do this."

"You think it's that bad? We couldn't even keep him in the chair?"

Stealth sighed and looked at him. "While Zzzap has often referred to himself as a small star, the truth is that his energy form is far closer to a nuclear bomb, one frozen in the instant after detonation. It is his conscious will that keeps the explosion from proceeding."

St. George set an onion down on the cutting board and cut it in half.

"Consider the possibility of him seeing hallucinations as well as hearing them. If Zzzap were to fire one of his blasts at street level within the Mount, my best estimates have over sixty people killed or wounded, increased to one hundred fifty in the attempt to contain fires and damages."

"If he's insane."

"Correct," said Stealth, "although I have seen nothing yet that makes for a convincing diagnosis of any type. As I said, there is currently nothing we can do."

"We can keep an eye on him. Let him know we're here." He finished chopping the onion and added it to the pot.

She came back to the kitchen. "I assumed that was a given."

He set a handful of mushrooms on the cutting board. "I'm still not sure sometimes."

"I care about his well-being," she said. "Zzzap is a valuable asset to the Mount."

St. George smiled. "That's what you used to say about me."

"It is still true. Any personal feelings I may have do not change that fact." She gathered up the glasses. "I am no longer certain this is a wise course of action."

"Not confronting him?"

"Dinner."

"It's going to be fine. You'll be fine."

She walked back to the table. "I feel very exposed."

"It's dinner," he said. "Not reconnaissance."

"Neither Barry nor Danielle is expecting to see me here, let alone in a casual situation."

St. George finished slicing and added the mushrooms to

the pot. "Look, they have to find out sometime, right? I'm surprised no one's figured it out yet. So this is a fine way to do it."

"I am not convinced of that."

"Are you getting scared?"

She stiffened. "Of course not."

"It'd be totally natural if you were a little nervous about this."

She stared at him. "I am not scared and I am not nervous. You may stop your clumsy attempt at reverse psychology, George."

"I thought it was clever and subtle."

"It was not."

"Cute and endearing?"

"On a childish level, perhaps."

Someone knocked on the door, tapping out a rapid drum solo. St. George smiled at her. "Last chance to vanish into a shadow."

"Do you wish to answer the door or shall I?"

He wiped his hands on a dishtowel. "I'll get it. Don't want to freak everyone out right off the bat."

She dipped her head and set the glasses on the table.

Danielle and Barry waited in the hall. His wheelchair was aimed at the door, ready to enter. She stood behind him, one of her hands clutching the chair's handle.

"Hey," said St. George. "Thanks for coming over."

"Free food, good friends, a night away from the chair," Barry said. He tipped his bald head back and smiled. "You know I'm all over that."

Stealth was right. Barry looked calm. His thin frame was relaxed, free of the odd jerks and tics the energy form had developed over the past few months. He looked . . . normal.

Danielle snorted. Her strawberry-blond hair was tied back in a messy ponytail, away from her freckled face. He could see a collar of black spandex under her shirt, the Cerberus contact suit. It served as her security blanket outside the armor.

Her knuckles were white on the wheelchair's handles. She lifted her free hand to reveal a bottle. "I brought presents."

It took him a minute to register what she was holding. "You actually have wine? Real wine?"

"I've been saving it," she said with a shrug. It was a tight, contained movement. "You said tonight was something special, so . . ." She shrugged again.

Barry looked between them. "Special? What have you two been keeping from me?"

"Beats me." She pushed the wheelchair into the apartment and her shoulders relaxed by a few degrees once they were inside. "Is it just us?"

"Not exactly," said St. George.

"Please tell me it's not Freedom," said Barry. "I'm sorry, but that guy can be so upti— . . . oh."

Stealth stood by the table. Her arms hung straight at her sides.

St. George stepped forward and took her hand. Her fingers wrapped around his. "Guys—Barry, Danielle—this is Karen."

Danielle's eyes went wide. Her shoulders tensed back up. Barry gaped.

Stealth shifted under their gazes. "Good evening," she said. A moment passed and her free hand went up to sweep a strand of ebony hair away from her face. As she lowered it, she paused to tug at the collar of her blouse.

The silence stretched out for another few seconds before Danielle cleared her throat. "Hello," she said. "I wasn't expecting . . . we . . . We didn't know George was . . . seeing anyone."

"You," said Barry, "are very pretty."

Stealth's lips twitched and she dipped her head to him. "Thank you."

Danielle set the wine down on the table. Then she picked it back up. "George, do you have a corkscrew?"

"Yeah, I think so."

The redhead nodded, glanced at the other woman again,

and vanished across the room. St. George separated his fingers from Stealth's and followed Danielle into the kitchen.

She turned on him as soon as he stepped through the doorway. "It's her, isn't it?" whispered Danielle. It wasn't a question.

"What?"

"Don't play stupid, George."

"I'm not playing."

She glanced back at the living room with wide eyes. They could hear Barry filling the air with small talk. He was quizzing the dark-haired woman on her favorite movies.

Danielle looked at St. George. "Want to know something? Women size each other up all the time. We're way more competitive than men. That's why no one ever knows who I am out of the armor."

"What are you getting at?"

"I know those hips and that rack, I just never see them without black spandex and leather straps stretched across them. And besides, I screened her when we moved into the Mount, remember? I didn't see her face, but I know she's black."

A wisp of smoke sighed out between his lips. "Don't say anything, okay?"

"Don't say anything?!" Danielle swung the bottle back at the doorway. "What the hell is going on?"

"She's trying to socialize, okay? She hasn't dealt with anyone without her mask on in three years."

"And you know what that says to me? She's going to kill us all because we've seen her face."

"Please," he said. "Just be cool about this. For me. She needs it."

She glared at him for a moment, then thrust her hand out. "Corkscrew."

He pulled open a drawer, fumbled through the collection of kitchen tools, and held up a corkscrew. "Thank you," he said.

She pulled it from his fingers. "Don't thank me yet." She took a deep breath and headed back into the living room. She ran into Stealth in the doorway. They stood eye to eye for a moment.

"Have you started the pasta?" Stealth asked.

Danielle swallowed. St. George shook his head. "No, I was just about to."

"I will take care of it," she said. She stepped to the oven. Danielle vanished back to the living room.

Barry gave a couple frantic waves when St. George returned, and the hero crouched by the wheelchair. "Where?" demanded Barry. "Where in God's name did you find a woman like that?"

"What?"

"Her. Karen. Where'd she come from?"

He blinked and exchanged a glance with Danielle. "Are you serious?"

"Of course I am."

"You . . . you probably just never noticed her before."

"It's the Mount," hissed Barry. "You can't hide someone who looks like that. Was she from Yuma?"

St. George shook his head. "No, she's been with us all along."

"Liar. I know her from somewhere, though."

"Maybe right here?"

"Your Jedi mind tricks won't work on me. I'll figure this out." He drummed his fingers on the arm of his wheelchair.

Stealth stepped back into the main room. "Dinner should be ready in fifteen minutes," she said. "The wine should have just enough time to breathe."

"It was only a step above Two Buck Chuck before the end of the world," said Danielle. Her lips twitched into a smile. "I'm not sure if breathing's going to help it any."

"Still," said Barry, "it'll be better than that fruit cider–stuff they're brewing down in Larchmont."

"I've got a bottle of that, too," said St. George. He tipped his chin at Danielle. "Did you finish gathering up all those helmets?"

She shook her head. "Not yet. I went out with Cesar riding shotgun and got maybe two-thirds of them. We might've missed a couple." She sank the corkscrew into the top of the wine bottle. "Something kind of strange I meant to tell you. There's a lot of military helmets out there."

"There were several units of Marines and National Guard in Los Angeles before the fall," said Stealth.

Danielle nodded. "I'd expect some, yeah, with all the stuff Legion scavenged. The percentage just seems kind of high. I mean, didn't we gather up a lot of that stuff when we were setting up the Mount?"

"Has anyone else thought that we need a new name?" asked Barry. He'd already started in on the first loaf of bread. "I mean, this is the Mount here, yeah, but are we going to call everything inside the Big Wall 'The Mount' or what?"

"That would be up to the civilian government," said Stealth, "would it not?"

"Yeah," he said, "sorry. Shouldn't bore you with shop talk."

The cork popped on the wine. Salad was tossed. Pasta was drained. Danielle sat down across from Barry. St. George and Stealth flanked them. They passed the salad and the bread. St. George poured the wine.

They paused with their glasses in the air. He realized they were looking at him. "Toast from the host," said Barry.

"Yeah," Danielle said. "This may be the last bottle of real wine in the world. Let's do it justice."

"There are nineteen pre-outbreak bottles in the Mount," said Stealth. "Several families hold on to them for special occasions." St. George gave her a look and her shoulders slumped. She gave a forced, awkward shrug. "Or so I have heard."

St. George raised his glass. "I guess . . . to bringing the world back to life."

"In the good way," smiled Barry.

"In the good way," agreed St. George.

Their glasses chimed together over the bread basket. Stealth put her lips on the rim, but barely let a drop touch her tongue.

Barry began to load up his plate. Danielle, seated across from the dark-haired woman, had another sip of wine and seemed to relax. Stealth tore off a small piece of bread, then set it down on her plate. She pushed at some of the pasta with her fork, impaled it on the tines, and then pushed it back off onto the plate. She reached for her wineglass.

Danielle watched her fidget. "Is everything okay?"

Stealth straightened up with the wineglass. "I usually eat alone," she said. "I feel somewhat self-conscious."

Barry shoved another wad of tomato-soaked bread into his mouth. "Don't worry," he said around the food. "Everyone's watching my horrible table manners. Especially now that I've drawn attention to them."

Stealth's lips twitched into something close to a nervous smile and she stuck her fork back into the pasta. She guided the bite around the plate.

Danielle ate some pasta and swallowed some more wine. "So," she said, "how long have you two been . . . together?"

St. George and Stealth exchanged a glance. "I never really thought about it," he said. "It just sort of happened over time, y'know?"

"So . . . weeks? Months?" The redhead set her wine down and picked up a piece of bread. "How long have you been keeping this little secret from us?"

"It wasn't really a secret," said St. George. "It just wasn't something that comes up in casual conversation."

"It does for most people," said Danielle.

"The first time we slept together was five weeks after the convoy returned from Yuma," said Stealth. "Is that what you wished to know?"

"Not exactly, no."

"Wait a minute." Barry banged his palm on the arm of his wheelchair and turned to Stealth. "I know who you are."

She tensed in her chair.

"You were on *Jeopardy!*," he said. "About a year before the exes appeared. You were champion for, like, a week and a half, weren't you?"

"Six days."

"And you won almost half a million dollars. You beat the highest-earning day ever and then you beat your own score three days later. It was amazing. People were talking about it for months. They all had you pegged as the next Larissa Kelly or Ken Jennings. You played two games where the other players didn't even get to buzz in. You just swept both boards."

Stealth gave a hesitant nod, then swept back the lock of black hair that fell across her face. "There was only one game where no other player buzzed in, but there were two games where no other player scored."

"Amazing," said Barry. "What'd you do with the money? Take a trip or invest it or what?"

"I invested some," she said. "I spent the rest on clothing and equipment."

"Ahhh," he said. "You're a sports nut."

"Something along those lines, yes."

They all glanced at St. George. He made a point of shoving a piece of bread into his mouth.

They made small talk through dinner, and St. George surprised them all with some peanut butter cookies from the bakery. For a few hours, they were just friends having dinner together. When he saw them to the door, Barry bumped knuckles and Danielle gave him a hug. "Thank you," she said. She even tried to hug Stealth, but then both of them thought better of it.

St. George closed the door and turned to the dark-haired woman. "Well," he said, "that didn't go too bad."

"Danielle knew immediately."

He sighed. "Yeah, I know."

Like That George Romero Movie
THEN

July 28th, 2009

Dear Diary,

My eyes opened when I heard the gunshot and the bullet
hit the ground six inches in front of me. The sand poofed
up and everything, just like on TV.

I know that sounds kind of staged, but it was really
just like that. Eyes open, <u>poof.</u> I almost peed my pants. I've
never been shot at before. It's scary as hell.

Dad warned us stuff like this might happen. Some
people weren't doing well with the zombies. That's one of
the reasons calling them exes stuck. It was a psychology
thing. He told me the term for it, but I don't remember.

Anyway, he said some people just went crazy. They
were shooting at anyone they thought was a zombie or
who they thought might be infected with the ex-virus that
made them into zombies. Other people were shooting at
people to get whatever food and stuff they had, or because
they thought they were coming to take <u>their</u> stuff. And
some people were just shooting at anything that moved.
It was all pretty stupid. It was like everyone's IQ dropped
forty points just because they were scared.

Writing it out makes it sound like I was all uber-cool and everything, like it was just a game or something. Bullets whizzing around me and I sat there thinking about psychology and stuff. The truth is, a second bullet made my hair move and I just ran. I rolled over two or three times and crawled on my hands and knees until I got to my feet and then I ran as hard as I could. Being on the track team finally paid off.

I think I realized then that I only had one shoe on, but all I could really think about was running away from the gunshots.

I ran maybe a hundred yards and saw an ~~zombie~~ ex-person.

Dad says it's better to call them ex-people, no matter what. They aren't zombies, he says, because zombies are made-up sci-fi things and exes are real.

I'm doing it again. I'm writing stuff like I was really cool and calm but I was screaming and running around. It's been four hours now and I think I'm hidden pretty good. I know I should try to be more organized.

Okay, so I was running away from the gunshots and I ran into an ex-person. It was a girl about my age, but she had blond hair. She was walking away from me, so I don't think she saw me. Well, I know she didn't see me, because I skittered away and hid behind some bushes and rocks and stuff and she didn't follow me.

I hid there for maybe a minute and then I heard something and realized there was another ~~zom~~ ex-person coming from the other direction and this one was looking right at me. So I got up and ran again. It was like that for two or three hours at least. I'd run and stop and there'd be another ex, so I'd run again. I'm lucky I'm in good shape. If I hadn't been a runner already I would've gotten tired and they would've gotten me. There were so many of them.

I think I've found a safe place for now. After running

around for a while I found some tall rocks. There were one or two exes around them, but none up on them. I don't think exes are good climbers. I ran between two of them and got up here. I looked around and found a nice little space between some boulders. It's like a little canyon with one entrance. I can put my back to the wall and watch the opening. I think I could shimmy up to the top if I needed to get out, too.

I'm not sure where the place I woke up is from here. I was just running around dodging zombies for so long and I didn't keep track of directions. It could be right by this rock or miles away. I ran a half-marathon right after New Year's and I think I ran at least that much getting away from all the exes.

I got up on top of the rocks and looked in all directions, but I don't see any lights. I don't see any lights anywhere except the stars and the moon.

I don't know how I ended up here. I mean, out-in-the-middle-of-nowhere here. I remember I was in the car with Mom—we were going to meet up with Dad somewhere safe—and then I woke up and someone was shooting at me. I don't remember falling asleep, or even being sleepy.

My clothes are shredded!!! Really totaled. Janine has those retro rocker jeans she wears sometimes with like two dozen rips and tears in them, but they still cover more than my pants do right now. The seat of my jeans is gone and my ass is hanging out. No wonder I'm cold. I wish I'd listened to Mom and not worn a thong.

My shirt and coat aren't much better. One of my sneakers is gone and the one that's left is all sticky with something black. My bra is more or less in one piece, so my tits aren't on display. Not much, anyway.

The coat has big pockets. The left one is torn open. It had some lip gloss, my house keys, and my phone. They're gone. The other one had my diary and two pens. I've still got those, obviously.

It's like someone let a bunch of dogs play with my clothes while I was out cold and then dressed me back up in them. I'm wearing rags. And I've got sand in a bunch of itchy places from rolling around on the ground but I really don't want to take my clothes off so I can shake them out, even though there's nobody around.

OMG Todd in sixth-period English would jizz himself if he saw me like this!!!

God, I actually wish that little creeper was here. Or anyone. I'd rather have someone staring at my tits and ass than just being out here alone.

I've got no idea where Mom is. We were supposed to be together, that's all I can remember. Dad wanted us safe and together.

I don't know where I am. I don't know where they are. I don't have any food or water. I barely have clothes.

I need to figure out what I'm going to do next.

July 28th, 2009

Dear Diary,

There's enough light from the moon to write this, so I'll try to get it all in order.

I woke up and I didn't know where I was.

I was between some big rocks out in the middle of nowhere. All my clothes are ripped up so much I'm almost naked. One of my shoes is gone.

I don't know how I ended up here. I remember I was in the car with Mom—we were supposed to be joining Dad somewhere safe—and then I woke up tucked in between these rocks. I don't even remember falling asleep.

Writing it like that makes me sound calm and stuff, but really I kind of freaked out. I mean, WTF waking up somewhere different. Realizing maybe people did stuff to you. ~~It didn't feel like anyone had~~

I crawled out between the rocks and ducked back in. There were a couple of ~~zombies~~ ex-people out there. They didn't see me. I tried to remember some of the reports I'd seen, and I don't think they look around much. I was high enough up they wouldn't notice me if I didn't make too much noise.

How did I end up out here—wherever the hell here is—with the zombies???

My bra covers more than a bikini top, so I took what was left of my shirt off and used it to cover my ass. It's my little butt-cape right now. I figured I still had what's left of my coat to keep the sun off my top.

I took off my shoe, too, and tied it onto one of my belt loops with the laces. I might as well keep it in case I find the other one. Socks in the sand will be okay for now. I didn't want to be lopsided if I had to run.

The big pocket on the left side of my coat got torn open somewhere. I've lost my phone, plus my keys and some lip gloss. I looked around but couldn't find them anywhere. The other pocket's still fine. It had my diary (I'm writing in it) and some pens (I'm writing with one of them).

I climbed up on top of the boulder and looked around. I couldn't see anything in any direction. It was so bright my eyes hurt. I wish I had sunglasses. I had to squint and shade them just to see anything. But there's no buildings or cities or anything as far as I could see. Just sand and dirt and a few ~~zombies~~ exes wandering here and there.

Dad says it's better to call them ex-people. They aren't

zombies, he says, because zombies are made-up things in movies and exes are real.

There were only two or three of them around the rocks I was on. It was pretty easy to time it so they were all on the other side when I ran. I got away and decided to head west. I figured I'd hit a road and I'd be able to wave down a car or something. I was pretty sure someone would stop for an almost-naked teenage girl in the desert.

I think it was around noon when I found the car. The sun was pretty high up in the sky. I saw tracks first and followed those for a little bit. The car was a big SUV. A Land Rover or something. It had New Mexico license plates. The driver's door was open and there was a woman in the driver's seat. The ~~zomb~~ ex-people had eaten a lot of her. I only know it was a woman because of her clothes and hair. Her face was gone down to the bones ~~and they'd eaten her boobs and her stomach and her th~~

I found her purse. There was a New Mexico license with a picture of a woman with the same color hair as the corpse. Her name was Bernard, Sarah J. She was nine years older than me.

How did I end up in New Mexico?!?!?!?

I looked in the back of the car. There weren't any bags or suitcases or anything. She didn't have anything with her. Just her and the car.

I think Sarah J. Bernard pulled off the main road to get away from exes. Maybe she thought she'd be safe out in the middle of nowhere. She drove until her SUV was out of gas and then the exes got her anyway.

That doesn't make sense, though. Things aren't that bad, and they've got the National Guard and the Army out taking care of these things. Heck, all the superheroes are out fighting them. Gorgon and the Mighty Dragon and all those guys are cleaning up the West Coast, and Dad said they've even just sent this super-armor woman out there, too.

So why did Sarah J. Bernard drive out into the middle of the desert to be safe??? Without any food or clothes or anything???

And another thing. Her car was all dusty. There was sand on the hood and it had blown into the front seat. It was like it had been sitting there for a couple weeks.

Then I did the ick thing. It still creeps me out, thinking about it.

When they ~~ate~~ killed her, it looks like they pulled her shirt open. So her shirt's still good it's just stained and dirty. I poked her with a stick a few times to make sure she wasn't an ex. Then I undid her seat belt and pulled her out of the car. She'd been in the sun so long she didn't smell bad. Her skin was kinda dry. I tried not to touch it.

The shirt still had two buttons on it, near the top. I think the rest popped off when it got pulled open. It's not great, but it's better than nothing. Better than what I had. Which was pretty much nothing. I rolled her over and got it off her arms and then I rubbed it in the sand for a while to try to clean the ick off it. Some of it was still sticky.

The shirt's small in the shoulders. I couldn't take her pants. I know I needed them but she died in them and they smelled like old piss and shit and I didn't want them on me. I could live with my butt-cape for now.

Why is everything old and dusty? I think I might have traveled in time. I'm in the future or something.

I thought about staying in the car, but there was still a lot of daylight left. And I could follow Sarah J. Bernard's tracks back to a road or freeway or something.

I walked for another seven or eight hours. I had to hide from exes a couple times, but I saw them before they saw me. They're pretty dumb. I don't know how so many people have gotten bitten.

I found a couple bushes with a little space between them where I can hide. I'm going to spend the night here. There's something near the horizon that might be a freeway, five or six miles away. I could probably make it, I'm not that tired, but I don't want to wander into a ~~zomb~~ ex-person at night when I might trip over them.

I'll head for the freeway in the morning. I've got to figure out where Mom went.

July 28th, 2009

Dear Diary,

Today's been really freaky.

Yesterday, Mom and I were going to meet Dad. Today, I woke up in some bushes in the middle of nowhere. I don't know where I am.

I don't know where Mom is.

I woke up wearing a shirt that wasn't mine or hers. It was missing buttons and had blood on it. A lot of blood.

My clothes were all ripped up. My coat was shredded and my pants were a mess. Janine has those retro rocker jeans with two dozen rips and tears in them, but they still cover more than my pants did. My shirt was tied around my waist and if it wasn't my ass would've been hanging out for everyone to see—the seat of my jeans was ripped out. Mom was right. I shouldn't wear thongs.

One of my sneakers was tied to my jeans. It's got something dark and sticky all over it. I think it's blood, too. I couldn't find the other sneaker anywhere. I was just wearing socks. They're dirty, like I've been walking in them for a long time.

My phone's gone. That pocket was ripped open. So I can't call for help or use my GPS. I lost my house keys and some lip gloss, too. My diary (Hello!) was in the other pocket with two pens.

There were a couple zom exes nearby when I woke up, but none of them seemed to notice me. I saw some reports saying they don't look around much. If you didn't happen to be in their field of view, you didn't exist. I guess I was lucky none of their heads were turned enough this way.

Off in the distance, to the west, was something that looked like a road. Maybe a freeway. It was a dark line just a little bit above the ground. There were some tire tracks near the bushes leading off that way. I had to wait a few minutes, but eventually all the exes were facing away from me and I could slip out of the bushes. I got scratched up by the branches, but not bad enough to bleed.

It took me four hours to reach the highway. I could've made it faster but I had to crouch down a couple times and hide from some exes. I didn't think there were this many of them. Maybe it's just wherever I am. Maybe I'm near one of the cities that got hit bad with the virus.

The road is two lanes. Dotted yellow line. No street signs. No cars. If it wasn't built up a little bit I never would've seen it. I decided to head north. I'm pretty sure I'm in the Southwest. That's where Mom and I were heading. So there's more of the country north of me.

I walked for another five hours before I found the car. It's a Mini Cooper. A red one. Dad said he'd get me one just like it if I graduated with an A average.

It has Arizona license plates. The doors were open. There were no people. No bodies. Dead ones or not-dead ones. I checked under it and in the ditch next to the road. No blood or anything, either. Someone just stopped his car in the middle of the road and wandered away. Or ran away.

There was a duffel bag full of clothes in the backseat. They were men's clothes, and they were a little too big for me, but it was better than what I had. Jeans, T-shirt, flannel, socks. I had to roll the cuffs up on the jeans. Whoever owned the Mini wore boxer-briefs, which felt a little funny but comforting after having my ass hanging out all day.

I changed right there next to the car. There wasn't anyone around for miles, not even exes, but it still felt kind of scary and naughty and sexy. Outside in broad daylight with all my clothes off.

No shoes. I took my one sneaker off my rag-jeans and tied them to the new ones.

I found a bathroom kit in the duffel bag. I wasn't going to use someone else's toothbrush, but I figured the toothpaste was better than nothing. There were some eye-drops, which is great because my eyes have been killing me.

There was a whole box of food, too. Lots of cans and some granola bars and bottled water and stuff. I didn't realize how hungry I was until I saw it. I hadn't eaten anything since lunchtime yesterday. There was a can of pork and beans and I thought it would be good comfort food. I knew they were something I could eat cold, too. Mom and Dad liked to cook out in the summer and we'd have beans with hot dogs and hamburgers. And then Dad would tell me gross stories about all the stuff in hot dogs.

But the beans had started to go bad and tasted awful. All I could eat was the pork. Which was kind of gross cold but still a lot better than the beans. It doesn't make sense, the beans going bad before the meat, but a lot of stuff isn't making sense today. I still ate all of it I could dig out of the can and then brushed my teeth with my finger and some toothpaste.

It was pretty close to sundown by then, so I decided I'd spend the night in the car. I can fold the passenger seat all the way back and use a sweatshirt as a pillow. I'm writing this by moonlight because there's not even enough power in the battery to turn on the dome light.

Where am I? Where's Mom?

~~July 28th, 2009~~

August 1st, 2009

Dear Diary,

Okay, this is messed up. I sat down tonight to write about all the freaky stuff that happened today. I mean, I woke up in a strange car wearing someone else's clothes—different UNDERWEAR—and that's not the messed-up thing.

Normally I just flip to the first empty page of my diary and start to write, but tonight I looked back through it and there are three entries that all say it's July 28th and I don't remember writing any of them. More to the point, I'm sure today is July 28th because yesterday was the day Mom and I were going to go meet Dad, the 27th.

I woke up in a red Mini Cooper. I don't remember falling asleep in it, but the last entry in the diary is about finding a red Mini Cooper with clothes and food in it. Mom wasn't there but all three entries talk about her vanishing. There was a bloody shirt in the car and there's one entry about finding a dead woman and taking her shirt—EWWW—and one mentions tossing it for the clothes here in the Mini. There was a half-full can of pork and beans on the side of the road and an entry about eating pork and beans. Well, pork. And the can looked like all beans when I checked it. They smelled bad.

I don't remember writing any of that. It's pretty clear in each one I don't remember the one before it. So if I thought it was the 28th for three days in a row, then today must be the first of August.

Unless there were days I didn't write in my diary and I can't remember them, either. But each one seems to begin where the last one ends, even if I didn't remember it then.

I wonder if I had a head injury. Dad said short-term amnesia's kind of common with head injuries. I think I'm fine now, and I don't feel any bumps or blood or anything. Maybe I got knocked out of the car (truck? jeep? They told me the name of it but I don't remember) and hurt my head and wandered around for a couple of days.

Why didn't they come get me, though? If I fell out of the car wouldn't they come back for me? Unless they couldn't for some reason.

And how did my old clothes get ripped up? Could that happen just from falling out of the car? Maybe if I rolled through some bushes or something? Or crawled out of a car crash?

There was a duffle bag in the Mini. I took out some of the jeans and bigger-cut clothes and filled the empty space with food and water. Was I looting? Stealing? When does it become okay to take other people's stuff? I couldn't find any sign of anyone else there. When I first saw the bloody shirt I thought it belonged to the car owner, but my diary says I found it in an SUV miles away.

I spent today heading north, away from the Mini.

There were a couple zombies, but I saw them before they saw me. They're pretty easy to dodge. I think they need to be in big groups to be dangerous.

I passed a few more cars. They all have different license plates. Arizona. New Mexico. California. Nevada. There aren't enough of any one type for me to figure out where I am. Some of them have dead people in them. Some of the dead people are moving, but they can't figure out how to open the doors. They don't react to me when they're in the cars. I figured that out pretty quick.

In some of the safe cars I found some more food and water. Some clothes closer to my size. Still no shoes or underwear. I hope this bra holds up because it's thrashed.

I need to find a new phone or maybe a watch or something. That'll help me keep track of what day it is. And I need to find Mom.

~~July~~ August ~~1st~~ 2nd, 2009

Dear Diary,

This is going to have to be qui

August ~~1st~~ 3rd???, 2009

Dear Diary,

Dammit, I know yesterday was the day I found out it was August 1st. I remember it. But there's another entry. Part of one. I stopped writing and I don't know why. Did something interrupt me? Did I fall asleep?

I think I have that Memento disease. The special amnesia that guy had. I shouldn't've been making out with Rick all through the movie. And we even skipped back so we'd have more time. First time at second base doesn't seem quite as important anymore in the big scheme of things.

Should I start writing stuff on my arms like he did? I remember that part. Maybe I should try sleeping with the journal in my lap so I always read it when I wake up.

I woke up in a drainpipe under the road. It was pretty dry. I don't think it's rained out here in a while. I was using the duffle bag as a pillow. I had one of those tinfoil space blankets I don't remember picking up anywhere. There's nothing in the journal about it, but it says I found cars with stuff in them. Maybe I found it and didn't write it down.

I found a road sign. It was right above the drainpipe. Now I'm wondering if I might've found a bunch of them and just didn't write them down.

It's a green shield that says **95**. Interstate 95 is on the East Coast, but I'm not sure where highway 95 is. Maybe there's more than one? I'm supposed to be in Arizona and every car I've seen is from a Southwest state, except for one from Virginia I saw this afternoon. It had a dead family in it—a man and woman and two little boys. They were rotting and dead and I was really glad they had their windows rolled up. Their car was off the road but pointed south.

It still feels like yesterday was the day I was in the car with Mom. Like when you have a long day and you think "Wow, was that only yesterday?" Except for me it wasn't yesterday and it feels like it was.

I wonder if Mom made it to Dad? I wonder if they're looking for me. I've got to figure out where I am so I can try to find them. Got to be smart, though. Dad always says to think first, think second, and then act third. If I keep heading north I'll find something I can locate on a map, and then I can figure out how to get where I'm supposed to be.

I need to find a new phone, or a watch, or something. That'll help me keep track of days and stuff better.

I need to find Mom and Dad. It's been almost a week. They're probably worried sick about me.

February 15th, 2010

Dear Diary,

Okay, WTF?! I have no idea how but it's February. Halfway through February. How did seven months go by and I didn't know? Yesterday was August ~~1st~~ **3rd**! I know it was!

I woke up and I remembered to check my diary. I remember writing that page. Today was August 4th. I knew it was the 4th because yesterday was the 3rd. But this watch has hands and a digital readout. The time matches up on them. The date on the digital part says 2-15-2010.

I missed Valentine's Day. Dammit.

I wonder if I only remember the 3rd because I wrote it down. Maybe I did a lot of stuff yesterday (the real yesterday) and the day before that and the day before that, but I didn't write them down, so I can't remember them.

I woke up in the back of a pickup truck. There were some blue quilted blankets in it and a couple tarps, so it was kind of comfy. It had really huge tires—Janice calls them "compensation tires"—so nothing could see into the back if it walked by. It seems like a good place to sleep. I don't remember finding it and there's nothing here in the diary about it.

There were a couple ~~zomb~~ exes wandering around outside the truck. I ducked down quick and none of them saw me. I opened a can of beef stew and tried to eat. All the potatoes and carrots tasted wrong and slimy, like the beans in the pork and beans. There was a can of P&B in the truck with all the beans left behind.

I remember Dad said the ex-virus did something to the exes to make them last longer. Maybe it's doing something to the meat, too? But how did it get in the cans? And does that mean I've been eating meat filled with virus?!?!

The exes wandered off after an hour or so and I slipped away. I walked north for two hours before I found the watch. It was on an older guy, lying on the side of the road (lying or laying? Honors English student but I can never get that right). He had silver-gray hair and a beard and glasses. His skin was all dried out, but it was still creepy touching him. There's another journal entry that says I took a shirt off a dead woman because my clothes were ripped up and I was practically naked.

The watch is this big, gold thing. A retirement watch, I think. It's like a bracelet on my wrist, even when I make it small. It looks expensive.

February still doesn't make any sense. Dad said the desert was freezing in the winter. It's cold, but I don't think I could've been walking around half-naked and with no food for three days. Although it doesn't feel really cold now. Maybe the date on the watch isn't right? Do digital watches go fast when they start to run out of power? That doesn't make sense. Things go slower, right?

My feet hurt and they look bruised. I think I've been walking a lot. For a long time. But they're not cold. Shouldn't they be cold if it's really February?

I just had an awful thought. What if it really has been seven months somehow? I was looking back through my diary and the last entry said I was going to keep heading north. But what if I found something and started heading south again? Or east or west? If I didn't write it down I'd just wake up and head north again. I could've been walking back and forth for seven months now!!!

Mom and Dad might think I'm dead!! They don't know I'm wandering around out here with a head trauma or something!

I'm on top of a Ford Explorer tonight. It's all locked up tight and there's a body behind the wheel and another one in the backseat. The one in the backseat is twitching but it can't smell me, so it isn't really reacting.

I think there's a city a couple miles north of here. There's a big sign another two miles down the road from here. I can't make out a lot of details. Far away things look hazy, like there's thin clouds in the air or something. Or maybe it's me. My eyes hurt like I've got a couple cat hairs stuck under my eyelids or something. I tried rubbing them all morning and it didn't help. The old guy with the glasses and the watch had a little bottle of eyedrops. They helped a lot, but the far stuff is still hazy.

Can a head injury make you nearsighted?

February 23rd, 2010

Dear Diary,

This is messed up.

I woke up and found a big gold watch on my arm. It said it was February 23rd, which I knew was wrong because yesterday was August 3rd. But then I sat down tonight to write in here and the last entry was dated the 15th. And I read it and I remembered the truck and finding the watch and that was yesterday. I'm sure it was yesterday and I'm only remembering days wrong.

I think this watch might be broken. I read the last entry, but I just can't believe five days slipped by without me knowing about it. I need another watch. That way I can tell if this one is right or not. A control watch, that's what Dad would say.

It'd be easy to find a watch in a city, but there's no sign of that city I mentioned in the last entry. I climbed up on the roof of this big-rig to look for it. I'm back in the middle of the desert again. No sign of any big population centers. No road signs.

I wonder if I should start making a list of cars and trucks. Or just their license plates. I could use them as landmarks so I can tell if I'm doubling back over somewhere I've been before.

I wonder if I got into the city, wherever it was, and didn't have time to write anything. They're all probably overrun with exes at this point. I might have just been dodging undead the whole time.

I wonder if I should try to find a gun. Maybe a shotgun or something, or some pistols so I can go all Milla Jovovich on any undead I find. I've never fired a gun before. I mean, I've played GTA and some Call of Duty, but I don't think that counts.

I wonder where Mom and Dad are. I wonder if they're looking for me. I hope they're okay and not too worried.

~~February~~ May ~~21st ???? 23rd~~ WHO CARES?!?

Oh God!!! Oh God this can't be right!! ~~I can't be one of them.~~ They don't have minds! They can't think or feel or anything. That's what Dad told me. He said they were just corpses. Just corpses walking around because of a virus.

There was a gas station and I thought I could spend the night because there's no exes here ~~except.~~ There's a big mirror by the register so you can see people behind you.

I can see the mirror. I'm looking at myself in the mirror right now. I can see my skin and my eyes. ~~I look like them.~~

I want Mom and Dad! They'll still love me. Dad can fix this. He's one of the smartest people in the world. That's why they hired him. He can fix it!

I CAN'T BE DEAD!!!!!!!!!!

Six

NOW

"**BOSS**," **ILYA SHOUTED** over the gunfire, "it's worse!"

He pointed behind them, to the north side of the street. More exes were stumbling out of a nearby storefront that might have been a Blockbuster at one point and a pizza place on the south corner. Exes wearing helmets. Some of them even had tactical vests and other scraps of body armor.

There were another hundred of them, at least. Maybe even two hundred. With the ones already swarming around *Big Blue*, that meant close to a thousand. The sound of clicking teeth almost drowned out the truck's engine.

The scavengers had driven into the valley through the Cahuenga Pass and followed the road all the way into Sherman Oaks. St. George and Cerberus were along as escorts. There hadn't been any problems until they passed the pair of gas stations flanking Van Nuys Boulevard. There was a minor pileup of four or five cars down the road at the next intersection—nothing compared to some of the trainwrecks across Los Angeles—and the armored titan had gone ahead to deal with it.

Cerberus had tossed two of the cars against the side of the road and the noise had attracted a handful of exes. Two of them staggered over from a street-side patio and another pair stumbled out from behind an oversized pickup truck. She batted one of them away with the BMW she was holding and dropped the car on another. A quick kick from the battlesuit sent a motorcycle skidding and sparking across the pavement to knock down the others.

Then more had staggered out of the Second Spin store to the south, and some pushed out of the comic shop to the north. A lot more than should've been in such places. They piled out of the novelty gift shop with the tattered banner and the Panda Express and the Sprint store. Hundreds and hundreds of them. Far too many with military helmets protecting their skulls.

Most of the scavengers were in the back of their truck. Billie, Jarvis, and a former Project Krypton soldier named Taylor stood around the half-lowered tailgate. Taylor was swearing between every shot. They'd started calling out targets as they fired, but the calls came slow as people took more time to line up. More than a few were called out twice as bullets flicked off the exes' headgear or lost too much force to penetrate.

Cerberus had tried to use the stunners built into her gauntlets but with the slow gunfire from the scavengers the dead overwhelmed her faster than she could put them down. St. George leaped over *Big Blue* to land near the titan and the two of them battered the exes back. They'd held back the tide as best they could.

And then Ilya had seen all the other exes pouring into the road behind them.

No question about it, St. George thought. Legion had figured out how to set a half-decent trap. He wasn't supervising it, but he didn't need to. It wasn't difficult to predict what would happen when a bunch of exes surrounded a dozen or so humans.

The hero soared back over the truck and landed a few yards behind it. A bullet smacked into his shoulder and he glanced back. "Sorry, sir," shouted Taylor. "You got in my shot."

"Striped suit," shouted Ilya from the truck, lining up on his target.

"Teenybopper," called out someone else.

"Red shirt," Lady Bee yelled from her perch on top of the truck's cab.

"Press pass."

"Parking enforcement," called Jarvis with a bit of glee.

St. George brought the edge of his hand around like an ax and chopped through an ex's neck. Its head wobbled in the air and dropped to the pavement. He whipped around just as a teenage boy in a camo-wrapped helmet grabbed his other hand and started to gnaw on it. The dead thing's teeth broke against his skin and clicked against the pavement. He grabbed it by the shoulder and hurled it at the crowds spilling out of the Blockbuster.

A trio of exes stumbled toward him, their jaws snapping open and closed. A pair of gunshots rang out and thudded off the Kevlar helmets. The dead men stumbled for a moment from the impact, then lurched forward again. The hero heard Taylor swearing behind him.

He drove his knuckles through the closest one's face and it dropped off his fist. One of the stumblers, a dead woman, grabbed at his arm. Two of its teeth—implants, probably—were still whole and brilliant white among the cracked gray stumps. He slammed his hand against the ex's chest and sent it flying back. The body knocked down three or four others before it hit the ground. He slammed his hands together and crushed the skull of the last one, helmet and all.

There were too many of them. He'd put down two dozen, the scavengers had dropped another forty at least, and they hadn't made a dent in the horde. The body armor was making them harder to kill. Just hard enough. He didn't think it was going any better at the front of the truck.

He backhanded another ex away. "Cerberus," he shouted. "Get back on board."

From this angle, St. George could only see the titan's blue and platinum skull and its broad shoulders over the truck. A little over a foot of bulky, armored spine was visible on its back. Cerberus grabbed an ex in either hand, slammed them together, then looked back at St. George. "There's too many up front," she bellowed.

Billie hopped up onto the tailgate and stomped twice. "Turn us around, Luke," she shouted.

"Fucking comic-book guy," growled Taylor. He put a round in an overweight ex in a Superman T-shirt and cracked its helmet. The zombie fell over backward.

The truck's engine revved and it lurched forward. An ex that had made it past Cerberus, a bulky man with blood-splattered eyeglasses under its helmet, dropped under the bumper and the large tires crushed its legs and one arm. Taylor and Jarvis took a few steps, keeping close to the tailgate while they called out more targets.

St. George grabbed a dead man by the neck and waist, lifted the ex up, and marched forward with it like a battering ram. Other exes tried to reach past the body and became a tangle of grasping arms and snapping jaws. He heaved and sent a score of them sprawling back. Their bodies tripped another dozen heading for the truck.

A quartet of the undead wrapped their arms around St. George in a group hug. The hero shrugged them off and hammered his fists down hard on their helmets. The impact cracked helmets and crushed three of their skulls. The fourth, a girl in a soccer uniform, he batted away. She plowed into another ex and they both tumbled back into a third.

Big Blue was halfway through a three-point turn. Taylor had leaped up onto the tailgate. Jarvis was still walking alongside it. The truck surged back again and knocked down another ex with the edge of the tailgate.

The air tingled and St. George heard the crackle of electricity over the chatter of teeth. Cerberus was firing up her stunners again. Arcs twisted around the titan's gauntlets and exes dropped at her touch.

An ex reached for St. George. He grabbed the claw-like hand

and swung the dead thing into the air, bringing it around like a club. He swung it once to the left and once back to the right, knocking down a dozen zombies as he did. The ex broke apart on his third swing, its cartilage crumbling like old jerky.

He spread his arms wide and marched away from the truck. He caught three exes against himself. The one by his face was a Latina with chalky eyes and no helmet. The dead woman tried to bite his face and its teeth scraped off his nose. St. George snapped his head forward to crack its skull.

The ex slumped against him and was pinned there when he walked it back into another one. He was pushing six exes at two steps, ten of them at four, and by the time he shrugged them off almost twenty exes were knocked to the ground.

They were already closing back in around him. He leaped into the air and they reached after him with withered fingers. He pushed himself through the air, back to the truck, and a half-dozen exes tipped over as they tried to twist and follow him. A tall one latched onto his boot and he dragged it a few yards before it dropped away.

"Son of a bitch!" shouted Jarvis. There was a sharp edge to his voice. The older man kicked his leg and swung his rifle down to shoot something on the ground. At point-blank range, its helmet did nothing against a rifle round. St. George got a quick look at the twisted thing before its head exploded. It was the ex *Big Blue* had run over, still wearing the red-flecked glasses. It had used its one good arm to crawl under the swerving truck to where Jarvis stood.

The salt-and-pepper man swore again. A wet stain blossomed on his left calf, just above his boot. He stumbled and grabbed the edge of the lift gate as the truck shifted gears again.

He'd been bitten. Bad, from the look of it.

"Get him in the truck," shouted St. George. "Now!" He flew down, grabbed another ex that had gotten close to Jarvis, and hurled it away.

Taylor had been part of the same super-soldier program that

had given Captain Freedom his enhanced physique. He wasn't anywhere near as powerful as Freedom, but he was still three or four times stronger than most of the people in Los Angeles. He grabbed Jarvis by the collar, heaved, and set him down in the back of the truck. Bee leaped down from the top of the cab and pulled a first-aid kit from her shoulder bag.

Big Blue lurched back and Cerberus stepped up onto the lift gate. The truck's suspension sagged and squealed. "Go," shouted Ilya, banging on the back of the cab.

St. George hurled back a last few exes as the truck surged forward. He grabbed one ex by the throat, a dark-skinned woman with a gash in her cheek. The corpse smirked at him.

"Still feel smart, dragon man?"

It let out a coarse chuckle. The hero brought his fist around and shattered the dead woman's jaw. The laugh echoed from a dozen exes around him. He lashed out and destroyed four more. Legion laughed at him the whole time.

Big Blue was a block away and picking up speed. St. George flew after the truck and landed in the bed next to Cerberus. "How bad is it?"

"Just a scratch," Jarvis said through clenched teeth.

"It's bad," said Bee. "Think it might've hit a vein." She was crouched next to Jarvis. Hector de la Vega was across from her. He'd slashed open the bloody jeans to expose the bite and held the leg up in the air.

The ex hadn't taken any meat, but it had sunk its teeth in deep. Bee washed the wound clean with a bottle of water and half the liquid ran down to stain Jarvis's crotch. For a moment the ragged bite pattern was visible on his calf and some of the loose flesh flopped back and forth like a dying fish. Then more blood streamed out and splashed onto the wooden planks that made up the back of the truck. She pulled a second bottle from her pack, hydrogen peroxide, and the wound sizzled. Jarvis hissed and twisted his face.

Bee tore his jeans open more, felt her way up his leg, and

pushed her fingers into his inner thigh. The salt-and-pepper man grunted and set his jaw. "Sorry," she said. "Got to slow the blood flow."

"Cheer up," said Hector. "Least they're not cutting limbs off anymore."

"Yeah," said Bee. "Now first aid just means I grope you for the ride home."

Jarvis forced a grim smile. "It too late to request the amputation?"

"Watch it," she shot back. She slapped a wad of gauze over the bite with her free hand and pressed down hard. The gauze turned red under her fingers.

The truck rolled past a grocery-store parking lot. A few exes between the dusty cars turned their heads to follow the vehicle. They took staggering steps to chase it but it had already driven on before they covered a few feet.

St. George's eyes went from the older man's grimace to the puddle of blood. Drops rained into it. It was the size of a dinner platter and still growing.

Cerberus loomed over the operation like a statue, held steady in the swaying truck by her gyros. "It's going to take us at least an hour to get back," she told St. George.

"I know."

"You're going to have to fly him."

"I know." He set a hand on Lady Bee's shoulder. "Tie it off," he said.

She nodded and let go of the gauze. In a moment she'd pulled a rubber tube from her kit and wrapped it around the wounded man's thigh. She pulled it tight and knotted it. The bloody gauze sloughed off and splatted into the puddle.

St. George bent down and gathered the wounded man into his arms like a child. Bee pressed two fresh pads against the bite and wrapped them with a bandage. It took a little longer for them to turn red. They all knew that could be good or bad.

"Jesus, this is embarrassing," said Jarvis. He sounded drunk.

"Could be worse," said St. George. "You ever ride a motor-cycle?"

"Not since I was a dumb kid."

"Just keep your eyes closed. It's going to be cold up there but it'll only take us a few minutes. We'll be moving fast, so the wind'll be the worst part." He glanced up at Cerberus and back to the scavengers. "You guys going to be okay?"

"We'll be fine," said Ilya.

St. George shot up into the sky. He carried Jarvis up above the buildings, until they were higher than the hills and could see Hollywood proper on the other side. He took a moment to orient himself off the larger landmarks, found the Cinerama Dome, and followed the street another block to the corner of the Big Wall.

The same corner he'd beat Legion back from a few nights earlier.

"Damn," said Jarvis. He shivered in the chill air. "Forgot to tell you I'm scared of heights."

"Yeah," said St. George, "you should've brought that up. Hang on."

He focused between his shoulders and the Valley rushed below them like a speeding river. Jarvis tensed in his arms, and the older man's white-streaked beard flattened against his face. His skin looked pale, but St. George wasn't sure if it was from the flight or the wound.

He raced past the NBC Universal building, over the Bowl to Hollywood and Highland, and then dove toward the Wall. He caught a quick glimpse of the sentries and then he sank through the air to the Hollywood Community Hospital.

Churches and apartments weren't the only thing the people of the Mount had gained when the Big Wall went up. They had a real hospital now, a six-story white building with full facilities and offices. It was another symbolic structure, even if it was undersupplied and understaffed.

The guards looked up when they heard his jacket rustle

above them and focused on Jarvis in his arms. After the outer walls, the hospital was the most guarded place in the Mount. Armed men and women stood ready for when a patient died. It was their job to put a bullet between the eyes of each dead body before the ex-virus reanimated it.

"Wounded man," called St. George. "Make a path." His boots touched the pavement and the guards stepped aside, pulling the doors open as they did. He marched past them.

The lobby was dominated by the large warning sign they'd brought from the old Zukor building, listing potential symptoms of infection. Another symbol. St. George shouted for a doctor while he headed for the emergency rooms.

Jarvis looked up at him. "Boss," he said, "you got to promise me one thing."

"What's that?"

"You know what."

"Yeah, don't worry about it. You're going to be fine."

"I don't come back. Don't let it happen."

"Nobody comes back. You know that."

"I don't want my body stumbling around drunk, embarrassing me. Hurting anyone. Y'all make sure that doesn't happen."

"It won't happen if you don't get drunk next weekend."

"I ain't joking."

"Neither am I," said St. George. "Nobody comes back."

Seven

NOW

SERGEANT EDDIE FRANKLIN, sometimes called Doc Ed despite all his protests, took in the ragged jeans with a glance and peeled the gauze pads away from Jarvis's leg. The skin around the bite was pale and clammy. "How long ago?"

"Maybe ten minutes," said St. George.

"Did he hook onto you, sir," the doctor asked Jarvis, "or'd you get him off quick?" Like most of the former soldiers, Franklin was still formally polite with most people. He'd been a combat medic with the 456th Unbreakables, which made him close enough to a doctor for most people at the Mount.

"Not even two seconds," said St. George. "He kicked it right off."

"And then shot it," added Jarvis.

Franklin had two fingers against the salt-and-pepper man's throat and a palm on his forehead. "You're cold."

"I was just a thousand feet up in the air doing a hundred miles an hour. Damn right I'm cold."

Franklin nodded and pushed the gurney down the hallway to a room. St. George followed for a moment, but knew he'd only be in the way. He found Jarvis's eyes. The older man gave him a smile and a thumbs-up. Then the doors closed and he vanished.

* * *

One of the guards outside tapped his headset. "East Gate's calling for you, boss."

The hero bit back a sigh and nodded. He dug his earpiece out of his pocket and looped it over his ear. "Go for St. George."

"Hey, boss," said a voice. It took him a moment to recognize Elena, one of the regular wall guards. "Heard chatter you were back. Got a minute?"

"Yeah," he said. "What do you need?"

There was a brief pause. "I think it might be better if you came out here to see. East Gate."

"Okay. I'll be there in five." He pulled the earpiece off. For a moment he thought about crushing it. Then he thought about setting fire to every ex outside the Big Wall. And then he thought about just finding Stealth and curling up in bed for a day or two.

Someone cleared their throat. "Jarvis going to be okay?" asked one of the men in front of the hospital.

St. George met his gaze. "I don't know. Maybe. He was bitten."

The guards sighed and shook their heads. "Damn," said the man. "That sucks. I really liked Jarvis."

"Everyone likes Jarvis," said St. George. He thought about crushing the earpiece again. Instead he focused and soared up above the buildings.

* * *

The East Gate was a misleading name. It was still just a solid line of stacked cars running north to south through the center of Melrose and Western. Where the gate would someday be was marked with a few bright lines of yellow spray paint. Since the scavengers had done most of their work on the east half of the city already, the East Gate was the last side of the Big Wall scheduled to get a working entrance.

Elena, Derek, and a bald man St. George didn't recognize waited on the wooden platform at the top of the stairs. They had an oversized umbrella and a few big chairs from the nearby furniture store set up there. All three of them looked out at the intersection of Melrose and Western. A few hundred exes staggered in the street between a bank and a storage center. Building the Big Wall had used up so many cars the roads around the barricade were wide, empty spaces.

His feet thumped on the platform and they turned. "Hey, boss," said Derek.

"What's up?"

"Something kinda weird," said Elena. Her finger stretched out and pointed down Melrose. "See the white building a block down on the right, just after the red one?"

St. George nodded. From his angle, the building looked like a large house or maybe a small apartment building. Curved bars that looked more decorative than functional stretched over the windows.

"Okay. Keep an eye on it." Elena took in a deep breath and cupped her hands around her mouth. "Hey!" she shouted. "You still there?"

Her voice echoed down the street and the exes at the base of the Wall shifted their focus to her. Their heads leaned back and their hands stretched up toward her. Their snapping jaws got more frantic. Another two dozen or so moved toward the wall and joined the mob flailing for the humans on the platform.

A block away, an arm stretched out between the bars of one of the second-story windows. It waved up and down a few times. "I'm here," a voice yelled back. It sounded female. "They're still all around the door."

"Hang on just a little longer!" Elena shouted back. "Someone's coming soon."

"Okay."

St. George watched the arm slip back into the building. "Why didn't you send a team out for her?"

"We almost did," said the bald man. "Then Derek noticed the exes."

The hero glanced down at the crowd of undead. "Are they doing something odd?"

"Not exactly," Derek said. "They're not doing anything."

St. George looked out at the street for a moment and then his brow furrowed. His eyes went from the flailing exes below the platform to the ones down the street. There were at least a dozen of them in front of the white building, still milling around. "They aren't, are they?"

"At first we thought it might be acoustics or something, the way her voice echoes between the buildings," said Elena. "Maybe it was confusing them. But we've been talking to her for two hours now, and it's been a good hour since we started watching the exes for reactions."

Derek nodded. "Someone shouts at the top of their lungs, waves their arms around, and not one single zombie heads in her direction. Just seemed wrong."

"Yeah," said St. George. "Good call, not going to check it out."

"You think it might be Legion setting up another trap?" asked Elena.

"Doesn't sound like him," said the bald man. "He always talks with an accent."

"It better not be," said the hero, "if he knows what's good for him." He took a few steps and launched himself into the air, sailing across the street. Some of the exes reached up and made feeble attempts to grab at him, even though he was well out of their reach.

He drifted over and above the storage building so he could come at the white building from the back. The curved bars were only on the street side of the building, and it took a moment to find a second-story window that had been smashed at some point in the past few years. He spun in the air and slid into the building feetfirst.

He was in a bedroom. A withered body stretched across the bed. It had been there for a long time, long enough St. George couldn't tell if it had been a man or a woman. He guessed the pistol and the dark stain on the far wall had been there just as long. Had they lost someone they couldn't live without, the hero wondered, or just decided they didn't want to risk the exes getting them? How long were they living here after the dead rose?

It crossed his mind that whoever it was could've been here even while the heroes were setting up the Mount. Someone just a hair too far away to hear the sounds of safety, or too scared to raise their voice and call for help. He wondered, not for the first time, how many other people he'd just missed saving during the outbreak.

The bedroom door was open and he walked out into the hall. The carpet muffled his boots. It was a small apartment. Bigger than the one he'd had before the Zombocalypse, less than a mile from here, but not by a huge amount. The far end of the hall looked like a bathroom, across from him was a kitchen. At the front of the house was a living room, or maybe another bedroom.

A stairwell down to a ground-floor door had been blocked with an upended table and a few chairs. They weren't dusty. It was a recent barricade.

He heard something move, and the shadows in the living room shifted. A few strides carried him down the hall. He peeked into the room, then took a single step in.

Across the room from him, staring out the window, was a small woman. He guessed woman from her hips and general build. She had on two or three layers of ragged, mismatched clothes, and another layer that was pure dust and dirt. Some long locks of dark hair hung out from under a Red Sox cap she wore backward. A sequin-covered sneaker dangled from her waist and glittered in the afternoon light streaming in the window.

Sitting near her on a coffee table was an overstuffed duffel bag. It had just as much dirt on it as she did. The shoulder strap had been padded with an old towel and wrapped in duct tape. She'd spread a sleeping bag across the couch.

"Hey," said St. George.

The woman shrieked and spun around. A pair of oversized sunglasses hid her eyes, the square ones elderly people wore over their regular glasses. She'd tried to hide her size and age with the layers of clothes. St. George bet she was twenty, absolute tops. Probably not even out of high school. If high school was still in session anywhere.

When she saw him standing there she fumbled at her belt and pulled out a revolver. It was huge in her hands. "Where did you come from?"

He tipped his head back down the hall. "Through the bedroom window."

The girl took another deep breath and calmed herself. She leveled the pistol at his head. "We're on the second floor," she said. "I've been watching the street. Where did you come from?" Her lips curled down. "Have you been here all along? Were you watching me sleep?"

"I'm telling you, I came in through the window," he said again. "You called for help, so I flew over to check it out."

She took another deep breath. "I know how to use this," she said, dipping her chin at the revolver. "It's loaded and I'm a pretty good shot."

"I'm serious," he said. "I used to be called the Mighty Dragon. Maybe you've heard of me?"

"Get over yourself," she said. "You're way too skinny to be the Dragon."

He smiled. "Afraid not."

She used both thumbs to pull the hammer back on the pistol. It made a loud clack in the room. "Last chance."

St. George took in a deep breath. He felt the tickle in the back of his throat, and let it sigh out. The flames trickled from his mouth and lapped up and around his head.

Her brows went up above her dark glasses and her mouth fell open. Her grip slipped on the pistol and it shifted in her hands. The weight settled on her trigger finger. The hammer slammed down.

There was a thunderclap of noise in the small room and the bullet punched St. George in the shoulder. He yelped. The girl shrieked and jumped back against the window. The deformed round clattered on the floor.

"Ohmigod!" she said. "Oh, God, I'm so sorry."

"It's okay," he said. He rubbed the top of his arm and patted the smoking hole in his jacket. "I'm fine. It just stings a little."

"Boss," shouted a voice in his ear. "You okay? We heard gunfire."

"No problem," he said. "Just a misunderstanding. Everyone's fine."

"It's really you," she said. Her arm went down and the pistol slipped from her fingers. It thudded on the carpet. "You're the Mighty Dragon."

"Told you."

"Oh my God," she said. Her body slumped with relief. "Oh my God. I just . . . you don't know what it's like out there."

"I've got a pretty good idea," he said.

"I've barely seen anyone in ages, and the people I did see kept trying to make moves on me. One guy stole some of my food and another one was this creeper who wanted me to do him and some people just shot at me and I . . ." She paused to breathe, dipped her head, and something like a smile crept onto her face. "I haven't been able to trust anyone for a while now."

"You can trust us," he said. "Inside the Wall's clean and safe. We've got food, electricity, and . . ."

Her glasses slipped down her nose when she lowered her head. She met his eyes and rushed to push the oversized lenses back up. "Please," she said, "just let me ex—"

St. George marched forward and snatched the glasses off her face, crushing them to splinters in his hand. She tried to turn her head and close her eyes, but he saw them again. There was no mistake. They were gray and chalky. The veins were dark against her pale irises.

"Don't hurt me," she said. She skittered back across the floor with one arm up, trying to hide her face. "Please! I'm not one of them."

St. George marched after her, grabbed the dead girl's shoulder, and tossed her across the room. She hit the wall and fell onto the couch. "Rodney, I swear to God, after what you did—"

"Please don't!" she shrieked.

"—the last thing you should be doing is wasting my time with another stupid . . ."

He stopped.

The girl was crying. A single tear made its way down her cheek. It left a path of clean, pale skin behind it. She was taking in raspy breaths as she cried, her chest moving up and down. Her cloudy eyes had gone wide with fear.

"Please," she said. "I'm not one of them. I swear. I swear I'm not."

St. George opened his hands wide and stepped back. "I . . . I'm sorry," he said. "It's okay. I thought . . . I thought you were somebody else."

She slid off the couch and skittered away from him. The trust had vanished from her face. Her eyes flitted to the pistol on the floor.

"Who are you?"

The dead girl lowered her arm a bit. "You're not going to hurt me?"

"I'm sorry," he said again. He raised his hands a little higher, spread his fingers a little wider. "I'm not going to hurt you. I promise."

A cloud of drywall dust drifted down from where she'd hit the wall. They both glanced at it. She set her jaw and glared at him.

"I'm really sorry," he said. "We've had trouble with . . . well, we've kind of got a low-level supervillain here in Los Angeles. He calls himself Legion but his real name's Rodney."

She blinked. "And you thought I was him?"

"He controls all the exes in the city," explained St. George. "He can talk through them, see through their eyes, make them act just like a person. He's tried to trick us before, so I thought you were him. Because you're . . . you know."

"I'm not like them."

He nodded. "I can see that."

"I'm not!"

"Okay, then. Do you want to come in? I think there are some people who'd like to meet you."

She stood up slowly. "How do I know I can trust them? Or you?"

He gave her a smile. "I'm the Mighty Dragon, remember? One of the good guys." He held out his hand. "Most people are calling me St. George these days."

She looked at the hand for a moment, then reached out and wrapped her cold fingers around his. "I'm Maddy," she said. "Madelyn Sorensen."

Eight

NOW

"CAPTAIN?"

"Sorry, sir," said Captain Freedom. He'd been staring at the girl for two minutes. He turned to St. George. "It's just . . . does it count as seeing a ghost if you never saw the real person?"

Madelyn sat inside one of the hospital's observation rooms. They'd cleaned everything out of the room except for a pair of chairs and a small table. Stealth had posted two guards inside the room and two more outside.

Franklin and Dr. Connolly had wheeled in their own table to take samples and check a dozen or so different vital signs. The dead girl winced as another needle went into her arm, but she stayed in the chair. It wasn't by choice. She'd agreed to let them strap her down until Stealth was convinced the girl wasn't Legion.

Madelyn had stripped down to a pair of threadbare jeans and an oversized T-shirt. The arm they were taking blood from had three wristwatches on it she refused to remove. A restraint ran between two of them.

St. George and Freedom stood outside with Stealth, watching the tests. Freedom stood with his hands behind his back, at ease. It pulled his duster open across his broad chest. Stealth's head moved inside her hood and her gaze settled on the huge soldier. "It is Madelyn Sorensen? There is no question in your mind?"

Freedom nodded. "I'd bet my pension on it, ma'am," he said. His mind flitted back three years, to the day he'd sent a team out to bring Dr. Emil Sorensen's family to Project Krypton. It hadn't ended well, for any of them. He still remembered the young girl being pulled across the sand, dodging the exes surrounding the base. He'd added her name—all their names—to the long list of people he'd failed to protect.

He shook the thoughts from his head. "I only saw her in person on the day she died," he continued. "But Dr. Sorensen had a dozen pictures of her and her mother in his office. I must have seen them a thousand times. If that isn't her . . ." He shrugged. "As I said, I'd bet my pension on it."

"So," said St. George, "she's dead and an ex, but it seems like she's still talking and thinking. Anyone got an idea how that happened?"

"More to the point," said Stealth, "how did it end up in Los Angeles, four hundred miles from the site of her death?"

Madelyn locked eyes with St. George through the window and he gave her a reassuring nod. She managed a weak smile back.

"Sir, ma'am . . . a point, if I may?"

St. George nodded. "Yeah?"

Freedom's mouth twitched. "Dr. Sorensen was always insistent Madelyn was still alive," the captain said. "Every now and then he'd have these moments of clarity about his wife, just little flashes when you could tell he knew what had happened to her, but couldn't bring himself to say it out loud. But he was convinced Madelyn would've survived the attack that killed them. He wouldn't back down on that." His eyes drifted back to the dead girl. "He said she was special."

Stealth's posture shifted. "Special?"

The huge officer shook his head. "I don't know, ma'am. I

always assumed it was fatherly instincts bleeding into his mental instability, that losing his daughter was somehow worse than losing his wife."

In the room, Franklin slid a needle out of Madelyn's arm and pressed a piece of gauze against her vein. She asked him something they couldn't hear through the glass and he answered with a few words and a nod. Then he followed Connolly out with the rolling table and left the girl alone with the guards.

"It wanted eyedrops?" Stealth asked Franklin.

Franklin's brows went up and he glanced at the window. He glanced at Captain Freedom out of habit, then nodded at the cloaked woman. "Yes, ma'am. I told her I'd get her some."

"Why does it need them?"

"I'm guessing because her eyes hurt. Her tear ducts probably aren't working well."

St. George looked over at Connolly. "So?"

The doctor shook her head. "Well, she's definitely an ex," Connolly said. "No pulse, no respiration, body temperature is seventy-point-five. I think it was cooler but she started warming up once we got her inside."

"But she's conscious," said Freedom. "She knows who she is. Or was."

"She seems to."

St. George looked through the window again. "Is she Legion?"

"It would not appear to be," said Stealth. "Legion consistently displays the same dialect and body language. Whoever or whatever this is, it is demonstrating numerous tics and habits different from his."

"Whatever *she* is," said Connolly, "she's pretty sure she's a seventeen-year-old girl."

Freedom's brow wrinkled. "She said she was seventeen?"

The doctor nodded.

"This is a discrepancy in its story?" asked Stealth.

"I'm pretty sure she was seventeen when she died," said Freedom. "I remember Dr. Sorensen talking about having her eighteenth birthday at Krypton."

"Well, it's not like she's aging any more, sir," said Franklin.

"No," said Freedom, "but if she's conscious why wouldn't she think of herself as twenty? Physically she might be the same, but almost three years have passed."

"Three years?" echoed Connolly.

"Two years, nine months," said Freedom. The images and sounds rushed through his mind again. "I lost four good soldiers that day, along with Sorensen's family."

Franklin set his jaw and gave a faint nod.

St. George looked at Connolly. Her lips twisted. "Something else wrong?"

She stared through the window. The dead girl was tapping her fingers on the end of the chair and looking around the room. "I'd never've guessed she's been dead for that long."

"The ex-virus does slow decay significantly," said Stealth.

"It does," agreed Connolly, "but it doesn't stop it. And it doesn't do anything to halt rigor mortis, evaporation, or basic wear and tear. I would've said she's been dead for a month at most. And a pretty gentle month."

"What are you implying, doctor?" asked Stealth.

"Just that I'm probably going to want to do a lot more tests after all this blood work's done. If that's okay." She glanced through the window at the dead girl. "With everyone."

Stealth nodded once.

The two doctors left the heroes standing at the window.

"So," said St. George. "Now what do we do?"

"We interrogate it," said the cloaked woman. "Captain Freedom, you are the most familiar with Madelyn Sorensen. Would you be able to confirm its identity?"

The huge officer straightened up and his face got hard. "That depends on what type of interrogation you're asking me to do, ma'am. I won't hurt a teenage girl."

"For the moment, a verbal interrogation should suffice. If

you are satisfied with the results, there would be no need to go further."

* * *

One of the guards in the room, Cook, glanced at the dead girl. She smiled at him. "Hey," she said. "I'm Maddy."

He ignored her. "You think if she turns out to be an ex they might let us have her?"

His partner followed his gaze. "For what?"

Cook shrugged. "She's not that messed up. Can't touch her but she's still fun to look at."

"Hey, creeper," snapped Madelyn. She glared at him. "I'm right here, y'know."

"Shut up, corpse girl," Cook said. He leveled his rifle at her. Her eyes went wide.

"That's enough of that," said Freedom. He stepped through the door and made the room look small. He walked over to Madelyn and gave Cook a hard stare. "You can wait outside, gentlemen."

Cook opened his mouth to speak but thought better of it. The other guard cleared his throat. "Stealth'll have our heads if we leave our posts."

"Your dedication is admirable," said Stealth from the doorway. "Wait outside as the captain instructed."

She made no move to get out of their way. The two guards turned sideways and pressed themselves against the wall to get out of the room without touching her. Once they were gone, she walked in the rest of the way. St. George followed her in.

"I apologize for that, ma'am," Freedom told Madelyn. "There's no reason for them to be speaking like that to you."

Her eyes flitted from St. George to Stealth and up to Freedom. "It's no biggie," she said. "I've heard worse in gym class."

"I'm still sorry." He reached over to her and pulled the straps open. She stretched her arms out and flexed her wrists.

They'd cleaned Madelyn up, even though she still wore the inner layer of her ragged outfit. Her slim body had started to fill out with the shape of maturity, but she couldn't've weighed more than a hundred pounds. Her skin was the dusty gray of the long deceased. She had her mother's dark, wavy hair, and it brushed her shoulder blades. Freedom recognized the shape of Dr. Sorensen's eyes, even though they were pale and cloudy.

She stared at him for a moment. "Are you Captain Freedom?"

Something twinged in his chest. He paused, half crouched into the other chair. "Yes, ma'am. How did you know?"

"Dad told me about you. I know he wasn't supposed to, but he was really excited and proud of how you guys turned out. Especially you." She smiled. Her teeth were bright and flawless. "I like your coat."

"Thank you." Freedom spread his duster and settled into the chair. It creaked under his bulk but held him. He glanced back at Stealth and St. George. The hero stood by the door. The cloaked woman had settled behind Freedom, near the window. "And your father is . . . ?"

"Emil Sorensen," Madelyn said. Her thin brows furrowed up. "He's the doctor out at Project Krypton. Your military base, right?"

Freedom nodded again. "How do you know about that?"

She raised an eyebrow at him. It let more of the light hit her pale eyes. "Because you guys flew me and Mom out there to meet him."

"When was that?"

"Just a few . . ." She closed her eyes for a moment. "It was July of 2009," she said. "We got on the plane late on the twenty-sixth, landed in Arizona a little before noon on the twenty-seventh."

"Okay."

"Why are you asking me all this?"

"We need to make sure you are who you say you are, ma'am."

"Is this what St. George was talking about? You think there's someone else talking through me or something?"

"More or less," Freedom said. He paused for a moment and studied the girl's face again. The twinge grew to a small knot. "Do you remember what happened after you landed?"

She nodded. "Some of Dad's soldiers . . . your soldiers, I guess . . . picked us up at the airport. There were exes there. They shot most of them, and the noise really freaked Mom out. One of the guards was bit, but I couldn't tell how bad it was and nobody wanted to say. Then they got us into a big armored jeep-thing and we headed for the base."

"It's called a Guardian," said Freedom.

"Okay, cool. So, we were driving along. I remember we could see the base up ahead. Mom was relieved and I was excited to see Dad and his new lab. And then . . ."

"Yes?"

"Then the guy driving the jee—the Guardian—shut it off. He turned the key and said the gas tank was empty, even though the gauge said it had half a tank. The woman in charge, Sergeant Washington, she said it was empty, too. I thought it was some kind of joke, just to see if they could make us scream or something. Then there were some explosions, and the exes were trying to get into the car. Their teeth were super loud. And all the soldiers kept saying there wasn't any gas, and they were *serious*. They really thought it was empty. So they were calling for help and me and Mom were freaking out and begging them to start the car back up and then one of the soldiers started freaking out and . . ."

She stared past Freedom to St. George. Her hands crawled toward each other and knotted together.

The memories crawled through Freedom's mind. The team had been brainwashed by Agent Smith and his mind-control powers. They'd looked at the gauge, seen empty, and believed it. One of the soldiers, Adams, decided it was better to try running through hundreds of exes to reach the gate. He'd dragged Madelyn with him and they'd both been torn apart right in front of Dr. Sorensen. The whole team had died.

He'd never been sure why Smith had done it. Maybe it had been to punish the doctor or keep him in line. Or maybe Smith had done it just because he could.

Freedom brushed the thoughts away. He took a slow breath to help cover the pause. "And then?" he prompted.

"I don't remember," she said. Her fingers shifted in their knot. "I think that's when I died."

"Do you have any idea how this happened to you? Why you came back with your mind intact?"

She shook her head. "Nope."

Freedom set his hands on the table. They looked massive across from hers. "Do you know what your mother's name was?"

"Eva."

"Do you know what year—"

"Wait," said Madelyn. Her eyes got huge. "What do you mean, was?"

Freedom's chair creaked again. The knot by his heart caught fire. He glanced over at St. George, then studied the tabletop for a moment. His voice dropped a few decibels, but it still rumbled in his huge chest. "I regret to inform you, ma'am," he said, "but your mother died with you in the Guardian attack."

The knot of fingers unraveled and she wrapped her arms around herself. "Are you sure?"

"Yes," he said. "I was there. We tried—I tried to stop them, to save both of you and my soldiers. I . . . I'm very sorry for your loss."

A lone tear raced across her cheek. Her chest heaved. With her eyes closed, she almost looked alive. After a few moments she wiped her face with her arm and opened her chalk eyes to look at him. "Does Dad know?"

Freedom paused again, then nodded. "He did. I'm afraid he died last summer, while we were evacuating Project Krypton."

Madelyn shrank a little more in her chair.

"Your father loved you both very much," said Freedom. "In all the years I knew him, I don't think we had more than a dozen conversations where you didn't come up. Losing the two of you was a huge blow to him."

She sobbed for a few minutes, but there were no more tears. Freedom's chair creaked again as he turned to look back at St. George and Stealth. The cloaked woman nodded once.

"I knew with all the stuff going on . . ." Madelyn stopped to blow her nose. "I knew they were probably gone, once I realized how long it had been. I just . . . I hoped." She sniffed again and wiped her dry face with the back of her hand.

Freedom let her sit for another minute. "May I ask you a few more questions?"

"Sure," she said. She sniffed hard and her voice got strong again. "I've got nowhere to be."

"I'm sorry," he said. "I just need to be sure."

"I get it," said Madelyn. "Ask away."

"What was your sister's name?"

"I don't have a sister. Or a brother."

"Do you remember the names of any of the other soldiers who picked you up at the airport?"

"I don't, sorry. I just remember Sergeant Washington because I thought of the president, and then she said her name was Britney."

He nodded. "So how'd you end up here? Why not Phoenix or Las Vegas or someplace closer to where you . . . closer to Krypton?"

"You can say where I died. I've gotten used to the idea."

"Okay. So why here, ma'am?"

"And please stop calling me ma'am. You make it seem like I'm some ninety-year-old dowager or something."

"I can make do with Madelyn," he said. "So why here?"

"I saw fireworks."

"What?"

She sighed. "Could I get my bag back?"

Stealth nodded to St. George. The hero stepped outside and a moment later he carried in the dusty duffel bag. It was un-

zipped and some clothes hung out of it. Madelyn pulled a battered book from one of the side pouches. She flipped through
the pages, then handed the open book to Captain Freedom.

July ~~1st~~ 4th, 2011

Dear Diary,

There were **fireworks** out to the west! West and south.
They must've been huge for me to see them from out here.

"That was almost nine months ago," he said. "It took you
nine months to get here?"

"Sort of," she said. She tapped her head with her fingertips.
"I have trouble remembering things since this happened to me.
If I don't write stuff down, it's like it didn't happen. There may
have been a couple days I was backtracking and didn't know it."

"Nine months, though?"

"Maybe a lot of days." She looked him in the eye. "I know it's
been almost three years since this happened. I can see it written
out in my journal. But it feels like it was a couple of weeks ago."

St. George spoke up. "Is that what all the watches are for?"

She nodded. "Yeah. I kept forgetting days, so I thought the
watch was broken, so I got another one. Then I thought maybe
they were both broken. But three saying the same thing have to
be telling you the right date and time." She closed the journal
and pulled it into her lap. "Are you sure there's no chance Mom
or Dad survived? I mean, maybe they're like me or something."

Freedom set one hand on top of the other. "No, I don't believe so."

"You're sure?"

"In your father's case . . . no. I'm sorry to say there's no way
he could've come back." The huge officer paused for a moment.
"Your mother's body was never found. We'd assumed she reani-

mated and walked away, or she'd been . . . damaged to such an extent that her body was destroyed."

Madelyn stared at him for a long minute. She didn't blink. It occurred to Freedom that she didn't need to. Then she lowered her eyes and sighed.

He gave her another moment. "Why did you try to hide your . . . condition from us?"

She looked down at the straps. "Not counting the chair, you guys have been great, but not everyone's so chivalrous to a seventeen-year-old girl on her own." She leaned back in her chair and crossed her arms. "Some of them thought me being dead made it okay to do things to me."

The captain's face hardened. "Did anyone . . . Were you assaulted in any way?"

Madelyn shook her head, then shrugged. "Not like that, no. I got groped a couple times, but that's it. Some people stole my stuff. I lost my shoes once. Most of them got freaked out by me being dead and still, y'know, smart. I could get away without too much trouble."

"And the pistol? Where'd you get it?"

"I found it in a car, under the seat. It was empty, but there was a box of ammunition in the glove compartment."

"Your father taught you how to shoot, correct?"

"Yeah, right," she said. "Dad and Mom hate guns." Her face fell. "Hated guns. It was pretty easy to figure out, though. There wasn't a clip or anything, just the . . . Are you still testing me?"

"Yes," Freedom said, "and it's called a magazine, not a clip." He turned his head back to Stealth again and nodded.

Stealth stepped forward. "We are prepared to accept you are who you claim," she said. "You are not Legion."

"Cool," said Madelyn.

The cloaked woman turned to St. George. "However," she said, "this poses a question. How is she not Legion?"

"Maybe because she's conscious," St. George suggested. "His powers may need the . . . the space of an empty mind."

"Perhaps she doesn't count as a regular ex," said Freedom. "Some tweak to the virus or something similar. If Legion's possession ability is very narrow-ranged, she might fall outside its parameters."

"According to everything we know," said Stealth, "the virus never mutates."

Madelyn tapped her fingers on the tabletop. The rhythm was from a song, something popular before the outbreak, but Freedom couldn't place it. "So," she said, "what happens now?"

St. George cleared his throat. "If you're up for it, I think the doctors want to run some tests on you and try to figure out why you are . . . well, the way you are."

"What does that mean?"

"To be honest, I couldn't tell you. I'm not a doctor."

"Am I . . . am I under arrest or anything?"

Freedom straightened up from his chair and shot a look at Stealth. "I don't think so."

Madelyn stood up, too, and swayed side to side. She was smaller than all of them. "Can I go out and walk around? It's been a while since I could just, y'know, walk and not worry about bumping into exes or anything."

St. George caught the shift in Stealth's body language. "Maybe we should ease into that," he said. "Most people probably won't react well to seeing a dead person inside the walls. Just for now, you shouldn't go anywhere without an escort."

"And until we are certain why you are the way you are," said Stealth, "we should make running tests our main priority."

Madelyn's face dropped. "Yeah," she said, "I could see that." She looked at St. George. "Where am I going to stay until then?"

"We shall have a room prepared for you here," said Stealth. "Captain Freedom will set up a liaison for you to take care of whatever needs you may have."

The dead girl glanced at Freedom and her lips twitched for a moment. "You mean, a guard to watch me."

"To protect you," said Freedom.

Madelyn looked ready to say something else when St. George's earpiece squawked loud enough for them all to hear. He slapped his hand up to block the sound, then yanked the plug out. He held it an inch from his ear. "Calm down, Barry," he said. "Yeah, yeah, I'll be right there." He looked at Stealth and Freedom. "You didn't hear that?"

She shook her head. "What does he need?"

"He says we've got to talk in person. It's urgent."

* * *

St. George found Zzzap in Stage Four, pacing in the air outside the electric chair. *Is it true?*

"Yeah," St. George said. "We've got an intelligent ex and it's Dr. Sorensen's daughter. But we're not sure how she—"

The other hero shook his head. *No, not her. Jarvis was bitten?*

The reminder hit St. George in the chest. "Yeah, he was. Sorry. I thought you would've heard by now."

Only rumors on the radio. He glanced at the entertainment center and gave a little nod. His hands did something in front of his chest, a motion lost in the glare of his body. *Is he going to make it?*

St. George shook his head. "There's a chance, but probably not. Sorry."

Zzzap nodded and continued the odd motion with his hands. St. George realized the wraith was tapping his fingers together. He glanced at the television again.

Okay, this is going to sound a little weird but . . . we need him.

"We need him for what?"

No, not you and me "we." I mean—yeah, shut up. I've got this.

"What?"

His body. When he dies, you can't destroy his brain. Just strap him to the bed or whatever and let him change.

St. George took in a slow breath. "What the hell are you talking about?"

We just . . . I need you to trust me on this, okay? Don't let them put him down.

He looked at Zzzap and tried to inhale the wisp of angry smoke around his nostrils. "How can you even ask something like that?"

Because . . . The gleaming wraith looked over at the television. *Yeah,* said Zzzap. *I think it's time we told him.*

"Told who what?"

Told you. No, just let me do this my way, okay?

"Okay."

Zzzap waved a hand at him. *Not you, George. Sorry. I've wanted to tell you for a while, but we agreed it'd be better to keep it quiet until the opportune moment, so to speak.*

St. George felt something twist in his gut. His shoulders slumped. "You've been keeping something from me."

Yeah. I figured you'd notice. Or Stealth.

"She did."

Zzzap nodded. *I really suck at secrets,* he admitted. *It's a good thing the world ended or I would've blown the whole secret-identity thing inside of a year.*

A moment of silence passed.

"So," said St. George. "Are you talking to . . . people on the radio again?"

Yeah. No. No, this is me and you.

"You sure?"

What? Yeah, of course.

"Okay. So what's going on?"

Zzzap stopped tapping his fingers and started pacing in the air again. *Okay,* he said, *you know I don't really "see" anymore, right? Not when I'm like this, at least. Not the way you do.*

"I think so, yeah."

The wraith nodded. *I take in a lot of material from across the spectrum and my mind's sort of figured out how to process it all as visual information. Visible light, infrared, ultraviolet, radio, television, microwaves, gamma rays . . . I see all of it.*

"Right."

Okay. Well, see, sometimes, all these things I can see come together in certain ways—certain alignments, you could say—and I can see even more.

St. George crossed his arms. "More how?"

Like a lot more. About a year ago I realized I can see stuff no one else can. Not with any equipment or lenses or anything, because no one's ever been able to look at the world the way I do.

"Barry, what are you getting at?"

The wraith paced in the air for a few more moments. He made a buzzing noise like a sigh. Then he turned to face St. George.

I see dead people.

Do You See What I See?
THEN

I'D BEEN IN the chair for about eight hours when Max came in. I didn't scream this time, even when he walked through the wall and then through the table my stereo system was on.

I didn't scream the first time he showed up, either. That time he just walked in through the door and started chatting. It took me a couple minutes to recognize him, and then I just assumed he'd survived somehow and nobody'd ever told me. I mean, it's what superheroes do, right? We absolutely-for-sure-no-way-out-of-it die and then a few months later we're back with some miraculous tale of survival. And it had been about four months since George put the demon down, soooo . . . perfect timing.

I think we'd been talking for fifteen minutes that first time when I realized he wasn't actually there. And then another minute or two before I realized I was talking to a ghost.

And then I screamed.

People told me I blew out a dozen walkies and five headsets. Stealth was pissed. I told her I'd been watching *The Orphanage* and gotten freaked out by the old woman who got hit by the bus. One great advantage of the energy form—I'm the only person in the Mount who can lie to Stealth and get away with it. No real body means no real body language.

Anyway, Max.

I've got to be honest, I met Max two or three times when he was Cairax, but I always thought all this magic and demons stuff was just some gimmick he had. I mean, there was Nautilus out in Hawaii and a guy over in Iraq who could turn into a dragon, so turning into a big purple, scaly thing wasn't hard to believe. I figured he had some sort of mass hypnosis or psychokinesis power, made up this sorcerer story, and then was just one of those people who refuse to break character, even on their downtime. Like Schreck in *Shadow of the Vampire*.

Needless to say, being a ghost gave Max's sorcerer story a lot more weight in my book.

Anyway, hanging out for the past three months had killed all the thrill of talking to a ghost. Today he showed up and he was bored and chatty. It was a common thing for us. People could see and hear me, but I was trapped in the electric chair all day. He could go anywhere, but nobody could see, hear, or feel him.

He glanced at the racks of DVDs. "Do you have anything new?"

George brought over a couple things the other day.

"Well, let's start the show."

One problem, I told him. *I've still got the third season of* Smallville *in the player. The new stuff's not loaded yet. And since neither of us can touch anything . . .*

"Damn it." He reached up and scratched his head. It was always a little disturbing when he did that, since he didn't have a head or a hand to scratch it with. I figured it was like how I could see radio messages.

You could just go watch somewhere else, I offered.

"Nah," he said. "It's weird just sitting there with people. And they never laugh at my jokes."

Your jokes aren't that funny, I said.

"So, no movie." He twiddled his fingers in the air. "You want to practice the symbols again?"

I know we should, but not really.

"Y'know, I've told you before, you don't have to do the whole buzzing-air thing for me. Your thoughts are pretty easy to pick up when you're like this."

Yeah, and that's not weird at all.

"Says the man who gets radio messages beamed straight into his brain."

That's different.

"Not by much," said Max. "I mean, it's pretty much what we're doing now."

Well, I said, *I'm still getting used to it.*

"It's been a couple of months now."

You have to admit, this isn't exactly an everyday thing. And I say this as a guy who more or less turns into a small star.

"Which is why I'd think you'd have an easier time adjusting to it than someone like Geor—ahh, speak of the devil." Max's eyes moved past me and he started to chuckle.

I turned around. George was standing halfway between the door and the electric chair. It looked like he was wearing a Prince Valiant wig. Then I realized it was his hair. I remembered today was the day of the big haircut.

Wow, I said. *They really did a number on you.*

"I feel like I should call him Christopher Robin," said Max.

"Who were you talking to?" asked St. George.

Nobody, I said.

"Not suspicious at all," snorted Max.

I shrugged and waved my arm at the air. *People. On the radio.*

George nodded and ran a hand through his hair. "So, how's it look?"

You know what's big after the Zombocalypse? I told him. *Hats.*

"Seriously."

"It looks like you got mugged by a hairdresser with some mother issues," said Max.

I glanced at Max and tried not to laugh. *Remember when you were a little kid and your mom always made you get that page boy–looking haircut?*

George blinked. "How'd you know?"

It's what every mom did.

"So it looks like that?"

"It's so much worse than that," said Max.

Yeah, it's a little worse, I agreed. *It's like a blind person tried to do a page boy with a pair of hedge clippers.*

Max chuckled. George sighed. "Great."

I stretched in what I hoped was a casual way and fed some power into the electric chair. *You still heading out?*

"Yeah. You still nervous?"

I shrugged and Max caught my eye again. He was walking around George, examining the Prince Valiant look from every angle. "Doing this to his hair rated giving out raffle tickets?"

It's a big thing, I said.

Max chuckled.

I looked at George. *You and I have been over to the Valley a few times but really no one's gone there in almost two years. Hell, I think Danielle was the last one there when she came over with her Marines.*

"I don't think you're supposed to call them 'her Marines.'"

Whatever.

"We've got to go sometime," said George. "We've cleaned out everything we can find on this side of the hills. Now it's either the beach or the Valley, and the Valley's got a lot more resources."

"A lot of exes, too," said Max.

I know, I said, not really sure which of them I was answering. *You have to admit, though, it's just kind of weird. I've gotten used to the Valley being "somewhere else," y'know?*

George nodded. "There seems to be a lot of that going around," he said. "We're getting . . . insular, I guess. Is that the right word?"

Max nodded and I copied him. *Yeah.*

"Plus I just had a talk with Billie about the Seventeens. We've got to start including them more, starting now. She's going to have one of them come out with us."

Really?

Max scowled. "Seriously? Why not just park the truck and open up the back so the exes can get in?"

I remember I thought hard about Max shutting up. He was so lonely and so excited to have someone to talk to, it was tough for him to stop talking sometimes. And sometimes it made it really hard for me to hide the fact there was someone else in the room. So I thought about it really hard, and maybe one or two folks in the area even heard "Stop talking" come over their walkies.

Max heard it. "Sorry," he said, because we'd talked about it before. He turned away and went to examine the CD collection he'd memorized a month ago.

I tried to remember the last thing George had said. Something about the Seventeens. I went with an easy cover. *You sure you don't want me coming out with you?*

George shook his head. "We'll be fine. This way you can keep Danielle powered up here and still make it out to us if anything goes wrong."

Assuming you have time to set off a flare.

"If we don't have time to set off a flare, there's not much you'd be able to do anyway." He held up his hand and counted off three fingers. "Remember, red is trouble, blue we need you but it's not urgent, white means we're spending the night over there."

The thought of sleeping with exes all around creeped me out. When I get to sleep, I'm out cold. And when I'm human, I can't feel anything from my thighs down. An ex could chew on my legs for an hour and I could sleep through it. That's vulnerable in a way lots of people don't get. It was a recurring nightmare for a while, right after we started fighting the exes but before everything collapsed.

Better you than me, I told George.

He nodded. "Hey, it's my last choice, too." He knew about my nightmares. I'd shared them a few months ago during a Freddy

Krueger marathon. He told me he had one now and then where zombie children were overwhelming him.

That's the sort of guy George is. He trusts you. You trust him.

Actually, I said, *do you have a minute?*

He nodded. "Yeah, sure."

There's something I've been meaning to tell you.

Max perked up.

I'd seen enough movies to know this was the point where so many people get ignored. They've got something important to say and they come up with the dumbest possible way to say it. I didn't want to be one of those guys.

Okay, I said, *a couple months ago I saw something weird—*

And suddenly Max was there between us. "Please don't," he said.

Trust me, I told him.

St. George nodded. "Something weird. Got it."

"He's not ready to hear this, Barry," said Max. "And you've got no way to prove it."

I started to say something and bit my lip. So to speak. I think it makes a little sizzling sound in the air.

"You've got no physical evidence I'm here," the ghost said. "None at all. And you know Stealth is going to demand proof once St. George tells her. So at best they're going to think you're making it up and wasting their time."

I knew he was right. We'd had this conversation a dozen times already. This was the second time we'd done it one-sided in front of George. Once it was in front of Danielle. Heck, I'd just been having it in my own head.

"At worse, they think you're losing it," said Max. "And once they start thinking that, we'll never convince them when we're ready to do everything else."

Yeah, I said without thinking.

"We've got to wait until we can prove it."

George was still waiting.

You know what, I told him, *you've got stuff to do.*

"Sooooo . . . you didn't see something weird?"

It was just . . . just a movie. I wanted to tell you about it. It can wait.
Max sighed in relief.

George nodded. "Okay. Maybe if we find some microwave
popcorn out there we can do a movie night or something this
weekend. We haven't just hung out in a few weeks."

I smiled, even though it's wasted in the energy form. *Well,
I've been hanging out,* I said with a wave at the electric chair.

He smirked. "Got to go. I'm supposed to check in with
Stealth before we head out. We're trying the chain mail today."

Excellent, I said. *If it works out, tell everyone I'm going to be pushing for a reenactment of* Lord of the Rings. *With all the stuff Peter
Jackson left out.*

He chuckled and stepped outside. I could see him through
the walls. His aura flared and he sailed into the sky. I've always
meant to tell him it does that.

And then I remembered the other important thing. *Damn
it,* I mutter.

"What?"

I forgot to have him put the new DVDs in.

Max laughed. "Thanks for not telling him," he said. "I know
it's a pain, lying to him."

It'd be easier if you'd stop trying to butt into every conversation.

"Sorry."

I nodded. *So, we've got no new movies,* I said. *Let's start figuring
how we're going to prove you're real.*

"Sounds good to me."

Two smart guys like us, I said, *how long could it take?*

Ten
NOW

OKAY, SAID ZZZAP, *I think I've got it this time.*

Another burst of static roared from the stereo speakers. St. George and Danielle sighed. Stealth didn't move a muscle, but impatience radiated off her like heat.

"Barry, come on," said St. George. "I think this has gone on long enough."

Hang on, he said. *If this was easy everybody'd be doing it.* He focused on the stereo again.

The speakers popped and said, "Work this time?"

Got it, said Zzzap.

"Oh my God," said the stereo. "I was starting to think I'd never hear my own voice again." There were a few quick snaps and a squelch of static. "Can you all hear me okay? You can understand me?"

St. George looked at Zzzap. "Is this it?"

The brilliant figure nodded.

"So, we're hearing a ghost on your sound system?"

"Actually, you're talking to a ghost on his sound system," said the speakers. "I can hear you, too."

"If this is intended as a joke," said Stealth, "I do not find it amusing."

"Ask me anything," the stereo said. "I'll prove it's me."

"You being Cairax," said St. George. He glanced at Zzzap.

"Well, me being Max Hale, but that's probably how you think of me, yeah." The speakers popped twice. "George, you and I met down in Venice Beach right around Christmas. There were some rich kids beating up a homeless guy for kicks. I made two of them wet their pants. You were down there doing a random patrol and you thought I was attacking the kids."

"I've told you this story," St. George said to the glowing figure. "It doesn't prove anything when you say it's a ghost telling it."

I'm just translating, said Zzzap. *He's doing all the talking.*

"Sure he is," said Danielle. She glanced at Stealth. "Y'know, the armor's way behind in maintenance, and I don't like trusting it to Cesar and Gibbs. I should probably go."

"Barry," began St. George.

"Cerberus, you and I never met," interrupted the stereo, "but you ended up replacing me on one of the task forces in the fall of 2009. You'd been in L.A. for about a month and—"

"After three years," Stealth told Zzzap, "there are very few stories regarding the past you can tell which we do not all know. If you wish to convince us you are speaking for a ghost, you will need to tell us something you could not know."

I'm not talking. I'm just translating what he's saying into radio waves so you can all hear—WHAT?!? Zzzap looked at St. George, then Stealth, and then over at the corner of the room.

"What's wrong?" asked St. George.

The wraith looked at his friend again, then his gaze settled on Stealth. *You're Karen,* he said. *You're the woman from dinner.*

Danielle sighed again and Stealth crossed her arms. "This is nothing you could not have deduced on your own," said the cloaked woman. Her head shifted to St. George for a moment before she took a few steps toward the rings of the electric chair. "It might be best if you returned to human form for the time being," she said. "We should discuss certain matters which are better resolved before you resume—"

Max says you were on top last night.

Stealth froze. So did St. George. Danielle's eyes went wide, and her expression went back and forth from amusement to horror.

Sorry.

Stealth's pose shifted. Her arms hung straight at her sides. "That statement refers to which of us?"

The speakers popped again. "To you, Stealth," said the stereo. "I was wandering around, thought I'd check in on you two, and caught you guys . . . in the middle of things. At St. George's place. I can give more details if you like."

"That will not be necessary," said the cloaked woman. St. George saw her face shift beneath her mask. If it was anyone else he'd guess she was confused. The closest Stealth got to confusion was sudden reassessment.

A few moments of silence passed.

"Wait a minute," said Danielle. "This is real? Holy shit, Max, this is really you?"

"In the flesh. Just, y'know, without any actual flesh."

Stealth crossed her arms. "For the moment I am willing to accept the premise you are a separate being from Zzzap. I do not yet believe you are a supernatural entity."

"How'd you survive?" asked St. George. "I mean, I crushed your skull. Or your zombie's skull."

"I didn't survive."

"So you jumped bodies like Legion does?"

"No, George, I didn't survive. I died. That's where the whole 'being a ghost' thing comes into it."

Stealth crossed her arms. "So you claim you have been a disembodied spirit here at the Mount since your death?"

"Well, not exactly," said the stereo. "That's where it gets a little tricky."

"Go on."

The speakers crackled for a moment. "You all know I had my Sativus medallion that let me transform into Cairax. He's a demon from the Abyss and I was hijacking his body every time I put the medallion on. This is the kind of thing that can get you into trouble in the long run, so I had some backups installed."

"Installed where?" asked Danielle.

"On me. That's what a lot of my tattoos were. They were wards and guards to make sure Cairax couldn't get me after I died. Being dead was my safe house, if you like." The speakers crackled like a potato chip bag. "Demons can't affect the dead unless said dead person falls into their sphere of influence—if they're going to hell. Otherwise, they can't touch you."

"So your plan was going to heaven?"

"No, that's way too big a gamble for someone like me who's done a lot of magic," the stereo explained. "I was just aiming to make sure my spirit got bound to Earth so I'd have time to work through a few things and rack up a few more karma points.

"What I didn't count on was the ex-virus. The idea that my body could die and still be walking around on its own. All my preparations sort of jammed up and I got trapped in there for a year or so until George destroyed my physical body."

"Sorry about that," said St. George.

"Don't be. That's what let everything start working again."

"I hate to agree with Stealth," said Danielle, "but I'm still not sure I buy this whole 'magic' thing."

The stereo chuckled. "You realize you're saying that to a ghost, right?"

"A ghost according to you. I never did buy all your magic talk."

"Okay," said the stereo, "let's look at it this way. If you hold out your hand, turn your wrist, and stomp your foot down, does it transport you across the country?"

Only if you're wearing ruby slippers, said Zzzap.

"Don't interrupt," said the stereo. "It's important they all believe this."

"No, of course not," said Danielle.

"But if you're sitting in a car it works, right?"

"Well . . . yeah. But that's different."

"Not at all. It's the same thing. We're agreeing that if you make the right gestures in the right place it's possible to get a result you can't get by doing the same thing in other places or under different conditions. And once you've got the car moving you can change the location those gestures work at so you can do it again."

"And you claim this is how magic works." It wasn't so much a question from Stealth as a challenge.

"In a really simple way, yeah," said the stereo. "I mean, there's a lot more to why a car works than just pushing down on the gas. There's more to magic, too, but it comes down to knowing the right gestures and places and conditions."

"So what happens now?" asked St. George. "Do we need to do some ritual or exorcism or something to let you move on?"

"Not exactly," said the stereo. "I've been looking for a new body. I can move into one that's more or less whole and take control of it, that's not a problem. After a few hours my own animus gets absorbed into the cells and I'd be alive again. The catch has been where I do it."

"Explain," said Stealth.

"Well, it wouldn't do me much good to resurrect outside, would it? The minute the body came back to life I'd get attacked by a dozen or so exes."

"And there aren't any bodies inside the Mount because we blow their brains out the minute they die," said St. George with a nod.

"Right," said the stereo. "I tried it outside a couple times anyway. I figured I'd signal whoever was at the gate to let me in, but all the bodies outside are pretty far gone. They're stiff and most of their vocal cords are raw and useless. Every time I got up to the gates I'd get shot or piked before I could do anything. I even tried jumping into a dead actor once, a guy I found wandering around out by Raleigh. The one from that space worm–zombie movie, irony of ironies. I figured celebrity status might buy me a few more minutes. Plus it was when the Krypton guys were first showing up, so I was hoping people might be hesitant to start firing guns. We all know how that turned out."

St. George nodded. He glanced at Zzzap.

"This is why you wish us to let Hiram Jarvis reanimate if he dies," said Stealth. "You wish to use his body and resurrect yourself."

The speakers were quiet for a moment. "Yeah, that's basically it," said the stereo.

"I think maybe we should get Father Andy in on this," said St. George. "This whole discussion is getting into a weird area."

"Feel free," said the speakers. "Nothing against Barry, but I'm feeling very talkative."

"And then?" Stealth asked.

"Then what?"

"Why return yourself to life only to be mortal and face death again? What do you gain from it?"

"Well, I'm not dead, for starters."

"Not yet. All of us will face an end, though. Will you then attempt to cheat death again?"

"Believe me, Stealth," the stereo said, "in the end all of us try to cheat death. I was just better prepared to do it than most folks."

Eleven
NOW

SINCE THEY'D MOVED all the Mount's medical facilities to Hollywood Community, there was plenty of room for Dr. Connolly to have an actual office. There still wasn't enough of a medical staff for her to be far away from the patients, though, even with Eddie Franklin and some of the others. And being by herself in the mostly empty hospital gave her the creeps at night. Instead, she set up camp at the nurse's station of whatever floor had the most patients. It was where St. George found her.

"Morning, doctor."

"Good morning," she said. "To what do I owe the honor?"

"I'm visiting some of your patients."

She nodded. "Eddie's finishing up some tests with the girl, Madelyn. I should have complete results for you soon."

"What do you think so far?"

"About her?" Connolly shook her head and swept back a lock of crimson hair threaded with silver. "I can tell you I might have been wrong earlier. I don't think she's an ex."

"What?"

"I don't think she's an ex. She's just . . . dead."

"But she has to be," said St. George. "She's walking around and she—"

The doctor shook her head. "I've run her blood work twice. I can't find the ex-virus in her. Not a trace of it anywhere. Not a trace of anything, in fact. No secondary infections, no old scars, nothing. My first impression is she's in incredible health."

"Aside from being dead."

"Aside from that, yes. She just seems like a normal seventeen-year-old girl in so many ways. Did you know she sleeps?"

"What?"

The doctor nodded. "Twice now. She got tired and fell asleep the night you brought her in. When she woke up later I had to explain where she was and who I was. Last night she stretched out on the bed, wrapped her arms around her pillow to cry for a few minutes, and she was out cold. No pun intended. And when she woke up a few hours ago she didn't know who I was again. Or where she was." Connolly paused. "Or that her parents were dead."

St. George sighed. "Yeah, she said she had some memory problems."

"That's putting it mildly," said the doctor. "Captain Freedom sat with her and went over the whole thing again. I think it might've been harder on him than her, watching her go through it all again."

"Crap."

"It's not too surprising, to be honest." Connolly gestured at a chart on the counter. "I hooked her up to an EEG the first night before she fell asleep. Even exes give off basic readings. There's still electrical activity in their brains, it's just very, very low. Below comatose levels."

"And Madelyn?"

"Her readings aren't that different from your standard ex-human. I'm sure a specialist could spot some little nuances, but nothing stood out for me. Stealth might want to take a look."

"Okay."

The doctor held up a finger. "Then she fell asleep. Her EEG went to a complete flatline."

"Flatline meaning . . . ?"

"Meaning corpse. I got nothing from her. Absolutely nothing. A potato would give me more responses. It was more like she died—really died—than fell asleep."

"Is that what messes up her memories?"

"Maybe." Another shrug. "I don't know how she even has thoughts, let alone memories. Her brain completely shuts off when she sleeps. Her blood isn't circulating. Preliminary results from her tissue samples indicate her muscles aren't manufacturing lactic acid. Every test I know how to do says she's just . . . dead. I have no idea how she's thinking or talking or moving around." She shrugged. "Then again, I have no idea how you can fly. I've gotten used to things I can't explain."

"Great."

"One more thing," said Connolly. "She's been in a mild degree of pain because of lividity. Most of her blood's all pooled up in her feet and legs. I'd like to sever the arteries in her ankles and drain it off. It should take care of her pain issues and give me more material for further tests."

St. George's eyes went wide. "You're going to drain off her blood?"

"It's the easiest solution I can think of."

"Won't that . . ." He stopped himself.

Connolly smirked. "She's already dead. It shouldn't have any effect at all."

He frowned. "What if you're wrong?"

"I'm pretty sure she's dead, George. They did cover it in medical school."

He drummed his fingers on the counter. "How's Jarvis?"

The shift threw her for a moment, and then her face dropped. "Not good," she said. "He's on antibiotics right now, but there's at least three symptoms they're not affecting at all. I'm still waiting on blood work to figure out how many infections he's got so I can start targeting them better."

"How long will that take?"

She sighed. "Longer than he's got." She shook her head.

"I'm sorry. You know how this works. There's just nothing else I can do."

"How long's he got?"

"A day at the most. I'm amazed he lasted this long." She looked at her watch. "It's been almost forty-two hours since he was bitten. That's practically a record."

"Is he awake?"

Connolly nodded.

* * *

Jarvis looked dead. A web of wires and tubes ran like mechanical ivy from his chest and arms to the machines around him. His face was dry and pale enough that in places it blurred with the white and silver speckled in his beard and scalp. It made his hair look thin. Where he wasn't pale his neck and arms had patches of dark pink rash spotted with red. Something yellow clotted in the corners of his eyes. St. George could see it on the older man's mouth, too, even through the oxygen mask. The inside of the mask was flecked with blood.

St. George took in a breath. "How you doing, Jarvis?"

His eyes fluttered open and he lifted his thumb. "Peachy-keen, boss," he coughed. It was a wet sound that rattled in his chest and throat. "Thought the end of the world couldn't get any better. Then y'all went and got me this comfy bed. And a cute nurse."

"Is there anything I can get for you? Something from your place?"

His head shifted side to side on the pillow.

St. George looked down at the man in the bed. "I'm sorry."

"Weren't your fault, boss. Don't worry about it."

"I should've been there."

"You were there," he wheezed. "Just too much going on. It happens." He reached out and grabbed the hero's hand.

"It shouldn't."

"It does," said the older man. "Life's a bitch and then you die."

The hero took in another breath. "Look," he said, "Dr. Connolly . . . she's done all she can."

Jarvis closed his eyes. "Yeah," he said. He let out a long, rasping cough that left more spots on the inside of his oxygen mask. "I figured as much. Seen too many bites to think mine'd be special. How long I got?"

St. George gave the man's hand a gentle squeeze. He stuck his free hand in his pocket. A streamer of smoke curled up out of his nose.

Jarvis let out a tired sigh. "Yeah," he said. "I figured."

A moment passed. The machines linked to Jarvis beeped and blinked in a way St. George thought was too cheerful.

"I've got something to ask you," he said. "A favor."

Jarvis smiled and coughed again. "Not much I can do right now, boss."

"I know. It's what you can do after."

The salt-and-pepper man's face lost its smile. "What's that supposed to mean?"

St. George drummed his fingers against his thigh. "We need a body," he said. "A fresh one."

Jarvis waved his hand at his leg. "This one's not too fresh," he said. "And it's going to be walking around soon."

"I know. That's part of what we need."

Jarvis coughed and his eyes lost focus for a moment above the oxygen mask. "We said no one comes back," he wheezed.

"I know," said St. George. "That's why we're talking about it. If you say no, we'll make sure you don't walk."

"Why do you need me? Need my body?"

The hero tried to think how to explain it. "If we can use your body," he said, "we might be able to save someone."

"Someone," Jarvis said, "but not me."

St. George opened his mouth to speak, then closed it again.

Another line of smoke spiraled out of his nostrils. "Yeah," he said. "Not you."

The older man had another coughing fit. This one coated the inside of the oxygen mask with red and a few black lumps. He grabbed at the rails of the hospital bed to hold himself steady and the machines scolded him with a chorus of beeps. St. George pulled a few tissues from a box near the bed and wiped out the inside of the mask. He tried not to look at the stuff on the tissues as he settled the mask back in place.

Jarvis took a few slow breaths. His watery eyes found St. George. "Do you think exes remember stuff?"

"Stealth's pretty sure they—"

"Don't care what she thinks, boss. Want to know what you think. You believe all these nuts, that there's still people inside the exes?"

St. George thought about the talking stereo back on Stage Four.

"No," he said. "I think people move on. I don't know where they go, if they go anywhere, but they're not in there." He squeezed Jarvis's hand again. "They're gone."

For a moment neither of them spoke.

"Before all this," the salt-and-pepper man said, "I had a cat. Really old thing. Had her forever. Pretty much my only friend. She got sick about a year before all the zombie stuff went down. Stopped eating, started starving. I couldn't even afford to put her to sleep. Had to watch her twist up and spasm and die in my lap."

"That's awful."

"Yeah," said Jarvis, "it was. I cried like a girl for about three hours straight afterward. But in a way, I was kind of glad. I didn't have to make the decision to put her to sleep. I knew I was too scared to make it. What if she was going to get better? What if I was betraying her somehow? I wasn't brave enough for that call."

"You're brave when you need to be."

"No," said Jarvis. "I'm really not."

"Could've fooled me."

"Do it," he said. He bit back a cough. "If it can save someone else, y'all can do what you need to with my body. I give permission or whatever."

"You sure?"

"Boss, if you say it's the right thing, I trust you."

"St. George," echoed a voice in his earbud. "Legion's at the South Wall, maybe two blocks from the southeast corner. About three hundred exes. With ladders."

He sighed. "Copy that," he said into his mic. He looked at Jarvis. "I have to go. Trouble."

Jarvis squeezed his hand. "It's been an honor, St. George," the older man said. "Thanks for everything."

"I'll be back," he said. "I'll get back before . . ."

"Just walk away, boss. Y'all can let me fake being brave one more time."

"Bye, Jarvis."

"Bye, boss. Go save the day."

≈ ≈ ≈

The South Wall reminded St. George of medieval war movies. Trios and quartets of exes ran forward with aluminum ladders, slammed the bases down, and one of the dead people was halfway up before the tops of the ladders hit the Big Wall. Some of the exes even had baseball bats and clubs to go with their helmets. The guards at the top tried to shove the ladders back, or fired point-blank shots into the dead faces as they topped the wall.

Legion was getting good at controlling multiple exes.

Captain Freedom was already on the top platforms of the Big Wall. One shove from his boot sent a ladder flying away. As St. George sank down through the air, the officer unholstered Lady Liberty and turned a pair of exes into a pile of loose limbs.

St. George landed outside the Wall. A group of exes charged him with an A-frame ladder and he stopped it with one hand, knocking them off their feet. He swung the ladder in a wide arc and sent a dozen exes sprawling. He swung again and let it spin away. Another handful of exes dropped, their skulls crushed by the whirling metal.

The guards on the Wall started laying down suppressive fire. He'd given them the moment of breathing space they needed to turn the tide. Exes ran at the Wall and their heads burst or jerked back. One kept stumbling forward as a bullet thudded off its headgear and St. George put it down with a blow that shattered its forehead.

The exes twitched and slowed. Three of them staggered to a halt and their ladder crashed to the ground. Another one dropped the golf club it had been waving. The five-iron tangled in its legs and the dead woman tripped face first to the pavement.

St. George floated into the air and grabbed an ex from the top of a tilting ladder. The ex, a shriveled dead man with a monk-like circle of hair around its bare head, clawed at his arm. The hero drifted back up to the top of the Wall. "Good job," he told Freedom. "I feel like you didn't even need me."

"Every bit helps, sir," said the captain. "You probably just saved us half an hour before Legion got frustrated and gave up."

"Hey," said one of the guards. He pointed at the ex twisting in St. George's grip. "Is that Picard?"

A lanky woman shook her head. "I think he's too short."

"Damn," said the other guard. "That'd be some serious points, getting Captain Picard."

Freedom gave the man one of his practiced looks and the man turned his attention out beyond the Wall with a nervous salute. "It was clumsy," the officer said to St. George. "In a classic siege, your ladders are never taller than they need to be. It slowed him down enough that he lost the advantage his armor's been giving him."

St. George swung the dead man out over the edge of the Wall. "You've been involved in a lot of sieges?"

"I studied military history at West Point, sir."

St. George's earbud squawked again and he glanced either way down the Wall. "Go for St. George," he said.

"Sorry to bother you, boss," said a woman's voice. "Small problem."

"What's up?"

The voice paused. "Jarvis passed ten minutes ago," she said. "We were going to . . . you know, take care of him, and Zzzap said we needed to wait until we talked to you."

"That can't be right," said St. George. "I was with Jarvis half an hour ago. He was doing fine."

The airwaves were quiet for an uncomfortable time. Freedom's face had gone solemn across from him. St. George was struck by the thought of how many people were probably listening in. Other guards. Stealth. Zzzap, watching the signals pass back and forth through the air.

"Doc Connolly says he, uhhhh . . . he took his oxygen mask off," said the woman. It was Lynne Vines, he realized. She was pulling a shift at the hospital between scavenging missions. Just like Jarvis did. Like he used to.

"She thinks he did it right after you left," Lynne continued. "He was so weak he passed out and . . . well . . . By the time the machines went off it was too late."

St. George glared at the ex pawing at his wrist and then hurled it out over the houses as far as he could. It sailed across the street, bounced off a red-tile roof that was probably very expensive a few years ago, and hit the side of a tall apartment building. It left a dark stain on the wall before dropping out of sight.

"St. George?"

"Yeah," he said. "Copy that. Zzzap's right. Don't put him down. Get whatever restraints you can and strap him down to his bed. Once he's tied down tight, just leave him alone."

The Writing on the Wall
THEN

"ARE YOU WEISS?"

It was the third café I'd gone to looking for the man, and I was starting to feel anxious. On one level, I was in no rush and had no deadlines. On another level, this was even more urgent than getting to the right spot for the eclipse.

The guy I thought was Weiss looked up at me. He had long gray hair and a goatee that twirled into a rope under his chin. On a guess, he was seventy pounds overweight. "Who's asking?"

"A friend of mine in the States recommended you. Said you're the best tattoo artist in Paris."

Weiss shrugged. "I just get a lot of the expat trade," he said. He took another bite of his sandwich, a prissy little thing made out of a croissant. I could see white meat and bright green lettuce hanging out of the edges. It looked tiny in his fat fingers. "It's my day off, though. Sorry. There's some guys down in the eighteenth arrondissement who do great work. They can do whatever you need."

I sat down in the chair across from him. "Not as I hear it."

He frowned at me. "What are you looking for? A sleeve? Tramp stamp for your girlfriend?"

I shook my head. "Not exactly."

"Tell you what. Go see Laura in the twentieth. She's fantastic. She did one of Angelina Jolie's tattoos. She's got pictures and everything. Tell her I sent you and she'll knock ten percent off her prices. We trade back and forth all the time."

He turned his attention back to the prissy little sandwich. I let him take two more bites before I set my hands on the table and laced my fingers. He sighed and set his brunch down again.

"Perhaps I wasn't clear," he said. "It's my day off. Go fuck yourself."

"Perhaps I wasn't clear," I echoed. "I need a *tattoo*."

I stretched my arms and let one of the images on my left arm slide out from under my sleeve. His fingers stopped an inch from the sandwich. He eyed it for a moment, then leaned back in his chair. He studied my face. "Who's your friend in the States?"

"Ernie Redd. You might know him as the Go-Between Guy."

He smirked for a moment. "I know him as Ernie. He's still alive?"

I nodded. "He's probably never going to leave his house again, but he's alive. Most of him, anyway. He lost his left arm and six toes."

"Lucky bastard," said Weiss. "It could've been his head."

I nodded. "Or worse."

Weiss nodded, too. "Or worse." He pointed at my arm. "Who did the *arma dei*? It's a little rough on the edges. The lines aren't great."

"Yeah," I said. "I did it myself five years ago."

Weiss wrinkled his brow. "You know enough to come to me, but you tried to do one of these yourself?"

"It was a rush job. I didn't have time to consult an expert."

He studied my face again. "What's your name, kid?"

"Maxwell Hale."

He gave a slow nod. "Hale," he repeated. "Heard of you. Word on the lines is you're a cocky little bastard."

I smiled. "I'm only cocky if I can't do what I say I can."

"Like build a working Sativus?"

"Yeah," I said.

He looked at me for another moment and then his eyes went wide. "No shit?"

"No shit."

"Can I see it?"

"No."

"You just want me to take your word for it?"

I sighed and tugged out my travel wallet. "Don't try anything," I told him. "It's bound to me. Fifty-foot tether. We'd both be dead before you got to the end of the block."

He gestured at his bloated stomach. "Do I look like a big runner to you?"

"Appearances are deceiving."

"Fair enough," he said. "No tricks. Let's see it."

I pulled the medallion out by the chain, careful not to touch it. It'd been a week and the runes were still warm. The air cracked with fresh enchantments. At least, it did if you knew how to listen for them.

Weiss bit his knuckle. "That's amazing," he said.

"Thanks."

He leaned his head far to the left, then far to the right. "Amazing," he said again. "Of course, I find myself wondering why a cocky little bastard who can do something like this needs me."

I let the medallion settle back in the nylon folder, wrapped the Velcro band across it, and tucked the whole thing back under my shirt. It was warm against my chest. "Insurance," I told him. "Someday this thing might get loose and I want to have plenty of safeguards."

"Why?" Weiss noticed the second half of his sandwich and picked it up. "After being tied up in there, anything's going to be too weak and embarrassed to cause you any serious problems. It'd probably just spit a hex in your direction and run for home."

"Right," I said. "If it was weak to start with."

He raised the sandwich to his mouth. "Did you catch a nightmare duke or something?"

"No," I said while he tore off a mouthful of food. "It's Cairax Murrain."

Weiss sprayed croissant and Romaine lettuce across the table. "*What*?" he shouted. "Are you *insane*?"

The café was silent. Everyone turned to look at us. Mostly at him, but more than a few eyes flitted at me. "Sit down," I said in a low tone. "You're making a scene."

He glared at me, then at everyone else. In true French fashion, they all politely looked away and began to talk about us in hushed whispers.

He sat down.

"This is Paris," hissed Weiss. "There are over two million people here and you bring that thing into the heart of the city?"

"It's safe."

"It's Cairax Murrain," he said through gritted teeth. "You've got the Reaver Lord tied up with cobwebs and Chinese finger cuffs and you're telling me it's safe?"

"He's bound," I said. "It's a perfect Sativus."

"You think."

"It is. You saw it. If he wasn't bound do you think any of this would be here right now?" I gestured around us.

Weiss shook his head. "So what are you looking for?"

"I need a Marley."

He snorted. "You need your head examined."

"Can you do it? I know it's a specialty piece."

He sighed. "I can do it. I'm one of maybe three people on Earth who can do one for you." He sighed again and looked at me. "What's on your back right now?"

"There's a curse ward on each shoulder and a Crowley's Knot between them."

"What type of wards?"

"One Coptic, one Germanic."

"Anyone gunning for you right now?"

I gestured at the pouch under my chest. "Besides the obvious?"

"Yeah."

"Not that I know of."

He rubbed his chin and the rope-like beard swung back and forth. "Crowley's Knot isn't doing anything if you've got the *arma dei*," he mused. "I can move both of the wards around onto your chest or arms if they're bare."

I nodded. "I've got three Ka marks on my left arm, but that's it."

"I know a woman at a clinic who owes me a couple of favors. They do facelifts and stuff, and they've got a YAG laser. It'll hurt like hell, but we could have your back clean in a week and start working a week after that. I can get all the inks ready while your back's healing. It'll take another three days to do the tattoo."

"Sounds good."

"You know once you've got a Marley that's it, right? There's no going back, no getting rid of it. You're bound here forever if you can't resurrect yourself."

"I'm counting on it."

He shook his head. "You're one crazy motherfucker, kid."

"Will it carry through? The Marley?"

Weiss shook his head. "That's why you have to get it on your back, so you can't see it. If it carried through to the next life, it could seriously fuck up your soul."

I smiled. "Well, that's what I'm trying to avoid."

Thirteen

NOW

"IF I COULD interject for a moment," said Father Andy. He reached up and scratched his neck just above his clerical collar. "There are some bigger questions here, aren't there?"

St. George stopped staring long enough to glance up at Andy. "Like what?"

Andy gestured at the figure stretched out on the bed, the center of attention. Jarvis's body was handcuffed to the railings. Restraints ran across its chest and legs. A bright red foam brace, the kind used for neck injuries, held its head down. The corpse had started moving three hours after Jarvis died. It had been moving a lot more in the five or six since then.

Andy looked the dead man in the eyes. "You said there are lots of spirits here?"

The ex nodded. "A few dozen, at least," it said. It had Jarvis's voice, but the inflections were off, as if the salt-and-pepper man was doing a very good impression of someone. It sucked some air through its lips. "It's hard to be sure."

"Why so many?" asked Danielle. She stood by the door, across the room from Stealth. Her eyes were everywhere except the body. "Is it because so many people had violent deaths?"

The ex shook its head. "Ghosts aren't really that rare," it rasped. "There are all sorts of reasons for people to end up stuck here on Earth. The real trick is doing it deliberately."

"So there are a lot of ghosts here?"

Jarvis's body tried to shrug under all the straps and cuffs and its brows wrinkled for a moment. "Like I said, it's hard to be sure."

"Why?"

"This isn't like the movies, George. We're not all hanging out in the ghost clubhouse or something. It's a form of purgatory. Yeah, you get to see your friends and loved ones, walk through walls, sneak into movies, all that stuff. But you can't interact with anything. You can't even see other ghosts. There could be a hundred other spirits in the room with us right now. I can't see 'em."

"But you have said there are several dozen here at the Mount," Stealth said.

The ex nodded again. "I can sense them pretty much the same way you do. Cold spots in a room. Echoes that sound a little off. I've just got more experience spotting them and telling them apart."

"So who are they?" asked St. George. "Or were they, I guess?"

Another awkward shrug from the dead man. "No clue. I can tell them apart, but for all I know there's thirty or forty dog and cat ghosts wandering around looking for balls to chase or something."

"There are dog and cat ghosts?" asked Andy.

"Of course there are," said the ex. "You think dog heaven's something people just made up?"

St. George glanced over at the window. "What about you?" he asked Zzzap. "Can you tell who they were?"

The gleaming wraith hung just outside, shedding his excess heat to the open air. He shook his head. *I can see little wisps and glimpses of them,* he said, *like I'm seeing something out of the corner of my eye, but Max is the only one I've ever seen clearly.*

The ex tensed in the restraints for a moment. Its fingers stretched wide and then relaxed. "Damn," it said, flinching again. "That stings."

Worse than you thought?

"Not much."

"What is the problem?"

"No problem," the ex told Stealth. It flinched again and gritted its teeth. "Like I said, this body's coming back to life. The nerves are starting to fire again. It's a bit painful."

"Could they all come back the way you did?" asked Andy. "The ghosts?"

"Probably not." The ex dipped its chin as best it could at its body. The head restraints made it look like a spasm. "I'm a pretty practiced sorcerer and this took me six months of prep work. And a fair amount of luck."

Andy nodded. "But they could, hypothetically, come back? You could bring them back."

"The mechanics are a little different, doing it to someone else instead of yourself, but the principle's the same."

"Anyone?" said Stealth.

"If their spirit was still hanging out, yeah."

"Hang on another moment, please," said Andy. "This begs the next question—should we bring anyone back?"

"Why wouldn't we?" asked St. George.

"Because it violates God's plan," said Andy, "or the natural order, if you prefer."

I don't know if you noticed, said Zzzap from the window, *but the natural order's been violated from pretty much every angle you can imagine.*

"He's got a point," said St. George. "With all those things walking around out there, it's hard to make a case for God's plan."

"This is exactly when we need to make a case for God's plan," said Andy. He glanced at Stealth. "If you're an atheist, just look at it from a moral point of view. If we agree those things outside are abominations, that they're *wrong*, then what does it mean if we're doing the same thing in here?"

"Well, it's not quite the same," said Jarvis's corpse. Its fingers stiffened and relaxed as a spasm swept over its body. "Out there you can argue a few million corpses are getting desecrated by a virus. This is more like resuscitating someone. This body's restoring itself. It's going to come back to life. Real life, with a pulse and breathing and everything."

"Except you died," said Andy, "and it's not your body. You had your time and now you're trying to get more."

The dead man's head twitched again. "So you're saying it was God's plan I got bitten by a zombie and my soul was trapped in a demon's walking corpse for fourteen months? Doesn't that mean the abominations are part of the plan?"

"We are not here to debate ethics or theology," said Stealth.

"Then why am I here?" asked Andy. "I'm supposed to be a moral and spiritual counselor, yes?"

"Nothing personal, father," said the ex, "but I'm no longer a spirit and I don't need counseling."

St. George felt himself smile. Zzzap let out a hiss of static that passed as a laugh.

"I'm not trying to be a pain in the ass," Andy said. "I just want you all to stop and think what this is going to mean to people. There's about a thousand people out there in the After Death sect who think exes still have souls buried in them somewhere. There's already this girl you found getting them worked up. What's going to happen when they find out it's possible to bring people back from the dead?"

"We shall explain these were special circumstances which cannot be repeated," Stealth said.

"How?" The priest looked at her. "How are you going to explain to someone that 'special circumstances' let one of you come back but not their child or wife or husband?"

"One of you?" echoed Danielle.

"I'm sorry," said Andy, "but it's how people are going to see it. Superhumans getting something regular folks don't. Not to mention the backlash over every single ex we've ever put down that might've had someone's soul inside it."

"I hadn't thought of that," said St. George.

"I have," said Stealth. "I believe the results will be minimal."

"Well, then how about this? Something else I've been wondering about," said Andy. He gestured at the ex strapped to the bed. "How do you know it's him?"

"We have established this is not a trick," said Stealth. "He has shown awareness of certain facts no one else at the Mount could know."

"But would Max know them?"

Stealth's face shifted under her mask.

"If we buy his story," the priest said, "that he's a wandering spirit who once trapped a demon, then we're back in my territory. And the church has a lot to say about spirits taking control of bodies. This could be anyone—or anything—posing as Max. It's classic exorcism material."

"Are you saying you want to exorcise me?" asked the dead man.

Andy shook his head. "I'm just saying, how are we supposed to know it's really you?"

Jarvis's body gave another shudder and the ex clenched its teeth. The shackled hands flailed at its chest. "I could say the Lord's Prayer for you, if it makes you feel any better. If I can say it forward, it at least proves I'm not a demon."

Andy managed a faint smile. "I appreciate the gesture, but how do we know that's a real test?"

"It's real," the ex grunted. "It's . . . it's one of the only things the film got . . . right." The dead man convulsed, its arms and legs thrashing as well as they could with their chains. Its head fought against the foam restraints. The ex fell limp against the bed and then another spasm racked its body.

St. George stepped forward to hold Jarvis—the dead man—still, but Stealth gestured him back. "What is happening?" asked the cloaked woman.

"We're close," grunted the ex. "My heart's trying to start back up."

"That hurts?" Danielle asked.

"You think a heart attack hurts less when it's happening in reverse?"

St. George glanced at the hall. "Do we need to get one of the doctors in here?"

"Jesus, no," said the ex. It looked at the priest. "No offense, father, again. They'll try to save my life and they'll just end up killing me. This has to happen at its owwnnNNNAAHH-HHH!"

The corpse convulsed again, and its face twisted up in pain. Its back arched, pushing its hips up in the air, and then it slammed back down onto the bed. It sucked in a rasping breath.

St. George looked at the body. "Are you sure this is working?"

"Not really," said the ex. "I've never done it before." Its chalk eyes turned to the window. "Barry," it called out, "I think it's time."

You sure?

"Time for what?" asked St. George.

"The next one should do it," said the ex. It sucked in another breath. "All four cardinal points, just outside the Big Wall and the walls of the Mount. Make sure—" The handcuffs rang against the rails three times as the corpse flailed at its chest. "Make sure they're pointed the right way."

On it.

"Zzzap, what are you—" But the gleaming wraith was gone before Stealth could finish her sentence.

Another spasm shook the ex. "Oh, yeah," it said. "This is it."

St. George's earbud crackled. "Boss," said a voice, "it's Ilya. I'm up at the North Gate. Barry just flew by and torched a section of Bronson just outside."

He tapped his mic. "What do you mean, torched?"

"It looks like he drew a bunch of lines in the ground with his hand. Melted it right into the pavement. Still too smoky to see what it is."

"St. George," a new voice cut in, "Makana at West Gate.

What's Zzzap up to? He just burned something into the street here."

"Dave at South Gate for St. George—"

"This is Katie at North Gower—"

"Lemon Grove gate to St. George—"

"—just scared the piss out of all of us—"

"—like some kind of big circle with squiggles in it."

"—the hell is Zzzap doing?"

St. George stepped forward and set his hand on the ex's chest, pinning it to the bed. "What's going on?"

"Just a second," the dead man said through gritted teeth. "Time to do the Jesus thing." His eyes clenched shut and tears leaked out of the corners.

One of Stealth's pistols appeared in her hand and settled by the ex's head. "What is happening?" she demanded.

The corpse roared in pain. It tried to thrash but St. George's hand kept it pressed against the mattress. The handcuffs chimed as it strained to grab at its chest. The body went tense, rock solid, and then went limp again.

Light flooded the room. *Did I make it?* called Zzzap from the window.

"What the hell were you doing?" snapped St. George.

It's part of the process, said the wraith. *He's had me practicing all the symbols for months.*

St. George looked down at the corpse and his eyes went wide.

"Holy shit," said Danielle. Father Andy crossed himself and whispered something.

The pale skin was taking on the soft colors of life. The veins faded behind the flesh tones. The ex—the man—let out a slow sigh. Sweat glistened across his forehead. "Jesus, that hurt," he said. "I had no idea it was going to hurt so much."

St. George's hand flinched away from the man's chest for a moment. He set it down again, spreading his fingers. "Your heart's beating," he said. "You've got a pulse."

"Yeah. And a very itchy beard. How did Jarvis live with this thing?"

St. George and Andy both frowned.

The man opened his eyes and looked at each of them. Color was leaking back into the irises, like an old Polaroid photo where an image formed out of haze. "Sorry. That was tasteless. After years without a body, I'm a bit overwhelmed right now."

Welcome back, Max, said Zzzap.

"Thanks, Barry. I'm guessing you got all the symbols done or we wouldn't be here right now."

Stealth pressed her Glock against the bound man's eye. "What do you mean?"

"Hey," said Max, "take it easy."

"You have never mentioned these symbols before as part of your resurrection. You have now just implied disaster if they had not been arranged around the Mount. What is their true purpose?"

"I was going to tell you."

"You will tell us now."

He sighed. "I can show you, if you like. It might be easier."

* * *

The North Gate was a few blocks from the hospital. Like all the entrances through the Big Wall, there were a few hundred exes and the air crackled with the sound of chattering teeth. Half of them pressed against the gate. The rest staggered through the street.

In the middle of Bronson was a smoking set of lines, a scar in the pavement stretching from one side of the road to the other. The superheated material had turned a fresh, deep black that stood out from the faded charcoal of the street. Three exes had been slashed in half by Zzzap's burning touch, too slow to get out of the way and too mindless to realize their danger.

Steam still trailed from their severed bodies. A spray of gore marked where one had boiled and exploded.

Two parallel lines marked out a ring fifteen feet across. Inside the double circle was what looked like two triangles—or maybe an hourglass—surrounded by squiggles.

"Nice job, Barry," said the resurrected man. His handcuffs jingled as he gestured at the symbols. He swayed as he did, and St. George kept one hand on the man's shoulder.

Thanks.

"So what is it?" asked St. George.

"It's the Hexagram of Water," explained Max, "modified with six of the names of God and a thaumaturgic circle."

"A what?"

"Magic," said Stealth. "He is claiming this is a magical ward of some sort."

"Very good," said Max. "There's an appropriate one protecting us at each gate, and some stronger ones around the Mount proper." He waved his hands to the east and south. It was a clumsy motion with the cuffs.

Protection? said Zzzap. The gleaming wraith turned to the man with the salt-and-pepper beard and tried to ignore the glare from Stealth. *You said they were part of the resurrection spell.*

"Yeah, sorry," said Max. "It was easier to tell you that."

"Okay," said St. George, "so what are you protecting us from?"

"Hang on," said Max. He was scanning the crowd of walking dead. "Wait for it."

An ex a few yards away stopped in mid-stagger as its feet brushed the edge of the steaming circle. It had been a petite woman, a redhead with a mane of wild hair clotted with gore and dirt. It wore a tight green henley splattered with blood and filth. It turned, searching, and glared at the people on the Wall.

"There he is," said Max.

The dead thing raised a hand to point at them. It howled. It was the roar of a mammoth or dinosaur or some other huge, primordial beast. It echoed between the buildings. Half a dozen windows shattered.

St. George winced. Ilya and the other gate guards covered their ears. Even Zzzap flinched back.

The ex filled out, its desiccated flesh swelling with new life. The trembling limbs stretched and its jaw swung open to reveal a bear trap of ivory fangs and tusks. Blue flames burst out of the ex's eyes and set fire to its hair. Its fingers stretched out into talons. In just a few moments it was over seven feet tall, then eight.

Then the dead woman exploded in a spray of gore and blue fire.

What the hell was that? shouted Zzzap.

"Remember what I said about how being dead was my safe house? Nothing could touch me?"

St. George nodded. "Yeah?"

"Well, I'm not dead anymore." He pointed at the bright circle of gore that had been the undead woman. "That was Cairax Murrain. He's pissed I've gotten away and he's coming after me. And anyone he thinks might've helped me."

What?! shouted Zzzap. His head turned from the steaming remains of the ex to his friends. Stealth was statue stiff. Smoke leaked out from between St. George's lips.

"Yeah," said Max. "I probably should've mentioned this would happen a bit sooner."

Fourteen

NOW

"YOU HAVE PUT everyone in the Mount at risk," said Stealth. Her sharp voice echoed in the hospital room. She stood wrapped in her cloak, so it was impossible to tell where her hands were. St. George was pretty sure they were near her holsters. He didn't blame her.

"Don't be melodramatic," said Max from the bathroom. "We're not at risk as long as we stay inside the walls."

St. George stood by the window. Smoke was pouring out of his nostrils in a steady stream, and he hadn't been able to get the tickle in his throat under control. Part of him wanted to grab Max and shake him, but he didn't want to set off the fire alarms.

Freedom stood across from them, his arms crossed against his broad chest. He'd joined them after the radios filled with people talking about the creature outside the Big Wall. He wore his displeasure plain on his face.

The resurrected man tapped the razor on the sink and rinsed away another inch of salt-and-pepper beard. St. George always suspected Jarvis would look a good ten years younger without the beard. He still knew the face beneath it, but it seemed more like a mask now. Jarvis never had that confident, almost smug look in his eyes and tone in his voice. He didn't have a barely hidden swagger when he moved.

But he did now.

They locked eyes for a moment in the mirror while Max brushed the razor under his nose. For just a moment the confidence and swagger vanished and St. George saw two looks flash across the other man's face. Relief that he'd escaped a horrible fate. Worry that somehow he hadn't.

St. George also noticed Max's eyes were brown. Jarvis's eyes had been blue.

Then the moment passed and Max winked at him.

"And if someone did not stay within the walls?" asked Stealth.

"Well, if someone goes out there, one of two things will happen," Max said. He reached up with the razor and scraped away a little more of Jarvis. "More than likely Cairax will just kill them."

"But you're Cairax," said Freedom.

"No," said Max. "We're two separate beings. Always have been. I just borrowed his body now and then. And maybe a little of his mind-set."

"Which was your excuse for molesting a dead actress," said Stealth.

"Hey!" snapped Max. He turned from the mirror. "That's not what happened at all. The whole thing just got blown out of proportion. And none of you did anything to stop it, I might add."

Stealth didn't flinch under his glare.

"I slipped a dead woman the tongue and she bit it off. That's it. Considering what my perceptions were being filtered through, it's an amazing example of self-control."

"Well," Freedom said dryly, "at least now we know you didn't do anything disgusting."

Max turned back to the mirror. A moment passed. No one spoke while the resurrected man scraped at the bit of Jarvis on his chin.

St. George took a slow breath and managed to get the

flames in his throat under control. The trailer of smoke from his nose turned to a thread. "So it'll kill anyone who goes past your marks," he said.

"Yeah. Probably."

"How?"

"Well, you've seen the exes. He's got a good four or five seconds before those bodies explode." He stopped shaving and glanced over his shoulder. "You've fought Cairax, George. How much damage do you think he can fit into five seconds?"

Stealth's head shifted inside her hood. "What is the other possible result of passing the wards?"

"He might try to possess whoever goes out there. But the odds of pulling it off with an unprepared body are next to nil. Really, it's just another way he could kill people." Max splashed some water on his face and the last of the salt-and-pepper beard was gone. A few drops spotted his hospital scrubs.

"What do you mean?"

Max grabbed a towel and wiped off his cheeks and chin. He let it drop and ran his fingers across his scalp. "If it isn't suitably prepared with the right sigils and agreements, a normal human body just can't take the stress of demonic possession."

"Yours did," said St. George.

"Yeah, but mine was prepared, plus I had the safeties in the medallion. Anyone else would just burst like the exes. It's like boiling a frog—you've got to go slow to even have a chance of it working." The sorcerer gestured at himself. "Look how long it took me to work my way into Jarvis's body. He'd need at least twice as much time."

Max stopped and ran his fingers across his scalp again. "Weird having short hair. Kind of weird having hair at all, to be honest. Been a long time." His lips shifted and one of his cheeks bulged. "Jarvis was missing one of his back teeth, too. That'll take some getting used to."

St. George felt the hostility coming off Stealth. Max either didn't notice it or didn't care. The hero cleared his throat rather than smacking the sorcerer. Max glanced at him, then put his hands down.

"If what you are saying is true," said Stealth, "the demon could possess an ex just as you did."

Max shook his head. "He's too big. A demon needs a sentient soul to use as . . . as an opposing force, sort of. Without one, going slow isn't an option. They just rush right into a body, like filling a water balloon with a fire hose. Believe me, if the wards weren't up, people would be popping left and right in here. Cairax is just too impatient for his own good. That's why his kind didn't overrun the world millennia ago."

"If it knows that," asked Freedom, "why'd it try to possess the exes outside?"

"Why do people punch walls?" Max shrugged. "And it's pretty creepy, you've got to admit. It sends a message."

"If what you are saying is true," said Stealth, "demonic possession should still be a common occurrence."

"Well, it's more common than people think," said Max. "Up until the ex-virus, they couldn't come through on their own, and once it had wiped out ninety percent of mankind, there just wasn't a point. Why make the effort to manifest in this world for just a few souls? Y'know, unless they really wanted to kill someone."

"Wait," said Freedom. "Why couldn't they come through before the ex-virus?"

"Because of the Pope."

"What?"

"The Pope. That's the whole point of there being a Pope. He's God's chosen warrior against evil. You didn't think the son of God really wanted to create some borderline-fascist religious bureaucracy, did you?"

"You're joking," St. George said.

Max shook his head. "The fisherman's ring. *Annulus Piscatoris*. Ever hear of it?"

"Yeah, it's like the Pope's signet or something."

"Or something. The real one, not the decoy but the one that's passed down in secret, is an anti-touchstone. As long as it's on a living finger, nothing demonic can manifest on Earth in a material form within nine hundred and sixty-three miles of it. Did you know there's a cardinal whose sole duty is to hang out near the Pope so he can put the ring on if he dies unexpectedly? He's the one who wears it while they're choosing a new one, too."

They all stared at him.

"You," said St. George, "are making this up."

"So if we cannot leave," said Stealth, "what are we expected to do?"

"Just relax," said Max. "After a while he'll get bored of stalking around out there and head off to plot some demonic revenge against me."

"How long?"

"I don't know. A little time. Ten or twelve days, maybe."

"Ten or twelve days?" echoed Freedom.

The sorcerer nodded. "Two weeks tops."

St. George felt the fire building in his throat again. "You're saying we might not be able to go out into the city for two weeks?"

"Two weeks at the absolute most," said Max. "It'll probably be less than that."

"There's no chance we could sneak out?" Freedom asked. "A small team, maybe with a diversionary action?"

Max shook his head. "Cairax is a demonic spirit. He can be in multiple places at once and he can see every living thing inside the walls. There's no getting out without him knowing."

"The other option," said Stealth, "is we surrender you to this entity now."

Freedom's lips twitched at the corners.

"You could," Max admitted, "but we're the good guys. Besides, it probably wouldn't make a difference. Demons are legendary for holding a grudge, and there's no way you'd convince it I misled you."

"Lied," corrected Freedom.

"It's all in your point of view," said Max. "All of this will blow over in a couple of days. Trust me."

"I think we're all having a little trouble with that right now," said St. George.

There was a knock on the door and Billie entered with a duffel bag. "Hey," she said. "I got a bunch of his clothes. Did you want to dress him up for a funeral or something? He didn't have an actual suit."

"Too bad," said Max. "I like a good suit."

Her eyes flitted to the resurrected man and she gave a polite nod. Then she looked at him again and her eyes went wide with recognition. One hand rose up. The other one dropped to her holster.

Freedom set a hand on her shoulder. "At ease," he said.

"Jarvis," she said, "you're—"

"I'm not Jarvis," said Max.

"But you were dying," she said. "I came and saw you." After three years of dealing with the undead, St. George could see the conflict on her face. She wasn't sure if she should hug her friend or shoot him.

"It is not Jarvis," said Stealth. "His body is being used by another . . . person."

Max took the bag of clothes from her. "Thanks," he said. He held out his hand. "Billie Carter, right?"

Billie looked over her shoulder at Freedom, then at St. George. The hero gave her a small nod. She held out her hand.

"Maxwell Hale," he said. "Max. Pleased to meet you."

"You, too," she said. She stared at him. Her gaze flitted from his eyes to his chin and up to his hairline.

Max pulled a few different shirts from the bag. He reached back and pulled the scrubs over his head. His shoulders and chest were covered with elaborate designs. Four smaller ones on his back framed a perfect circle of bare skin.

"I didn't know Jarvis had so many tattoos," said St. George.

"He doesn't," Max said as he shook out a pinstriped shirt. "I do."

"That doesn't make sense," said Freedom.

"No, it does," the sorcerer assured them. He pulled the shirt on while he searched for another analogy. "It's like . . . Okay, you know how you have hair in the Matrix even if you don't in the real world? Because in your mind you picture yourself with hair?"

"Are you trying to explain this using *The Matrix*?"

"I've been hanging out with Barry a lot, okay? It's the same thing, though. The soul is all about identity, and the body is part of someone's identity. Granted, we all tend to picture ourselves a little taller, a little thinner, but past that there are always physical things we just accept as an inherent part of who we are, and these are the things that are hard-wired into our soul. They carry over in cases like this."

Max gestured down at his chest. "All these tattoos are part of me. It's how I see myself. You could say they were inked into my soul as well as my skin. But if, say, Billie here came back, she'd probably only bring her Marine Corps tattoo with her, not the rose or the dolphin."

Stealth shook her head. "Psychosomatic tattoos?"

"If you like."

"You've got a big bare patch on your back," said Freedom.

"Because that one wasn't supposed to carry over," said Max. "Big, soul-scarring magic. One use only. If I can't see it, it can't become part of my identity."

St. George looked at the ink patterns as Max buttoned the shirt up. Now that he knew what they were, he was surprised he didn't recognize them sooner. He remembered the night Cairax had beaten him bloody, and the tattoo-covered man the zombie demon had turned into.

Billie's hands knotted into fists as they all mulled over the explanation. "How," she growled, "do you know I have a dolphin tattoo?"

He rolled his eyes. "I was a ghost here for a year and a half. Believe me, I've seen every tattoo everyone has."

She fumed but said nothing.

The resurrected man pulled a pair of jeans and some underwear from the bag and let his hospital pants drop to the floor. A minute later he tugged on some socks and was searching the bag again. "This was all he had for ties?"

The thought of slapping Max passed through St. George's mind again. "I don't think Jarvis was ever worried about formal occasions," he said.

Max sighed, selected a tie, and tossed the rest back in the bag. "So how are we playing this?" he asked. "I knew my return wasn't going to get cheers, but I didn't expect it to be this cold. Am I a prisoner? A partner? A free citizen?"

St. George glanced at Stealth. "I don't think we need to make you a prisoner," he said.

"Good."

"However," said Stealth, "it would be best if you did not go anywhere unescorted."

Max knotted the tie around his neck. "Still worried about what Father Andy said? That I'm going to cause an uproar?"

"There is that possibility," she said, "but I still believe it is slight. There is no need to cause confusion with your borrowed body."

"It's not exactly borrowed," said Max. "I can't give it back."

"Stolen, then."

"I was going to suggest donated. My hair will change color in a day or two, that'll help," he added. "I think I might lose a few pounds, too."

Freedom gave him a look. "Just like that?"

"Coming back from the dead burns a lot of calories," said Max. "Speaking of which, I haven't eaten a meal in almost three years. Not one I'd want to remember, anyway. Any chance of getting some food?"

"Billie," said St. George, "can you show him around? Maybe keep an eye on him until Freedom gets someone assigned to him?"

She gave a sharp nod and looked at Max. "Ready when you are."

Max held out a hand to St. George. "Thanks again. I owe you big time."

St. George looked at the hand for a moment and then shook it. "Let's just get rid of the demon as quick as we can."

The sorcerer held out his hand to Stealth, but she stared past him. He pursed his lips, nodded, and left with Billie.

"We require a moment of privacy, captain," said Stealth.

"Of course, ma'am," said Freedom. He bowed his chin to the two of them and left.

"Well," said St. George. "What are you thinking?"

"I am thinking," said Stealth, "I do not believe his story."

"Which part of it?"

"The parts involving magic and an afterlife."

"So . . . all of it."

"Several superhumans across the world manifested similar abilities. The Iranian hero Marduk had powers almost identical to yours. The British hero Scarecrow had agility and speed on par with Banzai's. We know Legion has the ability to project his consciousness. It is possible Cairax survived in the same manner."

"Max," corrected St. George. "If he's telling us the truth, Cairax is outside the Big Wall."

"If he is telling us the truth," said Stealth, "but I do not believe he is."

"Why?"

"His body language is inconsistent. At the least he is withholding information from us."

St. George nodded. "So what do you want to do?"

"For the moment, we shall allow him the time he wants. There were no scavenging missions scheduled for another four days, so it changes nothing."

"Okay. And then?"

"Then we shall question him again."

There was a rap at the door. Dr. Connolly stood outside. "St. George," she said. "Stealth. Could I speak with you two for a minute?"

A moment passed before the cloaked woman turned her head to Connolly. "What is it, doctor?"

Connolly held up a clipboard, then paused. She looked over her shoulder. "I'm sorry," she said. "The man in the hall. Did . . . did Jarvis have a brother or cousin I didn't know about?"

"Sort of," said St. George.

She looked at the empty bed and the hospital clothes piled near it. "And his body is . . . ?"

"These are questions for another time, doctor," said Stealth.

She looked at the bed again and blinked. "Was that him? You let him reanimate and he's . . . he's alive again?"

"It isn't him," said St. George. "It looks like him, but—"

"Another time, doctor," repeated Stealth. There was an edge to her voice that cut through the conversation.

They stood in the hospital room for a moment. Then Connolly cleared her throat. "All of Madelyn's tests are done and they confirm what I suspected the other day. She's not an ex."

She held a clipboard out to St. George. Stealth intercepted it and flipped through the handwritten notes. "Explain," said the cloaked woman.

The doctor shrugged. "She doesn't have the virus. Her core temperature is actually a little higher than an ex's, even if it's still well below normal. All I can think is it might be a new strain we haven't identified, one our tests aren't catching."

Stealth shook her head. "The ex-virus does not mutate," she said.

"I know. Josh used to say the same thing, but it's all I can think of. Plus, all those blood and tissue samples we took? All the cuts and punctures from them are gone."

Stealth's gaze rose from the clipboard. "She is healing?"

"Healing's not really the right word. It implies a process of growth and repair on a cellular level."

"And she's not doing that?" asked St. George.

"No. She's just . . . getting better. The wounds go away. It didn't even occur to me that she doesn't have any injuries from the attack that killed her. Captain Freedom said she was torn apart in front of him, but her only injury is severe scratching on her corneas. I'm guessing it's because dust on her eyes causes consistent, ongoing damage. It happens as fast as it goes away.

"I also did an extended eye exam. Her irises react to light but at maybe a tenth the speed they should. I tried to get them to dilate and it took fifteen minutes."

"There are several recorded instances of people whose reactions and vital signs drop below normal ranges," Stealth commented. "They are often mistaken for dead."

"Those people are usually in comas," said Connolly, "not walking around having conversations. And Madelyn doesn't have low vital signs. She has none. Zero. She's . . . she's a corpse."

"A corpse which speaks, thinks, and only eats meat," said Stealth.

"She eats meat," agreed the doctor, "but she's shown complete control of herself at all times. It's just a regular appetite. I can try to come up with new tests, but from a medical point of view . . ."

"So, if she's not an ex," said St. George, glancing at Stealth, "what is she?"

Connolly shrugged again. There was something tired and frustrated about the gesture. "I'm at a loss. Sorry."

St. George drummed his fingers against his thigh. "You're sure she's not contagious?"

"I can't find a single infectious organism in her," said Connolly. "I even did a few mouth swabs just to check for basic bacteria. Nothing. It's more hazardous to let us walk around than her."

"What are her anaerobic bacterial levels?" asked Stealth.

"Nonexistent," said Connolly, "which wouldn't be surprising in an ex, either, but . . ." She sighed. "I'm sorry. This is just completely beyond me. She's walking around, she's conscious, and she's dead. And I have no idea why or how."

Fifteen

NOW

"ARE YOU OKAY, ma'am?" asked Freedom.

Madelyn looked up at him. "Can you not call me that? You make it sound like I'm some ninety-year-old dowager or something."

"Sorry," he said. "I forgot. You asked me that before."

"I did?" Her brow wrinkled up and she managed a half smile. "I guess I forgot, too." She took a few quick steps ahead and raised her arms to the afternoon sun.

He let her have the distance and kept his pace. "I remember thinking 'dowager' was an unusual word for a teenage girl to use."

"I had to read *Great Expectations* a few months ago for class." She paused in mid-step. "Well, a few years ago. The word was on the back of the book, but," she said, with a knowing tone, "Charles Dickens never actually used it himself."

"Is that so?"

"Yeah. And, yeah, I'm okay," she added. "This is great. It's just . . . it feels like forever since I've been out without all my gear."

Freedom still thought it was good she'd decided to wear a coat and long sleeves. Having her blood drained had left Madelyn's skin chalk white. It wasn't as noticeable in the bright sunlight, but it was still a stark contrast against her dark hair and the collar of her shirt. A contrast people were too familiar with. Even with her new sunglasses, the dead girl drew a few long stares from the people along Vine Avenue. Fortunately, not many people chose to live near the Big Wall.

Madelyn didn't seem to notice them. She took a few more twisting steps with her arms up, turning in a half circle with each movement. Then she stopped and looked up at the huge man again. "Did he suffer much?" she asked him.

"Who, ma'am—Madelyn?"

It got him another half smile, but her mouth went flat just as quick. "My dad," she said. "Did he suffer much when he died?"

An image flashed through Freedom's head of the body St. George had recovered just before they'd abandoned the proving ground's sub-base. The only recognizable parts of Emil Sorensen had been the bloodstained tie and half of a ragged gray beard. His clothes, and the flesh beneath them, had been reduced to tatters. They'd laid his body to rest in one of the base's watchtowers, out of the undead's reach.

Captain Freedom had seen it as a complete failure. The entire Sorensen family had died under his watch. Three civilians it had been a specific part of his orders to protect.

"No," lied the huge officer. "It was quick. He never felt a thing."

Madelyn nodded and a tear slipped out from under her sunglasses. She wiped it away and started walking again. "Sorry," she said. "I know I shouldn't cry. He's been dead for a year, right?"

"A little less," said Freedom.

"Sorry. I haven't had to do this with people much. The memory thing. I'm trying. Damn it."

The dead girl stopped and dug in her pockets. She came out with a bottle of eyedrops and spun the cap open. Her head tilted back as she raised the bottle.

Freedom made a point of examining the balcony of an apartment building across from the Big Wall. The sound of teeth from the other side of the Wall echoed off it. He knew a few people lived in the building. He wondered how they dealt with it.

Madelyn coughed and he looked back at her. The wetness turned her chalky eyes into pearls. "Thank you," she said.

"Of course, ma'am."

"You're doing it again."

"Sorry. Years of training."

She dropped the bottle back in her pocket and settled her sunglasses back across her face. "If anyone ever asks you, crying with dry eyes hurts."

Freedom nodded and gestured at the street. "Do you want to go back to your room?"

Madelyn shook her head. "No thanks."

"Is it comfortable enough? We could get you some books or music or whatever you might like."

She started walking down the street again. "I just don't like hospitals much."

"Ahhh," he said. "I've spent a lot of time in them, too."

"For Dad's treatments?"

Now Freedom shook his head. "Before that." He thought about saying more, but didn't feel like dredging up memories of other failures.

Madelyn didn't push it. They walked along in silence for a few moments. She took in a deep breath and let it whistle out between her teeth.

A young man rode by on a bicycle and did a double take as he passed the dead girl. He glanced back and forth between Madelyn and Freedom. The bike wobbled and he almost crashed. At the last moment he got it under control and continued down the street, glancing back over his shoulder.

She sighed and took another deep breath. "It smells good here," she said. "Everywhere I've been . . . everywhere I remember being, anyway . . . has been kind of musty. Or worse. It's really nice."

"There are several large gardens," said Freedom. "There's some currency floating around, but for the most part people are bartering these days. Growing crops is like growing money."

"That makes sense, I guess."

He watched her from a few steps back. "May I ask you a question, Madelyn?"

She gave him another glimmer of a smile. "Since you used my name, sure."

"Do you need to breathe?"

She shook her head. "I don't think so. I have to think about doing it, but it just feels weird not to. And it makes it easier to talk."

"Ahhh."

"So, we're in Hollywood now, right?"

"Correct."

She looked at the buildings across from the Wall. "Are there any celebrities living here?"

Freedom shook his head. "I don't believe so. There are a few actors, but no one I'd heard of before coming here."

"Oh." She rolled her shoulders. "How about dead ones? Have you ever seen any ex-celebrities?"

He thought about it. "That's probably a conversation for another time."

"How come?"

"I'd rather not say, ma'am."

"You're doing it again."

"That time was deliberate."

"Ahhh."

A trio farther up the street stepped off the sidewalk and started walking toward them. Two men flanking a woman. Each of them held something dark. They were half a block away when Freedom recognized the woman as Christian Nguyen, the former councilwoman running for mayor. The two men were familiar, but the officer couldn't place their names. They were holding Bibles.

Madelyn hunched as they got closer. The practiced slouch of someone trying not to be noticed. It made him wonder just how many bad experiences she'd had with strangers during her travels.

"It is you," beamed Christian. "I was hoping I might run into you. What a lucky coincidence."

The two men slowed down and let her approach alone. It was rehearsed enough that Freedom ruled out "coincidence." They were both tall, but still stood a head below him, and weren't half as broad. He took a single step, which placed him right behind Madelyn. "Good morning, Ms. Nguyen," he said.

"Captain." She tipped her head, then focused on the dead girl. "If I could just take a moment of your time," she said, "I wanted to introduce myself. I'm Christian Nguyen."

She held out her hand. Madelyn looked at it for a moment.

"It's okay," said Christian. "I know who you are. A friend of mine from the hospital has been talking about you nonstop for days now. I was hoping I'd get a chance to meet you."

Madelyn glanced up at Freedom. He gave a slight nod. She looked back at Christian and took her hand. "I'm Madelyn Sorensen."

"You're cold," said Christian. "But that's probably healthier for you, isn't it?"

"I guess," said Madelyn.

The older woman beamed at her. "You're amazing, you know that? So many of us hoped to see someone like you, but we weren't sure it would happen in our lifetimes."

The dead girl shifted on her feet. "Someone like me?"

Christian nodded and gripped her Bible a little tighter. "Someone who came back."

Madelyn looked around the street. Her brow furrowed above her sunglasses. "Came back from where?"

Christian's smile faltered, but she caught it before it fell. "From the mindless dead. Your soul's risen again in your body."

"Oh," said Madelyn. "Thanks. I guess."

"We're heading to evening services now. Would you like to join us? I'm sure everyone there would love to hear about your experience."

"Umm," said the dead girl. "I don't really know you. Or them. No offense."

"We're a good group," said Christian. Her smile, a rare thing the past few years, was beaming at news-conference brilliance. "People can depend on us when things get tough."

"That's . . . umm, cool." Madelyn looked up at Freedom.

He cleared his throat. "I'm afraid Ms. Sorensen isn't going to have a lot of free time for a while. Stealth and Dr. Connolly have her on a fairly extensive schedule of tests."

The smile wavered again. It came back just as quick, but this time it didn't touch Christian's eyes. "Of course they do," she said. "It's a waste of time, though, trying to explain a miracle with science, isn't it?"

"If it can be explained with science, it isn't a miracle," said Madelyn. When the cold eyes flicked at her, she added, "That's something my dad used to say. He was a scientist."

"Of course," said the older woman. Her smile warmed. "You're probably still in shock from learning you'd lost them. My condolences. But there's still hope."

"Yeah. Thanks."

"Well, we must be going or we'll be late," said Christian. "It has been a pleasure meeting you. I hope you'll take me up on my offer and visit our congregation sometime soon."

"I'll keep it in mind," said Madelyn. "Thanks again."

"Thank you for being so understanding. I know everyone wants to meet you."

Christian bowed to Freedom again and walked past them. The two men fell in step behind her like good assistants or bodyguards. One of them nodded to Freedom. The other gave Madelyn a long look.

They walked on for another half a block. Then Madelyn spun to walk backward so she could face Freedom. "What was that all about?"

"It's complex," he said.

"Was I wrong, or was she completely giving me a creepy 'chosen one' vibe back there?"

"It's complex," repeated Freedom. "There are some people who've come to believe certain things about the ex-humans. Your existence . . . well, like Christian said, they've all been hoping to see someone like you."

"But Dr. Connolly says I'm not an ex. And wouldn't your supervillain guy, Legion, count as back-from-the-dead, too?"

He smiled. His lips were tight and controlled, but it was a smile. "Not exactly," he said. "That's complex, too."

Something caught his eye. He looked past her and his brow furrowed. She spun back around.

Another trio, two women and a man this time, headed for them. Beyond them were two couples, looking and pointing at Madelyn. Her shoulders slumped. "Seriously?" she said. "How did I end up becoming the golden child?"

Freedom looked around. He held out his arm to Madelyn. "Ms. Sorensen," he said, "I believe you asked about the Big Wall?"

She looked up and smiled. "Yes," she said. "That'd be cool."

He picked her up, cradled her in one arm, and she threw her arms around his neck. The huge officer flexed his thighs and launched into the air. He landed on top of the Wall and the structure shook from the impact.

Madelyn's sunglasses tumbled from her face. She snatched them out of the air before they fell into the street beyond the barrier. She slid out of Freedom's hold and thumped onto the wooden platform.

The two guards there saw her face, the white skin and pale eyes, and brought their weapons up. Freedom stepped forward. "At ease, men."

One of the guards, a soldier named Truman, lowered his

rifle. The other, one of the civilian guards, kept his weapon up for a few moments and then let it drop it grudgingly. Both of them kept their eyes on her.

"This young woman is a guest here," Freedom said, "and should be treated as such. Her name is Madelyn Sorensen." He said the last with a pointed look at Truman.

The soldier's eyes went wide. "You mean she's the doc's—"

Freedom nodded once.

Truman shouldered his weapon and held his hand out. "It's an honor to meet you, ma'am," he said.

"Again with the ma'am," she sighed, shaking the hand.

"Your father was a great man," he said. "He made me who I am today. Literally."

Her mouth wavered and she pushed the sunglasses back over her eyes. "Thank you." She looked up at Captain Freedom, then back to Truman. "You're one of the Unbreakables?"

He nodded and stood at attention. "Alpha 456th, ma'am, at your service. You need anything at all, you just come looking for me." He tapped the name on his chest. "Sergeant Mike Truman."

"Thank you," she said again.

The other guard's mouth twitched. His eyes flitted between the sunglasses hiding the dead girl's eyes and the pale skin of her neck. His fingers did a subdued dance on the strap of his rifle.

Freedom gave him a look. "As you were, men," he said. Truman gave a sharp salute and turned to continue his patrol along the wall. The civilian guard stared at Madelyn for another moment, then turned to follow his partner.

She watched them walk away, then let her eyes drift down beyond the Big Wall. A hundred or so exes were there, pressed up against the stack of automobiles. The constant *click-click-click* of their teeth echoed even louder here. Their dead eyes followed the two guards as they walked away along the Wall. Many of the staggering corpses went after them.

"Do I really look that much like them?"

Freedom stepped up behind her and the exes shifted their attention to him. They reached up and grabbed at the air. "According to my mother," he said, "looks aren't everything."

"Your mom never went to high school, I guess."

The exes clawed at their side of the Wall for a few moments, trying to reach the platform. Then they grew still. Their chattering jaws went silent.

Madelyn's eyebrows went up. "What's going—"

"Hey, big guy," rasped one of the exes. It had been a tall, dark-skinned man with a thin beard. One of its eyes was missing, and the opposite arm. The bloody rags of the shirt fluttered as it moved.

Madelyn shrieked and jumped back. Her oversized sunglasses dropped again, and this time they fell into the swarm of dead people below. Freedom stared down at the dead man with practiced disdain. "Did you want something?"

The ex blinked. Its eyelids flapped over the empty socket. "Getting lazy, *esse*," said Legion. "Forgot to call me 'sir.'"

"I didn't forget," said Freedom. "I made a point of not using it."

The dead man barked out a laugh. It opened its mouth and a handful of exes around it spoke in sync. "Yeah, you the big tough guy, hiding behind a gate," they said. "Adams thought he was tough, too."

Freedom's jaw shifted.

"You remember Adams, right? He was one of your guys. Now he's one of mine."

"This is him?" asked Madelyn. "This is the guy who can talk through exes? He controlled them out at your base?"

"Yes," said Freedom.

Madelyn stared at the dead man. It ignored her and continued to glare at Freedom with its one good eye. She set her jaw. "He killed my mom?"

"Since we got a moment alone," said Legion, "I'm going to make you a deal, big guy."

Freedom made a point of turning his head away from the swarm of exes and looked Madelyn in the eye. "No," he said. "That was something else."

"But he controlled the exes?"

The dead man twisted his head, and the dull eye panned back and forth across Freedom's face. "Game's changing again, Cap," the exes said. "You guys're always too slow. Always playing catch-up. You running out of time to do that."

The huge officer crossed his arms. It was like watching two tree trunks braid themselves. "What are you saying?"

"Saying you've got a chance," said the dead people. "You gather up all your soldier boys and leave. Go back out to the desert or wherever you want. You just all leave Los Angeles. Nothing'll touch you. You can just drive away."

Freedom said nothing. He stared at the exes. It was another practiced stare. After a moment, the handful of dead people shifted their feet. Madelyn's sunglasses crunched beneath a heel.

"Damn it," she muttered. "Y'know, until I came here I don't think I lost a single pair of glasses."

"Here," said Freedom. He pulled off his headgear and handed it down to her.

"You sure?"

"I've got three," he said.

Madelyn adjusted the strap and tugged the cap over her head. It shaded her eyes enough someone would have to look twice to see her bleached irises. She smiled up at him. "Good?"

He nodded.

"That supposed to impress me?" asked the exes.

Freedom glanced down at them. "Sorry?"

"Magic tricks ain't gonna save the day," Legion said. "Don't go thinking you can distract me with bullshit."

The huge officer hardened his stare at the dead man. "I don't know what you're talking about."

The dead faces below twisted into a dozen identical scowls. "Don't play games with me, big man. Where the hell'd your hat go?"

Sixteen

NOW

ZZZAP FLOATED INSIDE the electric chair, annoyed as all hell, and shot little bolts of electricity out of his finger at one of the rivets.

It wasn't really his finger. It was just an outline, a shape his subconscious formed to help him relate to the energy form. It was closer to a mathematical model than flesh and bone. And he wasn't really shooting electricity. It just streamed off him as potentials shifted, like a giant Tesla coil. It was an easy trick to do with all the conductive material in the cage, and it only added up to half a pound or so of himself that he was burning off each day.

Truth be told, he wasn't even aiming at the rivet. He didn't have that kind of fine control. It was just excess power that struck there instead of somewhere else along the copper-wrapped rings. If he actually fired a blast of energy at the rivet, he'd annihilate the electric chair, most of his entertainment center, and the far wall of Four. Not to mention the east and west walls of Five across the street, Zukor past that, part of the old telecommunications building, the lobby of Roddenberry (which would piss off Stealth to no end), the Gower manufacturing mill, and a little office complex past that which had been single apartments for two years now.

So, really, he wasn't doing anything. Except being annoyed as hell.

St. George and Stealth were angry at him. And he knew they had every right to be. Max had played him like an idiot. Whatever was lurking around their home right now was there because Zzzap had helped the sorcerer. Which he'd only done because he'd been too stupid to tell the others what was going on.

Now he was stuck wondering just what Max had brought back with him. And what it was going to do. And how many people were going to get hurt because of what he'd done.

Something shifted by the door. Somebody was lurking there he didn't recognize. He turned to get a better look and the figure cleared its throat. "Excuse me? Mr. Zzzap?"

No need to be formal, he said. *You can just call me Zzzap. Or even Barry, if you like.*

The figure stared at him for a minute. It looked like a boy, maybe ten or so. Zzzap tried to pick out some more details, but it was always tough with strangers. There were only so many particulars he could pick out with a smear of electromagnetic and thermal energy over the visual spectrum. He was pretty sure the boy had blond hair cut spiky-short.

Seriously, he said, *it's okay. Come on in.*

The boy took another step. "I'm sorry," he said, "I can't understand you. It sounds like you're humming a lot."

He nodded and focused on his words. *Better?*

The boy's face lit up. "Yeah. I can hear you now."

Fantastic. I'm Zzzap.

"Yeah, I know. I'm Todd," he said. "Todd Davidson." He paused after the name, as if hoping Zzzap would have something to say.

When the boy didn't continue, Zzzap nodded again. *Okay,* he said. *What's up, Todd? To save time, the rumors are true—I have the finest collection of sci-fi movies in Los Angeles. If there's something you want, odds are I've got it.*

Todd smiled but shook his head. "Nah," he said.

Well, I'm sorry, but I don't loan out my comics to strangers. Besides, you've probably read them all, anyway. All my favorite titles stopped three years ago. I don't know about you, but I don't think it's a coincidence that civilization collapsed right after Spider-Man made a deal with the devil.

The boy walked forward and squinted at the wraith. "I wanted to know, that is, I was wondering if maybe you'd heard anything from my dad?"

Zzzap cocked his head at the boy. *Your dad?*

"Danny Davidson. Daniel, but nobody calls him that."

Not ringing any bells, sorry. A few threads of electricity crackled from his shoulders to the curving rings above his head. He wondered if the boy was lost. A lot of kids had grown up inside the walls of the Mount, and when the Big Wall increased their world tenfold a lot of them had been overwhelmed.

"He's about this tall," said Todd, holding up his arm as high as he could, "with blond hair like mine. He used to be kinda fat but he lost a lot of weight just before the zombies showed up."

Sorry, said Zzzap, *still nothing. Where would I know him from?*

"What do you mean?"

Is he one of the scavengers or a gate guard or something? Were you guys out at Krypton?

Todd shook his head. "No, we've been here all along. Mom and I live over in Fifteen with my little sister." He turned and pointed back at the door. "We stayed here after everybody else moved out."

Okay. So where's your dad?

"Well, he's . . . he's dead. He died just before we moved here to the Mount."

Zzzap's stomach dropped. It was a sensation he'd never felt in the energy form before. He didn't like it.

"Some people were talking about the corpse girl and the magician," said Todd. "They said you could talk to him when he was a ghost and that's how he came back to life."

Yeah . . . That's not how it happened.

"But you could talk to him. To the ghosts."

Not exactly. I mean, yeah, but Max—the magician—he was a real special case.

"Can you talk to my dad?"

Y'know, Todd-buddy, I think this is a conversation you might want to have with your mom. Or maybe Father Andy.

"It was Mom's idea," said the boy.

What was?

"Asking you. She thought you could bring Dad back, too."

Zzzap knew he didn't have a stomach in the same sense he didn't have a finger. The energy form mimicked the shape of his body, not his internal organs. But his stomach was churning now.

"I miss him a lot," said Todd. "Cloddy—she's my little sister, Claudia—she doesn't remember him as much, but she was sad for a long time when he died. Mom says she sees him outside the Wall now and then. He's hanging around because he remembers us, too, deep down inside."

Yeah, that's probably it, said Zzzap. *Look, Todd, I don't think you understand what you're asking me for.*

"I'm asking you to bring my dad back."

I would if I could, he said. *I swear I would. But it's just not how it works.*

"But you already did it once. Couldn't you do it again?"

But I didn't really do anything, he said. *It's like saying the radio has something to do with writing your favorite song.*

The boy scratched his head. "Maybe you could just let me talk to him for a while."

Zzzap wondered how much trouble he'd get in if he fled the Mount right at that moment. They had lots of solar cells and some storage batteries. *I can't.*

"Or Mom. She misses him, too. She cried a lot when we first moved here. I know she'd be happier if she could talk to him for a little while."

The boy glanced over his shoulder at the door. Zzzap followed his gaze and focused on the far wall. It wasn't hard to look through objects, it just made everything a lot blurrier. There were at least two dozen people waiting outside. Maybe closer to thirty. Men, women, children. He was pretty sure he recognized Christian Nguyen among them. Half of them were on their knees, their hands pressed together.

Oh, frak me, he muttered. It came out as a blast of static.

The boy flinched from the sound, but only for a moment. "Can you do it? Please?"

Todd, look, you've just got the wrong idea. All of you. It's not that—

"Is there a problem?" a voice echoed through Four.

Zzzap sagged inside the rings of the electric chair. *Oh, thank God.*

Stealth walked out of the far corner of the room. The one with the deepest shadows, of course. She moved across the chamber with slow, even steps, and her boot heels clicked on the concrete floor. Her cloak caught the small currents from the electric chair and drifted behind her like trails of smoke.

Zzzap saw Todd's temperature shoot up three degrees and his heart rate jump. He wasn't sure if the boy was facing his childhood boogeyman or his first prepubescent fantasy. Todd probably didn't know, either.

She stopped in front of the boy and crossed her arms. Even with her featureless mask, it was clear her gaze had fallen on him. "You are Todd Davidson," she said. "Age ten and three months, son of Marcie, older brother of Claudia. Not doing well in English class."

The boy's heart rate revved again, just as he was getting it under control.

"You should not be here unescorted."

There was a long pause before he squeaked, "My mom's right outside."

"Then why are you in here?"

The boy shivered. He hadn't blinked since Stealth had crossed her arms. "I . . . I just wanted to ask a favor."

"You are being unfair to Zzzap," she said with a gesture at the wraith. "He wishes to help, but you are asking for something he cannot give you."

"He helped the magician."

"You refer to Maxwell Hale?"

Todd nodded twice.

Stealth's head swung side to side within her hood. "You are mistaken. Zzzap did not help him. Maxwell made several preparations on his own which allowed him to survive. That is all."

"But he was dead," said the boy. "He was dead and he could talk to him." He pointed an accusing finger at the gleaming figure.

"It might appear that way," Stealth said, "but that is not what happened."

"But everyone's saying—"

"Everyone saying something does not make it true. You are old enough to know this." The cloaked woman let the words echo in the room for a moment. "Zzzap did not and cannot bring anyone back from the dead."

Todd sighed. His face slumped into the universal expression of a kid who'd been told something depressing that he'd suspected anyway. "Are you sure?"

"I am."

Sorry.

The boy stared at Stealth's boots. Zzzap could see him cooling off, and the hint of moisture at his eyes. "Okay."

"The crowd outside is going to be leaving soon," Stealth said. "It is not safe for people to block the entrance of an important building like this. You should return to your mother and explain this mistake to her." She paused for a moment, then reached out to set one gloved hand on the boy's shoulder. "Can I trust you to do this?"

Zzzap saw the boy's temperature go up another two degrees. "Okay," Todd said again. She lifted her hand away and he slogged across the room.

"And Todd," she added.

He stopped at the door and looked back. "Yeah?"

"Return your sister's doll."

The boy's heart rate jumped one last time. His eyes went wide, his nerve broke, and he ran out the door.

Well, Zzzap said, *that sucked. Thanks for not being too mean to the kid.*

"I am never deliberately cruel, Zzzap." She tipped her head and her cloak slid off her shoulders to wrap around her. "I saw him enter on my monitors. His mother is an active member of the After Death movement, and has used her children to gain sympathy in the past. It was simple to deduce she had arranged for him to make such a request." She gestured at the doorway. "I will arrange for a guard detail on this building so you are not disturbed again. By children or adults."

I can deal with grown-ups. It's kids that are rough. Zzzap pressed his imaginary hands against his imaginary head. *I feel like I just kicked a bunch of puppies and kittens in front of him.*

"It is better he realizes the truth before his false hope grows too powerful."

But it's going to keep happening. Even if they don't get in, people are all going to be thinking this and expecting it. And it's all my fault.

"Some of it is, yes," said Stealth, "but not all of it. It is a natural psychological reaction for people to turn to religion in times of crisis. As this is a never-before-seen type of crisis, it is only natural it should produce a unique response."

Outside a trio of guards had joined the crowd. Zzzap could see the radios sparkling on their waists and the dim magnetic pattern of their weapons. The guards waved people away from the building's door and they grudgingly moved on. He saw Todd walk away alongside a thin woman.

You guys thought I was crazy, didn't you?

"Yes."

He waited for her to say more. Another few dozen megawatts of power washed off his form while he did. The electric chair popped and buzzed in the huge room.

Well, thanks for being honest.

"Of course."

I'm not, you know. Crazy.

"That much is clear now. I apologize for questioning your mental state, as justified as those questions seemed at the time."

I'd think with all the stuff we've seen and been through, you would've given me the benefit of the doubt.

"One would think," she said, "with all we have been through, you would trust us with a matter of such obvious importance."

A few more threads of energy crackled off his arms and legs to snap against the copper rings.

I'm sorry, said Zzzap. *I wanted to help him, and I thought he'd be able to help us. And I didn't think you guys would've believed me until I could prove it. Especially you.*

"In that, you are correct," she said.

Another few megawatts arced from his body to the electric chair.

So, said Zzzap, *what do I call you now?*

She looked at him. "I beg your pardon?"

Are you Stealth while you're wearing the mask and Karen when it's off? Y'know like Batman and Bruce Wayne? Or can we call you Karen when it's just us?

She glared at him.

The gleaming wraith put his hands up. *I just want you to feel comfortable.*

"Then you will continue to address me as you always have."

He nodded slowly. *Stealth it is, then.*

Zzzap hung in the electric chair and she stared past him to the door. After a few wordless seconds she turned and walked away. Unlike the walk she had done for Todd, her boots were silent now.

So you actually know how he's doing in school? he called after her. *That's not creepy at all.*

She stopped and looked back at him. Her face shifted beneath the mask. "Before society collapsed, several studies showed boys between the ages of nine and twelve scored an average of fourteen percent lower than girls in English and reading classes," she told him. "Double that percentage claimed English as their most difficult class. With a mathematically viable population of children, I saw no reason to assume those numbers had changed."

And the bit about taking his sister's doll?

Stealth held his gaze for another moment, then turned and walked back into the shadows.

Seventeen

NOW

CERBERUS PATROLLED THE Corner on a regular basis. The guards liked seeing her. The rowdier folks were kept in line by the sight of the armored titan. It was a small enough area that she didn't burn through too much battery life patrolling it. And it was far enough away from everything else that Danielle didn't have to listen to people nagging at her about how much time she spent in the battlesuit.

The northeast corner had been a trouble spot when the survivors of Los Angeles started building the Big Wall. The Hollywood Freeway, often just called the 101, cut right across that part of the city. It was a paved canyon filled with dead cars that never moved and dead bodies that moved too much. There'd been some debate about whether the Big Wall should just avoid it. Some people had pushed for a zigzag path through residential streets. Others suggested running the Wall along Santa Monica Boulevard instead of Sunset, cutting the area inside by a third.

Stealth had brought the discussion to an end. She insisted on running the Big Wall along the exact lines they'd planned. "We shall not reclaim the city by avoiding challenges," she'd said, "only by meeting them."

She'd been right, of course. Making the Corner safe had brought together hundreds of workers. It was where the assorted peoples of the Mount, the South Seventeens, and Project Krypton had started to bond as a community.

The freeway ramps had been blocked by concrete traffic barriers set up years ago by the National Guard. The survivors added sections of chain-link fence that extended out along the sloping ground on either side of the ramps and also the overpasses that stretched above the freeway. Cars stacked two and three high pinned the chain-link in place. It wasn't as solid as the Big Wall, but at the time it had been assumed the uneven ground would add to the barrier. The mindless exes didn't deal well with hills, and more than a few of them tipped over before they reached the top of the ramps.

That was before the people of Los Angeles knew about Legion. In the months since, barbed wire had been strung along the top of the chain-link. Guard platforms were built at each ramp. Extra cars had been stacked to limit the possible ways through. Cerberus had stacked most of them herself.

It all left a small area of four blocks isolated on the other side of the man-made canyon. Not surprisingly, "the Corner" was where the rougher individuals among the survivors had ended up. A lot of the loners and former gangers lived there, and some of the soldiers, too. There were rumors of a black market, although what anyone could have a black market *with* nobody seemed sure. The one thing everyone knew was that the Corner was the one place inside the Big Wall where it was impossible to block out the sound of teeth.

Cerberus had seen the almost-pixie woman a few times before. Her dark hair wasn't quite short enough to be a pixie cut, but Danielle didn't know what else to call it. She was in her late thirties. Maybe younger—people had aged a lot over the past three years. She was skinny by build, not just in the way most people were skinny these days, and her clothes fit well enough to show off her figure, even with the stylish overcoat she was wearing.

Most days the woman stood on the overpasses and stared

down at the exes staggering between the dusty cars and trucks. Every now and then she'd be muttering a prayer or talking to herself. It wasn't unusual to see. At a distance, the undead were a good device for soul-searching.

This evening, though, the woman was on top of one of the stacked cars a half block or so from one of the guard platforms. It was a minivan with a broad roof, and she was cross-legged on the luggage rack, a heavy blanket under her. She looked down through the coils of barbed wire at the exes on the weed-covered slope. Her expression was peaceful.

She glanced up at the approaching battlesuit and smiled. Her eyes were dark brown, almost black, and they flitted to the stars and stripes on the armor's shoulders. "Hello," she said. "Am I supposed to salute or something? I've never been sure."

"Just hello's fine," said Cerberus.

"Is it okay for me to be up here?" There was an odd pitch to her voice. It was somewhere between a high-pitched squeak and the creak you might hear in an older person's voice. A cute voice that had been shattered by lots of screaming. "Am I in the way or anything?"

"Not at all."

"I'm Tori."

"Cerberus."

"Yeah, I know," she said with a faint smile. Her eyes drifted back down to the undead on the freeway.

Cerberus watched Tori's eyes flit from one ex-human to the next. It wasn't unusual behavior, but she felt an awkward requirement to carry the conversation a little further. "Are you looking for someone?"

"A friend of mine. Richard. Rich."

The armored skull dipped once. "Ahhh," she said. "Friend or boyfriend?"

"Just a friend," said Tori. Her lips curled again, but the smile faded from her eyes. "Almost-boyfriend, I guess, but the moment never happened, y'know?"

"Yes."

"We got close a couple times," said the almost-pixie woman. "Really close that last Christmas Eve after we'd had a few drinks at a party. I stopped us before it went too far. Kind of wish I hadn't." She perked up and pointed down at the freeway. "There he is."

"Which one?"

"Okay, see the woman at the bottom of the ramp? The one in the green tee with the missing arm?"

The armor swapped lenses and zoomed in on the crowd of exes. Danielle found the dead woman with a tangle of brown hair and the green tee. Her right arm looked like it had been twisted off at the elbow. "Yeah."

"Go past her to the left. There's a tall guy in a striped coat and a wild tie."

The man in the pinstriped coat was on the shorter side, but so was Tori. He'd been good-looking in an average sort of way. One of his ears was missing, and Danielle could see blood-stains on his shirt when his lurching gait swung the coat open. His tie was a garish floral print. "That's quite a combination."

"He had to wear a tie to work, y'know, before everything, so making them clash was his little act of rebellion."

"Ahhh."

"Rich's boss was a real bitch. When the outbreaks were happening, most places were closing down or letting people work from home. She insisted they all had to go into the office or they'd get fired." Tori pointed at one of the taller buildings over on Sunset. "They got trapped in there. Three dozen people. I talked to him on the phone for a couple of days. They were living off the vending machines and stuff in the break rooms. The National Guard found them and gave them some food. They said they'd be back with a truck so they could get everyone out."

"They never came back?"

Tori shook her head. "I don't think so. After a week he called me to say they were going to try making a break for it. He figured if he could make it down to the freeway he could go along on top of cars and avoid the zombies."

It wasn't the dumbest survival plan Cerberus had ever heard. It wasn't the brightest, either. She didn't say anything. She'd long since grown used to people needing to unload on someone. And a lot of people found it easier to spill their guts to a giant robot than to a person they had to look in the eyes.

"Anyway, he told me to stay put and he'd get to me. So I stayed put. And I never heard from him again."

The battlesuit shifted, and its toes scraped on the pavement. "I'm sorry."

"It's okay," said the almost-pixie woman. She took a long, slow breath. "It was a long time ago."

Down on the street, the ex in the pinstriped coat had caught itself on the side mirror of a car. The dead man kept turning in small circles and bumping into the side of the car or other exes. After a few revolutions its coat slipped free and it staggered on. It headed in the general direction of the overpass they were on. Tori straightened up.

"After the Big Wall was done I kept coming out here to look for him. I even got an apartment over there." She waved her arm across the freeway at the Corner, but her attention drifted back down to her dead friend. "About five weeks ago I found him down there on the freeway. He's been staying put, just like he told me to."

"He's still pretty clean," said the armored titan, unsure what else to say. "That must make him a little easier to . . . to see like this."

"He hates being messy," Tori said. "He's one of those people who're always washing their hands and brushing themselves off. He's almost OCD about it."

The tenses hinted the conversation was going off into a direction Cerberus didn't want to be involved in. She'd had a version of it with someone every other week for the past four or five months since the A.D. movement had gained momentum. "If you're okay, then," said the battlesuit, "I'm going to move on."

"Oh, sure," said Tori. "I'm great now that Rich is here. Thanks for talking."

Cerberus nodded, feeling like she'd dodged a bullet. She didn't have anything against the almost-pixie woman's religion—any religion—but she found dogma boring as all hell. Most people wouldn't want to sit through one of her discussions about exoskeletal motion-reactive processors, either, but she didn't feel the need to force the subject on anybody except Gibbs and Cesar.

Tori reached out an arm to wave to her former-almost-boyfriend as the titan thudded past. Cerberus looked up ahead and saw the two guards at the Sunset on-ramp wave to her. She was trying to remember their names when she heard the noise.

It was the hollow sound of bending metal. Part of her recognized it as someone moving on a car roof. Then she heard the rustling, saw a glimpse of movement through her rearview camera, and the two guards stood up and raised their voices. The battlesuit spun around just as the click of leather on pavement reached her.

Tori's blanket hung across the chain-link fence. It covered and flattened the barbed wire. The fence still trembled from her vault over it.

The almost-pixie woman walked down the ramp, into the late-day shadows and toward the exes. Her hair was fluffed up from the jump. She was half turned away from Cerberus, but the battlesuit's lenses could still see the happy smile on her face.

"Tori," yelled the titan, "get back here now!"

She turned around and shook her head. "Don't worry," she called back. "He recognizes me. It'll be fine."

Dead Rich swung its head around to look at Tori. Its teeth banged together as it staggered toward her. The one-armed dead woman moved in her direction, too. So did an ex with a broken lower jaw, one with fingers worn down to bone claws, and a half-dozen others.

Cerberus took a few huge steps back to the minivan the woman had sat on. The battlesuit was too heavy to climb onto the car, and the chain-link would never support the armor's weight. She didn't have her ranged weapons because ammunition was so scarce for them. There wasn't any way for Cerberus to get to the other woman except for tearing open a hole in the barrier. Danielle clenched her fists in frustration. "Tori," she shouted again.

The almost-pixie woman ignored her. She was halfway down the ramp, seventeen and a half feet from the one-armed ex, according to the armor's targeting software. The dead woman raised its stump and its one good arm.

A shot rang out and the ex's head cricked hard to the side before it collapsed. The guards on the platform were lining up shots with their rifles. Tori looked up at them and screamed as another ex shambled toward her.

Cerberus patched herself through to their radios. "Keep her covered," she ordered. "I'm going to try to get down there."

"Make it quick, ma'am," said one of the guards. "There's at least a dozen more on the move, heading her way." He was one of the unenhanced soldiers from Krypton. His name flitted across her mind for a moment and she pushed it away.

Tori broke into a run, heading down the ramp. One of the guards pegged the claw-fingered ex and the woman screamed again. Cerberus thought the woman had gone hysterical and was just running to get away from the gunfire.

Then Tori got to the bottom of the ramp. She threw herself between the rifles and her dead friend. The woman spread her arms wide and looked up at them. "Don't hurt him!"

The guards looked over at Cerberus. So did Tori. Danielle glared at the screens inside her helmet and slammed her steel fist down on the hood of the minivan. "Get out of the way," she bellowed in full public-address mode. Her words echoed down into the concrete canyon.

Ex-Rich wrapped one arm around Tori's waist from behind. The other one hooked over her shoulder and grabbed her left boob. Her face lit up for a second with a look of vindication and relief. Maybe even a bit of naughty excitement.

Tori turned to look at the ex. Her eyes went wide just as it sank its teeth into the base of her neck. She shrieked. Blood gushed out across her shoulder and soaked her overcoat. The dead man clawed at her chest with its fingers and she twisted away. Ex-Rich staggered back with a mouthful of flesh between its chomping teeth.

Danielle blinked and the lenses zoomed in. Tori was bleeding a lot, but it wasn't pulsing. The ex had missed any major arteries. If she got back to the fence there was still a chance. A good chance.

But the almost-pixie woman was in shock. Once she was free of her dead friend she stood there for a moment. Her hand went up to touch her neck and came back soaked in red. She looked over her shoulder at the ex who had been her friend.

"Get back here," yelled Cerberus. "Come on!" She tried stepping up onto the trunk of a car. It squealed and crumpled under her armored foot. She looked at the fence and tried to figure out if there was a way to open it that could be repaired quickly. The only way through was to shred it.

Another shot echoed across the freeway and an ex jerked but didn't fall. It had been a dark-haired man in an L.A. Kings jersey. It took another few steps and a second round put it down.

Now Tori was hysterical. She turned to run and slammed right into a car. She sprawled on the hood and left a splash of blood on the silver paint. She pushed herself up and made it a few yards back up the ramp before she stumbled. She tried to twist herself back up and grabbed at her ruined shoulder. It threw her balance and she tumbled to the ground.

Ex-Rich fell on her, pinning her face down against the pavement. She twisted around onto her side and tried to push him away, and his teeth closed on her fingers. Its jaws opened again and her hand slipped in to the next knuckle. She howled.

The broken-jawed ex flapped its mouth at her and tried to chew her arm through the heavy sleeve of her overcoat. She thrashed her legs, but her almost-boyfriend slipped between them. Her other arm was pinned under her, and Cerberus could see it grasping at the air.

The guards took out two more exes heading for the woman, but a third slipped past them, and a fourth. Tori's screams were already growing weaker when the two new exes fell on her. Her cries gurgled as if she had a mouthful of water and one of the exes stumbled back with pink meat between its teeth.

The steel fingers wrapped around the chain-link, and Danielle hollered at the exes as they ripped the woman apart. Then she stood up straight and bit back her tears. There was no way to wipe her eyes while she was in the suit, and she'd be useless if she couldn't see or run the optical mouse.

Not that she'd been very useful to Tori as it was.

Eighteen

NOW

THE COUPLE ON the other side of the street glanced at Madelyn. She tried to walk casually and watched them without turning her head. When their gaze didn't leave her, she gave them a nod, a tight smile, and a little wave. The woman returned the wave and whispered something to the man, but they stopped looking at her and kept walking.

It was the third time this morning her disguise had worked, and she was feeling pretty good about it. The collar of her jacket was turned up and Captain Freedom's cap sat low against her latest pair of sunglasses. She was lucky the hospital had a small stockpile of them. With her hands in her pockets, she was pretty sure she'd pass as a living person if nobody got too close.

She walked down El Centro, a residential street running parallel to Vine. At each intersection she could see the Big Wall a block to the east. If her notes were right, she was two blocks away from the gate she'd walked past with Freedom.

They were going to be annoyed with her for sneaking out of the hospital. The guards on her floor had been pretty lazy because they all thought her memory issues meant she was stupid. She'd heard them talk about how she'd probably forget the way out of the building or how to open doors. Adults were always underestimating her. It pissed her off sometimes.

And she'd been a lot better about writing in her diary since arriving at the Mount. She had a lot more downtime, after all. Dr. Connolly even found two more notebooks for her. It meant she was clearer than she'd felt in ages.

Which was why Madelyn decided she needed to run some tests. Her dad had been very big on teaching her to use rational thought and the scientific method in all things. Schoolwork, cooking, sports, even dating.

In the months she'd spent—*years*, she corrected herself—wandering the Southwest, she'd come to suspect the exes didn't react to her the same way they did to living people. It'd never occurred to her they couldn't actually see or hear her. Even if it had, who'd want to test that theory out in the middle of nowhere?

Madelyn turned down a side street and the sound of clicking teeth grew louder. She stepped out onto Vine. The West Gate and its guard shack sat just a little bit to the south at the next big intersection.

She stayed on the sidewalk and slowed down a bit. There were more people along the street here and she didn't want to scare anyone. Or get shot. A few of the guards on the Wall were dressed in uniforms, but all of them were carrying big military rifles.

She turned away from the Wall and fished her eyedrops out of her pocket. A quick glance confirmed there was nobody within a block of her, and none of them were paying attention to her. Her head tilted back and she pushed her glasses onto her forehead. The soothing drops washed across her eyes and the sunglasses slid back into place.

Through the gate she could see the exes. Dozens of them. Hundreds, she realized, as she got closer. A lot of them were looking up at the people on top of the Big Wall. Some of them stretched arms through the bars to flail at passing people who were far out of their reach.

She was about ten yards from the gate when one of the guards noticed her. He was a tall man dressed in military camos. She didn't recognize him. He saw her cap and gave her an approving nod. "Don't get too close," he called down to her. He had to raise his voice to be heard over the sound of teeth.

"How close is too close?" she called back. She tried to sound a little flirty. Guys let you get away with a lot more when they thought you were flirting.

She saw his chest move with a chuckle she couldn't hear. He pointed with his free hand. "See the line?"

Madelyn looked at the bright line painted in front of the gate. "Yep."

"Stay a yard back from the line and you'll be fine. They won't be able to touch you."

He was reassuring her, she realized. A lot of people probably came to the gates, looking for familiar faces. A lot of those After Death folks. She gave him a nod and he turned his attention back to the creatures on the other side of the Wall.

There were two guards in the shack, but they were eating lunch. One looked at her, and his eyes lingered long enough to worry her. Then he went back to his sandwich.

It was just her and the exes. There were dead men, women, and children. Young and old. Black, white, Latino, Asian. The ex-virus didn't discriminate.

Except for me, thought Madelyn. It doesn't want me for some reason.

On the plus side, the exes were falling apart and she wasn't. They were missing fingers and hair and skin. Some of them had dark sockets where there should've been eyes or noses or ears.

Most of the ones at the gate were watching the guards on top of the Big Wall. Their attention kept shifting to the nearest target as the men and women walked back and forth. It made them sway.

A dozen or so at the far end of the gate stretched their hands at the shack. The windows were large enough for them to see the two men inside. Their crooked fingers clawed at the air, trying to pull the structure closer.

She moved a little closer to the shack. The exes there had their eyes at ground level, but she didn't want to get near enough for the guards to get a good look at her. She took a few steps forward and stood a foot back from the painted line.

None of them looked at her.

She took a breath and held it for a minute. "Hi, there," she said. Her words were washed away under the torrent of clicking ivory. She tried again and it came out louder than she'd intended. One of the guards walking above her, a rail-thin woman, glanced down for a moment before continuing south along the Wall.

The exes didn't react to the sound at all. Their heads never moved in her direction. Their grasping hands didn't reach for her.

A dead man with sun-bleached hair stood right in front of her. It wore a tuxedo jacket over jeans and a brown T-shirt, and it took her a moment to realize the brown was all stains. It stretched its arms toward the guard shack. Two of its fingernails were missing on one hand.

Madelyn took another step and set her toes on the line. She pulled her hand from her pocket and moved it back and forth in front of the dead man's face. The ex's eyes stayed focused on the shack a few yards away. "Can you hear me?"

She glanced around. The guards were ignoring her for the moment, wrapped up in their breaks or their duties. She reached across the line and tapped the ex on the back of its grasping hand.

It paused for a moment, then went back to reaching for the guard shack. Both her feet were past the line. They could grab her. There were three of them who could reach her without even trying. But they didn't try.

Madelyn slid forward, lined up between the bars, and punched the ex in the shoulder. The tuxedo corpse rocked on its feet, but its focus never shifted. All the exes around it ignored her, too.

"Hey," yelled someone up on the Wall. "Get back behind the line!"

Madelyn looked up and saw the guard in the camos staring at her. His face was trying to decide if it was angry or scared. Two other guards were turning to see what he was yelling about.

Then everything happened at once.

An ex a few feet away, two down from the one she'd punched, shifted on its feet. It was a thin man in a long coat. It wore a helmet wrapped in digital-camo cloth. The ex looked around and she realized it was reacting. It was doing something different. Like the ones had the other day when she was out with Freedom.

It had a pistol. It slid the weapon out from under its coat and brought it up. The barrel pointed between the bars at the gatehouse. The dead man's face pulled into a grin.

Something landed behind her. The camo guard had leaped twenty feet through the air to land on the pavement. The name on his coat said JEFFERSON. His hand reached for her shoulder. He was looking at her, not at the exes. Not at the ex with the gun.

She acted without thinking. It was like soccer. The ball came at you and you leaped to block it. You didn't think. She knew the ex was going to shoot the guards in the shack, so she just acted.

She twisted away from Jefferson and pushed down on the gun just as the ex squeezed the trigger. The pistol jerked under her hand, and the blast sparked against the pavement in front of the shack. The arm fought back and she struggled to keep the weapon pointed at the ground. The barrel was hot now.

"Gun!" bellowed Jefferson. He leaped back and swung his rifle around. At the same time he grabbed Madelyn by the arm with his free hand and yanked her away from the gate. He was strong. Really strong. It crossed her mind he was one of her dad's super-soldiers just as her feet left the ground and she sailed through the air. If Jefferson hadn't held on she would've tumbled across the road. As it was her hat went flying and her hair spun in every direction. The landing shook her and knocked her sunglasses to the ground.

The guards up above looked confused. Some of them shot down into the exes outside the Big Wall. Jefferson fired through the gate. The ex with the pistol slumped with a hole in its head.

A dozen sleepwalking exes woke up. Their posture shifted, their eyes became alert beneath their helmets. Pistols and rifles appeared from under shirts and coats. Some of them aimed at the guard shack. A few leaned back to aim at the guards on top of the Wall. At least three aimed at Jefferson, enough to make him hesitate for a moment. Shots echoed across the street and one of the guards howled and grabbed at his arm.

None of the exes aimed at Madelyn. None of them even looked at her.

She lunged past Jefferson again and grabbed a pistol from the dead man holding it. The gun flew over her shoulder and she reached through the gate to yank a rifle away from the next ex.

The exes looked confused. "WHAT THE HELL?" they all roared at once.

The rifle was heavier than Madelyn thought it would be, so she let it clatter on the pavement halfway through the bars. She took two quick steps and grabbed a pistol with each hand. She tried to think of it like a game. The weapon-grabbing game. One of the handguns went off as she grabbed it, and another shot thundered near her head. She cringed away but didn't feel any pain.

"WHAT THE FUCK IS GOING ON?" The exes looked past her at Jefferson. Then up in the air and all around them. Their heads moved in sync, like dancers or those Olympic swimmers. They were so confused they'd only fired a dozen shots so far.

She smacked a pistol out of withered fingers and brought both palms down on a soldiery-looking rifle with a curved clip. The dead man holding it fought back and snarled at the weapon. Her fist flew through the bars to punch the ex in the nose and she twisted the rifle away. She threw a clumsy kick and another pistol spun into the air.

More gunfire exploded around her. She flinched away from the exes, and just as she realized the sound was coming from behind her Jefferson dragged her clear again. He held his rifle in the other hand, snapping off shots like it was an oversized pistol. The guards from the shack joined him.

A dozen exes dropped across the width of the gate. They roared and fell and the ones behind them picked up the roar. The guards up on the Wall fired into the mob of exes. There was some return fire but it didn't last long.

Madelyn took a few deep breaths. It had all happened so fast. She glanced at the watches on her wrist and guessed maybe five minutes had passed since she walked up to the gate.

The exes at the gate tripped over their fallen brethren. Jefferson moved in and slid the fallen weapons away with his foot.

Then he turned and his rifle settled on Madelyn.

She threw her hands out and shouted, "Hey, whoa!" Even as she did, she saw her sunglasses on the ground. She really needed to get a strap or a lanyard or something for them. She blinked, then closed her eyes. "Call St. George," she said. "Or Captain Freedom. I know what I look like but I'm not one of them."

"It's her," murmured someone. "It's the corpse girl I heard they were keeping at the hospital."

Madelyn opened one eye. Three of the guards up on the Wall were still watching the exes beyond the gate. The rest stared at her with awe. Jefferson lowered his rifle a bit. She guessed if it went off now, it would hit her in the gut instead of the head.

She took in a breath and cleared her throat. "That's right," she said. "I'm from the hospital. And I need to get back or St. George is going to be angry with me."

"She's still got her soul," said a woman on the Wall. She pulled a string of rosary beads from her pocket and crossed herself. "It's true. They can come back."

The guard by the shack murmured something. Madelyn realized he was praying. She looked at Jefferson. He glanced at the others and back at her.

Then she heard fast, heavy footsteps—someone running up behind her. Jefferson's face relaxed even as his shoulders squared up. "Sir," he said, "this young woman claims you know her, sir."

She turned and looked up into Freedom's face. He gazed down at her and set his jaw. "I do," he said, "and I've been looking for her."

Nineteen

NOW

ST. GEORGE STOOD in the air and examined the symbol burned into the pavement outside the West Gate. Even with a dozen exes meandering over it, he could see it was different from the one up on Bronson Avenue. That one had been an hourglass, but this looked more like a pair of overlapping triangles. He tried to read some of the words scribbled out along the lines, but the walking dead made it hard to see anything more than a few syllables here and there. It wasn't English, and it didn't look like any of the Spanish words he knew. If he had to guess, he'd say it was Latin.

The edge of the circle was twenty feet out from the Big Wall, past the crosswalk and across from a dust-covered bus stop. For a moment he thought about flying up and looking at it from above. Then he remembered the dead woman twisting and exploding at the North Gate. There were two stains on the far edge of the circle where the same thing had happened here. He decided he could see it well enough from where he was.

He looked at the swarm below him and picked an ex at random. It was an emaciated woman with blond hair and clothes that had been stylish before the end of the world. She'd probably been pretty when she was alive. Now the skin was stripped from its chin and half its neck. Its bottom lip was gone and the teeth were yellow and cracked.

He wondered if the wound was how the woman had died. Maybe an ex had torn off part of her face with its teeth, letting her get away only to die and rise. Or maybe it was something someone had done trying to put the dead woman down, a blow to the skull that had missed.

St. George swooped down and lifted the dead thing by the back of the neck. It twisted in his grip as the ground fell away beneath its feet. A few nearby exes made awkward grabs at him as he rose back into the air with his catch. He drifted across the Wall and settled down in the open space inside the gate.

His boots tapped the pavement but he kept his arm up. The dead woman saw Cerberus, Jefferson, and another guard named Derek standing in a loose semicircle. The ex stretched out its arms and made awkward grabs at them. It swung back and forth in St. George's grip.

Madelyn shifted behind Cerberus. She'd been skittish around the guards since Freedom left. St. George shook his head and gestured for her to come out in the open. "You're safe here," he told her. "No matter what happens, you'll be safe."

Jefferson stepped forward, his rifle braced in one arm. He batted away the grasping fingers, and gave the ex a quick pat-down with his free hand. "Clear," he said.

"Can't believe we need to start watching them for weapons," said Derek. "I mean . . . a zombie with a gun? It sounds like a joke."

"Not anymore," Cerberus said. She pointed at a pair of exes in camoflaged helmets. "Legion got to the armory out in Van Nuys. Weapons, ammunition, helmets, body armor." Her head shook back and forth. "For all we know he's got a dozen exes out there watching the walls through telescopic sights."

Derek grimaced at the thought. So did a few guards on the Wall within earshot. The casualness faded from their movements.

St. George gave the ex a shake and raised his voice. "Rodney," he shouted. "Time to have a talk."

His voice echoed out across the street for a moment and then the dead woman stopped thrashing. The clicking teeth stopped and its face shifted from a blank mask to a surly grimace. It reached back to swat the hero with one hand. "Told you plenty of times, dragon man," the ex said, "it's Legion now." Without a bottom lip, its voice was a drunken rasp, like the words were being dragged into the air across sandpaper.

Cerberus leaned forward with a hiss of servos and scraping armor.

St. George set the dead thing down. It shrugged a few times and turned to glare up at him. The ex had been a tiny woman, a good six inches shorter than the hero. "Got a question for you," he said. As an afterthought he added, "Legion."

The dead woman snorted. "The answer is fuck you."

"All that time you were hiding out at Krypton, while Dr. Sorensen was covering for you, were you ever going to keep your side of the deal you made?"

Madelyn stiffened at the mention of her father. Her face got hard and she took a bold step away from Cerberus. Her sneakers slapped hard on the pavement, almost a stomp.

The ex didn't even glance at her. "Don't know what you're talking about," it said to St. George.

"The one where you told him you'd find his family for him."

The dead woman sneered as best it could. "What's it to you?"

"Think of it as your big chance to prove you're better than I think you are," said the hero.

Madelyn took another few steps forward. The only person closer to the dead woman now was St. George. Madelyn stood up straight in front of the ex.

Legion tried to spit at St. George, but without a lower lip it just leaked thick oil over its chin. "Yeah, my word matters," it growled. "I looked for them, just like I said. Didn't make any difference. His old lady's dead and walking. Never found the girl's body. Figured it was easier to let the old guy think I was still looking."

"And it gave you a place to hide," said Cerberus.

The ex turned to the armored titan. Its gaze passed right through Madelyn. She even stepped to the side to stay in front of the dead woman's face. "Fuck you, *puta*," Legion spat at Cerberus. "I don't hide from nothing."

"Except me," she said. The titan held out one massive gauntlet at head height and squeezed it into a fist. The ex gave her the finger.

St. George nodded. "So you looked for his daughter and never found her?"

Legion returned the nod while Madelyn waved both hands in front of the ex's face. "Yeah. Never saw any sign of her. What's it to you, *esse*?"

St. George smiled. "Okay," he said, "I think that answers that."

"Answers what?" growled the ex.

"It makes sense in a way," said Cerberus. "I remember the military tried using dead bodies as bait for a while, but the exes only react to living people."

"Yeah, I remember something about that," said St. George. "The bait thing."

"Bait?" echoed Legion. "What the fuck you people talking about?"

"Doc Sorensen ran some tests out at Krypton, sir," offered Jefferson with a polite nod to Madelyn. "He said it's some kind of perception thing, like how the T. Rex in *Jurassic Park* can't see you if you don't move."

"*Jurassic Park*?" echoed Cerberus.

Legion's eyes flitted between them. "What the fuck you people talking about?"

Jefferson glanced at the talking ex, then back to the heroes. "I remember it because the T. Rex scared the piss out of me as a kid. Pardon me, ma'am," he added to Madelyn. "He said it was something to do with the reptilian brain. They see everything, they just process it different than we do. Living things get priority over dead things, moving things get priority over still things, things they see get priority over things they hear, like that. He said that's why they run into walls and stuff."

"They don't need it, so they don't register seeing it," said Cerberus. She looked at the dead woman. "And he's in the exes, so maybe he's stuck using their senses. Or not using them, I guess."

"And she's dead," said St. George with a glance at Madelyn, "so she's not a priority."

Legion looked down at the body he was wearing. One of the hands flexed open and closed. The ex's brow furrowed in confusion. "She who?"

"We know he can see nonliving things," said Cerberus. "Maybe it's a focus issue?"

Madelyn took her cap off and waved it in the air in front of the dead woman. "So, you're saying I'm not invisible, I've got a perception filter? Like on *Doctor Who*?"

St. George, Cerberus, and the guards all looked at her.

"*Doctor Who*," she repeated. "It's this sci-fi show from England."

"Yeah, I've heard of it," said St. George.

"Heard of what?" said Legion.

"Okay," Madelyn said, "well, there's this thing they use on it called a perception filter. It's like a force field that makes things inside it less interesting so you can't focus on them. So you're sort of invisible but not really. You're just . . . very forgettable."

She waved the cap in front of the ex again for emphasis.

"Well, there's one way to be sure." St. George took a few steps back and looked at Madelyn. "Go ahead and hit him."

"Her?" asked Madelyn, nodding at the ex.

"This some game, *pendejo*?" asked the dead woman. "Who you people keep talking to?"

"Yep," said St. George. "Go for it."

Legion looked up at St. George. "What?"

Madelyn let the cap drop from her hand. It hit the ground and Legion's head shifted to glare at it. The dead eyes went wide for a moment. "The fuck?" he said.

"See?" said Cerberus. "He saw that."

"That's the big guy's hat," said the dead woman. "Where'd that come fr—"

Madelyn slammed her fist into the ex's shoulder. It wasn't a great punch, but Legion staggered back a step and spun around. "What the FUCK!" he shouted. The ex reached up to probe its shoulder with its fingers. It glared at the heroes.

"He can feel getting hit," Madelyn said, "I just don't think he knows I'm doing it."

"Maybe it's because he doesn't know what to look for," mused Cerberus. "He can't prioritize you because he doesn't know you're there. It doesn't even seem like he hears you."

Madelyn leaned into the ex's ear. "Hey!" she shouted. "I'm right here!"

"Hear who?" said Legion. The dead woman looked up at Cerberus, then past Madelyn to the roof of a nearby building. "Stealth up there somewhere? This her idea?"

"Hit him in the face," said Cerberus. "For science."

Madelyn grimaced, but threw another punch. It caught the dead woman on her bare jaw. Legion stumbled and spun around, clawed hands missing Madelyn by a good three or four feet. The ex spat out a mouthful of Spanish swears and curses that made St. George's mouth twist into a smile. She poked the dead woman a few times from different directions, making it twist around, then placed her hands on its back and shoved it toward the gate. The dead thing stumbled and tried to get its balance back.

"Oh my God," said the armored titan. "Once again, science makes the world a better place."

Jefferson snorted out a laugh.

"This feels kind of mean," Madelyn said. "I mean, I know he's the bad guy, but he can't fight back or anything."

"You're not doing anything he doesn't deserve a hundred times over," said Cerberus.

"True enough," said St. George, "but I think we've learned what we needed to know, anyway."

"What is this?" snarled Legion. "Got someone invisible now, that it? Pushing me around and taking my guns?"

"Something like that," said St. George. "Might want to keep it in mind next time you try rushing the walls."

"I'll remember it," grunted the dead woman. It took in a hissing breath and so did a dozen exes pressed up against the gate. They all spoke with Legion's voice. "I'LL REMEMBER IT THE NEXT TIME YOU'RE OUTSIDE."

"Y'know, you're starting to overuse that trick," St. George said. "It's not as scary as it used to be."

The dead woman made another messy attempt to spit at him and then her jaw started chomping up and down again. Madelyn hopped away from the ex. The teeth clacked together half a dozen times before St. George grabbed the dead thing and pitched it over the top of the Big Wall.

"Game's changing again," Legion said from the gate. Now it was a dead man with a helmet and a series of silver loops running along each lip. "I got guns. I got armor. Next time we do this it's gonna be big."

St. George walked up to the gate. "Try it," he said. "One of these days—"

"What, dragon man?" The ex grinned at him. Half its teeth were cracked from banging against each other for months. "You can't stop me. Can't do anything. Go ahead and beat up a hundred stiffs. Two hundred if it makes you feel all macho. Can't touch me, and you know it."

Smoke curled out of St. George's nose as he glared at the dead man through the fence. He could feel things twisting at the back of his throat and swallowed the flames down. His fingers curled into fists and he had to fight the urge to drive one of them through the ex's face.

Someone stepped next to him. Madelyn reached out and poked the tip of the dead man's nose. Legion growled and stepped back from the gate.

"I can touch you," she said, "and you'll never know it's coming." She stood up straight and crossed her arms. "Damn it, that was totally cool and he couldn't even hear me."

The dead man squinted at the air next to Madelyn. Then its gaze flitted to the left and locked eyes with her. She took a quick step back.

"There you are," the ex growled. "All fuzzy and blendin' in, but I see you."

St. George snapped his fingers. Legion glanced at him, and when the pale eyes swung back they went past Madelyn. The dead man scowled and took a few more steps back.

"I'll figure that one out, too," Legion said. The exes stepped back, clearing a path for him as he marched away from the gate. "You go ahead and keep thinking I'm stupid. How many people that cost you so far?" He looked back over his shoulder. "How's your buddy with the beard doing? Jarvis?"

St. George's fists shook. He breathed out hard and licks of flame slipped out between his lips. He took in a breath to yell after the ex, or maybe send a ball of fire, and froze.

On the far side of the street, just across the symbol burned into the pavement, two of the exes had turned to face Legion. Their faces twisted into twin expressions of pure rage. Their eyes swelled and burst, spilling blue fire across their faces.

Uncertain muttering broke out across the Big Wall.

"Rodney," St. George called out. "Stop moving!"

The dead man sneered at him over its shoulder as it stepped onto the symbol. "It's Legion!" said the ex. "Not your fucking servant boy to call up when you want something. Remember that next time you want to play fucking games."

"Seriously," yelled St. George. "Look out!"

The exes at the seal bent and swelled. A third one opened its mouth to reveal a forest of long teeth. A fourth held up hands with dagger-like fingernails.

"You're pathetic, dragon man, and any day now I'm gonna—"

The distorted exes pounced on Legion as he stepped off the symbol. It was like watching cats fight, a ball of teeth and muscle and claws that spun and twisted too fast to see more than glimpses. More exes piled into the fight, some of them with burning eyes and some shouting in Spanish.

And then they started to explode. And Legion started to scream. It was a long howl of pure agony.

Instinct pushed St. George into the air. "Cerberus," he shouted, "get ready to go out there. We need to—"

He dropped out of the sky and hit the pavement hard next to the silver titan.

"Don't do it, George," someone said.

Max stood in the street behind them. Somewhere he'd found a charcoal suit. The sleeves were pushed up to reveal the tattoos on his forearms. He had his hands pressed palm to palm against each other so his fingertips touched his wrists.

St. George leaped to his feet, focused on the spot between his shoulder blades, and stayed on the ground. Something pushed down against him. He focused harder and the something pushed harder.

Max shook his head and raised his hands without separating them. "I can't let you go out there."

The hero glanced out the gate. The screaming was more ragged. Between the exes he could see the bursts of blue flame and dark gore. "It's killing him. We can't just—"

"No great loss," said Max. "But either way, you're the last person who should step past the seals."

"I can take care of myself."

"Not against that."

Cerberus took three huge strides and set an armored gauntlet on Max's shoulder. Her fingers flexed. "Let him go."

St. George tried to throw himself into the air again. He couldn't even jump while Max held him down. "Even Rodney doesn't deserve that."

"Not the point. You're not a normal human, George. You're tough. You're strong. Your body could take possession as is. He could use you."

"Boss," shouted Derek from the top of the Wall. "It's stopped."

St. George glared at Max. The sorcerer looked at the silent street through the gate and nodded. "Don't go out there," he said. "Seriously."

He glanced up at Cerberus and pulled his hands apart. St. George lifted into the air. The hero floated up and settled on the platform by Derek. Madelyn dashed up the staircase to stand next to him.

At least a dozen unmoving exes littered the street past the symbol, and enough parts and gray meat to make up another dozen. The remaining undead stumbled around like shell-shocked survivors of a bomb blast.

While they watched, another ex stopped and turned to look at them. A heavyset man in a bloodstained football jersey. It roared and flames poured out of its mouth and ragged nostrils. Its eyes boiled away. A hand came up and pointed a long spidery finger at the figures on the Wall.

"What the fuck is that?" muttered Derek. "A couple exes did that the other day."

"And why's it pointing at me?" asked one of the guards.

"It's pointing at me," St. George told him.

Derek shook his head. "Are you sure? It looks like it's aimed right at me."

"I'm sure. Calm down."

"So what is it?"

"It's death," said Max. He was up on the Wall next to them. "It's the most nightmarish death you can imagine."

The ex stretched and twisted. Tusks and fangs burst from

its mouth even as its spine arched like a snake. A forest of spikes sprouted across its back and arms, shredding the football jersey. The prehistoric roar echoed from its mouth again and shook the Big Wall.

The blue flames swallowed its head, burning it down to a bare skull. Its flesh tore at the joints and the dead thing burst like a water balloon. Dark blood and gore splattered across the street.

Max raised his voice. "Cairax Murrain is going to kill every living thing it can, anyone it can reach. Make sure everyone knows. Man, woman, child . . . superhuman." He looked at St. George and let his gaze drift over to Cerberus down at the gate. "Right now, the only safe place in this city is inside these walls."

The muttering that had echoed along the Big Wall turned into nervous discussion. Some of the guards crossed themselves. Others gripped their weapons even harder. They all stared out at the symbol burned into the pavement, just a few yards out from the gate.

And a few of them were on their radios, spreading the word.

St. George grabbed Max and leaped down to Cerberus. "Great," he snapped. "You just scared a bunch of people."

"Good," Max said. "Right now none of you are anywhere near as scared as you should be."

Madelyn pushed past the guards on the Wall to race down the staircase. She leaped past the last few steps to land in a crouch on the pavement. A few quick steps put her right next to St. George again.

He barely noticed, his attention focused on Max. "Look, it's your demon, right? If I can beat it alone, Cerberus and I can go out there and—"

"You didn't beat Cairax, George. You beat me."

"No, I think it was—"

"No." Max shook his head. "What you beat was a shadow. That was Cairax Murrain starved, handcuffed, gagged, and shoved in a sack. It's like punching Mike Tyson when he's asleep. And even then, the only way you beat him was taking the Sativus off and turning him back into me."

The sorcerer turned to gesture through the gate. "What's out there now is the real thing. No psychic chains, no magical restraints, no limits whatsoever. None. It's at full strength and it's seriously pissed off that I had it bound for over two years. Way, way more pissed than I thought it was going to be, and that's really saying something. So trust me when I say you do not want to go out there. Out there, you've got a life expectancy of two minutes if you're lucky."

Cerberus's feet scraped on the pavement. "You don't think he'd last that long?"

"No," said Max with a shake of his head and a meaningful stare at St. George, "I meant he'd be lucky if he died that quick."

Twenty
NOW

FREEDOM LIKED WALKING the streets. It reminded him of being on patrol, which was much more in line with what he was trained to do. Plus, after close to three years in the desert at Project Krypton, there was something luxurious about the trees, shrubs, and small lawns of Los Angeles.

He hadn't been thrilled with the idea of using Madelyn as a test subject, let alone with one involving exes. He understood how important it could seem on one level, but he also knew in the long run it wouldn't mean much. Freedom was a longtime believer in Bradley's old adage, "Amateurs talk strategy, professionals talk logistics." Having one person at the Mount who couldn't be detected by the exes or Legion would be more of a minor convenience than a major advantage.

Especially when the one person was a teenage girl.

"Six, this is Seven," echoed a voice over his earbud.

"Seven, this is Six," he responded.

Even though she'd grudgingly accepted her new position at the Mount, First Sergeant Kennedy still insisted on using military protocol and call signs over the radio. It had caused chaos at first as every Wall guard, deputy, and scavenger with a radio took on a self-assigned number. She'd finally sat all of them down for a series of lessons and explained why they couldn't refer to themselves as Sixty-Nine, Eight-Fifteen, Red Five, SG-1, or any of the others they'd picked.

And they all still just called for St. George by name.

"Six, this is Seven," Kennedy said. "Update on that domestic dispute at Raleigh. Got a little out of hand. We've got three in the brig, two injured. One civilian, one of ours."

"Seven, this is Six. Anything serious?"

"Six, this is Seven. All injuries are minor. I'll let you talk to the deputy when you get back."

Kennedy using the word *deputy* meant it was one of the civilian peacekeepers. If it had been one of her own soldiers, she would've called them out and used verbal shorthand to let Freedom know the exact infraction. It was a habit he noticed her using more and more, keeping civilians and soldiers separate.

When Freedom had taken command of the Mount's police force, it had been a disorganized mess. Looking back over the past months, he could admit they hadn't helped matters by expecting everyone to conform to military standards. The call signs had been the tip of the iceberg. After a few years of postapocalyptic life, his people were as unprepared to deal with civilians as the civilians were to deal with structured law enforcement.

It didn't help that there was a fair amount of animosity toward the soldiers. The people of the Mount had lost family and friends, lives and homes, and the U.S. Army hadn't been there to protect them. Freedom had overheard more than a few grumbles about the men and women of the Alpha 456th Unbreakables becoming part of the command structure in Los Angeles.

Which was the problem. Freedom and his soldiers were military trying to command civilians. It was a gray area they were still exploring. He was used to conditions of absolute authority, and the huge officer was very aware the only reason the civilian police listened to him or Kennedy was because Stealth had told them to.

He was close to the southwest corner of the Big Wall, on a street called Larchmont, when he heard a faint noise over the echo of teeth. He'd heard it before, in Afghanistan. A series of sharp pops echoing back and forth between the buildings. The sound of gunfire in a quiet city. There was nothing else quite like it.

He tapped his earbud. "This is Six," he said. "Report. I hear shots fired?"

Another squelch of voices stepped over one another before a voice stood out. A man shouted into his microphone loud enough to make Freedom wince and grab for his ear. "It's out," the man yelled. "It got out!"

"This is Six," Freedom said. "Calm down."

"It got out," repeated the man. "I think Katie's dead. It was so fast, and the bullets didn't stop it. They didn't even slow it down!"

"Twenty-Four, this is Seven," said Kennedy. "Stand by, units are coming to your position." She'd identified the man's voice and given Freedom the location. Twenty-Four was shorthand for second platoon, fourth squad. And squad four was inside the studio walls, broken into a few small teams to guard different positions.

Freedom started running. He was three blocks from the Mount. The long, north–south blocks of Hollywood. "Twenty-Four, this is Six," he said. "Coming to you."

"This is Danny—uhhhh, Twenty-One—on the Wall. It just went over the Wall right by the Melrose Gate."

Too much chatter and not enough information. He still didn't know who or what they were fighting. It didn't sound like exes. It sounded fast.

As Freedom passed an intersection he saw movement out of the corner of his eye. A figure dashed across the road parallel to him, two blocks over and heading south. He saw the pale skin and thought an ex was inside the walls, but no ex moved that fast, even the ones Legion controlled. The captain turned his head and got a quick glimpse of the figure—a blood-splattered old man wearing khakis and a white T-shirt.

Freedom made a snap call. He pivoted and went after the man. "Six to Seven," he called out. "Target engaged."

Whoever he was chasing was fast, even barefoot. Not as fast as Freedom or the other super-soldiers, but enough that for a moment he worried he was chasing one of his own. He closed the gap. The old man was a few yards ahead. And he was running out of road. Beverly was just a block ahead.

A new voice cut over the chatter. "Freedom, this is Stealth," she said. "St. George is moving to join you. Stop the prisoner at all costs. Use lethal force, nothing less."

The word *prisoner* stood out. So did *lethal force*. And so did the tone in Stealth's voice. He'd never heard it in all the months he'd known the woman, but it almost sounded like she was worried. Maybe even scared.

Freedom had enough sense to know anything that scared Stealth was something he shouldn't be second-guessing.

He stopped in a shooting stance, pulled out Lady Liberty, and fired off three quick bursts with the massive handgun.

A handful of red carnations blossomed across the old man's back and thighs. One grew out of his shoulder. He stumbled and flew through the air, carried by his own momentum and the impact of several twelve-gauge slugs at short range. His body crashed onto the pavement, rolled a few yards, and came to rest. It twitched twice.

Freedom walked over to the crumpled figure. The man wasn't as old as he'd thought. The hair was deceiving, and it was shockingly white against all the blood soaking the man's clothes. His gray eyes stared up at the sky. One of his hands looked withered and bony, like a corpse. His shoulder was a tangle of red sinews.

He took a slow breath and tapped his earbud. "Seven, this is Six," he said. "Be advised, target has been neutrali—"

The man rolled to his feet.

He locked eyes with Freedom and hurled something at the huge captain. It struck him in the shoulder, just past his body armor. It cut fabric and broke the skin, but even at the joints Freedom's muscle was too dense for it to penetrate far. He brushed it away and it clattered on the ground with a sound like wood.

The chalk-haired man was on the move and half a block away, sprinting like he'd caught his second wind. Freedom raised his pistol and fired again. The prisoner staggered but kept moving.

He raced out onto Beverly, headed straight for the Big Wall. The guards had heard Lady Liberty and were waiting for him. None of them were Freedom's soldiers. All five of them opened fire. Many of the shots sparked on the pavement—the guards weren't used to a fast target—but a good number hit. Freedom saw the man's limbs jerk and tremble, but he never broke stride.

Something uncoiled from the prisoner's shoulder like a snake and he swung his arm up at the guards along the top of the Wall. A long cord lashed out and wrapped around the neck of one of the guards. The man let out a wet cough. His companions stopped firing and leaped to help him, grabbing at the line.

The prisoner jumped. He went hand over hand up the thick cord to the top of the Wall. A dozen feet in seconds. The guards didn't even realize they were helping by pulling on the line until the white-haired man was on the platform with them.

Freedom was a dozen yards from the Wall. He flexed his legs and hurled himself into the air. The guards were too close to the prisoner for him to use Lady Liberty again.

The prisoner lashed out and a guard staggered. Another one opened fire. The white-haired man and a guard stumbled back, but only the guard dropped.

Freedom landed on the Big Wall. He heard two-by-fours crack under his heels, the wooden platform trembled, and the stack of cars groaned beneath them. For a brief moment the whole structure tilted.

"On your knees," he bellowed. "Get on your knees with your hands on your head." Even as the words left his lips, he remembered Stealth's insistence on lethal force and realized nothing had stopped the man yet.

The prisoner glanced at the captain, then at the crowd of exes gathered below.

Freedom lunged forward.

The white-haired man threw himself over the railing and plunged into the horde outside the Big Wall.

Freedom looked over the edge. The prisoner had vanished beneath at least twenty undead. They swarmed over him and the sound of clicking teeth seemed to grow louder.

He turned to the men on the Wall. The two who were still on their feet, the shooter and a cornrowed woman, just stood there. Freedom knew the look. They were up and locked. The shooter kept glancing between the railing and the man he'd shot. The woman was frozen with her mouth half open.

"You," he snapped at the shooter. He pointed at one of the bodies. "Check him. Now."

The man blinked awake and ran to the fallen guard. The woman was still frozen. Freedom ignored her.

The man who'd been shot coughed and spat up some blood. Freedom could see the dark stain spreading across his chest. Bleeding but not spurting in pulses and not whistling. Serious, but probably not fatal if he got care soon enough.

The other man had a blade buried in his chest. It looked like it had been carved from pale wood—more of a stake than a blade. He was still breathing, but it was erratic. The shooter was gripping his hand and speaking to him, urging him not to quit.

The last guard, the one who'd been throttled by the prisoner's line, unwrapped the last coil of it and tossed it aside. He was covered in blood. His hands were soaked with it, but there wasn't enough to be arterial bleeding. The rope had just slashed through the skin of his neck.

"Seven," Freedom said, "this is Six."

"Six, this is Seven," she replied.

"Seven, this is Six. Emergency medical to Big Wall south at Windsor. We have three wounded. One serious, one critical."

She signaled her acknowledgment and his eyes fell on the line. He prodded it with his boot, then crouched to look at it. His brow furrowed.

The rope was a crude whip. The long strands weren't leather, just sinew and tendons that had been dried and braided together. There were white barbs along the length of it, gathered in tight quartets. They gave the weapon a strong resemblance to a length of barbed wire. It took a moment for Freedom to realize he was looking at close to a dozen teeth woven into the whip's lash with their roots pointing out.

He heard a noise and looked up to see Stealth. Her cloak streamed behind her. "Where is the prisoner?"

Freedom nodded at the railing. "He's dead, ma'am. He threw himself off the Wall. The exes tore him ap—"

Stealth took three quick strides to the railing. Her hands flicked and her pistols were out. Freedom saw a quick ripple of movement within her hood as she scanned the street at the base of the Big Wall.

Then she fired both weapons, aiming at something across the street. Freedom unholstered Lady Liberty and joined Stealth at the railing just as her pistols ran dry. It took him a second to realize what she was shooting at.

The prisoner stood there, arms spread wide. His clothes had been shredded by the exes, and his skin was smeared with gore, but he was smiling. A dead woman latched onto his forearm and tore a mouthful of flesh away. Another one gnawed on his calf. The white-haired man didn't seem to notice.

Stealth's fingers shifted and empty magazines dropped from each pistol to rattle on the platform. She reloaded in seconds and was firing again. Freedom raised his own weapon and Lady Liberty thundered. The trigger-happy guard joined them, but Freedom could tell the man was just spraying bullets.

The prisoner flailed under the assault. His skin ruptured and blood sprayed across the lawn behind him. He staggered back and dropped on the grass. The exes chewing on him were torn apart by stray rounds from Lady Liberty's bursts. Their remains fell on either side of the man.

"If you don't mind my asking, ma'am," said Freedom, "what the hell was that all about?"

The cloaked woman ignored him. She reloaded again.

The prisoner rolled over and scampered across the lawn on all fours.

Stealth tracked him and led her shots like a decorated marksman. Freedom saw her score half a dozen hits before the prisoner got back to his feet. The white-haired man sprinted to the end of the block before glancing back, and Stealth rewarded him with three rounds in the face. His forehead burst apart and he slumped against an SUV, but he was moving again before he hit the ground. He shook off the impact, rolled under the vehicle, and vanished.

A shadow passed over them. St. George hung in the air. "Go," she shouted at him. "That way!"

The hero shot across the road after the escaped prisoner. He got to the SUV and shook his head. He raised his hands to his mouth and called out a name twice.

Freedom waited for the cloaked woman to turn to him, but she stared out after the prisoner. He took the moment to shove his earbud back in. The panicking man still monopolized the airwaves.

"Oh, Jesus," said the voice on the radio. "The Thing got out. It got out of the Cellar."

Twenty-One

NOW

LEGION FOUND HIMSELF in a dead man, wandering in the middle of a tree-lined residential street. Small houses and one or two apartment buildings. He glanced around and looked through the eyes of a dead woman at the end of the block. The street sign said Stetson, like the hat.

He expanded his view, spreading out across another dozen or so exes until he saw a few more nearby street names. Walnut. Harkness. Colorado. He saw big buildings framing a campus and the sign for Pasadena City College. He was about twenty-five miles away from the Big Wall, way out past Glendale.

His attention focused him into a new body, a heavyset Samoan stumbling through a store parking lot off Colorado. The dead man was intact except for a few scrapes and cuts. And one dead eye. He reached up to check the socket and realized it was made of glass. It'd be fine for now.

Legion looked around the parking lot. The store had faded pink awnings with a "99" logo on them. There were a dozen dusty cars parked at different angles. One of them was T-boned into another, totaling both. A driver's side door hung open, and he saw old blood splattered on the passenger seat. A primer-colored muscle car sat halfway through the store's big window next to the double doors. Purple shopping carts were scattered everywhere. Some had drifted with random winds, others were tipped on their sides like dead animals.

He glared at another ex in the parking lot. It was an older woman with a wrinkled face and a pair of bullet holes in her chest. "What the fuck," he asked her, "happened back there?"

The dead woman stared at him for a moment, then staggered into the side of a pickup truck.

For a moment he considered looking back at the Mount. There were almost ten thousand exes within a block of the Big Wall. He could sense them in a basic way, like someone knowing they were wearing shorts or going commando without checking. He just knew where they were, all through the city. It wouldn't take much effort to reach over and see through their eyes.

Whatever attacked him had taken his exes away, though. One moment they'd been there, the next minute a bunch of them were gone. He could still see them, but it was like part of him had gone numb, like a cripple looking at legs that weren't part of him anymore. They'd become something else.

And "something else" had kicked the shit out of him.

When the first one jumped on him he thought it was the Dragon's new trick. Somebody with telepathic-ness or whatever you called moving stuff with your mind. But none of the Dragon's people were that savage. Even when Stealth fought, she was intense, but never sadistic.

It was fast and brutal and ruthless, like wrestling with a hungry pit bull. A smart, hungry pit bull crossed with a piranha. He'd thrown more exes at it and it had fought back with more of its own.

Legion didn't have a real body anymore. He hadn't had one for a year and a half now. It had freaked him out at first. He even came close to crying once. Real men still cried now and then. Not often, but it happened.

But then he realized he'd become something bigger than just Rodney Cesares or Peasy. He'd become untouchable. Yeah, he didn't have a body anymore. He had millions of bodies, every one of them tireless and numb to pain.

Numb until today, anyway. Whatever was using the other exes had hurt him. A lot. He'd felt every body get slashed and torn apart. And for a few moments it had held him there, like holding a geek's forehead and watching them swing useless punches. He hadn't been able to shift away.

He hadn't been able to do anything.

Legion kicked one of the purple shopping carts and it rolled a few feet across the parking lot. He stalked over, slammed his foot into it again, and watched it bang into the side of a Lexus. Another kick raised a few wisps of dust and chipped some paint off the car.

He was pretty sure the thing at the Mount would've killed him. He didn't know how, but he felt it in his gut. If he'd stayed there it would've torn him apart. Somehow.

The thing that'd saved him in the end was the other exes were changing too fast. They didn't have time to do much damage. They got tall and sprouted fangs and claws, like were-wolves or something—enough to fuck up a regular person, easy. And then they'd pop open like hot dogs in a microwave and fall apart. There'd been a break and he'd thrown himself away, like diving off a bridge. He didn't care where he ended up, as long as he wasn't there.

It was kind of familiar, what the other exes had been turning into, but he couldn't put his finger on it. Maybe something from back during his months in the Army when they were pumping him and a bunch of other grunts full of drugs to make them bigger and stronger. There'd been a bunch of weird stuff going on then.

Legion picked up the shopping cart. The dead Samoan had slablike muscles that still had plenty of strength in them. He got the cart over his head, roared, and slammed it down on the windshield of the Lexus. The glass spiderwebbed from side to side. He picked the cart back up and slammed it down again.

The windshield collapsed in across the dashboard and driver's seat. He tried to drag it out, but one of the wheels had hooked on the steering wheel.

He growled and drove his fist through the driver's-side window. Then he brought both fists down on the roof and dented it in. He kicked the door and slammed punches into the hood and yanked at the cart until he'd deformed the steering wheel and knocked the last few bits of glass from the windshield frame.

Truth be told, he was bored as shit most of the time. Even with the extra effort it took, big projects like looting the National Guard armory or gathering up all the armor and guns and ammo in the city didn't take long when you had a hundred thousand bodies doing it. At least once a week he fucked up a car, just for the hell of it. Sometimes a house or an apartment building. He'd trashed half the food court over in the Glendale Galleria during one angry weekend.

After a couple of minutes of violence he calmed down and looked at the car. He'd messed it up pretty good. The roof was beat down, and the hood was pretty messed up. He'd smashed all the windows, one of the headlights, and most of the instruments on the dashboard.

The Samoan's hands were ruined, too. The fingers were broken and the flesh had ripped away from the knuckles. The foot he'd kicked the door with was pretty messed up. He focused on a skeletal little girl across the parking lot and shifted into her. He watched the Samoan stagger on its bad foot for a few steps before it fell over. The dead thing flailed on the pavement for a minute or so before it rolled over and crawled off.

Legion let his view flow out again for a moment, drifting through the Samoan's head for a few seconds, and then focused himself inside an older man in the middle of Colorado Boulevard. It was a big guy with a beard and loose skin. Legion liked being big. It reminded everyone he was strong.

Little soul.

He spun around and staggered. He'd picked an old guy with a bad knee. Maybe a whole bad leg, and being dead hadn't helped it any. He forced the body up straight.

Nobody behind him. He thought he'd heard a voice, a buzz in the air like glow-boy from the Mount. He had a lot on his mind, though. He'd already written off what had happened earlier and was ready to start planning his next assault.

How interesting you are, little soul.

This time Legion reached out to look through a dozen sets of eyes. He saw himself in the old man, and a heavyset woman with a missing hand, and a teenage boy, and a slim woman whose face and hair had been burned off at some point.

There was no one around who wasn't him. He stayed in all the bodies and marched across the street. He looked in cars and behind bus stops and in the small patio of a Starbucks.

He wasn't sure if he'd heard the voice or just imagined it. It sounded damned close, though. And warm. Not warm in a good way, but warm like sick with the shakes.

Little Rodney Cesares. Son of Juan and Gabrielle. Once so great in body, now a living soul with no flesh around it. How fascinating.

"Okay," called Legion. He found two exes up on the roof of a thrift store and one trapped on a balcony with a high railing. He looked down on the street through their eyes. "That you, Zap-man? Where you at, *hijo de puta*?"

Nothing. He couldn't see anyone anywhere. He reached out and guided a few more exes down to the intersection. Thirty different views, but nothing.

"You think you can hide from me?" The dead took in a breath and shouted in the street, "I'M LEGION! I'M EVERY-WHERE!"

The words echoed on the street for a moment. Then silence settled down across the street and coated everything. The air grew still.

Do you take the name of Legion in vain, little soul?

He poured himself back into the old man with the bad knee and grinned. "I am Legion, bitch," he growled at the air. "I'm death incarnate. I'm the guy who killed the world."

He had the unmistakable sense of someone standing right behind him. Behind all of him. Every ex within his reach felt a warm prickling on their backs and shoulders, a faint pull on the eyes. All his bodies looked around and saw nothing, but the feeling remained.

You insult the great name of my sibling with your ignorance and arrogance. Perhaps a lesson in humility is in order. If nothing else, it should relieve my boredom while I await my new vessel.

Legion rolled his fingers up into tight fists. All of the walking dead within three blocks copied him, guided by his anger. "Oh, yeah?" he spat. "Fucking coward. Come out here and give it your best shot."

And a few moments later, every ex in Los Angeles County screamed at once.

Twenty-Two

NOW

"MA'AM," SAID FREEDOM, "sir, with all due respect, this is your fault."

It made Stealth pause. St. George had said it was possible to catch her off guard, but this was the first time Freedom had ever seen it happen. He wondered how often anyone dared interrupt the woman.

He was in Stealth's meeting room with the other heroes. It was a rare thing for Freedom to be invited to these morning meetings. He understood they were informal, though, and the other heroes had known one another for years.

The cloaked woman stood on the other side of the conference table and stared at him. He'd learned to sense her stares, even through the blank balaclava she always wore.

St. George stood next to her, leaning against the edge of the table. He'd looked preoccupied for the whole meeting so far.

Barry was in his wheelchair off to the side. He was also much more subdued than normal. If fact, Freedom was pretty sure the man hadn't spoken yet.

Danielle sat next to the wheelchair. He'd come to learn what a rare thing it was for her not to be wearing the Cerberus armor if she had a choice. Even now, with Lieutenant Gibbs and the boy, Cesar, able to operate the battlesuit, it was still her wearing it more than half the time. He'd known a few tank officers who were the same way—not comfortable unless they were surrounded by steel.

The arrangement of the room also didn't slip by the captain. He'd been on this side of similar tables three times before. Two of them were for official inquiries into the deaths of soldiers under his command. The other was when he was brought into Project Krypton and had the full scale of the project revealed to him.

He still wasn't sure which type this meeting was. All four of the heroes looked uncomfortable. It could be going either way.

"Please," said Stealth. Her voice was ice. "Continue."

"I've been here for eight months now, ma'am, and this is the first I've ever heard of a high-security prisoner in the Mount. One being held a hundred yards from my own quarters."

"Are you claiming you have never heard of the Cellar?"

"Of course I've heard of it, ma'am," he said. "Everyone in the city has. And everyone has a different idea what it is. I've been told it's a quarantine area, storage for ex-humans, and where we keep monsters." He gestured at St. George. "One very excited little boy told me it's where you hide the magic lantern that gives you your powers, and you have to go down there to recharge."

Barry looked up at his friend. "You've had a magic lantern all this time and you didn't tell me?"

St. George smirked. So did Danielle. It didn't break the mood, but it cracked it enough for everyone to breathe.

Freedom plowed ahead. "Who is the prisoner? Why did you have him locked up? And where did he get all these primitive weapons from? Is it some . . . ritualistic thing?"

"Man, that'd be nice," Barry said. "So much simpler."

"Speaking of ritual," said Danielle, "wasn't Max supposed to be here for all of this?"

Without turning Stealth pointed over her shoulder at one of the numerous video screens in the room. The high angle showed Max in another meeting room somewhere. He was scratching notes and symbols on a huge whiteboard. His brow furrowed at the board as he went back and erased a pair of lines. "He has been notified twice," said Stealth. "It was a courtesy. We do not require his presence."

"Still working on his demon-banishment thing?" asked Barry.

"So he claims. Legion's scream seems to have worried him." Stealth tossed something onto the marble tabletop. It made a hollow sound as it bounced over to Freedom. "This is the weapon the prisoner attacked you with?"

He picked it up. "It looks like it, ma'am. I couldn't be certain. I only saw it for a moment."

It was a thick piece of pale hardwood. It had been scraped down to something that was almost a blade. He recognized the scratches down the length from crude weapons in Iraq. Someone had dragged the spike across rough stone or concrete to shape it.

Then he registered the thick knob under the handle.

"This is a bone," he said.

"Yeah," said St. George.

"Someone slipped your prisoner a leg of lamb when you weren't looking?"

"It is a human tibia," said Stealth. "To be precise, it is the prisoner's left tibia."

Barry tipped his head back and rubbed his temples.

Freedom set the bone down. "I'm pretty sure the prisoner had both of his legs."

St. George nodded. "Yeah, he did."

Freedom frowned and nodded at the table. "And the whip?" It had been coiled and stuffed into a large evidence bag. He wondered how Stealth had actual evidence bags when his people were using Ziplocs.

"Identifying exact muscle tissues is more difficult without certain tests," she said. "However, judging from the density and length of the sinews, I feel confident saying it is comprised of nine sartorius muscles. There are also eleven molars worked into the braid, to increase either traction or damage. Possibly both."

Danielle shuddered and looked away from the table.

Freedom pondered this for a moment. "So there are multiple victims," he said. "He killed other people before he got out and we missed it somehow."

St. George shook his head. "No," he said. "They're all his. The prisoner's." He tapped his fingers on the tabletop for a moment. "Looking at these and some of the evidence we found in the Cellar, we're pretty sure he was tearing out his own bones and muscles to make weapons and tools."

Freedom blinked. He opened his mouth to respond, then shut it again. After another few moments he spat the words out. "And you never noticed this how, sir?"

"We never noticed," said Stealth, "because he would grow new ones."

The huge captain dwelled on her words for a moment. "Before the fall," he said, "there was a hero with healing powers. The one named Regenerator."

"Also sometimes called the Immortal," said Stealth. "His real name is Joshua Garcetti."

"He was attacked and bitten in a field hospital, wasn't he?" Freedom glanced at St. George. "I thought he died near the end."

"Not exactly," muttered Danielle.

"Josh survived the bite," said St. George, "but it canceled out his powers. He was just a normal guy with a messed-up hand where the infection had gotten trapped."

Freedom recalled the prisoner's withered hand. "So he was in the Cellar? Why?"

St. George drummed his knuckles on the table. Danielle shifted in her chair. Even Barry squirmed a bit. Stealth stared at the huge captain.

"What did he do?" asked Freedom.

"You have to understand," said St. George, "Josh had gone insane. Seriously, honestly insane. He managed to hide it from us for a year while we were establishing the Mount. None of us knew."

"Knew what, sir?"

"Sixteen months ago," said Stealth, "we discovered Regenerator's affliction was an elaborate somatoform disorder, one where his abilities allowed his guilt to physically manifest as an injury."

"Guilt?"

Danielle reached up to wrap her hand over her mouth. She turned to study one of Stealth's video screens.

St. George looked at Stealth. "What you are about to hear, Captain," she said, "is known only by the four of us and now yourself. It does not leave this room under any circumstances. Ever."

They told him everything.

* * *

St. George had seen Captain Freedom mad before. Back at Krypton, when the officer had been brainwashed into thinking Stealth had killed his commander, he'd been furious. The icy calm that settled over the giant officer now, though, was even more disturbing.

"He did all of this," Freedom said. "Your partner is the source of the ex-virus."

"He is not our partner," said Stealth.

"I never even met the guy until we set up the Mount," said Danielle.

"This man is responsible for everything," hissed the captain. "For the deaths of millions of people."

"Billions," said Stealth. "By the last known population numbers and projected estimates, five-point-four-two billion people died in 2009 as a direct result of the ex-virus."

"My men died!" shouted Freedom. "That man caused the death of dozens of soldiers under my command. You knew this and you said nothing to me about it."

"Lots of people died, Captain," said St. George. A cloud of smoke rolled from his mouth as he said it. "Everybody here lost friends and family and loved ones. You think we haven't all thought about going down there and chopping him up until he stops healing?"

"And why hasn't anyone?"

"Because we're the good guys," St. George told him. "We remind everyone that sometimes you've got to do the right thing even when the wrong thing would be a lot easier and make you a lot happier. We're the ones setting an example so all of this doesn't turn into a *Road Warrior* movie. That's our duty. And yours."

It was enough. The huge officer calmed himself.

"He was being punished," said the hero. "We told everyone he went insane and killed himself. He was always so depressed about his wife, no one questioned it. He'd spent the last year and a half in a twelve-foot-square cell. He hadn't seen daylight that whole time. I was the only person he ever got to talk to. We even stopped feeding him once we realized he doesn't need to eat. Once there's some real stability here, we were going to turn him over to the people for a trial."

"As someone who understands morale issues," said Stealth, "I am certain you also understand the need to keep all these facts secret until then."

Freedom's jaw shifted. "Unfortunately, ma'am, I do."

"As such," she said, "our primary concern is not justice but containment. Which means recapturing him must be our highest priority."

"Problem," said Danielle. She tapped a finger on the map. "We can't go after him without crossing Max's magic symbols."

"If they are real," Stealth said.

"That thing outside looked pretty real," said Barry. "With

all the teeth and the fire and the twisting body parts. It was like a John Carpenter movie come to life."

"It exists," said Stealth, "but that does not mean it is a demon. Or that it is being held back by magical symbols." She gestured at the maps. "The exes will follow Regenerator as long as he remains within their range of sight or hearing. If St. George or Zzzap reaches sufficient altitude, they may be able to see a pattern of movement, much like a tide or current. This will give us a general sense of his current location."

"I've got a question for the floor," said Barry. "Is this really a bad thing?"

Stealth turned to him. "I beg your pardon?"

"Okay, so Josh got out. And he got out of the Mount. Out of our whole complex of New Los Angeles or whatever we're going to call it." He shrugged in his wheelchair. "So now it's him alone against Cairax McBitey and, what, five million exes here in Los Angeles. Six hundred million or something in North America. Not to sound harsh but . . . well, it sounds like the problem's dealt with."

"Or is it?" Danielle pulled her arms tight. "Can they actually kill him?"

"Forgive me for saying so," said Freedom, "but from what you've told me, can *anything* kill him?"

There was a quiet pause.

"To the best of my knowledge," said Stealth, "he has never been decapitated."

"Oh, come on," said St. George. "Are we going to hunt him down and chop his head off?"

She bowed her head inside her hood. "I was merely offering a possible scenario where his powers would not allow him to regenerate."

There was a brief lull, and then someone cleared their throat.

Max sat in a chair at the far end of the meeting table. His suit was navy blue with a paisley tie of red and silver. St. George realized he could barely see Jarvis in Max's face anymore. There was a little something around the eyes, a bit in the cheeks, but for the most part the salt-and-pepper man had vanished.

Another person consumed by the dead.

"Sorry I'm late," Max said. "I was up all night working out a couple ideas before I lost them. With Cairax being so determined and aggressive I figured I needed to put some serious thought into banishing him." He swung his feet up onto the table.

Freedom glanced at the door. "How did you . . . ?"

Max twiddled his fingers in the air and smiled.

"He is wearing rubber-soled shoes," said Stealth, "and the doors have pneumatic hinges."

"Do you have no sense of wonder in your soul?" Max shook his head. "Good news is, I've got it figured out. I'll need four days of prep and I can get rid of Cairax for good."

"Really?" said Barry.

"Yep. So, what did I miss here? Anything that's still relevant?"

"Josh's escape," said St. George, "and if we can go after him or not."

"Anyone crossing the wards before I banish Cairax would be bad," said Max. "Refresh my memory—who's Josh?"

Danielle sighed. Stealth stiffened and crossed her arms. "Joshua Garcetti," she said, "better known as Regenerator."

"Wait," said Max, sitting up. "Regenerator's still alive?"

"Yeah," said Barry. "You missed the big catch-up."

"No way? It's like we're getting the band back together again. Where's he been?"

"He was our prisoner," said Stealth, "until he escaped two and a half hours ago. He is somewhere in Los Angeles beyond the Big Wall."

"WHAT?"

Max leaped out of his chair so hard it skittered across the floor and hit the far wall. He looked at each of them in turn. His eyes were wide and his chest heaved. He pressed his hands against the tabletop. "Regenerator is out in the city? He's past the wards?"

St. George nodded and shrugged. "Yeah."

"Does he still have his powers? Just before everything collapsed I heard he'd lost his powers."

"Still got 'em," said Danielle.

"He took over a dozen twelve-gauge slugs during his escape," said Freedom. "They barely slowed him."

"Oh, Jesus," muttered Max. He reached back and grabbed the back of his head. "Oh, fuck, fuck, fuck."

Stealth crossed her arms. "Is there a problem?"

Max's eyes were still huge. "Problem?" he echoed. "Well, everyone in Los Angeles has maybe nine or ten hours left to live. But other than that, yeah, things are just fantastic."

Twenty-Three
NOW

"EXPLAIN," SAID STEALTH.

Max shook his head. "Okay, look, the whole reason Cairax Murrain can't manifest is because any host needs to meet two major conditions. They have to be alive and they need to be durable enough to survive the process of possession. That's why it was so important that George didn't go past the barriers. It could kill anyone, but it could actually possess him."

"Okay," said St. George with a nod.

"Well, now there's a body out there that won't die. Regenerator can take all that damage and keep going. He's viable. So the instant he says yes, Cairax is going to start moving in, just like I did. And once he's got flesh he's going to march in here and kill every single man, woman, child, and fluffy kitten in the Mount."

"But we're safe inside, right?" Barry waved his arm at the window. "That's the point of the symbols."

Max shook his head. "We're not safe. This isn't remotely safe anymore. This is like being out in the middle of the ocean, a thousand miles from anything, on a six-dollar pool raft with a great white shark circling you. Except the raft has a hole in it and the shark's armor-plated, on meth, and has a laser cannon mounted on its skull. That's about how 'safe' we are." He started to pace. "The wards only block his essence. They meant he couldn't make someone pop inside the Mount. Once he's got a body he can walk over those hexagrams just like you or me. And then everyone in here dies."

Danielle played with the edge of the map on the table. "You sure do talk a lot about how awful this thing is."

"Because I know you're not getting it," snapped Max. His pacing carried him from one side of the room to the other. "You all keep thinking back to George beating up a zombie, half-breed version of Cairax and telling yourself it's no big deal."

"And this is worse?" asked St. George.

"It's the worst thing ever. Period. Every book you've read, every movie you've seen, this is a thousand times worse. This is one of the things every single villain you've ever heard of is based off because he's *so* evil, knowledge of his existence leaks between dimensions. He's so terrifying that when a bunch of idiot Satanists set him loose in the fourteenth century his name entered the language and became the word for plague."

Freedom crossed his arms. On opposite sides of the room, it made him and Stealth look like a set of mismatched bookends.

"Remember when he bit you?" Max asked St. George. "Yeah, you do, don't you? First time anything had hurt the Mighty Dragon in, what, two years at that point?"

The hero reached down and rubbed his arm.

Max nodded. "You want to know what you tasted like, George? You tasted scared. Fucking terrified. I was dead and in a possessed body and I could taste your fear on my tongue. That's how strong it was."

He stopped pacing and pointed at the window. "That thing out there, his whole existence boils down to two things. Fear and death. Someone being scared of dying is like sex for him if sex gave you a full stomach and did your laundry. Someone dying is him getting that rush on New Year's Eve at midnight. And once he's got a host, believe me, it's going to be midnight here in the Mount for a very, very long time."

The room got quiet. They all stared at the window. Max put his hands on the table and let his head hang.

"Okay," said St. George. "What do we have to do?"

The sorcerer shook his head. "I'm not sure," he said. "This is way bigger than anything I ever planned on. I mean, even in my worst-case scenarios I never figured he'd get a usable host. Once he's flesh . . ." Max shrugged.

"You claim the demon was once set loose during the Middle Ages," said Stealth. "How was it defeated then?"

"I don't know," said Max. "The details are fuzzy. The popular theory is Pope Clement the Sixth tricked him into touching the fisherman's ring. Instant discorporation, but it killed Clement, too."

"So we need to find the ring," said Barry. "Okay."

"It is reasonable to assume the ring is on the far side of the planet," said Stealth. "At last report, Pope Benedict was sequestered in the Vatican during the outbreaks. It is likely the ring is still in that region."

"Knowing where it is doesn't help us if we can't get there," said Freedom. He looked at Stealth. "Unless there's more you've been holding out on me, I don't think we have a transcontinental jet anywhere in the Mount."

"I could fly it," said St. George.

"No offense, sir, but flying four hundred miles out to Krypton was tiring for you. We're talking more than twenty times that, half of which is over open ocean."

"Bigger issue," added Danielle. "It all involves going outside and crossing those spell-circles."

"The ring's a nonissue," said Max. He waved a hand at Barry. "The only one who could get there, find the ring, and get back in time would be Zzzap, and he wouldn't be able to pick it up."

"Why are you certain of this timeline?" asked Stealth.

"I told you, there's a bunch of rules to this. For any sort of conscious possession to work, astral cords have to be intertwined, souls married, contracts have to be agreed on, all sorts of stuff. It takes time."

"Contracts?" asked Freedom.

"Yeah, contracts. Agreements. A demon can't just jump into your body like it's a car with the engine running. You have to agree to it. It can lie and cheat and bend words, but there needs to be an agreement. A contract." He shook his head. "I think our best bet is going to be killing him."

"Killing him?" Freedom echoed. "Can we do that?"

"I didn't say it was a good bet. I just said it was our best." He pressed his fingers against his temples for a moment. "We're trying to kill a concept, an idea made flesh. So we have to fight it with an idea that's just as powerful. We'll need a sword."

"A sword?" repeated Freedom.

"Is there an echo in here?" Max furrowed his brow at the oversized captain. "Yes, a sword. A long piece of metal with a handle and a pointy end, symbolic since the Garden of Eden."

"Does it have to be a certain type of sword," asked Barry, "like a broadsword or a claymore, or would anything do?"

"We're not going to beat it with a collectible lightsaber, if that's what you're asking," Max said. "It needs to be a real weapon, not a display replica or something. Preferably silver or silver-plated. Even just silver inlays on the blade would be great. If it's spilled some blood, too, great. Past that, anything goes."

"There are three museums with historical edged weapons within a mile of the Big Wall," said Stealth, "and very likely several dozen personal collections with functional swords. However, all of them are beyond your wards."

"You said I was strong enough for the possession," said St. George. "Does that mean I could make it out to find a sword?"

Max shook his head. "Strong enough to survive it. It'd still feel like getting kicked repeatedly in the balls by a horse, even to you. Plus he's got a few million exes out there. Each body gives him a couple seconds to beat the crap out of you."

"I could take it."

"Be realistic, George. You know how hard he can hit."

"I could fly—"

"Even if you flew out of here, he could go for the possession and then beat you unconscious when you fell out of the sky."

"If we cannot go beyond the seals," said Stealth, "how do you expect to fight Cairax?"

Max shrugged and stared at the table for a moment. "We wait for him to come here."

"Whoa." Barry raised his hand. "Weren't you just saying him getting in here was extremely bad? Like crossing-the-streams, end-of-life-as-we-know-it bad?"

"We don't have a lot of options," said Max. "First things first. We need a sword."

"The scavengers," said Freedom.

"What about them?" asked Danielle.

"They carry a lot of nonstandardized weaponry," he said. "Lady Bee tells me some of them use knives, machetes, other things they find out on runs. Maybe someone's found a sword and brought it back here."

"Only one of the scavengers carries a sword," said Stealth. "Daniel Foe wears a replica katana in a back sheath. He wears it as an attempt to look imposing, hoping to impress Lynne Vines. He has never drawn it."

"There could be others, though," said St. George. "Maybe they don't use it, but somebody may have found one and just kept it as a trophy or something. We should ask all the scavengers and guards."

Freedom nodded in agreement.

"What about making one?" asked Danielle. "Maybe we could silver-plate a machete or something."

Max shook his head. "It's got to fit the symbolism, remember? The less we think of it as a sword, the less the chances it will work."

"There are also the studio prop houses," said Stealth. "It is possible there is a real weapon mixed in with the various fantasy and historical movie props."

"Good call," said St. George. "I'll put Ilya and Dave on it."

Stealth turned her attention back to Max. "What else would we require?"

"I'll need to prepare a few spells and protections," he said. "That should take a couple of hours. If any of you have a hotline to God, we could use an archangel to wield the sword for us."

"An archangel?" asked Stealth.

Max looked at her. "You know, a creature born from the radiance and divine will of God and shaped in his image. Think of all the stuff you think of when someone says 'holy,' and an archangel is ten times purer than that. I thought you were the smart one?"

Stealth crossed her arms.

"Sorry," he said. "A bit tense. Barring an archangel, we need the holiest, purest person we can find."

The heroes glanced at each other, then all turned to St. George. "I don't think any of us are that holy or pure," he said. "Especially after the past few years."

"I'm not," said Danielle. "You're the one named after a saint."

"Not by choice," he said. "I just kind of fell into it."

Barry shrugged. "I guess I'm an okay guy, but unless I'm going to fight the monster in my wheelchair I couldn't hold a sword anyway."

"I would be unfit," said Stealth after a moment. "I have been an atheist for thirty years."

They looked at Freedom. He shook his head. "I'm only human."

Danielle looked at Max. "What about you?"

He snorted back a laugh. "With all the magic I've done? I

may not count as evil but I'm a long way from pure. It's the nature of the beast. No pun intended."

"Father Andy?" suggested Barry.

Max shook his head. "Nothing against the good father, but he's not the warrior priest we need, know what I mean?"

"Okay," said St. George. "We'll work on that one. Let's start with the sword and go from there."

＊ ＊ ＊

"So," St. George told them, "that's where we are. We need a sword and we need it quick."

The scavengers and every free Wall guard were gathered at the Melrose Gate of the Mount, across from Gorgon's cross. Freedom and First Sergeant Kennedy stood nearby. She still dressed in her full uniform with her hair pulled back tight under her headgear. The surviving soldiers of the Alpha 815th Unbreakables stood behind her in tight formation, even if a few of them were missing one or two elements from their ACUs.

Danny reached up and tapped the hilt stretched over his shoulder. "You can have mine," he said.

"No offense, sir," said Freedom, "but this needs to be a real weapon."

"It's real."

"Real in the sense of actually made to fight with," said St. George. "Something that's not going to break apart on the second or third swing. I've got Ilya and Dave going through the prop house right now. Does anyone else have anything?"

"What about a Marine officer's sword?" asked Billie.

St. George shook his head. "Same thing, I think. It can't be ceremonial, it needs to be something that's made to fight with."

"They're made to fight with," she said.

He gestured at the folding table they'd set up in the street. "If you've got one we'll give it a try."

Al held up his square-topped machete. "I've got this." A man across from him held up a similar blade.

"Same thing. I don't think it'll work, but we'll try it."

Hector de la Vega cleared his throat as the crowd began to rustle with unsheathed steel. "I know where there's a sword. Just what you need."

St. George looked at him. "What?"

The tattooed man shrugged. "My grandpapa, he showed it to me a couple times. It was some old family thing. An heirloom or something."

Paul gave him a nudge. "Is it some Mexican army thing you brought up here?"

"Fuck you, *babosa*," he said. "My family had a ranch here before California was even a state." He turned his attention back to St. George. "It's an old saber from the eighteen hundreds or something. He told me once it killed over a dozen men."

"That sounds perfect," St. George said. "Is it here?"

Hector shook his head. "Never trusted my dad or me with it." He smirked and shrugged again. "Mostly me. Think he was worried I'd hock it or something. Kept it all locked up in his house."

"Which is where?"

"North Hollywood. Little place just past Universal City."

"Might as well be on the Moon," muttered Kennedy.

"We could put a small team together," said Billie. "Go in fast with a truck or maybe even some motorcycles."

"We could set up a distraction at one of the other gates," said another one of the scavengers, Keri, with a nod. "Get the thing over there so they can slip out."

St. George shook his head. "From what Max has said, it's not possible to get past this thing. It's got us surrounded, just the same way Legion does. We can't go out past the wards."

"I could get it," said someone in the back.

The crowd shifted and parted. A few of them jumped away

when they saw the speaker. Most of the guards and scavengers stepped back from her, and a murmur danced through the crowd.

Madelyn walked forward. She was wearing a black shirt that made her skin look pure white. Her sunglasses were pushed up on her brow, holding her hair back and showing off her dead eyes. "I could get it," she repeated.

"You're not supposed to be outside the hospital," said St. George.

"She's not supposed to be inside the walls," said someone else.

The hero glanced at the crowd. "What was that?"

Makana shrugged. It made his dreadlocks kink and shift. "I thought that was one of the basic rules," he said. "We don't let her kind inside the walls, no matter what."

"My kind?" said Madelyn. She gave the black man a look of disbelief that was clear even with her pale eyes.

"Look, corpse girl," he said, "nothing personal, but you're one of them."

"She's not one of them," countered Keri. "She's still got her soul."

"Don't use that soul crap as an excuse," said Lady Bee.

"Let's just toss her back outside," said Al. "She'll be fine and she doesn't need to be in here scaring people and eating up resources."

"Hey," snapped St. George. A burst of dark smoke rolled from his mouth. "Let's cut all this talk right now."

The murmur continued for a few more seconds before falling. The dead girl's mouth twitched into a faint smile aimed at St. George.

"Madelyn's not an ex," said St. George. "She belongs inside. She's one of us."

"One of you, maybe," muttered Al. Billie gave him a light smack on the back of the head and he batted her arm away. The murmur returned and swelled into rumbling.

"I can get the sword," Madelyn insisted, raising her voice over the noise. "Max said the demon's after living things. And Legion can't see me through the exes, so maybe this other thing can't, either. I'm the only person who can do it."

The phrase "not a person" flitted from a few places in the crowd. St. George ignored it. Freedom gave the crowd his well-practiced glare and the rumbling died down again.

"You can't go out there," St. George said. "We can't risk anyone going past the wards."

"But if it can't see me—"

"No one goes out," he repeated. He turned his gaze back to the guards and scavengers. "We'll take every blade we've got. Machetes, bowies, ninja swords, whatever. Start gathering stuff. Maybe between our stuff and whatever Dave and Ilya find, Max can find something usable." He patted the folding table and pointed across the crowd. "You too, Danny. We need everything."

"You heard the man, people," bellowed Kennedy. She clapped her hands together twice. "Let's get moving."

The scavengers and guards scattered. Some of them emptied sheaths right there. A dozen knives and daggers appeared on the table with Al's square-bladed machete.

Madelyn walked the rest of the way to St. George. "Let me do it," she said.

Freedom shook his head. "Absolutely not."

"I can do this. I want to do it."

"We are not sending a seventeen-year-old girl alone into hostile territory."

She glared at him. "Hello? In case you forgot, I spent the past three years in hostile territory."

"And you don't remember most of it," said St. George. "We let you out there, it could be weeks before we see you again. Maybe years."

"I'll be careful. It won't happen."

He shook his head.

She crossed her arms. "You have to let me try. I mean, it's like my duty and stuff, right?"

Freedom's brows went up. "I'm sorry?"

"I mean, I've got responsibilities, even to some of those jerks. I'm like you guys, right?"

"How do you figure?" asked St. George.

"I've got superpowers," she said, waving a hand at herself. "The exes can't see me or hear me. They don't sense me at all."

Kennedy snorted. "I don't think being dead counts as a superpower, ma'am."

"It does for me," Madelyn said. "Come on, it'll be easy for me. I can just bike over there, grab it, and be back here in a couple hours. It's . . . it's dead simple."

Freedom rolled his eyes.

"Dead clever?"

"Just stop," Kennedy said.

"I'm also dead sexy," she added, batting her eyelids at St. George.

"Okay," St. George said. "Look at it this way. Suppose I let you go, you get out there, and it turns out the demon *can* see you. Then what?"

"I . . . I'd just keep away from it. I'd run."

He shook his head. "What if it turns out it can jump into you the same way it jumps into the exes? What if you take two steps past the ward and you just explode like they've been doing?"

"I'm not like them," she snapped. "I'm like them but different. I'm . . ." She lifted her arms and crossed her wrists over her heart. "I'm the Corpse Girl," she said with a tight smile.

"You're a seventeen-year-old we're responsible for," said St. George. "I appreciate that you want to help. I really do. But I think right now it'd be better for everyone and a lot less distracting if you went back to the hospital."

Twenty-Four

NOW

"FATHER ANDY?"

He looked down the aisle to the huge shadow blocking the church door. "Hello, Captain," he said. "I thought you'd be out on the walls."

Freedom walked down to meet the priest. He held his cap in his hands, and his boots thudded on the carpeted aisle. "Soon enough," he said. "I apologize if you were finishing up for lunch, sir, but I have a request and I'm afraid it's urgent."

Andy met him near the midpoint of the aisle, brow furrowed. "Something from me?" He glanced around the church. "I don't have much, but if it helps it's yours."

Captain Freedom stood at ease and explained what he needed.

Father Andy listened without a word. His jaw shifted when the captain finished. "I see."

"Is there a problem, sir?"

"Possibly."

"In Iraq and Afghanistan, the chaplains assigned to us would do similar things for some of the men."

"Some of the men," the priest said, "but not you?"

"Hopefully you'll forgive me, father," said Freedom, "but I'm actually a diehard Baptist. In this case, though, I'm hedging my bets."

Andy reached up to run a finger along his collar, giving it a slight tug. "I'm not actually a priest, you know," he told the captain. "I was never ordained by anyone. The responsibility was thrust upon me."

"You wouldn't be the first to say such things," the huge officer said with a solemn nod.

"What I've been preaching isn't really Catholicism. It's more of a general Christian mishmash to give solace to as many people as possible."

"I understand," said Freedom. "We've all been a bit loose with our denominations over the past few years."

"It's just that what you're asking for is . . . well, it's pretty hard-core Catholic. I've never done it before. Never even seen it done, so I'll be winging it. And this needs a lot of weight behind it, especially considering the circumstances." Andy's hand dropped away from his collar. "I just want you to be clear there's a good chance this won't work. Not the way you want it to, anyway."

"All the same, sir," said the captain, "I'd feel much better if you could."

Father Andy turned back to the altar. "We've got plenty of candles. I just filled the aspersorium this morning. Let me go get my vestments." He looked over his shoulder. "If you want it done right—at least, what I think is right—it's probably going to take forty minutes or so."

Freedom followed him to the altar.

* * *

Max ran his fingers along the futuristic katana's blade. The engraving looked like printed circuits. He tossed it back on the table. "It's crap," he said. "The tang's not much more than a steel bolt and it's just riveted onto the blade."

"What does that mean?" asked Billie. She'd supervised the pile of weapons being brought in from guards and scavengers.

A few civilians had heard about the search and donated fencing sabers and ceremonial weapons.

"It means it's crap," said Max. "You could wreck this thing by twisting the pommel two or three more times. Hitting something with it will just make the blade snap off in your face." The sorcerer waved his hand at the table of weapons. "Most of this stuff is crap. The only blades that are any good are ones that wouldn't work for this." He reached up and grabbed the back of his head and took a few slow, deep breaths.

"So," said Stealth from the gates, "we have nothing."

Max let go of his head. "Yeah."

"There's got to be something we can do," said St. George. "You trapped this thing once before, can't you do it again?"

"It took three years of preparation and an eclipse," said Max. "If you can scrounge up an eclipse in the next seven hours, I'll see what I can do about the rest."

"Can't you just make a stronger barrier?" Billie asked.

Max reached up to loosen his tie. "With the right materials and a few months of research, sure. This just isn't something I ever planned on, facing off with a physically manifested demon."

St. George drummed his fingers on the table. "Can it be hurt?"

The sorcerer raised an eyebrow. "Without the sword, you mean?"

"Yeah. Once it's physical, can we hurt it?"

"Technically, yeah," said Max with a shrug. "You've got to understand, everything we've got in the Mount—even some of the big stuff you brought back from Krypton—it's going to be like hunting dinosaurs with slingshots. And if it's possessing Regenerator, it's going to have his powers, too. We'll have a minute, tops, before it heals from whatever we do to it."

Stealth looked at the table of blades. "Including wounds from the sword?"

"No. Well, it's hard to explain."

"Please attempt to."

"You don't even have the right knowledge for a frame of reference. It's like trying to explain quantum physics to one of those isolated tribes in the rain forest. I can give you some neat analogies, but that's about it."

"Then, again, please do so."

Max sighed. "Okay, in simple terms, if the demon believes it can be hurt, and we believe we can hurt it, it'll be hurt. It's like Jung on steroids. That's why all the big symbols are so important. It's the same reason silver bullets have been able to kill werewolves ever since Siodmak wrote the *Wolf Man* screenplay."

Billie's brow furrowed. "What?"

"Never mind, bad example," he said, shaking his head. "Okay, you know how you can be in the Matrix and even though you know it's all just in your mind—"

"You're using *The Matrix* again?" asked St. George.

"You don't like it, get Barry some new DVDs," snapped Max. "Even though you know it's all just in your mind, the injuries will still translate through to the real world because the illusion is so perfect. The sights, the sounds, the feelings—no matter what you know, your mind can't deny all the information coming in. Belief trumps knowledge, like a psychosomatic injury."

"I do not accept that," said Stealth.

"Look, just trust me, okay?"

"Okay, then," said St. George. He picked up one of the swords from the table. "So what's our best choice here?"

Max shook his head. "We don't have a best choice here. If this is it, our best choice is getting some pointed sticks and painting them silver."

Billie stepped forward. "I'll make sure they all get back to their owners," she said.

"Don't bother," said the sorcerer. "They'll all be dead by tomorrow anyway."

"We have to do something, Max," snapped St. George. Fire

flashed in his mouth. "Anyone can sit around and bitch about how bad things are. We're the ones who are supposed to fix it."

"We can't fix this," said the sorcerer.

"Well, that's the difference between you and me, then," said St. George. "I'm going to try."

"Meaning what?"

"We can't just wait for it to get in here," said the hero. "Ilya and Dave should be done with their search soon. If we're lucky, they'll have another dozen swords and one of them will work, or at least be useful. Supposedly I'm tough enough to stop it from possessing me, so I just need to hold it off as long as I can while I look for Josh."

"If what Max says is true," said the cloaked woman, "the odds are it will kill you."

Twin streamers of smoke curled up from his nostrils. "Probably, yeah."

Max cleared his throat and killed the moment. "Not probably," he said. "You'll be going to your death."

Stealth glared at him. They could all sense it, even through the mask. "If you continue to speak in such a demoralizing manner," she said, "I will paralyze your larynx."

Two fingers on each of his hands curled back. He met her glare through the blank planes of the mask. Max didn't back down, but was aware Stealth was two inches taller than him, not counting her cowl. After a moment his face calmed and she turned away.

St. George looked at Max. "Symbols are important, right? I'm the guy who beat him before, so maybe it'll remember me and be a little scared or something. It might give me an edge."

"It will," said Max. "Not much, but it'll help."

"Then that's what we'll do," said St. George. "We'll get the best sword we can and I'll go out to find Josh and face the demon. Maybe I can slow it down and give the rest of you time to figure out another plan. If I'm really lucky, I'll get Josh back here somehow."

Max let out a long sigh and closed his eyes. "I'll go with you," he said.

Billie raised an eyebrow. Stealth crossed her arms.

"Give it a rest," he said. "You're right, okay? George is right, I'm a cowardly pessimist, let's move on while there's still time to save the world."

"What are you thinking?" asked St. George.

Max shrugged. "I'm the only other person remotely protected from Cairax. I can draw some of his attention, maybe. Give us a little more time."

"You don't sound too confident," said Billie.

"Honestly, two of us aren't going to confuse him much more than one."

"Well," said St. George, "then I guess we hope the guys find a good sword."

Max nodded. "Maybe I can make something up for you. A simple shield spell or a glamour. Something so he can't lunge right into you."

St. George felt smoke trickle out of his nose. "If you can do that, I could've gone to get the other sword."

"No, you couldn't," said Max. "This'll be a one-time-only trick, and I'm not even sure it'll work the one time."

"This should have been mentioned before," said Stealth with another glare.

"Yeah, real sorry about that," Max said. "I was going under the stupid assumption we didn't want anyone marching out to a horrible death."

They stared at each other for a moment. Then Billie gathered an armload of blades from the table and headed back into the Mount. "I'll check on the guys," she told St. George.

He gave her a nod and looked at the sorcerer. "How soon do you want to head out, then?"

Max looked up at the sun, then traced a few paths across the sky with his eyes. "We've got a little over seven hours, if all goes well. Odds will be slightly in our favor if we go earlier and maybe catch one of them before they start to bond. We should go see what your guys have found for weapons so far." He stopped and looked around. "Do you hear something?"

"There is a crowd approaching," said Stealth. Inside her hood, her head turned to the west. "I would estimate between thirty and forty people."

As she spoke, the crowd flowed around the south corner of Gower Street. St. George guessed there were three dozen of them, and spotted a few children holding hands with parents. At the front of the crowd was Christian Nguyen. She was talking with a few people around her, and every few steps she'd raise the Bible in her hand a little higher for emphasis. When she saw the heroes she waved.

"They are all members of the After Death movement," Stealth said.

"Great," said St. George. "Any idea what they want?"

"With Ms. Nguyen's aggressive nature, I have been expecting them to make some list of demands under the grounds of religious freedom. There are several possible things they could be prepared to ask for."

"Or maybe they're just all out for an after-lunch stroll?"

Stealth looked at him. "I find that unlikely."

"At least they're not carrying torches and pitchforks," said Max. "That's always a plus in my book."

The crowd got closer and St. George took a few steps toward them. "Christian," he called out. "Always a pleasure. What can we do for you After Death folks?"

"We don't use that name," she said, closing the gap between them. "It's a term others have applied to us. We just think of ourselves as Christians." She held her Bible with both hands and gave a thin smile. "No pun intended."

"Of course not." It occurred to St. George that he kind of missed the old Christian, the one who just hated the heroes and fought against anything they suggested or any action they took. She was troublesome, but she was predictable. Since she'd found religion, talking to her always gave him the sensation of walking in a minefield.

"We have a request," she said.

Stealth shifted her posture enough to make her cloak ripple. "This cannot wait until the district meeting next Tuesday?"

"I plan on bringing it up there as well," she said, "but many of us felt this was a matter of extreme urgency." There were nods and echoes of agreement from the crowd.

"George," said Max, "we're on a tight schedule here."

"Mr. Hale," said Christian, "you of all people should appreciate our worries. This is a matter of immortal souls."

He blinked. "What?"

"You're living proof the dead can come back," she said. "You can lead the way for all our loved ones. The girl, Madelyn, is a flawed creature, but you've returned unharmed."

"I'm two inches shorter and I'm missing a tooth," said Max.

Christian let her gaze slide back and forth between St. George and Stealth. "We'd like you to stop shooting the exes outside the Big Wall."

St. George coughed in amazement. It came out as a puff of smoke threaded with yellow flames. "I'm sorry?"

"Perhaps explore some nondamaging way to stop them," said the former councilwoman. "We're concerned you may be injuring them spiritually, and perhaps ruining their chances of returning to this world."

Max snorted. "They aren't coming back."

His words threw Christian for a moment, but she recovered. "You can bring them back," she said. "With enough time and help, you could bring all of them back and restore the world."

Max glanced at St. George. The hero gave a faint shrug.

"Look," the sorcerer said, raising his voice, "I get that you need to cling to something. But those things out there aren't your loved ones, and I can't turn them into your loved ones. They're just meat. The people you knew are dead. They've moved on."

"Like you did?" A faint glimmer of something familiar crossed Christian's eyes. It was her old haughty, confident look, the one she used to give in council meetings. The one that showed up when she thought someone had made a mistake she could exploit.

"Maxwell was a special case," said Stealth. "He should be considered the rare exception, not the rule."

"But there could be other exceptions," said someone in the crowd.

"No," said Max, "There aren't."

"The Bible talks about all this," said another man. "The end of days, the dead coming back as zombies. It's all true."

"There's dozens of resurrections predicted in the Bible," agreed Max, "but even the ones in Revelation aren't about zombies rising up to attack mankind. They're just saying when the end comes, the dead get to enter Heaven first because they've been waiting the longest." He waved his arm out at the Big Wall, at the distant sound of teeth. "I know it's comforting to believe this stuff, but it's just not true. I've got suits with more personality left in them than your average ex. Everything you loved about them is long gone."

"But I've seen my sister," said one man. "She's still wearing her favorite shirt."

"She's wearing clothes, Mr. Diamint," said St. George. "It's just what she died in, like a lot of other exes. Captain Freedom can tell you just because they're still wearing a uniform doesn't mean they're thinking like soldiers. Last time we were over in Burbank there was one wearing a cell phone costume. It doesn't mean he's still thinking about his phone contract."

"How do you know?" shouted one man. Harry, one of the part-time drivers for the scavengers. He tended to follow Christian around. His nose was still crooked from being broken a year and a half ago. "How can you know what's happened to their souls?"

"I know," said Max. "I was there, remember?"

Again, his words tripped them up. Harry glanced at Christian. Doubt flickered on her face.

"When it comes to cheating death," the sorcerer told the crowd, "I'm the only guy who brought a parachute. Everyone else fell the whole way. And believe me, having been dead, they were the lucky ones. The last thing you should be wishing for is that they've spent the past three years in the purgatory I did. I was ready for it and it almost drove me insane."

A woman in the back sniffled. "You don't know what you're talking about," Christian said. "You're just confused because of your journey."

"You can't have it both ways," said Max, raising his voice a little more. "You want to believe I'm the way to bring your families back? That's great, but if you believe me, then I'm telling you it can't happen. Your friends and loved ones are not outside the Big Wall waiting for someone to flip a switch so they can be alive and hug you again. The real world doesn't work that way. Real problems don't get solved with a snap of a finger. The exes are just walking corpses. They're dead. That's it."

Diamint's shoulders slumped. It was a gesture of resignation, but St. George saw a little relief in it, too. Another man looked up at the sky and pressed his eyes shut. The sniffling woman started to sob. A man put his arm around her. Christian clutched her Bible in a death grip.

"Don't you get it?" said Max. "You're not praying, you're just . . . wishing. And wishes don't come true."

Someone else started to cry. Diamint drifted away and led a woman with him. Another man slumped against one of the oversized potted plants flanking the gateway into the Mount.

"I'm sorry," said St. George.

"You're just saying this to make us look foolish because of our faith," Christian said. "That's why people believe in me just as much as you. People can depend on me when things get tough."

"What's that supposed to mean?"

"It means you . . . you have to ruin everything, don't you," she snarled. "Keep all the good things for yourselves. You can't even let people have hope, you have to ruin it."

"This is a false hope," Stealth said. "Nothing good can come of it."

"It lets people cope," snapped Harry.

"It allows people to deny the reality of our situation," said the cloaked woman. "That is a luxury none of us can afford."

"We have to look forward," said St. George. "If we just cling to what the world was—what our lives were—we're never going to accomplish anything."

"Speaking of looking forward," said Max with another glance at the sky, "there are some things we need to do here if we want there to *be* a future."

Christian looked ready to tear her Bible in half. St. George was sure the woman would've if she'd been strong enough. She glared at him for a moment.

Then the anger went out of her and she tucked the book under her arm. "We'll discuss this more soon," she said. "Believe it."

She turned and marched through the crowd. Some of them followed her. Others seemed confused and drifted in the streets.

Stealth took St. George's arm. "Ilya has tried to reach you," she said, gesturing at the dangling earbud. "He has found three swords he believes may suit our needs."

"That's great," said St. George.

"We have also received an urgent summons from Dr. Connolly. She says it cannot wait."

"Okay. I'll catch up with you la—"

"We, George. She wishes to speak with both of us."

Max nodded. "Go," he said. "I need some time to figure out a good shield spell I can paint on you instead of tattooing."

St. George held out his hand and Stealth grabbed his wrist. They shot into the sky.

Twenty-Five
NOW

ST. GEORGE AND Stealth landed outside the hospital. The receptionist told them Connolly was in one of the small labs on the fourth floor. They walked across the lobby to the stairwell.

They were on the second landing when Stealth spoke. "In some religions," she said, "your willingness to sacrifice yourself could be seen as making you more honorable and holy."

He tried to smile. "That's good. I think I'm going to need every edge I can get."

"I would not put much trust in Maxwell's offer to assist you."

"Why not?"

"Despite his bravado and professed expertise, I believe he is far more an amateur than he would like to admit."

"Ahhh."

They passed the door for the third floor.

"Also," she said, "he is lying to us."

"You could've led with that," said St. George. He stopped on the landing and turned to her. "Why do you think so?"

Her cloak settled around her. "I cannot say," she admitted. "I am positive something he has said is a lie, yet I cannot confirm why. The uncertainty is frustrating."

"What did he say?"

Stealth went up the next flight of stairs without a word.

"Well?"

"He knows Billie Carter has a dolphin tattoo."

"Is that . . ." He looked up at her and cleared his throat. "Is that wrong? I mean, besides the obvious way it's wrong he knows that?"

Stealth's head shifted inside her hood. "No. I performed her screening when we first took survivors into the Mount. The tattoo is on her left pelvic where it would be hidden by most items of clothing or underwear. From the color bleed, I would estimate she received it close to her seventeenth birthday."

St. George followed her up the stairs. "So what's the problem?"

"As I said, I am unsure. Yet I am convinced Maxwell has lied to us and it ties back to that statement."

He pulled open the fourth-floor door and held it for her. The guard in the hallway directed them a few doors down to the pathology lab. Connolly was sitting in front of a microscope attached to a battered laptop computer. She glanced up as they entered, then back at the screen, as if she was worried what she'd been looking at would vanish. Her face was a mix of emotions.

"This had best be important, doctor," Stealth said. "We do not have much time."

"It's important," said Connolly. She waved them over to the counter and tapped a few keys on the laptop. She turned it so St. George and Stealth could see better.

On the screen St. George saw a trio of delicate shapes. They looked like silver spiderwebs, or maybe simple snowflakes, set against a white background. Each arm or branch looked like it was made of short segments. They drifted in the image, like underwater plants. One of the shapes shifted and St. George realized the arms extended out in several directions, like a Christmas tree ornament.

"Are they some kind of bacteria or something?" asked St. George. "Is it the ex-virus?"

Connolly shook her head. "They're macromolecular complexes. Those arms are nanotubes, like flagella, but they're all composed of different chemical compounds. The center mass is a mix of proteins and DNA, like you'd find in a virus. This whole structure's approximately forty microns across."

St. George blinked a few times and his mouth twisted up. "None of that means anything to me."

"They're nanites," she said.

"A what?"

"A piece of nanotechnology," Stealth said. "Machinery built or grown on a cellular level. Where did you find them?"

"They came from Madelyn."

St. George looked up from the screen. "What?"

"Yesterday morning I decided to do a straight visual inspection of her blood at a higher magnification. Since the ex-virus mimics white blood cells, I thought it might be a way to spot a possible variation. I know it's not supposed to mutate, but it was the only thing I could think of. That's when I realized none of her blood cells were actually blood cells."

She tapped her keyboard and a new image came up. The nanite webs had rolled their arms into coils and wrapped themselves into double-layered discs that were thicker at the edges. "These are from another one of her blood samples."

Stealth's head tilted inside her hood. "Their form now resembles erythrocytes. You are certain they are the same structures?"

Connolly nodded. "That's why I didn't notice them before. They were shaped like red blood cells and acting like them." She hit a key and called up another picture. In this one dozens of webs were stretched out long and thin. The arms were gathered in parallel bundles. "These are from a tissue sample we took. Hundreds of them linked together to form bone muscle fibers."

The doctor cycled the pictures back to the extended spiderweb and took in a controlled breath. "These things reshape themselves to mimic different cells, depending on where in the body they are. Blood cells, muscle cells, skin cells. They can even work together to imitate nerve cells." She paused for a moment. "Do you have any idea what that means? An artificial neuron? That's past Nobel Prize, that's just . . . It's impossible."

"Clearly it is not," said Stealth.

St. George tipped his head at the microscope image. "So these are in Maddy? They have something to do with her . . . condition?"

"They're not in her, George," Connolly said. "It's all she is."

He blinked. "What do you mean?"

"I mean . . ." The doctor took a breath. "Okay, I'm just guessing here because this is all way, way out of my league, and at this point I haven't slept in two days." She looked at Stealth. "You super-genius types can do what you want with this. Maybe you'll come up with another way to interpret all the data."

She took another slow breath and collected her thoughts.

"I think Emil Sorensen invented something amazing," Connolly said. "He figured out how to biochemically engineer the dream nanite sci-fi writers have been talking about since the seventies. Almost a self-guided, synthetic stem cell, if you will. And, for some reason, he used them on his daughter. Maybe she had some injury or a disease or something. I don't know her history well enough to guess what happened. But they ended up in her body, and they started multiplying and fixing things. Maddy got older, became athletic, and they supported and enhanced her whole system. If anything went wrong—muscle tears, injuries, whatever—the nanites would zoom in, multiply, and replace it until her own systems could catch up."

"And then she died," said St. George.

The doctor nodded. "And then she died. And they tried to fix it."

They looked at the spiderweb on the screen.

"From what you and the captain have told me," continued Connolly, "she was probably mangled, missing a lot of tissue mass. So the nanites did what they're supposed to do. They re-

placed the damaged and missing sections. And they kept repli-
cating and replacing until they made her whole again. But the
body was decaying, maybe getting eaten by scavengers. It was
an uphill battle, and by the time it was done . . . there wasn't
much left of the actual body.

"Plus they weren't designed to do the job they were trying
to do. Not something on this scale, anyway. So there were gaps.
They built memories that were hardwired instead of flexible.
They replicated a cardiopulmonary system, but it doesn't work.
And it doesn't need to.

"This is also why she sleeps. After watching them for a
while, I can see a regular pattern where the nanites expend all
their electrochemical energy and then become dormant until a
sufficient gradient rebuilds. As they start to shut down she gets
tired, and then when they start back up they reset themselves."

"And she forgets the previous day," said Stealth.

St. George thought of the smiling girl he'd left a few hours
ago. The Corpse Girl. "So you're saying Madelyn's . . . what?"

"Maddy Sorensen isn't real," said the doctor. "She doesn't
have any life signs because she's a . . . a robot. An android. She's
a pile of nanites working together to duplicate the individual
parts of a teenage girl on the cellular level, and they don't realize there's no actual girl left. They rebuilt a working model of
a corpse."

The spiderwebs drifted across the screen.

"Does she know?" asked St. George. "Did she see any of
this?"

"No," said Connolly. "I was working alone on this all day
yesterday and she was out earlier with you, right?"

St. George nodded.

"That's why I figured now was the best time to talk to you
about this."

"Does she pose a threat?" asked Stealth.

Connolly blinked. "How do you mean?"

"Is she a threat to the population of Los Angeles?"

The doctor shook her head. "I don't think she has any evil programming or something, if that's what you mean. For all intents and purposes, she's still just a teenage girl. No stronger or faster. It seems like she's got more endurance and her pain response is a lot lower than it should be, but I think that's a function of her . . . well, not being alive."

The cloaked woman turned her head to the image on the screen. "Could her nanites be dangerous to other individuals here in Los Angeles?"

The doctor shook her head. "I don't think so." She reached out and tapped the screen. "I've only scratched these things, granted, but it seems like they're Madelyn-specific, designed to her DNA, and they won't last long outside on their own." Connolly shrugged. "Like I said, this is a little over a day's work. There's still so much about these things I don't understand. I could keep a research team busy for their whole careers."

"So," said St. George, "now what do we do?"

Stealth's head tilted inside her hood. "What do you mean?"

"Do we tell her?" he said. "Do we tell her what she is? Or what she isn't, I guess."

"In a few hours," said the cloaked woman, "her knowing these facts may be irrelevant."

"She still deserves to know," said St. George.

"That does not mean she would be better off knowing," Stealth responded. "It is more likely such knowledge would cause her considerable mental and emotional stress."

Connolly nodded. "When I was an intern I saw people get close to complete breakdowns over all sorts of things. Tumors. Paternity tests. STDs. This is going to be just as life-changing for her as any of those. Heck, just the philosophical angle could keep you—"

"This isn't philosophical," St. George said, "it's a person. We can't just—"

"Either way," snapped Stealth, "this is a matter best discussed tomorrow."

St. George took a breath, then let it drift out between his teeth. "You're right," he said. He glanced at Connolly. "Where is she now? Is she in her room?"

Connolly's brow wrinkled. "No, of course not."

"Of course not?" echoed Stealth.

The doctor looked at St. George. "I thought you had her doing something."

"What do you mean?"

"That's why I decided to talk to you—I knew she'd be gone. She came in about two hours ago and said you'd given her a mission."

Twenty-Six

NOW

MADELYN'S BICYCLE SKIDDED to a stop and she double-checked the address. Hector had run a piece of duct tape down the arm of her jacket and written out the street number with a fat Sharpie marker. "Don't want you getting halfway there and forgettin' where you're going," he'd said. He'd also given her a few map pages from something called a Thomas Guide that lined up to show her the route out of Hollywood and into the Valley.

It hadn't been hard to convince him to help her. Despite her mom's constant warnings, Madelyn was pretty sure not everyone in Los Angeles with a tattoo would slit your throat if you asked a question or flashed your headlights to remind them theirs were off. Hector de la Vega was gruff, and he stared at her boobs just a little too long for her liking, but he got the urgency of the mission a little more than St. George did. Hector had a cross on each arm, and the numbers of a Bible verse on his collarbone. She wondered if he was religious and had a better idea of what the demon represented.

By the same token, she was also pretty sure Hector wouldn't be too broken up if she never came back. She'd seen the big man recoil when his fingers brushed the back of her hand. Nobody liked the feel of dead flesh, and he'd been one of the ones giving her looks at the big meeting.

Getting out of the Mount hadn't been half as hard as she thought it'd be. It reminded her of a line from an old Houdini movie her mom loved—had loved. Nobody made safes to keep people from breaking *out* of them. She'd scaled the Wall while the guards were facing the other way and slipped down into the crowd of exes below. It'd been creepy as hell, being surrounded by them, but it wasn't any worse than a school hallway between classes. Hundreds of people around you but not one of them seeing you while they moved. They jostled her, but none of them reacted to her.

Stepping past the seals took a little more work. She'd stood on the sidewalk with the tips of her sneakers against the invisible line for almost five minutes, staring at the circular symbol ahead and to the right. Inside the Wall it was easy to tell herself she was safe, but out here, with chunks of meat and pale limbs scattered across the ward, she'd found herself wondering what it would feel like to catch fire and explode.

It was just like a high dive, she'd told herself. Just like being on the board. A hundred things could go wrong, but none of them really would. She could do it. Her team was counting on her to do it.

"I'm the Corpse Girl," she told the exes around her. "It can't see me. It can't touch me."

She closed her eyes and took three quick steps. There'd been a brief moment of panic, the knowledge she couldn't go back. She squeezed her hands into fists, ready to fight however she could.

Nothing happened. An ex bumped against her and wandered past, its teeth clicking away. Another one tripped over the curb in front of her and sprawled on the sidewalk.

She'd found a bike with a rattling chain a block and a half from the Big Wall. Most of the bike's owner was a few feet away, but she'd decided to skip the helmet. It took her an hour to get to the address.

Denny Avenue looked like a pleasant place. Yeah, there were

a couple of dead bodies and a burned-out pickup truck, but the houses were nice and there were lots of trees. Even the exes shuffling in the street looked a little cleaner.

Hector's grandfather lived in a cottage behind the main house. She followed the driveway around the building and found a garage and a tall wooden fence with a matching gate. There was a mailbox on the fence with the street number on it. She checked the address on her arm again and knocked the bike's kickstand down.

Something thudded against the far side of the fence. It made Madelyn jump back from the gate, but she didn't flinch at the second or third sound. She was getting into the whole "invisible to exes" thing. She stepped forward and flipped the latch.

An ex staggered out of the gate. It stumbled past her without a look and crashed into the parked bicycle. The bike fell over, but the ex managed to stay on its feet.

It had been an older man, an inch or two shorter than Madelyn. The bristly hair was the same gray as its skin. It was dried out and leathery, but still weighed twice as much as she did.

The dead thing had the same jaw and cheekbones as Hector. She decided right then to say she hadn't seen any sign of the old man. She wouldn't want to know her family was still walking around.

She left the ex standing in the driveway and walked through the gate. There was a flowerbed that had grown out into the small yard. A few cobblestones in the grass led up to the big wooden door. It swung open when she pushed on it.

She was looking for a wooden box three feet long and eight or nine inches square. It was padlocked shut. Hector thought it might have a little plaque on the lid, but he couldn't remember for sure.

The cottage was small, and there weren't too many places to hide something that size. Madelyn looked in both closets, under the bed, then went through each drawer of the dresser. She checked under the couch and behind the washer and dryer.

There was a loft above the washer, but it was just filled with dusty paperbacks. Hector's grandfather had loved science fiction. She wondered how he'd felt when the dead started to walk.

The fridge was disgusting. The kitchen cabinets were jammed full of pots and pans of every size and a huge selection of dishes. She even looked in the dishwasher. Someone had run it before the end of the world. The glasses and silverware were still sparkling clean.

The cottage didn't have a basement, which seemed weird to her. Growing up on the East Coast, almost everybody had a cellar. It just felt like the old man's home was missing something important.

There wasn't a real attic, either. She found a small hatch in the ceiling of the bedroom and got up into it with a footstool from the kitchen. Twenty minutes convinced her there was nothing but old clothes and Christmas decorations up there.

Madelyn checked her watches. She'd spent an hour biking into the Valley, and another hour searching the house so far. According to watch number two, sundown was in ninety-three minutes. And Max's deadline was in four hours.

There was a small shed in the backyard, one of the ones that looked like a big Tupperware container, but it was nothing but garden tools and a lawn mower. She even tipped over a few bags of potting soil and fertilizer to make sure the box wasn't hidden behind them. Nothing in the tight gap between the shed and the backyard fence, either.

Even though the garage was connected to the cottage, it didn't have a connecting door. She tugged on the big door but it was locked. Or maybe the motor was holding it shut. She walked around the garage and found a side door opposite the cottage. It was also locked.

A quick trip back inside let her find the basket by the door. It had a very overdue parking ticket, some loose change, two key rings, and a small remote with a single button on it. Madelyn squeezed the remote a few times before she remembered the power had been off for a few years at this point.

Back outside she started testing the key ring against the door. Hector's grandfather had shuffled down the driveway and found a friend. A tall ex with a plaid shirt and a limp. They'd bumped shoulders and were turning together in a creepy slow dance. They didn't notice her or the sound of jingling keys.

And how is that, she wondered. There was a certain logic to them filtering her out, but shouldn't they see and hear other things she had contact with? Were the exes seeing an empty suit of clothes walking around, or a set of keys floating in the air, or did the filter have range?

The first key she tried on the second ring fit the door. She glanced at her watches again. Fifteen minutes trying to get into the garage. If she didn't find the box soon, it'd be dark by the time she got back to the Mount. She pushed the door open.

The garage was a lot like hers back home, an example of controlled chaos. A huge Lincoln filled most of the space. There was a trio of bikes parked—stacked, really—against the back wall. Metal shelves held some canned food, jars of nails and screws, a plastic toolbox, and a few more paperback books. It looked like Piers Anthony and Alan Dean Foster had been banished from the loft. An upright piano stood under a drop cloth and some empty flowerpots. An old painting—a guy with a mustache and a sash—hung on one wall next to a pair of rakes and a folding ladder.

Madelyn pulled everything off the piano and opened the lid. She pressed her hands against the Lincoln's windows and looked in the backseat. She got down on all fours and looked under the car. It wasn't until she climbed back to her feet that she bothered to look up.

Just like her own mom and dad, Hector's grandfather had saved space by putting stuff up in the garage's rafters. He'd even wrestled a sheet of plywood up there to use as a huge shelf.

She could see suitcases, old boxes, and what looked like a big stuffed bear.

Stretched between two of the beams, right over the big door, was something wrapped in a black trash bag. It was about three feet long.

It took her a minute to get the ladder off the wall, and another two to get it in front of the Lincoln. As she was trying to set it down, one of the legs swung up and broke the Lincoln's tail light. Nobody would ever know, but she still felt bad. She kicked out the ladder's legs and climbed up to the top. It wobbled a little, but she'd never been scared of heights.

A few tugs and the plastic bag came loose. The box was dark wood, just like Hector had said, with narrow iron hinges. It looked old. She slid one side free and let the whole thing settle into her arms. It took a moment to get her balance and then she worked her way back down the ladder without using her hands.

The box reminded her of a coffin, even though she'd only been to one funeral in her whole life. There was a crest engraved in the lid with a few words in Spanish—she'd studied French in school. There was a latch made from the same black iron as the hinges. The padlock on the latch, however, was steel and new.

Madelyn looked around the garage for a minute and found the plastic toolbox. There was a flathead screwdriver right on the top tray and a hammer underneath that. She pushed the screwdriver through the padlock's hasp and whacked it with the hammer. The screwdriver slipped loose and spun across the garage. She chased after it, repositioned, and pounded a few more times. The padlock didn't budge, but the latch tore free from the wood. It made her pause for a moment, then she beat on the screwdriver a few more times until the box cracked and the latch ripped away.

She heard a thump behind her and spun around. Grandfather de la Vega and the other ex were pressed against the garage door, their heads framed in the large windows. Well, the top of grandfather's head. The wood muffled their clicking jaws. Another ex, a skinny woman in a dress, stumbled up the driveway behind them.

Less than an hour until sundown. She needed to get moving. She threw open the box and tossed aside an old black sheet that had been folded over the contents. And there was the sword.

After seeing the first *Pirates of the Caribbean* movie she'd convinced her parents to let her take fencing lessons. It'd been a huge letdown. Junior-level fencing wasn't as action-packed as the movies made it out to be, and competition-legal foils just didn't measure up to the gorgeous sword Orlando Bloom had made for Commodore Norrington or the one Inigo Montoya's father had made for the six-fingered man.

This sword did, though. She didn't know anything about weapons but she could tell this was a piece of art. There weren't any fancy jewels or gold or anything, but it was still beautiful. The blade was thin and covered with hundreds of curls and scrolls that reminded her of her dad's paisley ties. Above the handle—the hilt, she remembered—was a circle of metal, curved down to guard the hand. It was cut and engraved to look like an elaborate flower. A thick rod of metal stretched side to side beneath the circle, and a matching one curved down to make the knuckle guard.

She wrapped her fingers around the hilt and lifted it out of the box. It was a little heavier than she'd expected, but it balanced in her hand really well. There were a few faint nicks on the blade, but they'd been ground down and polished out. The sword had been used a lot, but somebody had taken care of it. The edge was still sharp.

"Corpse Girl for the win," she said with a smile.

Another thump convinced her to get moving. There wasn't any scabbard or anything in the box, so she hiked up her coat and slid the sword through her belt. It was a little awkward, but she was pretty sure she'd be able to ride a bike with it.

Grandpa and his tall friend ignored her and kept trying to walk through the garage door. The female ex stood in the middle of the driveway as if lost in thought. There was a stringy piece of something caught in her teeth and it flapped up and down as her jaw moved.

Madelyn swung her leg over the bike and edged the kickstand up with her foot. As an afterthought, she reached out and tugged the gate closed. The exes twitched when the latch connected, but none of them made a move toward her. She guided the bike past the dead woman and back down to the street.

She peeled the tape off her sleeve and took another look at the Thomas Guide pages. Just over three hours until Max's deadline. A lot of the trip into the Valley had been uphill. Hopefully the way back would be faster.

Twenty-Seven
NOW

"ARE YOU SURE this is the best way to go, sir?" asked Freedom.

"This is where Josh got away," said St. George. He gestured at the railing, then nodded across the street to the blood-splattered SUV the prisoner had been shot against.

"That's not quite what I meant." The huge captain glanced out at the street. "There've been no sightings of Cairax from the south."

"It doesn't matter," said Max. He'd pushed up the sleeves of his suit and unbuttoned his shirt to display more of his tattoos. "Like I said, he's all around the Mount. He saw Josh leave. He'll see us leave."

"How can he be all around the Mount at the same time?" said one of the guards.

"Bilocation," Max said. He shook out his hands while he talked, letting his fingers bounce and snap at the edges of his palm. "It's not just for saints. A lot of the higher and lower entities can manifest that way."

The guard's lips twisted into a frown. "What's that mean?"

"It means he can be all around the Mount at the same time."

St. George shifted his hips again. He was used to carrying various pouches and pieces of gear on his belt, but the sword was something different. It swung like a lopsided pendulum and pulled at his waist. Even with his strength, it felt odd.

The weapon they'd settled on had come from one of the old prop houses. Ilya had found it in a barrel with two or three dozen others and—after Max's halfhearted approval was given—spent an hour putting an edge on the safety-dulled blade. It looked like a classic knight's sword, with a square crossbar for a guard and wire wrapped tight around the hilt. The pommel was a big wheel of metal with a large ruby in it, although St. George was pretty sure the gemstone was cut glass at best.

It looked like a real sword when he held it in a shaft of sunlight. It felt like a real sword. Hopefully that would be enough.

Stealth stood off to the side. Her cloak had settled around her, and she'd let her hood sink over her head. She said nothing as they made the final preparations.

Max finished his hand exercises and looked at the cloaked woman. "Look," he said to her, "I know you're not going to like this, but if something happens . . . well, don't come after us. No matter what you hear or see, don't come out."

Stealth stiffened beneath her cloak. St. George was sure he was the only one who caught it. "Why not?" she asked.

"We're either going to stop Cairax or not. If we do, you've got no reason to go out past the wards. If we don't, well . . ." Max shrugged again. "The walls and wards will give everyone a small degree of protection. Not much, but use them as long as you can."

Stealth glared at him for a moment. Then she nodded once in assent.

The sorcerer turned to St. George. "How do the runes feel?"

"They itch," said the hero. Max had painted a series of symbols across St. George's back and chest with a fat brush he'd found in one of the scenery shops. He hadn't used regular paint. It was something oily that just smelled wrong. He'd mixed it up while the two heroes had talked with Dr. Connolly. "It feels like a peeling sunburn."

"Good," said Max. "That means they're working. Should

give you an hour or two if we're lucky." He looked up at the sky. "We should get going. We've got half an hour or so until sundown. Maybe an hour till full dark."

St. George nodded. He exchanged a solemn look with Freedom, then turned to Stealth. He had a sinking feeling this was the last time he was going to see her, and she had her mask on.

"I'll be back soon," he told her.

Her head dipped ever so slightly inside her hood. "I am certain you will."

He waited a moment, wondering if she was going to crack and hug him or something. He thought about hugging her. He thought about pulling her mask up and giving her one last kiss.

But she was cool and professional. She didn't crack. It would be demoralizing to the guards if she did. So she walled herself off and didn't give any hint of what they'd shared. She was cold and strong and merciless so no one else had to be. So everyone else could just live.

It was who she was, and it was part of the reason he loved her.

He hoped he survived to tell her.

Max traced one of his tattoos with his finger and looked at St. George. "I can levitate pretty easy, but I'm not fast. How do you want to do this? Piggyback?"

"God, no," said the hero, turning away from Stealth. He gave a wink to the guards. "If I'm going out to my death I don't want to look pathetic doing it."

They all chuckled. The mood rose a little bit.

He focused on the spot between his shoulder blades, floated into the air, and held out his hand. Max grabbed it wrist to wrist. They rose up and floated out past the Big Wall.

The exes below tilted their heads back and followed them through the air. They snapped their jaws open and shut. Their desiccated fingers stretched up to claw at the empty space below Max's feet.

"A little higher would be nice," said Max.

"You'll be fine," said St. George.

They drifted over to the circle burned into the pavement. The shambling dead hid it well from the Big Wall, but from overhead it was easy to see. St. George paused in the air just before it. He looked down at Max. "As soon as we're over it? Or once we're past it?"

"Past it. The seal itself is the end of the safe area. He'll see us, but you should be safe from any level of possession."

"Should?"

"For a while, anyway," said Max. "If he wants to kill either of us, he'll have to do it the old-fashioned way."

"Great."

They floated a few more feet. A cluster of exes shuffled below them and brought the sound of clicking teeth. One of them stumbled and fell over backward. The others trampled over it, still reaching for the heroes.

"Hang on tight with both hands," St. George said. "If it comes at us, I'm going to move fast."

"If it comes at us, you're going to want me to have a hand free," said the sorcerer.

St. George took in a deep breath. He glanced over his shoulder at the Big Wall, where Stealth and Freedom stood watching him. The breath hissed out of his nose as black smoke. He tightened his fingers around the sword and swallowed.

They crossed the seal.

Nothing happened.

St. George turned in the air. There were a hundred or so exes in his line of sight, but none of them was streaming blue fire or growing claws and horns. He swung the sword once and it made a whipping noise.

Still nothing.

"So far, so good," said Max. His free hand was up with the middle and ring fingers folded flat against his palm. A set of devil horns. "Which way are we headed?"

St. George rose another foot or so in the air and headed west.

* * *

"And that's sunset," said Max twenty minutes later.

They drifted between trees and buildings down La Brea Avenue. It was one of the more urban sections of Los Angeles, and he'd heard it called "Beverly Hills–adjacent" a few times back when people talked about apartment locations for something other than looting. Several lanes wide, a fair number of trees, and a mix of warehouse-like stores and small shops. Hard to believe just a few blocks to the east it looked more like a small town than a big city.

"It's not actually down," St. George said. "It's just lower than the buildings. We've still got another ten minutes or so."

"And then it gets even harder to see anything."

Exes staggered after them, like paupers to a banquet. St. George and Max had collected a large crowd of followers as they flew back and forth across the neighborhood. Some fell behind as others joined the chase. There were sixty or seventy of them at the moment, trailing behind the flying men in a loose fan. They shuffled between cars, dragging against the sides, and added the scraping noise to the sound of their clicking teeth.

St. George panned his eyes across the road again. There were a lot of cars, all covered with dust. It meant lots of places to hide. "Isn't there some kind of locator spell you can cast or something?"

"Yeah," said Max, "but gosh-darn-it, I missed that day at Hogwarts."

"You don't need to be an ass about it."

"Sorry. A little tense. I didn't think it'd take this long to find either of them. Or for Cairax to find us."

Something moved quick in the corner of St. George's eye and he heard a sound over the *click-clack-click* of the exes. He spun and brought the sword up, inhaling hard as he did. He felt the tickle at the back of his throat and realized it was just another zombie, a tall man who had been coming to join the pack. It had stumbled off the sidewalk and fallen against a Mercedes.

He let the breath out slow and smoke twisted from his nose and mouth. He glanced down and saw Max's outstretched hand was shimmering like a hot sidewalk. The other man sighed and let his fingers relax.

"So," said St. George, "you thought we'd've found them by now?"

"Well, yeah," Max said. "Cairax wants to get me, so either he was going to keep Josh close until the possession took effect, or he was going to be waiting at the seals to pounce the moment I stepped outside. I'm not really sure what's going on."

St. George checked the crowd of exes below them. His eyes flitted down to the tooth on his lapel and came back up. "He should be pretty tough to miss. Long tail, purple hide, ten feet tall."

Max grunted. "That isn't what Cairax really looks like, y'know."

"No?"

"That's what it looks like when it's squeezed into my shape, if that makes sense. Sort of like how a filet-o-fish is shaped like a bun, not like a real fish. It's not natural, it's just easier to swallow."

"So it's going to look different?"

"It's going to look a bit more pure."

St. George turned and brought the sword up again. "Interesting choice of words." The quick movement had been an ex's shadow this time, stretched out long as the last rays of sunlight slipped between two buildings.

"Just take what you remember and dial it up to eleven," Max told him.

"It was already at eleven."

"Then take it to thirteen. More fitting, anyway. Hey, can we take a quick break?"

"What?"

"You're the super-strong guy who can fly, but I've been dragged by one arm for half an hour. My shoulder's going numb."

St. George looked around and spotted a flat area on the roof shared by an oversized pet shop and a huge lamp store. He flew over and set Max down. The sorcerer swung his arm in a circle a few times, then rolled his shoulder back and forth.

St. George turned and looked down at the street. The shadows were getting darker. "How long do you need?" he asked Max. "We probably shouldn't stop for long, right?"

"Just a minute." He said. He shook his hand out like a pitcher getting ready for a big game. "I'm not going to be much use if my arm doesn't work."

On the street below, the crowd of exes spread out. Some of them lost track of the two men on the roof and stumbled away. A dozen or so were trapped on the far side of cars, helpless until dumb luck moved them around. They kept their blank eyes on St. George and clawed at the air. Others pushed their way through the lamp store's broken display windows. The sound of crunching glass made its way up to the roof.

"I don't suppose there's a chance the demon just left? Didn't you say he might just decide you weren't worth it?"

Max walked to the edge of the roof to stand by St. George. He rolled his shoulder again. "It never works out that way. D'you remember any fairy tales where the devil makes a deal with someone but then never bothers to follow through in the end?"

"Not off the top of my head."

"There's a reason for that." He shook his head. "He's too pissed to leave. We just need to find him before he finds . . ."

St. George followed Max's gaze. Across the street was a small storefront that might have been an art gallery or some kind of showroom, something that looked more East Coast than Los Angeles. He remembered searching it years back and finding nothing useful. The huge picture window had been smashed ages ago, if the leaves on the inside floor were any sign.

Josh stood inside the gallery, watching them. He was just

far enough in that they never would've seen him if they'd been floating down the center of the street. A deep sigh moved his chest as he locked eyes with St. George.

The man formerly known as Regenerator was tall and broad. His build was solid, despite months in a cell with no food. His white hair almost glowed in the gallery's dim interior, while his gray eyes were just dark enough to be black in the fading light.

St. George risked looking away for a moment. There were at least sixty exes between the lamp store and the gallery. Too many to have a conversation at street level.

He glanced back. Josh hadn't moved. He looked tired.

Max shrugged. He put his fists side by side to make a row of tattooed knuckles, then rolled them back-to-back. A few murmurs slipped from his lips as he pushed his fists forward and opened them. He whispered a few more words, closed his eyes, and swung his hands away from each other.

Twin clouds of dust and dry leaves rose up off the street. A few of the cars squealed and lurched in either direction. The exes slid across the pavement as if they were being swept aside. Some of them fell over and kept moving. One of them, a dead woman in shorts and a gory tank top, kept trying to stagger forward even as she was swept back.

Max opened his eyes and looked at the pristine path across the street. "Looks great when you do it with water," said Max. "Very biblical."

"You can keep them away?"

Max let his hands drop. "It'll stay for a while. It only goes side to side, so watch your back."

The hero stepped off the roof and sailed down to land in the center of the street. His boots tapped the pavement and he took a few steps forward. The white-haired man watched him come.

"Hey, Josh," St. George said. He glanced over his shoulder and saw a few exes staggering inside the lamp shop. One of them, a dead woman, had already spotted him. It would take a few minutes to reach him.

Josh stepped out of the gallery. He'd found some new clothes that fit him pretty well—a pair of dark slacks with stained cuffs and a rumpled jacket with a pair of bullet holes in one shoulder. He still wore the plain white T-shirt from his imprisonment, soaked with blood from his escape. His feet were still bare, and broken glass crackled under them as he walked. "Coming to talk with me twice in one month," he said. "I'm starting to feel special."

"We don't have a lot of time," St. George said. "We need to get you back inside."

"Back in my cell, you mean." His hands hung at his sides, and the withered hand twitched at the mention of imprisonment. The sleeves were too short for his long arms, and the pale bite was just visible past his wrist.

"Honestly, right now it's just important we get you back inside the Mount," said St. George. "Even just inside the Big Wall. We can talk in there."

Josh chuckled. "I don't think Stealth or the others are going to be in a talking mood."

A few feet away, an ex stumbled toward them and hit Max's barrier. It swayed for a moment, its jaws gnashing at the air, and then tipped over backward. Its skull hit the pavement with a solid *thunk* and it went limp.

"I know you're not too happy with us," said St. George. "I know you've got no reason to go back, but you've got to believe me. We have to go and it'll be quicker if you don't fight."

"And if I did fight?"

"Please," he said, "we really don't have time. There's something out here looking for you, and if it finds you . . . it's not going to be good for anyone."

"So?"

St. George took another step toward the man. "Don't give me 'so,'" he said. "You still care about people, Josh. You're still one of the good guys at heart." He nodded at Josh's pale and shriveled right hand. "You've been showing everyone how guilty you feel for years."

Josh glanced down and shook his head. "You're too late, George."

"We can still work something out," the hero insisted. "Please, just come back with us. We can make everything—"

"No," said Josh. "You're too late." Blue fire sparked in his eyes. His mouth opened in a broad smile made of long, alien tusks. "It found me hours ago. We've been waiting for you to come to us."

Later, as his life drew to a close, St. George would look back on the moment with perfect clarity, each and every detail seared into his mind. Josh's clothes shredded apart and his entire body turned inside out, twisting along unnatural lines and angles. The hero could see gleaming bones and stringy muscle and glistening organs, all painted with blood. The man's insides churned along those strange angles, and then they pulled together and were back where they belonged, hidden beneath the flesh.

Not the same flesh, though. This skin was the color of a fresh bruise and stretched drum-tight over a skeleton more than twice the size it had been a moment before.

It loomed over the hero, a dozen feet tall. Saucer-like eyes dominated its face, portholes into a world of cold fire. A crown of curling horns wrapped around its skull and became a crest down its back. Its tail whipped back and forth like an enraged snake.

"St. George," it said. The smooth voice sounded like an English baritone imitating Josh. Despite its polish, it made his skin crawl and left a foul taste in the air. "George Bailey. The Mighty Dragon. Such a great man does not need so many names."

Cairax Murrain reared up, stretched back its lips, and a mouth filled with a thousand tusks and needles grinned down at St. George.

"Such a delight to see you again."

Twenty-Eight
NOW

MADELYN PICKED HERSELF up off Highland Avenue and checked the sword. She'd landed on it, but it didn't look damaged. Her right hand was torn up, though. There were a bunch of long gashes on her palm from sliding on the pavement, and she was pretty sure her middle finger and ring finger were broken. Dislocated, at least.

She walked back and kicked the bike. The rear wheel had locked up and sent her flying while she was swooping around an ex. The master link had fallen off the chain, and now one end was wrapped around the gears and axle. She was pretty sure she could have fixed it if she had tools. And light. And the master link.

And the time. According to her two watches with glow-in-the-dark faces, she had about two hours until Max's deadline. One hundred and ten minutes until hell on earth.

She waved at the ex, a desiccated man her dad's age with a bald head. Bloodstains blended with the dark red flowers on its Hawaiian shirt, and ran down onto its shorts. "You can have the bike," she said. "I didn't like the color anyway."

Madelyn checked the sword again and started walking south. She wanted to run, but her eyes didn't work well in the dark and she didn't want to risk another accident. While she walked she grabbed her two twisted fingers with her left hand.

They throbbed, but they didn't hurt as much as she knew they should. Dead nerves.

She took a deep breath out of habit more than anything else and pulled hard. There was a double pop and a flare of sharper pain. She wiggled the reset fingers. Not great, but she'd be able to use them.

It took her ten minutes of brisk walking to reach Sunset. She cut across the parking lot of a strip mall. If she remembered right, it was a mile to the northeast corner of the Big Wall. There was a pair of bodies on the far side of the lot. Two kids about her age, from their size and clothes. She glanced over her shoulder and across Highland to the gray shape of the high school. She wondered if your parents had to be in the film industry for you to go to Hollywood High School.

There were dozens of exes wandering in the street, but they were spaced out enough for her to dodge them. Madelyn set one hand on the sword and started jogging. Not a full run, but faster than walking. She was pretty sure she'd still see anything dangerous before she tripped over it.

After another ten minutes the abandoned cars started to thin out and the exes started to get a little denser. The noise of their jaws got louder. Another two blocks and she saw Amoeba Records and the Jack in the Box facing each other across the street. A few more yards and the Cinerama Dome loomed up in the night. She was a block from the Big Wall. She grabbed the sword and broke into a run.

The Corner came into view, and she could see the guards standing on top of the Wall. Three or four hundred exes clogged the intersection below them. The dead pawed at the stacked cars and reached for the men and women on the platform.

Madelyn didn't want to risk being another face in the crowd. She stopped near the back of the horde and waved her arms. She jumped up and down a couple of times. "Hey," she yelled to them. "Over here!"

One of the guards straightened up and peered out at her.

A few flashlights lit up and searched her out. "Here," she said. "I've got the sword!" She pulled it out and waved it over her head.

She heard them talk over the sound of the exes, but couldn't make out any words. They gestured at her a few times, but it seemed like it was part of the discussion, not signals intended for her. One of them raised a walkie-talkie to his mouth. She started forward through the crowd and two of the guards leveled their rifles in her direction.

"Hey!" she snapped over the sound of chattering teeth. "It's me, the Corpse Girl. I'm on your side."

The discussion on the Corner platform had turned into an argument. One woman reached out and pushed the guard's rifle away. He resisted and brought it back to settle on Madelyn. They were waving and pointing.

She looked at her watches. Just over an hour until the Hellmouth opened or whatever was going to happen. "I have the sword," she shouted. "Get St. George or Captain Freedom or someone on the radio." She shoved an ex aside and took three more pronounced steps forward.

The two guards with rifles freaked out. One of them lifted his gun to his shoulder. The other fired from chest height. The shot echoed across Sunset Boulevard, drowning out the *click-click-click* of teeth for a moment.

The ex in front of Madelyn twitched and gore sprayed out of its shoulder. She felt a tug on her sleeve and smelled hot metal. The bullet had missed her. Barely.

She dove back and crouched low behind another ex, an obese man that stank of filth. A second shot rang out, and then shouts from the platform. She wasn't sure if they were shouting at her or each other. The dead man stumbled toward the Wall, attracted by the noise, and she shuffled to stay hidden behind it. She glanced down and something dark dripped out of its pant leg.

It crossed her mind that maybe they wouldn't let her back

in. She'd snuck out without permission, and maybe they had firm rules about contact with exes. A good chunk of the population inside thought she was a prophet or omen or something, but there were also a lot of folks—probably including the two men shooting at her—who thought she wasn't different from any other dead thing.

They had to let her back in! They needed the sword.

All her stuff was inside. She hadn't brought her backpack or her heavy coat or anything. It had just been a given they'd let her back in. Honestly, she was hoping to impress St. George and convince him she could be useful to him and the other heroes. It would be cool to have someone like St. George impressed with her.

But maybe that wasn't going to happen now. She glanced back down the dark road, back the way she'd come. There'd be a backpack somewhere in the high school. Now that she knew she didn't have to hide, it'd be easier to scavenge for supplies.

Her diary was inside the Mount. If she didn't find something to write on, she'd wake up tomorrow and maybe not even remember being there. Her memory had been getting better, but she didn't think any of it would stick without the diary.

If they didn't let her back in, she was going to die all over again.

Then the sounds from the Big Wall died down and a voice bellowed out across the intersection, thundering over the sounds of dead teeth.

"Madelyn!"

She waited a moment. She'd played enough video games and seen enough movies to know what happened to someone who poked their head out to look. The obese ex shuffled a few more feet and swayed back and forth.

"Madelyn, are you still there?!"

This time there was less echo. She recognized the voice and leaped up. "Yes!" she yelled back. "I'm here. I've got the sword!"

Captain Freedom stood on the platform, looming over the guards. One of the men who'd shot at her had vanished. Even from this far back she could tell the other one was sulking.

The huge officer waved her forward and she pushed her way through the swarm of exes. Closer to the Wall they were packed in tighter. She elbowed and shoved her way past the mindless dead.

When she was close enough, two of the guards tossed a rope down to her. She wrapped it around her wrist and they hauled her up to the platform. The exes clawed at her legs, and she had a moment of terror her invisibility had worn off somehow, but it was just random grasping as they tried to reach the people above them.

She stood on the platform before Freedom. He glared down at her. "You snuck out."

"Yeah," she said.

"You were ordered back to the hospital."

"I went back to the hospital. And then I went out and got the sword. You can ground me later." She flipped the sword over in her hand and held it out to him hilt first, just like in the movies.

"You did good, soldier," he told her, "but it's too late."

She blinked. Her lids made a faint whisking noise across her eyes. "What do you mean?"

"St. George and Maxwell left thirty-nine minutes ago," said a voice. Stealth stepped from behind the dead girl. "They hope to find Regenerator before the demon does." The cloaked woman moved past Madelyn and down the staircase to street level.

"But what about the sword?" She held it up a little higher. "They need the sword to kill the demon, right?"

"Mr. Hale decided one of the swords that were already here on the lot would work well enough," said Freedom. He gestured her down the stairs to Vine Street. "Now it's time for you to go back to the hospital."

"That's stupid," said Madelyn. "Why'd I even go get this thing?"

"You were told not to," Stealth said without looking back.

"No, I mean it was a total waste of time," Madelyn said. She hiked her coat up and slid the blade through her belt again. "You'd think with all the time he had as a ghost he would've known there was a good enough sword here."

Stealth stiffened up. Her fingers curled into fists, but loosened right away. The tremor flowed through her cloak like a miniature shock wave. "Captain Freedom," she said, "we will be heading out to assist St. George in ten minutes. Make whatever preparations you see fit."

The huge officer was a step behind her. "I'm sorry, ma'am, what was that?"

"You heard me, Captain. Zzzap?"

His voice echoed back over their radios. "What's up?"

"We are switching to battery power. Meet me on the South Wall at Larchmont in nine minutes."

"Got it."

Her pace increased. Freedom found himself shifting to a slight jog to keep up with the woman. "Madelyn," she said, "I believe we will have use of your abilities. Under no circumstances are you to hand the sword to anyone until I tell you otherwise. Guard it with your life."

"Okay."

"Ma'am," said Freedom. "What's going on?"

Stealth stopped and spun on her heel. "Maxwell's illogical statements about magic and an afterlife distracted me from a clear line of reasoning. Once I accepted them as fact, his lie was obvious."

"I'm not sure what you're talking about."

"Maxwell claims he has been here for just under a year and a half as a spirit," said the cloaked woman. "Long enough to say he has seen every tattoo on every resident of the Mount."

Freedom glanced at Madelyn. "You think she's right about the sword?

"Not the sword," said Stealth. Her masked face turned to him inside the hood. "After eighteen months, how could he not have known Regenerator was our prisoner?"

* * *

St. George leaped forward, his weapon raised. He'd never used a sword before, but he figured between the cutting edge and his strength he could do a fair amount of damage with one.

He'd forgotten how fast the demon was. It had been fast as an ex. It was a blur now. The sword came down and Cairax was three yards away.

The monster's tail lashed out and parried the blade, almost knocking it out of his hand. St. George tightened his grip and felt the hilt crumple under his fingertips. He swung again, but the sword sliced air. The demon was behind him.

It laughed.

St. George spun and let the weapon swing wide. Cairax sidestepped, this time moving slow enough for him to see how easy it was. The demon glared down at him and its tail shot forward like a striking rattlesnake. It shot past his guard to punch him in the chest. The world blurred and the last panes of the pet store's plate glass exploded against his back. He managed to hold on to the sword.

Behind the demon, Max leaped from the rooftop and drifted toward the ground. Clouds of light billowed off his hands like steam. His lips were moving, but St. George couldn't hear the words.

Cairax Murrain stalked forward and St. George threw himself at it. He thought of every *Conan* and *Beastmaster* movie he'd watched as a teenager and brought the sword down with a roar. The demon put up its arm and the blade bit into the flesh. It felt like cutting into a tire. The hero pulled back and swung the blade again. It cut into the meat of Cairax's forearm and hit a bone that could've been solid rock.

Something snapped in the sword's handle. St. George felt the *twang* of breaking metal and the blade rattled against the guard. He pulled his arm back and the sword fell apart in his hands. The pommel and guard dropped away. The blade tipped and fell back over his shoulder. They all clattered on the pavement.

He stood there for a moment holding the hollow hilt.

The demon let out a deep laugh. "You face me with toys, little hero?" it rumbled. "You dishonor your namesake."

There was a blur of motion, a hot rush of pain, and St. George was hurtling through the pet store. He shredded his way through two sets of shelves, smashed some glass terrariums, and plowed into a checkout counter. He hit the wall, felt the cinder blocks crack, and dropped to the floor. His chest was wet, and a few spots of blood spread across his tattered shirt.

The floor was trembling, like a low-level earthquake, and by the time he recognized the rhythmic tremor as footsteps Cairax had grabbed him by the head and hurled him back out into the street. He struck the rear of a car. The bumper wrapped around him, the trunk collapsed, glass shattered, and St. George found himself in the backseat.

The ground shook again. He pushed himself free of the wreckage. He grabbed the loose bumper and swung it like a bat. It hit Cairax in the side of the head with a shriek of metal on bone, tore in half, and sent the demon stumbling back. St. George leaped into the air, pulled back his fist—

—and plunged back to the ground. He hit hard, and the confusion of it dropped him to his knees. He tried to push off, to get himself moving again, and the ground pressed up against him. His body was too heavy to move. His head settled against the ground and he heard Cairax Murrain moving behind him. It was chuckling.

Max stepped into his line of sight. The sorcerer pressed his palms hard against each other, his fingers tickling his wrists. A crackle of static surrounded his hands, like the St. Elmo's fire that marked doomed ships.

"Told you to watch your back," said Max. He walked over to stand by the demon. "You're not going to believe me, but I'm really sorry it had to go down like this."

Denial, Grief, Bargaining
THEN

MY FIRST THOUGHT is "No."

Just "No" over and over again. I end up shouting it. Not that anyone can hear me. When you're dead, people tend to ignore you.

Of course, I'm not really thinking or shouting. I have no language in this state. Barely have consciousness. Just enough to know how screwed I am. The image of Burgess Meredith with broken glasses appears and vanishes before I can understand why it's relevant.

This can't be happening. It's stupid. It's ridiculously stupid. I planned for everything. Broken wards. Magical interference. Demonic vassals. I even took precautions against my death. Only an amateur wouldn't.

I didn't think about undeath, though. I mean, why would I have planned for a zombie apocalypse? The whole idea of it's ridiculous.

This can't be happening!

I died. I know I died. The death shudder, the last breath, the silver cord parted. I even pissed myself. I'm dead.

I should be free, but I'm trapped in here.

No. No. No. No. No.

The Marley's gone wrong. I can feel it. It's like a door that opened enough to let you see out, but not enough to fit through it. I'm bound here. Right here.

I'm trapped in a zombie. Stuck inside the reanimated corpse of a demon. A scrap of consciousness in the back of a dead brain. At least until one of these trigger-happy soldiers decides to . . .

Oh. Oh, no. Oh, Jesus. I'm bulletproof. They can't shoot me in the head. I'll be trapped in here forever. No, no, no, no!

No, be calm. No, I won't. Stealth had the Dragon putting down all the superhuman types who changed. He'll find me—find Cairax—break his neck or crush his skull, and that'll be that.

Of course . . . we fought once before and it's not like he hurt me. Hurt Cairax. He won the fight but only because I backed off.

I realize I'm much more conscious than I should be. Enough so that I can understand that I shouldn't be able to think about why I can think. Something has changed in the dark corners of the mind. Something has been added to the mix, something *not-me* I can differentiate myself against.

And then I realize what it is. I realize what's just woken up in here with me. Oh, no, no, no, no, this can't be happening. This cannot have gone so wrong. It just can't.

The Marley's trapped him in here, too.

Trapped him in here with me.

* * *

I scream for a month. Or maybe two.

If I was using vocal cords to scream, they would've gone hoarse ages back. They might have snapped. But this is a silent scream. It goes on and on.

Again, I have no language, because I've been blinded to everything except the pain. Now that we're alone at last, Cairax

Murrain is making me pay for binding him in the Sativus. Lacking his usual tools, he's forced to use what he has at hand to torture me.

My memories. Memories of every scrap of physical, emotional, or spiritual pain I've ever suffered. Thirty-three years of agony.

I'm hurled across the room during an exorcism and my elbow breaks as I hit the far wall. I find the letter from Marie-Anne saying she's left me for Anselm. A tooth cracks as I bite down and the cold air hits the nerve. The flu wrenches my stomach and my throat convulses from food and bile going the wrong way. An excruciating hangover at nineteen. The bitter cold outside the womb. A sharp kick to the testicles six months before I die, followed by a rifle butt to the jaw.

And of course, again and again, the feeling of my flesh turning inside out when I use the Sativus medallion to take possession of Cairax's body. Every muscle in my body spasms. Horns tear through my forehead. New teeth shred my gums and lips. Talons rip open my fingertips. He appreciates the irony in this. What was torture for him is now torture for me. After my death I make the transformation tens of thousands of times more than I ever did in life.

After two months of screaming, or maybe three, he stops. I don't know why. When he talks to me, it's with the voices you hear in the back of your head. He speaks with the sound of imagined conversations and half-remembered dreams.

It shall give me great pleasure to destroy you for this disgrace, little soul.

I shout back, "No." My voice only sounds different because I want to be heard. In this place, in the state we're in, neither of us has a real voice.

To make one such as me a mortal plaything is a dishonor beyond measure. To sully the unholy titles of Cairax Murrain with acts of selflessness and charity. To make mortals cheer my name when they should shriek and cower and beg. Such a painful insult must be returned in kind.

I manage another "No" before he begins again.

My screams are the chorus for a symphony of pain that goes on for another four or five months without interruption. Almost half a year with every agony of my life on a loop. The tattoo needles stab down again and again. A kneecap shatters on my twenty-eighth birthday. Three fingers burn on the stove when I'm four. An absolutely gorgeous dead woman bites down on my tongue and tears it away. My skin crawls with infection while the straps bite into my wrists and ankles. My dog, Muggsy, hit by a car and dies in my arms when I'm nine. A broken nose in a bar fight. Marie-Anne tears away a clump of my hair for the doll and leaves my scalp bleeding.

Cairax stops again. The pauses let him enjoy the torture even more. He's a gourmand of agony, making himself wait so he can savor each sweet morsel of my pain. He breathes in my suffering.

You shall long for the feeble torment of this imprisonment. You shall look back at our time here together with such pleasure and happiness. These shall be the happy memories that sustain you.

My head is spinning from the lack of torture. It doesn't know how to work with the constant agony, but it's hit the point I'm having trouble without it. Part of me wants to give up and just accept it. On some level, I always knew this is how I would end up. Despite all my attitude and style, I knew nobody beats the house in the long run.

I don't beg. Begging will just make it worse. I don't know how it could get worse, but I know it will. "We both know this wasn't supposed to happen," I say. "This isn't my fault!"

Only the worst of craftsmen blame their tools for their failures.

But I sense there's a puzzle piece in front of me, one of the edge pieces that tells you how everything fits together. And Cairax hasn't seen it. There still might be a chance to get out of this.

Your cries shall ring out through the Abyss for ten times ten generations. My hands shall deliver unto you every pain and affliction and violation that has ever been known to man or beast. It will take you ten thousand years just to reach the brink of oblivion, and another ten thousand to fall in. And every moment of that time, my sole purpose shall be to make it worse for you.

I realize what he's missed. Or maybe what he didn't want me to notice. We're still here. Still trapped in a mass of rotting tissue by a short-circuited spell inked into my skin.

I manage a chuckle and Cairax glares at me.

What aspect of your future is so pleasing to you, dearest Maxwell?

"It's your future, too," I remind him. "And we're not there yet, are we? It's been, what . . . six months? Maybe seven?"

I feel the smile on his face. It's a terrifying expression, even when it's just a mental construct. Did I miss something else? Some detail that slipped past me? I decide to press on.

"Over half a year since we died," I say. "And no one's shot us in the head or disposed of us somehow. We're still both trapped in here. How long will you be able to keep this up? A year, maybe?"

He laughs. I want to drink bleach to clean out my head from the sound. His laughter just gnaws away at my essence, at my fabric of being.

Dearest little Maxwell, he tells me, *we have only been here together for a day now.*

And then he makes me start screaming again.

*　*　*

I don't know how long it's been. The rest of the day? Weeks? Months?

The only things left in my mind are memories of pain, and memories of memories of pain. There's no space for anything else. I can't remember a time when there wasn't constant agony racking every inch of my body and mind. I've lost all concept of what order my life happened in, because it's all dependent on the pain.

At some point, Cairax gets bored and decides to let me breathe for a few minutes. It's like pulling a burn victim from a fire and leaving them sitting on the ground. I've hit the point the lack of torture isn't any better than the torture itself. Even with the pain gone, I writhe and flail from a thousand aftershocks. I have an excess of agony to process before I can think.

Ahhh, the exquisite torture you have to look forward to in the Abyss. The eons we shall have together before your soul is rent and fed to the lesser reavers. And then . . .

"And then what?"

Cairax Murrain turns to me.

I've said the words without thinking. Now I need to think fast. "Then what?" I say again, trying to buy myself an extra moment or two.

And then I see it. It's like magic. Magic isn't on the surface, it's the ninety percent below water. I know how I'm going to get out of this.

"There isn't going to be anyone else," I say. "I'm the last soul you'll ever get."

His spines rustle like a buzzard ruffling its wings.

"I was right before. We're still in here. No one's put us down. And considering we'd be pretty damned dangerous as one of the walking dead, I think it's because there's nobody to do it."

Cairax stalks around me. He's angry, but the anger's not directed my way for the first time in . . . well, a long time.

"If we ever make it out of here," I say, "you're going home to a dwindling kingdom in the Abyss."

Your prattling tires me, dearest Maxwell. Your screams are such better company.

He raises a claw to begin again.

"Wait!" I shout. "Wait! What if we made a deal?"

Your gall is beyond measure. The jailer is willing to bargain when his prisoners free themselves and rise up against him. What could you possibly offer that could serve as compensation for the dishonor you have brought upon the name and title of Cairax Murrain?

But he's amused now. Interested. He thinks it can see where I'm going, but it wants me to say the words. That's how these things always go. Even when the deck's marked and they're holding all the cards, demons want it to seem like you're the one with the strong hand, you're the one controlling the game.

"The world," I tell him.

And there it is. A steel wheel, five-high straight flush. I can't think of anything he could have to beat this. This is how desperate I am. That I'd try this game with these stakes.

Cairax is caught off guard. At this point, most losers are promising to sacrifice six hundred and sixty-six people or some such idiot payment. It's where some of the world's best serial killers have come from. The demon's annoyed and interested I've offered him something else. Considering the circumstances, I hope he's more interested.

The rustling spines settle down. His talons tap together.

The world, as you have pointed out, is empty. It is devoid of all but the soulless ones.

"It's not empty," I say. "You and I both know that. There'll be survivors. Only a few millions, but they'll be there. And they could be all yours. Every living soul on Earth. It could be the Black Death all over again."

He makes a dry sound like the death rattle of a snake. He's sighing with pleasure at the memories.

And, assuming your terms were pleasing to me, what would we need to do for this, dearest Maxwell?

"Once this body is destroyed, the Marley will operate correctly. You'll return to the Abyss, I'll remain on Earth as a bound spirit. I can begin working to prepare a body for you. Depending on who survives, I may have the perfect one for you."

Or perhaps you will flee and try to avoid your debts.

I shake my head. "I can't flee. You know that. The Marley leaves me bound in spirit form. I can either stay a spirit or find a new body and die, which brings me right back to you."

We talk. We talk for a long time. I know how the game goes.

If I leave anything to chance or miss one loophole, this could all go wrong for me.

Eventually we stop talking. The demon mulls things over. I'm just starting to think he's going to reject my offer when he speaks.

This would seem to be a beneficial contract for both of us. Your terms are accepted.

I breathe a sigh of relief. I've done it. I've beat the devil.

And your offenses? How shall we balance the books on those?

"I'm offering you the world, Cairax Murrain. The goal of every fallen one and demon since the beginning of time. Surely such a gift makes up for any inconvenience I've caused you in the past."

No. It does not.

"I . . . I don't have anything else to offer."

Oh, but you do, dearest Maxwell. You can entertain me until this body is destroyed.

And now I'm screaming again.

Thirty
NOW

ST. GEORGE COULD lift almost seven tons under perfect conditions. Fourteen thousand pounds. He was strong enough to pick up a car if he could balance it, and move a semitrailer when he had the right leverage. He could snap steel aircraft cables without breathing hard. His fingers could crush brick and concrete and pavement.

He took a deep breath, gritted his teeth, and pulled.

The glistening red cords that held him weren't much thicker than shoelaces. They had no knots or fasteners. The lines looped around his wrists and ankles, barely tight enough to touch his skin. Max and the demon had him strung up between a streetlight and the signpost for a Trader Joe's on the north side of 3rd Street.

Smoke whistled out between his teeth. His eyes watered from the effort. His shoulders burned and his wrists screamed with pain but the thin lines didn't budge. He took a few deep breaths and tensed his shoulders again.

"Flex and strain all you like, my dear little hero," said the demon. Cairax's legs raised a little too high and reached a little too far, like a huge spider. It stalked across the road to stand face-to-face with him. "These are blood ties. They cannot be broken."

This close St. George could see the scaly texture of the demon's skin. The burning blue eyes locked on his, each one the size of his palm, and dared him to look away. It felt like a staring contest with a rattlesnake. The slitted nostrils trembled as Cairax sucked in air and exhaled on the hero. The monster's breath was hot. It reeked of disease and meat.

Max bent over the road with a dagger he'd pulled from his coat and put the final touches on the circle he'd scratched into the pavement. He straightened up to stretch his back. "Anyway," he said, picking up as if there'd been no interruption, "breaking Josh out was the easiest part. It's not like he needed much convincing, either. A bit of alchemy turned the cell wall to water vapor for a minute, he walked out, and the bars and mesh reformed behind him. No sign of anything being tampered with. I'm sure it drove Stealth crazy."

St. George risked looking away from the demon's eyes. "She knew he had outside help."

"Because nothing else made sense in her little worldview," said Max. "Your girlfriend has one big blind spot, George. She's inflexible. She can't think outside the box. The box she does think in is gigantic, I admit, but she can't put her brain outside it even just for a moment."

The sorcerer twisted at the hips, then leaned to either side and stretched his arms out. He bent over to scratch a few more Latin words along the edge of the circle. "After that it was just a matter of getting you alone out here, so Josh's escape killed two birds with one stone. Thanks for letting me paint all those sigils and agreements on you, by the way. It saves us about an hour and a half."

St. George tried to ignore him and looked at the demon. It gazed back at him with its saucer-like eyes. He was pretty sure it was smirking, but the forest of teeth made it hard to be sure.

"Josh," he said, "you've got to fight this. I know you hate all of us because of what happened, you hate the world because of what happened to Meredith, but you can't let—"

"You waste your final hour calling to your friend," said Cairax. The demon reached up and tapped its fingers against the crown of horns. They made a noise like the crack of billiard balls. "His lonely mind was broken long before what was left of it accepted our offer. He submitted to dear Maxwell's preparations, turned over his mortal form, and retreated to nonexistence with no resistance or second thoughts. Through me he found the end he has searched so long for."

The demon twitched a finger and the red cords holding St. George pulled tighter. Not much. Just another half inch. He felt it in his joints.

He managed to glare back at the creature. "Next you'll tell me your only weakness is wood," he said. "Before you know it you'll give your whole plan away."

"Such bravado," said Cairax. Its tongue darted out and snapped like a whip in front of St. George's face. "You are a credit to your namesake after all, my little hero, but soon your soul shall be my plaything. We shall see how brave you are then."

"Just try me."

Its tooth-filled mouth twisted into another grin. Fangs and tusks pointed in every direction. The demon looked over its shoulder at Maxwell as he scratched more symbols inside the new circle.

"It's easy to be brave when you're ignorant," said Max without looking up. "Believe me, if you had any idea what's going to happen to you, you'd be wetting your pants right now."

"Yeah?"

"Oh, yeah."

Smoke streamed out of St. George's nostrils. "Is that your excuse for siding with this thing? For betraying all of us? You're scared of what it could do to you?"

Max shoved the dagger into his belt and walked up to the bound hero. Cairax moved out of his way with one step of its long legs. The move was graceful and unnatural all at once. "Yeah," he snapped, "I am scared."

"You used to be a hero."

"I used to be a paperboy, too. So what?" He shook his head. "Let me tell you something, George. I know what Hell's like. I've seen it. I've felt it. And you know what?" He waved his arm over his shoulder, back in the direction of the Big Wall. "I will sacrifice *anything* not to go through that again. You, Stealth, Barry, Danielle, my parents, every girl I ever loved, every single person in the Mount—Cairax can have all of your immortal souls as long as it means I don't go to Hell."

St. George took in a long, slow breath. "You're a coward."

"No," Max shook his head, "I'm a realist. There's only so many ways this can go down, and they all involve a lot of people dying. I just made the choice not to be one of them. Like I told Stealth, I chose to survive."

"And that's the way it is?"

"Yeah," said Max. "That's the way it is."

"Then I don't feel too bad about this."

St. George exhaled hard, spraying fire down at the sorcerer. It was a good-sized cone, enough to cover the man from head to toe. The blast exploded over Max, and splashed out across the pavement. The flames lit up the street for a block in either direction. They burned for a few seconds and then sputtered out.

Cairax Murrain's hand stretched out in front of the sorcerer. The fingers spread wide in front of Max's face. A last few licks of fire danced on the knuckles and talons, like flies caught in a spiderweb. The demon closed its hand into a fist and the flames were crushed.

Max wasn't even singed.

The demon snorted and pulled its impossibly long arm back. It strode halfway across the street and snatched up an ex through the barrier. It spun the dead thing in its claws, plucking off arms and legs and then the head.

"That was foolish," said Max. "Even if Cairax wasn't here, I've got two different fire wards on me."

"Maybe I don't give up as easily as you."

"I didn't give up," said Max. "I made a deal."

"Come on," St. George said. "Do you think that thing's going to hold up its side of the bargain? After everything you've told us about it? What's going to stop it from killing you?"

"Well," said the sorcerer, "one is the contract. I've offered it a lot of prime souls in exchange for its leniency. A bunch of heroes. And a deal's a deal."

St. George glared at him.

"Two is that I'm going to be a lot harder to kill in about twenty minutes or so."

He wrinkled his brow at the sorcerer. "How so?"

Cairax Murrain picked up another ex, a dead woman, and tossed it from hand to hand. A chuckle slithered up out of the demon's throat. It caught the ex and scissored the woman in half with its talons.

Max waved a hand at his chest. "Stealth was right. This isn't much of a cheat. Jarvis was in pretty good shape, but in five or ten years I'll just need another body. Unless I found a better one sooner than that. One that was strong, almost completely invulnerable, and would last a hundred years or so with no problem."

He gestured at the circle and symbols he'd been scratching into the pavement, then looked the bound hero in the eye.

"That's where you come into the deal, George."

Thirty-One
NOW

ON A GUESS, said Zzzap, *maybe over there?*

He pointed to the southwest. Even in the unlit night, the clouds piled up black over that part of the city. They flickered with sparks of light. Distant thunder echoed across the city.

Zzzap hung in the air above the corner of the Big Wall, just south of the After Death church. Stealth, Freedom, and Madelyn were on the platform below with half a dozen guards and First Sergeant Kennedy. Cerberus stood in the street behind them.

"I estimate it is centered over La Brea Avenue," said Stealth. "Somewhere between Third and Wilshire."

Looks like your boyfriend lives in the corner penthouse of spook central, if you ask me.

Captain Freedom cinched the strap of his glove around his wrist. He'd shrugged off the leather duster in favor of his full combat gear. "Are you sure about this, ma'am? The rest of the Unbreakables are on alert and ready to go. We can have them assembled here in five minutes."

Stealth's head shook inside her cloak. "A small group gives us our best chance of success while still leaving the Mount protected. The Unbreakables shall stay behind with Cerberus."

The armored titan made a noise that might have been a grumble, but nodded.

Freedom nodded down at Madelyn. "And she's coming because . . . ?"

"The exes do not sense Madelyn because of her unique nature," said Stealth. "This invisibility extends to items she is wearing or carrying. From what Maxwell has—"

"Corpse Girl," said Madelyn. She pulled her mouth into a tight line. "I'm the Corpse Girl now."

"From what Maxwell has said," continued Stealth, "Cairax Murrain's senses are similarly tuned to living things. Corpse Girl's trip to North Hollywood supports the premise that her invisibility also includes the demon, which means there is a good chance it does not know we have the sword. She will carry the sword and perhaps give us an element of surprise. At the least, she will still be able to help control the exes in the area."

Madelyn gave a sharp nod. She pulled her camo cap from her coat pocket and tugged it down over her hair.

Ummmm, I hate to once again be the voice of reason in these discussions, said Zzzap, *but if Max has been lying about everything else, why do we think he was telling the truth about needing the sword to kill the demon?*

"Maxwell is clever enough not to overcomplicate his story with unnecessary lies," said the cloaked woman. "He believed we did not have the necessary tools to destroy Cairax Murrain, so there was no danger in telling us the truth."

Cerberus's armored head swiveled to look at her. "That's what your whole strategy is based off? That's kind of thin."

"If you prefer," said Stealth, "I can tell you that we have no other options and that the 'thin' path is better than taking no action at all."

The titan sighed and shook its head.

"I can get behind the overcomplicated idea," said Madelyn. *I love this plan.*

"From what he told us, though, even with the sword, it seemed like a long shot," Freedom said. He adjusted his helmet and pulled the strap across his chin. "The better play might be waiting here behind the protective seals."

"Assuming the seals even work," said Cerberus. "If all of this was a plan to get Josh and the demon together, the seals might just be clever graffiti."

"We have more than just the sword," Stealth said. "Based on the information Maxwell gave us, I believe we have all the requirements needed to kill the demon."

* * *

Stealth and Freedom went from rooftop to rooftop. She moved in graceful bounds, her path traced through the air behind her by her flowing cloak. He attacked the air, every leap and landing a show of brute force and mass that shattered roof tiles.

Madelyn had another bicycle to help her keep up. One of the guards at the Corner platform had "volunteered" it. It was in much better shape than the one she'd ridden out to the Valley. She swerved around the shambling exes and tried to keep an eye on the two figures moving across the rooftops. She kept one hand on the sword. It was still tucked in her belt.

Zzzap flitted back and forth, keeping them all well lit. The ink-black clouds blotted out the sky and reminded him of a hero named Midknight who'd died during the uprising. Then he'd died again when Zzzap reduced the hero's animated corpse to ash. It wasn't a pleasant set of memories.

They had to go through the broad expanse of the Wilshire Country Club. It would take too long to go around. It meant a quarter mile of open ground with nowhere to hide. "No firearms," Stealth told Freedom, "and no energy blasts. We must maintain silence."

Freedom and Zzzap both nodded. Madelyn let her bike drop to the sidewalk. The cloaked woman flipped up and over the vine-threaded fence, and the captain leaped after her.

Zzzap hovered over the chain-link while Madelyn worked her way up the fence. As she got near the top, he passed his hands through the barbed wire and the coils melted away with a few sparks and sizzles. "You couldn't've just made a hole through the fence," said Corpse Girl with a smile.

Hey, he told her, *the more fences there are in L.A. these days the better.*

They plowed ahead. Zzzap's brilliant form attracted every ex on the golf course. Madelyn ran ahead, shoving exes or tripping them. They were halfway across the green plain before the undead became too numerous for her.

Stealth made a quick movement with her hands and her batons swung into the ready position. "Keep moving," she said. "Time is of the essence."

Captain Freedom lashed out with his fists. Even his glancing blows sent exes staggering back. Stealth's batons swung back and forth, up and down. Skulls and necks shattered around them.

Zzzap tried to clear a path for them and swung his hand at an obese ex. He missed severing its head. The fat of its jowls sizzled and the zombie turned into a pillar of fire. The burning flesh spit and popped, and the flames swelled as the dead man's T-shirt caught fire.

Madelyn leaped away from the fiery ex. Freedom stepped forward and drove his boot into its chest. The overweight dead man staggered back and tumbled over. It kept burning as it struggled to get back to its feet.

Another rumble of thunder blasted across the greens. To the southwest, they could see lightning twist in the dark clouds, as if it didn't dare reach down to the ground. A cold wind dropped down out of the sky.

This doesn't look good, said Zzzap. *I should run ahead and buy us some—*

"No," snapped Stealth as she brought her baton across an

ex's jaw. "We must stay together. Timing is essential if our plan is to succeed."

Freedom dropped a dead man with a wide backhand, then grabbed a dead woman by the head and twisted her neck before she could react. "Just keep moving," he said. An ex grabbed his arm and bit down, but the Kevlar weave of his jacket stopped it from breaking the skin. He slammed his fist into its forehead and it fell to the ground. "If we stop they'll overwhelm us."

Madelyn put her hands on an ex's chest and tried not to think about the fact she was touching the dead woman's boobs. She pushed hard, knocking the ex back into another one behind it, and then catching a third in the shoulder. The zombies dominoed, five of them crashing to the ground.

Zzzap made another pass and heads vanished off a dozen exes. One of the skulls popped like an overboiled egg. Their bodies dropped.

The far fence of the country club came into view. A hundred yards to go. The heroes smashed, tripped, kicked, and punched their way across the last stretch.

They reached the fence and Stealth vaulted up and over it. Three quick swings with her batons put down the trio of exes gathered on the other side. A few more leaps took her to the roof of a nearby house.

Freedom lifted Madelyn up by the arms, put one hand on her ass, and hurled her over the fence. She flew through the air and landed on top of the house near Stealth. The cloaked woman grabbed her by the wrist. A moment later Freedom hit the roof next to them. The tiles shattered and they heard a beam crack beneath him.

The shadows shifted and Zzzap hovered above them. *Okay,* he said, *now for the hard part.*

Thirty-Two

NOW

ANOTHER RUMBLE OF thunder echoed across the city as Max finished his circle and stepped back. "This should do it," he said. He glanced over his shoulder. "Sorry, George. Time for you to go."

Cairax Murrain turned to them. A pile of dismembered exes had grown near the demon. The heads still shifted and twitched. Their lack of leverage muffled the *click-click-click* of their jaws. "At last," it said. "Claim your prize, dearest Maxwell, and then both sides of our contract have been fulfilled."

Smoke poured from St. George's mouth and nostril. The tattoos were tingling under his shirt. It felt like they were moving. "You don't want to do this, Max," he said. "I know you're better than this."

"Sorry," the sorcerer said. "I guess you don't know me."

St. George scowled and sucked in a little more air.

Max shook his head. "Don't waste your time. It still won't do anything."

"It'll make me feel better."

"If I cared how you felt, I wouldn't be trading your soul to a demon. But, if it helps, your body will change just like this one did. I won't be tricking anyone into thinking I'm you or any of that sort of—"

A shot rang out and the air blurred by Max's head. Something appeared near his temple, a small lump of gleaming metal. Two more reports echoed across the street. St. George could see the trails as the rounds slowed down and came to a halt.

Max turned and plucked one of the bullets out of the air. "Well," he said, tossing it aside, "I guess the cavalry's shown up after all."

Stealth leaped off the pet store, her cloak billowing out behind her. A Glock thundered in each hand and half a dozen rounds traced their way to Max. She hit the ground running, and another six rounds led the way.

The sorcerer held up three fingers and the bullets dropped to the pavement.

Cairax Murrain stretched up to its full height and stepped forward. "Ahhh, how truly wonderful," the demon said, "the star-crossed lovers, reunited for the end. George Bailey, trying to live up to the impossible example of his parents, and Karen Quilt, desperately running away from the legacy of hers."

Stealth froze, just for a moment, and Cairax beamed its shark's smile at her. It pulled back a massive talon to swat the cloaked woman and a brilliant light from above washed the darkness away. The demon looked up and blinked its leathery eyelids.

Zzzap had one hand out. The air rippled around his brilliant palm for a moment and then a burst of energy struck Cairax in the face. It splashed off the monster like the spray from a garden hose. The demon roared and swung at the gleaming wraith. Zzzap flitted away and fired another energy blast.

Stealth raced past them and dove at Max. The sorcerer cut his hand through the air and a tornado blast of wind sent her hurling away. She hit the pavement near the line of exes, rolled, and threw herself back at him.

Max brought his hand up again, but before he could gesture the Glock spun in her fingers and smashed down on his knuckles. He yelped, stepped back, and Stealth drove both of her boots into his chest. She flipped over in a whirl of cloak and Max flew back to crash against a Honda.

Stealth looked up at St. George. "Are you unharmed?"

He nodded. "I might be two inches taller, but other than that, yeah."

She holstered one of the pistols and a black-steel blade appeared in her hand. It lashed out twice, but the red cords binding St. George resisted. Her face shifted beneath her mask and she brought the knife down hard on the line.

"I think they're magic," he said.

Stealth turned with her pistol out and fired two shots at Max. The bullets clattered to the ground between them. The sorcerer slashed his hand up and the cloaked woman was hurled into the air.

St. George breathed out more flames, but Max waded through them. "Don't get your hopes up," he said. "I told you, there's only one way this can end." He pushed his sleeves back up and yanked open his shirt. The tattoos on his chest and arms were blurred, as if they were trembling on his skin.

He marched after Stealth.

* * *

Zzzap dodged another claw and hit Cairax with two more blasts. A nearby car caught fire, but the demon's skin just steamed like a wet sidewalk on a hot day. Getting hit with enough raw energy to superheat steel didn't seem to be slowing the thing down at all.

It was time to try something drastic.

Zzzap steeled himself for the wave of nausea that always came when he touched solid matter in his energy form. He dipped a little lower in the air. Cairax Murrain's talons lashed out and ripped through his side.

The claws passed through Zzzap and left the gleaming

wraith shuddering in the air. It wasn't just the churning stomach he usually felt. It hurt. A lot. He let out a cry like a hiss of steam and static. The pain left him dizzy and lightheaded and cold. Guts open to the air cold, if he had to guess. He glanced down at his hands and saw his fingers blur into a thick shape at the end of his arm.

The demon raised its talons. The skin was charred and smoking, but the fingers flexed without effort. They filled out and healed as it studied them. "Not accustomed to being touched, are you, crippled one?"

Its tail sliced up through the air.

Zzzap dodged the tail and pushed himself higher into the air, out of the demon's reach. His head spun. He focused on his hands and tried to get his fingers to re-form.

Cairax reached over and picked up a dust-covered motorcycle. It could've been a toy. The demon swung its arm back and whipped the bike up at Zzzap.

He spun in the air and dodged it, but Cairax had already grabbed an oversized pickup truck. The vehicle went up over the monster's head with a squeal of metal and rust. Zzzap thought about blasting the truck, but he was still fuzzy.

Captain Freedom landed between them. His boots rang out against the pavement and kicked up a cloud of dust. His arm swung up and leveled his monstrous sidearm at Cairax.

About time, said Zzzap, clenching his hands into fists. *I've been going easy on him so you'd have something to do.*

"John Carter Freedom," said the demon with a grin. "What a pleasant surprise. Such a deliciously bright soul. So proud despite the many, many lives lost in your name. What hope does such a failure of a man have against me?"

Freedom set his jaw. "You'd be surprised."

Lady Liberty roared. A triple blast of white flame exploded against the monster's chest and knocked it back. Cairax Murrain shrieked and the truck crashed to the ground. The huge officer leaped clear and fired another burst, catching the demon in the side.

Cairax fled, a flailing, squealing mass of long limbs and thrashing tail. Freedom stalked after it. The pistol thundered again and again. The monster stumbled away, arms up to deflect the blasts that tore chunks of flesh from its body. When the weapon ran silent, the captain let the drum drop free and pulled another one from his belt.

What the hell? said Zzzap. *Are those napalm rounds or something?*

Freedom shook his head while he reloaded. "Blessed ammunition," he said just before the demon's claw caught him in the chest. The huge soldier flew back and slammed shoulder-first into a tree trunk.

Cairax straightened up and snarled at the huge officer. "For that, your skin shall be my victory sash," it growled through gnashing fangs. "And you have my word you will live to see me wear it."

* * *

St. George watched Stealth empty her pistols at Max. The rounds spun off in random directions or dropped to the ground. She attacked with her batons and they sparked off the air around the sorcerer.

Their fight carried them away from the bound hero. St. George took another breath and pulled hard on the cords. They were the immovable object to his irresistible force.

"Hang on," someone called. "I'm coming."

He looked over his shoulder. Madelyn pushed through the crowd of exes. Even more of them had been drawn to the sounds of battle. At least three hundred of them crowded Max's barriers on the north side of the street. None of them reacted to the dead girl shoving them out of the way.

She got to the barrier and stopped. Her brow wrinkled, and for a moment she looked like a bad mime working with a wall.

"What's this?" she called over to St. George. "Some kind of force field?"

He nodded. "It's keeping the exes out."

Madelyn frowned and leaned into the barrier. "Good thing I'm not one of them, then," she said.

"I think you can go over it," he said. "The others did."

Her pale fingers stretched wide and she pushed harder. Her hands inched forward. She took a heavy step, the movement of a deep-sea diver, and then another. On her third step she stumbled forward and grabbed the side of a car before she fell over. The sword tucked through her belt clattered against the body panels.

"Once again," she said, "Corpse Girl for the win."

She loped over to where St. George was strung up. "You can't break these?" she asked, looking at the lines. She tapped one holding his leg and rubbed her fingers together.

He shook his head. "Magic. Something to do with blood."

"Gross." She grabbed the cord and pulled. It didn't budge. She swung her legs onto the line, hung on it, and heaved her hips a few times. It didn't even quiver.

* * *

Zzzap flew past the demon and gave Captain Freedom a quick once-over with infrared, X-rays, and the visual spectrum. There were three red lines across his chest where the demon's claws had shredded his body armor, but the huge officer didn't have any broken bones, and Zzzap didn't see any of the hot spots he associated with internal bleeding. The man was built like a Mack truck.

He heard Cairax stomping up behind him. He spun, and put some distance between himself and Freedom. Cairax reached for him and he put a blast of heat and light into the demon's eyes.

Cairax Murrain didn't blink. It lashed out with its talons

and followed through with a swing from its tail. The stinger tore through the air and missed Zzzap by inches. He let off another bolt of raw power that singed the demon's horns.

The monster laughed at him. The needle-like teeth sounded like knives being sharpened. "Poor little cripple," it said, "do you think your pale heat is anything compared to the fires of the Abyss?"

Apparently not, said the gleaming wraith. *So I guess there's no reason to hold back.*

He threw both palms forward and the night turned to high noon.

The blast washed over the demon like a tidal wave. The pavement around it turned to liquid tar and boiled away. A manhole cover melted to slag. So did a nearby car.

Freedom threw his arms across his face. So did Madelyn. St. George clenched his eyes shut and felt the heat of a sunburn on his face. Even Stealth and Max paused.

The world turned white as light and heat poured out of Zzzap. The paint on the buildings caught fire, and then the concrete itself. The air roared. A dozen nearby exes charred and collapsed into dust that was whipped away by superheated winds.

When it was over the wraith sagged in the sky for a moment. His brightness faded. Then he seemed to take a deep breath and straighten up in the sky.

What was left of Cairax Murrain swayed back and forth in a crater stretching across four of the street's six lanes and part of the sidewalk. Steam boiled from a few long-dead sewer pipes that glowed red-hot. The gravel and sand beneath the road had fused into a glassy surface.

The body was a twisted thing of gristle and charred bone. Three of the horns were blackened stumps. One eye had boiled away, the other had taken on the dull hue of an ex. The molten floor of the pit had cooled around its ankles. Zzzap wasn't sure if the faint hiss was breathing or the sound of sizzling meat.

Then the scraps of muscle bubbled and expanded. Flesh wrapped around the skeletal frame. A new eye swelled up and filled the empty socket.

Son of a bitch, said Zzzap.

Cairax Murrain shook its head as the last patches of purple skin healed across its frame. The floor of the crater shattered as it pulled one leg free and then the other. It looked up at the gleaming wraith and its face split in a grin of tusks and fangs. "A valiant attempt, my poor little cripple," it hissed, "but this is such a marvelous host Maxwell has found me."

The demon stalked forward, its long legs carrying him up and out of the pit.

* * *

Captain Freedom tossed aside his cracked helmet. He knew he'd never get another one in his size—double extra large was custom headgear and there were no more quartermasters. He shook his head, blinked a few times, and glanced around. The arm of his coat was singed and smoking. Zzzap was fighting Cairax Murrain—the demon had Regenerator's powers, all right. And then Freedom saw what he wanted by the rear tire of a truck.

He snatched up Lady Liberty. There was no sign of the drum he'd been loading. Depending on where it had landed, the whole thing might've cooked off during Zzzap's light show. He pulled a fresh one from his belt. He only had one more drum left after this one. Half his ammo gone already.

The drum locked into place. Freedom leaped into the air and his boots slammed into the demon's back right between the shoulder blades. He grabbed one of the long spikes running down Cairax's back to steady himself and slammed Lady Liberty's muzzle against the scaly neck.

He pulled the trigger and the demon roared. The twelve-gauge rounds, blessed and anointed by the last known priest left in the world, ripped huge gouges out of the purple flesh. The kickback was enormous. No firearm was meant for continuous point-blank fire. A normal man would've lost fingers to the bucking weapon, and possibly shattered his wrist.

Then Cairax reached up and wrapped its spidery fingers around Freedom's arm. The demon twisted the huge pistol up and away. The captain held on to the spike for a moment with a steel-like grip, but the demon tore him away. It pulled Freedom off its back.

Freedom dangled by his arm for a moment, then lashed out with a kick that cracked two of the demon's teeth. He pulled his boot back and lashed out again with his heel. It connected, but the demon pulled him away, holding him at arm's length.

Cairax's wounds were already healing, bubbling shut. New teeth pushed up through its gums to replace the broken ones. "Tell me, bright little soul," it said, "how does it feel to fail yet again?"

"I'm with the U.S. Army," snarled Freedom. "We don't know how to—"

The demon slammed the huge officer into the ground and flung him away. Freedom smashed into the charred remains of a bus and tumbled to the pavement next to the glassy crater. He didn't move.

Then Cairax turned and glared up at Zzzap. Cold flames boiled out of its eyes. "This game bores me, little cripple. It is time to end it."

* * *

"Oh, God," said Madelyn as Freedom crashed into the ground.

"Get back," St. George told her. He thrashed at his bonds again.

"Hold on," she said. "I'm going to try cutting them with the swor—"

"No, get back!"

Madelyn looked up and saw Max racing at them with Stealth right behind him. The dead girl twisted to get behind St. George, but the sorcerer had her by the wrist. She swung around and punched Max in the nose. He snarled and wrenched her arm back behind her. Madelyn fought but he grabbed her other shoulder and dragged her around to block Stealth.

"Back off," he snapped. His tattooed hand came up and he pressed his palm against her throat. Two of his fingers curled under his hand to touch her collarbone.

Stealth halted a few yards from him. Momentum carried her cape forward to wrap around her and swipe at Madelyn's legs.

"I'll break her neck," said Max. "Internal decapitation. You're fast, but I can sever her spine in half a dozen places before you reach me. She'll be an undead quadriplegic."

Madelyn tried to twist away but he pushed her arm up even farther behind her back. It was a sharp pain that made her dead nerves spike into life.

Stealth's batons spun in her hands and collapsed. She slotted them back into their holsters. Another flick of her wrists and the Glocks were back in her hands.

Max put pressure on Madelyn's arm and placed himself a bit more behind her. "You have no idea how desperate I am," he said. "Don't try anything."

The cloaked woman's fingers moved between her pistols and her belt as she exchanged spent magazines for fresh ones. She did each weapon one-handed. It was the quick, effortless motion of someone who'd practiced something thousands of times and then done it a thousand more. She never looked away from him.

"Let her go, Max," shouted St. George.

"Drop the guns and step away," the sorcerer told Stealth. "I'm counting to three, and if you haven't I'm going to—"

Her left pistol came up and shot Madelyn three times in the chest. The dead girl's eyes went wide. So did Max's.

"What the hell?!" shouted St. George.

Max let go of Madelyn and staggered back. Blood stained the front of his shirt. He tried to speak and coughed up a few dark red drops.

"She was already dead," said Stealth.

Madelyn wheezed twice and reached up to touch her chest. "Okay," she squeaked, "that felt really weird." Air whistled out of the holes in her shirt when she spoke. She poked a finger at one of them.

Stealth stepped past the dead girl and swept Max's wobbly legs out from under him. He hit the pavement and coughed up more blood. She reached down, pushed his arms out of the way, and pistol-whipped him across the jaw. One of his teeth skittered across the pavement and he slumped.

The cords holding St. George turned to liquid. He hit the ground as they splashed on the street. He shook his wrists and took a few awkward steps. "You okay?"

Madelyn looked up from her bloodless wounds. "Yeah," she beamed. "Try telling me this isn't a superpower."

He looked at the cloaked woman. "Kind of risky."

"Not at all," said Stealth. "His abilities are most likely some form of psychic projection. It stood to reason their effects would cease if he lost consciousness."

"Yeah," said St. George. "About that . . ."

The clicking of teeth rose up over the sound of Zzzap's superheated energy bolts. Hundreds of exes shuffled across the line of Max's barriers. Their jaws snapped open and shut as they headed toward the heroes.

Thirty-Three

NOW

CAPTAIN FREEDOM SAT up and felt something flare in his side. A broken rib, maybe two. Fractured at the very least. He'd had enough of them over his career to know the feeling.

The sky flared with blue lightning and he heard the clicking of teeth beneath the rumble of thunder. Whatever had been keeping the exes off this city block had vanished, and now they were shambling toward him. Out of the corner of his eye he saw some of them stumble toward the demon. Cairax was swatting Zzzap and didn't seem to notice.

Freedom risked a glance behind him past the glassy crater. Stealth and Madelyn had St. George free. The sorcerer was down. They were about ninety seconds from being overrun with exes themselves.

Lady Liberty had maybe five or six rounds left in her, plus one drum on his belt. He didn't want to waste the ammunition on the undead, but he also wasn't sure how much longer he'd need to hold off the demon.

The first of the exes closed in on him. It was a noseless man in a gore-splattered lab coat, a former doctor or scientist. Then Freedom saw the grocery store name tag and realized the dead man had been a butcher. The ex reached for him and he grabbed both its wrists in one hand. It bent its jaws to his knuckles and he cracked its forehead with one punch. He swung the withered body around and hurled it at Cairax Murrain.

The demon was still looking in his direction, even while fighting Zzzap. The knife-like talons lashed out and caught the corpse in midair, slicing it in half.

Freedom looked at the approaching wave of undead. The cracked ribs flared as he turned. His legs flexed and he hurled himself away from the crater.

As he landed a dozen exes reached the edge where he'd been. They tumbled in. The first few hit the glassy floor with the loud cracks of breaking jaws and noses. The dead made no attempt to break their fall. Some of them crawled away before the second wave fell on top of them, but not many. In a minute the pit had become a mass of undead limbs and chattering teeth.

Three other exes reached Freedom. He lashed out with his massive fists, breaking teeth and skulls and glad for his Kevlar gloves. The zombies dropped around him, but there was a small pack of six or seven headed his way. Two of them wore bloodstained police vests, even though only one was wearing a uniform.

There was another hiss of superheated air from off to his left. Cairax Murrain was saying something to Zzzap, but Freedom couldn't understand it over the sounds of shuffling feet, clicking teeth, and sizzling pavement. He glanced right and saw St. George scoop up the sorcerer's body.

Freedom pulled out Lady Liberty and fired off two bursts at the pack of exes, emptying the drum. He aimed low. The shells blew out knees and shattered shins. Four of the zombies collapsed, and two more fell on top of them. It gave him a few moments, but there were still more coming.

Stealth caught his eye as he reloaded. It was hard to be sure with her mask and cloak, especially in the dark, but the woman seemed to be staring at him. She made a series of quick gestures and Freedom realized she was using Army Field Manual hand signals. And at least two unique to the Unbreakables.

She repeated her instructions. He signaled his under-standing.

* * *

St. George leaped into the air. He set Max down on the roof of Trader Joe's. The sorcerer was safe from exes, but he'd die if they didn't get him to a hospital soon.

"You can't beat it," wheezed Max. A few drops of blood came up with the words. He looked pale. "You don't have the tools."

"I guess we'll see."

Max shook his head. It was a loose gesture without much control behind it. "No chance," he muttered. "Why bother?"

"Because if we didn't try," St. George said, "we'd be no better than you."

He floated down to the ground. Madelyn and Stealth held their own against the swarm of exes. The dead girl tripped and shoved the exes as they got close. The cloaked woman had her batons out and battered skulls and jaws.

St. George ripped a parking meter out of the sidewalk. He spun it once in his hands and then swung it like a bat. The lump of concrete at the end crushed half a dozen exes into jelly. The impact sent another dozen flying back. He glanced over at Freedom battling more exes and Zzzap dodging the cars Cairax threw at him. "I hope the plan went past getting me free," he said over the *click-click-click* of teeth.

"It does," Madelyn piped up. "You just need to grab the demon."

"Sorry, what?"

"You must distract Cairax Murrain," said Stealth, "and then pin it so it cannot move."

St. George swung his oversized club again. The weight of the concrete bent the pole in the middle. He sent it spinning into the exes. "I don't understand."

"And it needs to be facing me," the cloaked woman added.

"Are you serious?"

"There is no time to explain," she said. She whirled and drove her heel through the jaw of a dead construction worker. "You must trust me."

He nodded. "Got it." He glanced down at his bare arm and the cobweb of scars stretched across it. "Taking on the demon again."

St. George rose into the air, took a deep breath, and hurled himself at Cairax.

*　*　*

Zzzap still felt cold. Most of the effect of the demon's claws had worn off, but there was a chill at the center of the energy form. He wondered if it was all just in his head, then realized when he was Zzzap everything was just in his head.

Freedom leaped up to the roof of a car. The back half of the vehicle was melted to slag, a victim of Zzzap's megablast. He leveled his huge pistol at the demon.

Then St. George shot forward and tackled Cairax. They tumbled across the street, over a low wall, and struck the corner of a Ralph's grocery store. The brick facade crumbled around them and a few last shards of glass in the picture windows dropped and shattered on the ground.

The building exploded in flames as St. George poured fire onto the demon. Scraps of paper bags and cardboard signs ignited around them. When Cairax tried to push its way out of the rubble, St. George punched it twice in the face. He seized two of the demon's large horns and slammed the creature's head down into the floor again and again. He found a chunk of concrete ribbed with rebar, raised it up, and smashed it over the demon's skull.

Cairax lay still just long enough for the hero to relax. Then St. George caught a backhand with enough force behind it to knock over a bus. He sailed into the intersection, bounced twice off the pavement, and crashed into the side of a street sweeper.

The demon stalked out after him. "This is most welcome," Cairax hissed. "My defeat at your hands was a gnawing insult. How pleasant it will be to right those accounts."

Zzzap blasted the demon in the chest. Freedom hit it with two bursts from Lady Liberty. Cairax glared at them, cringed away from Freedom's shots, but didn't slow its march toward St. George. Blue flames sparked behind its teeth as it roared.

The hero was waiting for it. St. George tore the door off the street sweeper and flung it at the demon. The amount of raw force behind his throw made up for his lack of finesse. It struck Cairax in the shoulder, sprayed dark blood across the pavement, and knocked the monster back a few feet.

Freedom leaped over a dozen exes to land on the roof of an SUV. It crumpled under his impact. He winced as his ribs shifted in his chest.

Zzzap circled around to the monster's far side and let his feet drag through a crowd of the dead.

St. George yanked the plastic seat out of the cab and hurled it at Cairax. The demon put up a hand and shattered it in midair.

The plastic shrapnel sprayed back over Captain Freedom, and he threw up an arm to protect his eyes. When the rain of fragments stopped and his arm came down, the demon's tail was a foot from his neck. He spun and the barb tore at his shoulder instead of his throat, but the move made him slip on the uneven roof of the SUV. He grabbed the closest thing he could. It was rough and scaly, even through his glove, and writhed in his grip. When the scorpion tip whipped up he let Lady Liberty tumble away and grabbed the tail with both hands.

Cairax glared over at the huge officer and St. George slammed a fist into the side of the demon's head. It was like punching a statue. He threw two more punches, scratching his knuckles on the barbs and horns covering the creature's skull.

The demon hissed at the hero. Its tongue snapped out between long teeth and lashed at St. George's face. It drew blood at his temple. The long arms lashed out in wide swings, but the hero soared back and out of reach.

Stealth charged forward. Her batons cleared a path through the exes. She leaped into the air, sheathed the batons, and drew both Glocks as she landed next to Freedom on the SUV. Bullets tore through the meat of the tail.

Cairax shifted its hips and its tail slashed through the air, yanking Freedom off the SUV and away from Stealth. The tail smashed the huge officer against the pavement, then flipped him into the air. Freedom's hands slipped and he spun into the sky, then back down.

It met him halfway. The barbed tip speared him in the side, just under the ribs, and the impact knocked him back into the air again. He slammed against the roof of a bus and the recoil tumbled his body down the street and into the crater full of exes.

The barbed tail curled around Cairax like a snake. A good six inches of it dripped Freedom's blood. The demon chuckled.

A tall ex, a dark-skinned man with a bullet-ridden torso, reached across the roof of the SUV for Stealth's leg. She stomped down on the dead man's hand, pinning it to the roof, and then shattered the wrist with a swipe of her pistol. A snap kick sent the ex stumbling back into the swarm. She looked back up and bullets tore through the air, pinging off Cairax's horns and teeth.

St. George grabbed a Mini Cooper and heaved it into the air, but the door ripped off the frame and the car tumbled out of his hands. It crashed to the ground on its side and sprayed glass across the street. He shook his head and lunged at Cairax again. He drove his knuckles into the demon's chin hard enough to shatter the bones of a normal man. His next punch could've crushed cinder blocks. He locked his fists together and brought them down with enough force to dent steel.

Cairax dropped to one knee. Its tail twitched and trembled.

St. George stood in front of the demon—still taller on its knees than the hero—and grabbed one of the horns growing from its skull. He slammed his fist into the monstrous face again and again. Then he seized another horn and launched himself upward.

St. George dragged Cairax into the sky. The demon's long limbs flailed at the air for a moment and then it laughed. The sound almost made St. George lose his concentration, and they dipped for a moment.

Cairax reached up and clawed at the hero's chest. The talons gouged his flesh and set his nerves on fire. He gritted his teeth and tried to ignore the wetness spreading across his body. He went another thirty feet into the air, spun the demon around, and hurled the creature at the ground. Cairax plummeted down and the pavement cracked under the impact.

Zzzap flew up to hover by his friend. He nodded at the slashes on St. George's chest. *You okay?*

"I'll live," he said. "How about you? You look a little pale."

That thing can take some serious punishment. I've burned up half my reserves.

"Are you going to be okay?"

I'll be fine, but I don't think I can do anything else big if we're going to pull this off.

"Pull what off?"

Just get him pinned. This is going to be so awesome if he doesn't kill us all. Whoops.

Zzzap pointed his hands down and blasted Cairax Murrain as it leaped up at them. The demon pushed through the blast, like a shark forcing its way through a wave, but the heroes had flown higher into the sky. Its claws swiped at the air below them and it plummeted back to the ground.

The demon landed hard, crushing a trio of exes beneath its hooves. It roared up at the two heroes, crouched to leap again, and white fire exploded in its eyes. Cairax howled and stumbled back.

Stealth braced her leg and fired Lady Liberty again. The pistol was huge in her hands, a cut-down combat shotgun with nowhere to hold on. She had one hand on the grip and the other in front of the drum magazine to steady it. The trigger stayed down and Lady Liberty bellowed her magazine at the demon. The shells burst into white flame against the dark flesh of Cairax's face and chest, like flares in the darkness. The demon threw his claws up and staggered back.

St. George dropped out of the sky and drove his heels into Cairax's skull. He wrapped one arm around the thick neck and hooked the other under the beast's shoulder. He couldn't reach far enough for a half nelson, but he grabbed one of the demon's long spines and held tight.

The huge pistol ran dry and Stealth let it drop. She spun to her left and held out her hand. Her fingers went wide to catch their target and signaled to Madelyn to—

Madelyn was nowhere to be seen.

Thirty-Four

NOW

CAPTAIN FREEDOM STRUGGLED to his feet. He remembered riding in the back of a cargo truck in Afghanistan where the crates slid and shifted under his feet. Standing in the crater was like that, except the crates kept reaching up to drag him back down.

He was in a lot of pain. If his ribs hadn't been broken before, they were now. He'd heard people say pain felt like needles or blades, but anyone who'd felt real pain knew it was a screw. It kept twisting deeper every time you thought it was done. His side was filled with white-hot screws.

Where the tail had skewered him, he felt his pulse and wetness on the inside of his jacket. Half of his torso had a faint chill that reached into his arm and was working its way up his neck. Even with his basic first-aid training he knew it wasn't a good combination of feelings.

The floor of the crater shifted again. A dead hand reached up to grab at his knee. He bit his lip, drove his heel down, and heard bones crunch beneath him. He kicked at a few exes grabbing at his legs. A dead woman with a patch of bare skull tried to gnaw on his boot and knocked out its own rotted teeth. A mangled, genderless thing caught its fingers in Lady Liberty's empty holster and made Freedom stumble for a moment.

Half the exes in the crater had made it to their feet. He

slammed his fist into one, then brought his arm around to bat-
ter away another. It flew back, taking two other exes down with
it, and Freedom felt the burning screws in his ribs sink a little
deeper. He gritted his teeth.

The pause gave a dead woman with matted hair the chance
to grab his arm. He could feel the teeth through his combat
uniform, but the material held. A quick shake knocked the ex
off. A pair of arms wrapped around his leg, and he let his fist
swing down like a hammer.

Even as that ex dropped, another one grabbed him by the
waist. Its withered arms squeezed tight enough to set off the
fire in his ribs. He turned to shake it off and the screws tightened down even more. The dead man made a wet noise as it
slipped away and white spots danced in the captain's eyes.

The wet noise hadn't come from the ex. The side of his uniform was soaked in blood from his armpit to mid-thigh. The
wetness hadn't gone away. He'd just gone numb. Shock. He was
going into shock.

He battered away another dead man and struggled through
the growing crowd of exes. He just needed to finish the mission.
He had to get to the demon.

Then he could rest.

* * *

Madelyn ran to her high point. The sword bounced and swung
on her hip. An ex stumbled into her path and she elbowed it
out of the way. She was supposed to climb the remains of the
street sweeper. She needed to be high up and close enough so
she couldn't be blocked when she saw Stealth's signal.

She pulled herself up into the cab and swung her legs
around onto the hood. A quick twist and she crawled over the
windshield onto the roof. It wobbled under her weight.

There were exes everywhere, more than she'd ever seen before. A thousand of them, at least. The sounds of the fight were

drawing them in from all over the city. The clicking teeth and the rumbling clouds drowned out almost everything.

St. George dragged the monster up into the sky where Zzzap waited. Stealth was on the roof of an SUV, right where she said she'd be, with the big shotgun-pistol Captain Freedom called Lady Liberty. And Freedom was . . .

Then she saw him, covered in blood and vanishing beneath the swarm of exes in the crater.

There was a sound like a falling redwood as Cairax hit the pavement. She glanced at the fight and back to the huge captain who'd been friends with her dad.

Madelyn leaped off the street sweeper and ran to the crater, shoving exes as she went. Throwing herself into the pit was just like stage diving, at least from what she'd seen on TV and in movies. She dragged herself though the crowd, pushing and shoving and kicking at the exes. It was a struggle. They all wanted to get to Freedom as much as she did, maybe more.

She jumped into the air and kicked off a dead man's hip. It got her close enough to grab Freedom around the neck. She threw her legs around his waist and pulled herself tight against him.

He winced and his eyes went wide. "What are you—"

"Trust me," she told him. She pressed her body against his and squeezed with her legs. She could hear his heart thumping through his body armor. He was cold. She could feel his blood seeping through her jeans and into her coat and tried not to think about it.

The exes slowed their frantic pawing. Their grips loosened and their dead gazes drifted away. The chattering teeth moved away from Freedom. The ones on the edges of the mob wandered off. The closest ones bumped against him a few times before stumbling away.

Madelyn smiled. "Welcome to my world," she said.

"Finish the mission," he told her.

"We're going to. Come on." She loosened her grip on him

and shifted her weight so she could slide over his shoulder. He put up a hand to help her. A moment later she was riding piggyback on his broad back.

He wheezed, but didn't cry out. "Where to?"

"Get me to the far side of the street," she said. She shook her hips and the sword swayed on her belt. "I need to be able to hand this thing off to Stealth."

* * *

Cairax Murrain rolled its shoulder and broke St. George's half nelson. The hero fell away and a shrug from the demon knocked him back. Cairax turned on him with a growl.

St. George went to throw a punch and an ex snagged his arm. The zombie bit down on his wrist and its teeth crumbled against his skin. He shook it off in an instant, brought his fist around, and Cairax's tail wrapped around his throat.

The thick rope of muscle heaved him into the air. It wasn't strong enough to choke him, but he couldn't get enough leverage to pull it loose. He focused on his shoulders and tried to haul Cairax back into the air, but the tail shook him hard and dragged him back down.

Cairax pulled him close. The demon's teeth whisked against each other as it spoke. Its breath smelled like rotted milk. "If dear Maxwell dies," Cairax said, "it may save your soul, but your heart shall still be my feast."

"I hope you choke on it," he gasped over the tail.

Gunfire echoed behind the demon and it turned with a growl. As the horn-covered head turned, St. George saw rounds spark off the jutting points and one of the wider tusks. It sounded like someone with a machine gun.

Stealth stood on the roof of the SUV, her Glocks firing in each hand. They ran dry and she let the magazines tumble into the crowd of exes below. The guns spun in her hands, her fingers danced between grip and belt, and she was firing again. Bullets sprayed across the demon's face like heavy rain.

Cairax took a few steps toward her, and her guns hit empty again. Its hooves thudded against the pavement and trampled a dead woman beneath them. It brushed a trio of exes out of the way with a sweep of its arm.

Then it glanced down.

The three exes had wrapped their arms tight around its long forearm. Each one held on without biting, or even gnashing their teeth at the air. They glared up at the demon.

"You ready for round two, *pinche pendejo?*" they asked in unison.

Cairax had time to snarl before the exes pounced on it. The tide of the undead shifted as all the exes in the area charged the demon. A dozen grabbed its other arm. A platoon's worth of them tackled its legs while a score more threw themselves on the tail. They swarmed over the demon like ants on a lion.

Three dead people sank their fingers into the coil holding St. George and yanked at it. They loosened it enough for him to get his hands in. He pried the tail open and dropped away. St. George took in a deep breath.

An ex loomed over him. It had been a heavyset man with a goatee, dressed in a filthy tee and wool cap. "Your lucky day, dragon man," growled the corpse, "'cause I actually hate this fucking thing more'n I hate you."

St. George nodded. "We need to hold it," he said. "Stealth needs a clear shot at its chest."

The ex nodded and hurled itself onto the demon's back. Over a hundred dead people clung to the monster, burying it beneath their bodies. They shifted to expose its bony chest.

St. George leaped into the air, soared over the demon, and landed next to Stealth. "I think Rodney just gave us our edge."

"Agreed."

"Ready to tell me the big secret plan?"

"Symbolism," she said. "We have the sword and an arch-angel."

"What?"

"A creature of radiance and will, shaped in God's image."

The phrasing stuck in George's head for a moment. Then Cairax Murrain lashed out with both arms and dozens of exes went flying. The barbed tail skewered three and shook them off. It reached up and seized the dead woman who'd wrapped herself across its eyes.

"Stealth!" someone shouted.

The cloaked woman turned. So did Cairax Murrain. Captain Freedom slumped on a car near Madelyn. She was on the roof, holding the sword over her head.

The demon's saucer eyes squinted as if it was trying to focus on something. Then it snarled.

It could see her.

"Hold the demon!" snapped Stealth.

St. George hurled himself through the air. His boot slammed into Cairax's face, knocking the demon's head back into a small tree. The monster tried to bite down on his leg but only tore the heel off his boot. Cairax swung one arm at him and glared at the hero.

The Corpse Girl tried to remember everything she'd seen in pirate movies about throwing swords. None of it seemed instructional. In the end she just swung her arm back and hurled the weapon in Stealth's direction.

As the hilt left her hand Cairax's eyes got even wider. It hissed through its forest of tusks and lunged forward. Another dozen exes stumbled forward and threw themselves at its hooves. They grabbed at its calves and thighs.

St. George grabbed the demon's arm and twisted it back. The odd proportions made it hard to use leverage, but he got the claw up behind the spike-covered back again. The spidery hand flexed in front of his face and the movie *Aliens* flashed through his mind.

All at once George knew why "in God's image" sounded familiar. It was a phrase from the Bible. It was what people always said about humanity.

The blade spun through the air like a propeller. Stealth took three steps, reached up, and snatched the whirling saber out of the air halfway between Madelyn and the demon. Her fingers shifted on the grip and she pulled it back over her shoulder. For a moment she was a statue. Then she hurled the sword at Cairax Murrain like a javelin.

Light flashed between them. A sonic boom cracked the air. Zzzap placed himself between Stealth and the demon.

A creature composed of radiance and will, shaped in God's image.

A man made of light and thought.

Zzzap reached out an arm so his palm was blistering the creature's hide and hoped he wasn't about to die.

The sword melted the second it touched the gleaming wraith's shoulder. The blade dissolved into a stream of steel and silver. The intricate engraving blurred together and was gone. The leather grip incinerated, a small cloud of ash that vanished in a swirl of superheated air. Almost a third of the sword boiled away to vapor and broke apart in the furnace that was his body, reduced to mere atoms.

For Zzzap it was every type of discomfort his mind could pull up as an analogy. Having something physical inside him, even just for a tenth of a second, was past nauseating—it was agony. It was food poisoning and charley horses and getting kicked in the nuts and broken bones and smoke inhalation all at once. He sensed the sword's path, right where Stealth said it would be going, and forced his arm to stay up with his fingers spread.

The stream of molten metal shot from his palm. Free of his internal fires, it shed heat into the air around the demon. Inertia shaped it into a gleaming icicle of steel as it crossed the open space.

The sword in Zzzap's hand punched through the demon's skin and slid between two ribs. Smoke poured from the wound as it pierced Cairax Murrain's heart. The blade slid even farther, and used the last of its momentum to bury itself in the bone plates of the monster's back.

Cairax Murrain roared. It was a howl of pain and anger and frustration and fear that shattered glass and made eardrums bleed. The demon threw off the exes holding its arms and lashed out at Zzzap. The talons tore through the wraith with a sizzle and a loud crack. It thrashed and howled and hurled St. George across the wide street.

Zzzap stood there with his arm extended as the sword boiled away around his palm. The jagged piece of steel never moved. It was solid in the air between Zzzap and Cairax Murrain. White flames shot from the demon's mouth. The wound sparked and flared and caught fire. The blaze started to build and swell around the demon.

St. George saw Stealth dive behind a truck. Madelyn tugged Captain Freedom down behind a car. The exes were still throwing themselves at the demon. They were laughing even as the flames charred them down to the bone.

St. George closed his eyes and crossed his arms over his face.

Everything went white. There was a sound he felt more than heard. And then nothing.

Thirty-Five
NOW

SOMEONE VERY FAR away pushed on his shoulder and called a name. They kept pushing and calling. It echoed down to him and he recognized it. "St. George?"

He regretted it. Admitting he knew his name meant consciousness. Consciousness brought a lot of pain with it.

The face over his was pale, with chalky eyes framed by ragged hair. He pulled his hand back to strike before he recognized the Corpse Girl. Her dark hair hung down, shadowing her face and making unfamiliar lines.

"Don't be a jerk," Madelyn said.

She helped him sit up. His knuckles ached. His chest itched and burned where the demon's claws had raked his flesh. He was willing to bet the wounds were infected.

He looked at her. Her coat had sizzled away, and her jeans and shirt were singed. Charred in places. So was her hair. One of her arms and part of her face were burned.

He nodded at the arm. "How are you?"

Madelyn nodded. "I'll be fine," she said. "I think Captain Freedom's really bad, though. He's got broken bones and a fever."

St. George stood up. The last of his leather jacket crumbled away like burned parchment. The tattered shirt below wasn't much better off, but it held together for now. He hobbled when he walked, and remembered the demon had bitten one of his boot heels off.

A wide spiderweb of white ash stretched across the street. It covered cars and the cracked pavement and the bony remains of hundreds of exes. The dust hung in the air like a white haze. He looked up at the moon, lighting the whole scene. The dark clouds were gone.

They were halfway to Freedom when St. George saw the black boots stretched out beneath an ash-whitened truck. He grabbed the chassis and flipped the truck up. What was left of the tires broke apart and the battered Chevy crashed onto its side.

Stealth's cloak wrapped around her like a shroud. Parts of it had burned. He could see glimpses of dark skin where her bodysuit had been torn or charred away.

He set his fingers against her wrist to check for a pulse. She grabbed his arm and pulled herself up, the knife in her other hand aimed at his own throat. The blade scraped off his Adam's apple before she stopped herself.

She took a few ragged breaths. A third of her mask was gone. He could see her cheekbone and the smooth line of her jaw and the edge of her lips at the corner of her mouth. "You survived," she said.

"Yeah," he said. "We did."

She wrapped her arms around him and allowed him to lift her up. She settled on her feet and took a few cautious steps. "I appear to be uninjured."

"Good."

Madelyn waved them over to Freedom. The huge officer lay on the far side of the street, sheltered by the car the dead girl had dragged him behind. His hand wrapped over the bloody wound in his side. His breathing was ragged.

St. George looked around. "Try to find Barry," he told Madelyn.

She nodded and darted away. Stealth followed her.

He crouched and set a hand on Freedom's forehead. It was burning hot. His eyes blinked open and he looked at the hero. "I take it we won, sir."

"Seems like it," said St. George. "You look like crap, Captain."

"I think the demon's tail might've been poisonous. And I've lost a lot of blood."

"Can you walk?"

"No idea."

St. George helped the big man to his feet. He swayed for a moment, then fell against a car. "I think I'll wait here, sir," he coughed.

"Zzzap's alive," Madelyn called from a few yards away. "And he's . . . uhhh, naked."

"That's normal," said St. George. "Are you sure you're okay?" he asked Freedom.

"I've had worse."

St. George glanced around for something to cover his friend as he made his way across the rubble. He didn't have much left in the way of clothes himself. Pretty much everything that could burn near the demon had burned.

A few yards from Barry was the center of the spiderweb. Dozens of long bones lay there in a heap. A distorted skeleton, like the remains of a dinosaur. Scraps of charred flesh hung on the long bones. A long shard of gleaming metal stood between two ribs. It was the only thing not covered in dust.

Stealth tapped the horned skull with her boot and it fell free of the pile. It looked swollen and round. The sockets were too large. The jaw bristled with teeth like daggers. The spine dragged after it, bound together with threads of gristle.

Barry sprawled on the pavement. His dark skin was covered with ash. St. George remembered the ghastly look from 9/11 footage. The hand that had held the sword was still spread wide open, as if it had cramped that way.

Madelyn's fingers danced down her shirt and she shrugged out of her flannel. Her bra and her skin were the same shade of white. She draped it across Barry's lap. The other man's eyes fluttered as she did.

Barry looked up at them. "You guys are still alive?"

"Yeah," said St. George. He kneeled. "Barely."

"Am I still alive?"

"I hope so. We don't need any more ghosts."

Barry nodded. "Cairax?"

St. George tilted his head back toward Stealth. "You got him."

"Wow." He started to relax, then his eyes snapped open. "Oh, crap," he said. "Crap, crap, crap."

"What's wrong?" Madelyn asked.

"Are you okay?" St. George tried to check his friend's body and wondered what he wasn't seeing.

Barry's eyes were wide with terror. "I can't feel my legs. I think . . . I think I'm paralyzed."

St. George looked at his friend for a moment, then burst out laughing. Madelyn giggled. Barry kept the act up for another few seconds before a grin broke out across his face.

"Well, damn," Barry said after a minute of laughter. "I always wanted to do that."

"Do what?"

He smiled at them. "I think we just saved the world."

* * *

St. George stood up to join Stealth and saw the exes.

At least three hundred of them stood halfway down the street, near the crater. They stretched across La Brea Avenue, blocking it, at least four or five rows deep. Their arms were crossed. Their jaws didn't move. He glanced over his shoulder and saw a similar line behind them, and one in either direction on 3rd Street.

They were surrounded.

"I have no ammunition," said Stealth. "I assume the captain is incapacitated. Is Zzzap well enough to fight?"

"Maybe," said St. George. He did a double take and stared at her face. The hole in her mask had vanished.

"Focus, George," she said.

"How did you—"

"I carry a spare mask in my belt." She tipped her head to the line ahead of them. "Be ready."

One of the exes marched forward. It had been a tall, lean black man once. Two fingers were missing off its left hand. A gaping hole in its side was clogged with ropy lengths of meat that had probably been intestines before they were hit with a shotgun blast. It had both eyes, and St. George could see Legion's expressions behind its face.

The ex stopped ten feet away from them, just past where the spray of ash and dust ended. St. George rolled his fingers into fists. He felt Stealth tense next to him.

"Could kill all of you fuckers right now," said the dead man. The fingers of its mangled hand curled into a fist, then went loose again. Its jaw shifted side to side.

The heroes didn't move.

The ex shook its head. "You got an hour."

St. George waited a few moments. He let a few curls of smoke twist out of his nose. "Meaning what?"

"Got an hour to get back behind your Wall," Legion said. "Nothing'll bite until then. After that, you're on your own."

"Just like that?" said St. George. "After all this time, you've got us down and beat and you're just walking away?"

"No," said the ex. "*You're* walking away. I'm lettin' you."

"I do not believe you," said Stealth.

"The fuck do I care if you believe me or not?"

St. George looked the dead man in the eye. "Why?"

Legion waved the mangled hand at the web of ash. "I ain't stupid. *El demonio* here was gonna trash my city. You helped stop it. Gets you a pass. One time only."

St. George and Legion stared at each other for a moment, and then the hero nodded. "Okay," he said. "Thank you."

"Yeah, fuck you, too," said the ex. "Last thing I want is to owe you anything."

"One hour, then," said St. George.

Legion grunted at the hero and glanced at Stealth.

She crossed her arms. "This changes nothing."

"Damn straight."

"You are a murderer."

"Take a look in the mirror, *puta*," the ex snorted. "We're all killers. I just killed people you liked more, that's all."

The dead man turned and walked away from them.

"And what happens next time we're outside?" called St. George. "We'll just go back to trying to wipe each other out?"

Legion looked back. "Guess you'll find out," he said. "You got an hour."

The dead man's face went slack and it stumbled on its next step. But its jaws didn't move. The lines began to break up and the silent exes staggered off in different directions.

St. George looked at Stealth. She stared after the dead man. "Now what?"

"Captain Freedom requires medical attention," she said. "Zzzap, Corpse Girl, and I will make our own way back to the Big Wall. If Legion keeps his word, we should have no problem reaching the South Gate within an hour."

"And if he doesn't?"

"We shall find a secure location and await your return. For now, you should get the captain to the hospital."

"Yeah," said St. George, nodding. "He was looking pretty . . . damn it."

He hurled himself into the air and headed back to the Trader Joe's.

* * *

The puddle of blood around Max wasn't as wide as St. George expected, but he was still pretty sure the sorcerer was dead. The man's skin was as white as Madelyn's, and his chest was soaked in red where the bullets had punched into him. He didn't move at all as St. George landed on the rooftop.

Then he shook and coughed up a spray of red. His eyes fluttered and he looked up at St. George. "Ahhh," he croaked. "So . . . you won."

"Yeah."

"Congrat . . ." He coughed again and flecks of blood came out of the holes in his chest.

"Save it," St. George said. "I'm going to get you to the hospital."

Max's head trembled side to side. He raised his hand an inch and tried to wave the hero back. "No," he wheezed. "Done this enough times now."

"You have another cheat lined up?"

Another minimal shake of the head. "I'm done. Glad . . . glad you killed him."

"Is this your deathbed conversion?"

The sorcerer managed a weak smile. "Was on your side all along."

St. George shook his head. "Sorry. I don't buy it."

"Why'd I . . . Why'd I tell you how to kill him, then?"

He looked at the dying sorcerer.

"Every word I said . . . almost every thought I had . . ." Max paused to suck in some air and the chest wounds wheezed. It was a wet sound. ". . . had to convince one of the nine lords of the Abyss I was on his side."

"I wish I could believe you," he said.

"That's . . . that's the trouble with the real world, George." He took another wheezing breath. His last one. "Good and evil are never . . . that black . . ."

Max let the air out of his lungs. St. George waited a moment, making sure the man was gone. He left the body on the rooftop.

* * *

Madelyn reached down and tapped the gold band on the skeletal finger. It swung back and forth. She shivered. "Do you think he's really dead?"

Stealth looked at the skeleton. "Cairax Murrain or Regenerator?"

The dead girl rubbed her arms. "I don't know. Either of them?"

"I believe the demon has been killed or banished."

"And the . . . the other guy?"

The bones of the arms and legs looked shorter. The teeth in the skull were still long, but not the tusks they'd been just a few minutes earlier. The horns were little more than lumps across the frontal and parietal bones. It might've been a trick of the dim light from the moon. Or maybe some aspect of the possession wearing off.

Stealth shook her head. "We do not know the upper limit of his healing ability. He may, in fact, be dead. It is also possible he will be fine by morning."

"Wow," said Madelyn. "Is that . . . that's good, right?"

Stealth's boot lashed out and caught the skull right at the base. It snapped off the spine and spun twice on the ground, away from the pile of bones. Her foot whipped forward again and sent the skull sailing down past the intersection of La Brea and 3rd. It hit the pavement with a loud crack almost twenty yards away, right at the entrance to a furniture store parking lot, and skittered south even farther. It settled in the gutter in front of a ransacked yogurt shop.

"Just to be safe," she told Madelyn.

First Impressions

THEN

I WAS DOWN in Venice. I don't go there often. I'm not a big swimmer, and I've never surfed once. As the Mighty Dragon . . . well, there's a lot of wind coming off the ocean. Even with the cape-wings, I can't really glide down there, so my mobility gets cut down. It all just becomes exaggerated hops. And it makes me feel kind of silly. Yeah, I'm hopping fifty or sixty feet at a time, but it just seems undignified for a superhero to be bouncing around.

But there'd been some weird stories coming out of Venice over the past month. People said a monster was stalking the boardwalk. I'd seen a news report saying it was a giant purple dinosaur (and, wow, did Fox make a lot of lame jokes about that). A few homeless folks who'd seen it said it was one of the aliens from the Sigourney Weaver movies.

I knew of four heroes who'd taken up in L.A. There was me. There was the guy with the headgear, Gorgon. There was Midknight. And there was the ninja-Batgirl woman. I'd caught her watching me one night while I dealt with some muggers, but she was gone by the time I finished with them.

I generally worked around my home. Hollywood, Los Feliz, a bit of Koreatown. Midknight was out in the Valley, Burbank usually. Gorgon was over on the west side, Beverly Hills and

West Hollywood. The ninja-woman stayed around downtown and the Rampart district, but sometimes I'd hear stories of her in other parts of the city.

No one covered the beaches. So after the fourth or fifth report of the monster, I decided to check it out. I drove over, parked in a corner of that big lot right at the end of Venice Boulevard, the one before the beach, and changed into my costume in the backseat. I figured enough surfers probably changed in and out of wetsuits there that I wouldn't draw too much attention, even at night in December.

It's kind of silly, I know, but it surprised me when I learned the Venice Boardwalk was made of concrete. It's just a big sidewalk. You hear "boardwalk" and you just think . . . well, wood. I thought the whole thing would look like the Santa Monica Pier.

Anyway, I was coasting around in the sky as best I could and came in for a landing on one of those tall apartment buildings right on the waterfront. A few homeless people saw me and pointed. I'd been doing this for almost six months now. People tended to recognize the costume by this point. One guy with a shaggy beard saluted.

Then I heard the wail. Somebody in a lot of pain. They yelled again and I saw a few of the people on the boardwalk scatter.

A few steps launched me through the air and north along the beach. The wind knocked me around. I went maybe twenty or thirty yards and managed to land on a shop without slipping off and crashing.

The cries were clearer now, but as I tried to pinpoint them they shifted. New voices started yelling. And they were scared. I was hearing screams, not yells.

I got a better sense of where it was coming from, about two blocks away down the boardwalk, and just as I did three teenagers came running out of an alley. Three boys. They were gang age, but weren't wearing any colors. What they were wearing looked a little too high-end for gangs, too. All just a little too shiny and new. I wasn't an expert on footwear, but I was pretty sure those weren't Payless sneakers.

Whoever they were, they were terrified.

I stepped off the rooftop to soar down to street level.

The last kid was maybe a yard out of the alley when something reached out after him. At first I thought it was a spear or a board. Something long and thin that somebody'd thrown after them. Then the end split open and wrapped around the kid's head like something out of a horror movie. The arm yanked him back into the alley.

I was halfway to the ground. I shifted my cape and glided toward the alley. The other two kids ran below me. One of them gave me a glance, but they never looked back. The closest one smelled like piss.

I ran over to the alley. It took a second for my eyes to adjust to the gloom and see what the arm was attached to. I was right. It was something out of a horror movie.

On a guess it was maybe nine or ten feet tall, but it was tough to be sure because it was hunched over. It was more or less human-shaped, but the proportions were off. It was too tall and thin, like a person who'd been stretched out on a rack and stayed that way. It made every step and swing of its arms seem unnatural. It had a tail that looked like a cross between a dinosaur and a scorpion.

Its head looked like a fish. One of those deep-sea fish with the huge eyes and teeth so long it could barely close its mouth. Half a dozen stubby horns circled its scalp like a weird crown or something.

It had the third kid by the ankles, hanging him upside down so the boy's eyes and its were level. Its tongue was out, this long thing like a snake. It was poking the kid on the nose. The kid was bawling, almost drowning in his own snot. There was a glossy stain on his jeans and it was creeping into his shirt as it followed gravity.

"Hey," I shouted. "Put him down, whatever you are."

I felt stupid as soon as I said it. Monsters don't generally understand English. It was going to take a bite out of the kid if I didn't hurry up.

But it didn't. It turned to look at me. Its eyes shifted and it bared even more teeth.

And then it spoke.

"Well, well, well," it said. It had a deep, cultured voice. If I didn't know better, I'd think it was that old British actor, Lee something, who'd been in *Lord of the Rings* and *Man with the Golden Gun*. "The Mighty Dragon," it continued, "what a wonderful surprise this is. Please believe me when I say I am a great admirer of yours."

It flipped the kid in its hand—a huge, long-fingered hand, like its arms ended in spiders—and set him down on his feet. He ran as soon as his shoes were on the ground. I let him race past me to get clear.

The monster took a step toward me. I noticed it was wearing a silver necklace, some pendant or something, the size of a half-dollar. Its claw-tipped fingers wiggled with excitement. "I must say, what an exquisite cologne you have on," it said. "What is that scent?"

I took a step back. Then another one, out of the alley. "I don't know what you're—"

It followed me out onto the boardwalk. It wafted the air around its face and took in a deep breath through slitted nostrils. "Ahhh, of course," it rumbled, "now I recognize it." Its back curled and it leaned its head down toward mine. The pendant swung back and forth on its neck. Its mouth split in a toothy grin. "Fear."

I was a little freaked. It's one thing to be fighting street gangs and pitching in on Amber alerts. It's another when some CGI nightmare slithers out from between a few garage-stalls.

In retrospect, my reaction was a little . . . well, comic-book, I guess. I mean, he could've been a stranded alien or something.

I didn't know. I just saw this big nightmare thing loping down the alley at me talking about fear.

So I punched it.

It hurt. Whatever it was, it was a lot more solid than it looked. It staggered back a few feet, but the tail lashed around to help it keep its balance. It reached up and felt its jaw, just like a person would. Its fingers were all stretched out, too, with big claws on the tips. I bet it could've palmed a car tire.

I braced myself for it to charge and felt the tickle in the back of my throat that meant I had fire waiting.

For a moment its face twisted up in a scowl. Pure rage. I was about to die. No doubt in my mind. But maybe I'd keep it from hurting a few more folks.

Then it took a deep breath and let it out through the forest of teeth. "Ahhh," it said. "Forgive me. I do sometimes speak out of turn."

"What?"

It stood up straight, or as straight as it seemed able to do, and bowed. "Allow me to introduce myself. I am Cairax Murrain, infernal viscount of the Abyss, Reaver Lord, and newly arrived hero of Los Angeles." Its tail thrashed at this. It took a chunk out of one of the concrete trash cans that dotted the boardwalk.

I was still a little confused. I think I said "What?" again.

"We fight the same battles for the same cause, oh Mighty Dragon," it said. "When I adopt this form, all my strengths and powers are set to the causes of truth, justice, and so on and so forth."

I risked a glance over my shoulder. "What were you doing with the kids?"

The monster shook its head and made a clicking sound with its tongue. "Such a shame," it said. "The bourgeoisie youths releasing their primal instincts on a helpless drunkard."

It gestured behind it. A homeless man with a bloody face

was curled in a ball. While I watched he glanced up at the thing looming over him. He shook his head, whined, and buried his face deeper in his arms. AA was going to have a new member in the morning.

"A nonviolent lesson was in order," continued the monster. "Fear is such a wonderful deterrent, and whets the appetite as well. Although," it said, striking a thoughtful pose, "was I all that different as a boy? Or is that just Cairax adjusting how I see my own memories?"

I wasn't entirely sure what it was talking about, but I thought I was starting to get the gist of it. "You . . . you're a person? A human being?"

"Indeed. Hidden within this frame is one of the greatest sorcerers of our generation."

"Okay," I said. I guess as back stories went it was interesting. "What was your name again?"

"Cairax Murrain."

"Cairax," I echoed. "Sorry about, y'know, the punch. I just saw a monster with a kid."

"Of course," said Cairax with a dip of his head. "Although, what is it they say about first impressions?"

"You only get one chance with them?"

The monster grinned. "So often, they are correct."

Epilogue
NOW

ST. GEORGE HUNG in the air over the water tower. It wasn't the highest point inside the Big Wall, but it was familiar to him. He needed a good dose of familiar.

It had been two nights since Cairax had died or been banished or whatever. St. George had flown Freedom to the hospital. Stealth and Madelyn passed through the South Gate of the Big Wall forty minutes later, and ten minutes after that the exes were banging their teeth together again. There hadn't been a sign of Legion since then.

His own wounds were healing. As he'd learned the last time he fought the demon, his immune system was powerful enough to handle any disease he encountered. Dr. Connolly took a trio of blood samples this time. "Who knows how long it'll be before something breaks your skin again," she said.

Freedom was still in intensive care. His ribs had been set and taped, and he'd received several transfusions. Freedom's massive frame held over fifteen pints of blood, and he'd lost more than six. His soldiers had lined up to donate. Even the ones who didn't match his type insisted on donating to the slowly growing blood bank.

He was racked with disease. Connolly was pretty sure Cairax Murrain's last gift to Freedom was a fast-acting case of the bubonic plague. The huge officer was in quarantine with three different IVs filling him with fluids and antibiotics. St. George had wanted to try a transfusion, to see if his blood would help Freedom fight off the disease, but he was the wrong blood type. "Besides," Connolly told him, "I'm not entirely sure your blood wouldn't treat his whole body as an infection."

Last St. George had heard, she was prepping an ice bath to bring the captain's temperature down but expected him to make an eventual recovery. "It would've killed anyone else by now," she said, "but the man's got the constitution of a bull elephant."

The sun came up seven hours early and bathed the water tower in brilliant light. St. George's musings vanished with the darkness. *I thought I might find you here.*

"Hey," he said. "What are you doing out of the chair?"

I asked Stealth if I could come talk to you.

"And she said yes?"

Yeah. Most folks are already asleep, and there's hours of battery life.

"So," he asked his friend, "what's up?"

I just wanted to say good-bye.

St. George smiled. "You flew over here to tell me you're going back to Four?"

No, George. I came to say good-bye.

A faint chill shimmied down St. George's back. "What do you mean?"

Now that I know what I am, I realize I'm not supposed to be here.

"What?"

Zzzap tilted his head back and looked out into space. *It's time to return to my place in the heavens. Time to embrace my destiny.*

"Barry, what the hell are you talking about?"

Good-bye, George. You've been a good friend. I'll miss you.

"Wait, you can't be seri—"

The gleaming wraith shot up into the sky, a falling star in reverse. In an instant he was one pinprick of light among thousands. Another star in the night.

And then he was gone.

St. George stared up into the sky, his jaw still open, unsure what had just happened. The after-image of Zzzap still burned his eyes. He shouted his friend's name, then yelled it again over their private radio channel.

No response.

He sank down and the heels of his new boots clanged against the roof of the water tower.

Then a bolt of light shot down out of the night and halted in front of him.

Nah, I'm just screwing with you, said Zzzap.

"You bastard," said St. George. "I think I just had three different heart attacks."

Let's be real. This place would fall apart inside of a week without me.

"So you don't think you're an archangel now?"

Oh, hell no, said the gleaming wraith. *Last thing I want is to be a religious figurehead. Plus, isn't there a law or a commandment about impersonating God or something like that?*

"Maybe the one about false idols?"

Yeah, that sounds about right. Besides, I was just a good symbolic representation of an archangel, not the real deal.

They hung there for a moment, looking down at the city. So many people had moved out when the Big Wall was done, the population of the Mount itself had dropped to almost nothing. It was clearest at night, when they could see how few lights there were at the center of their square mile of city.

So, Zzzap said. *Maddy Sorensen's really the Swamp Thing, huh?*

"What?"

Swamp Thing. "Anatomy Lesson" by Alan Moore?

"I have no idea what you're talking about. Is this another television show?"

No, said the wraith. *Well, yeah, but that's not what I'm . . . You know what, forget it. It's not my fault you've got huge holes in your education.*

"Fine."

I was referring to the fact she's ninety percent nanites or whatever she is.

"How'd you hear about that?"

Dr. Connolly told me about it while I was getting checked out after we got back. We were talking about Freedom and Dr. Sorensen, and then Maddy came up.

"She's supposed to be keeping it a secret."

Zzzap nodded. *She is. I think she just figured since I was one of the cool kids I'd be hearing about it sooner or later.* He turned in the air and looked northwest, toward the hospital. *Are you going to tell her?*

St. George shrugged. "I don't know. This is up there with 'you've got cancer' or 'your wife is dead' or that sort of thing. I think if we decide to tell her it needs someone better trained than me."

I think it's probably better if it comes from you.

"How do you figure?"

You know she's got a huge crush on you, right?

"What?"

Yep.

"Ignoring the twice-her-age thing, I thought she was into Freedom."

The gleaming wraith shook his head. *He's the big brother she always wanted. I think he's fine with that, too. It's letting him deal with that rucksack of guilt he's always carrying around. You're the one she's having schoolgirl dreams about.*

"I doubt it."

George, trust me. One thing life in a wheelchair has given me is amazing powers of perception regarding when women are interested or thinking of you as a friend.

St. George chuckled. "Great."

That's how I can tell Stealth's really in love with you.

"What?"

I mean, I could tell at dinner, I just hadn't figured out who she was. But she's crazy about you, George.

"Thanks," he said. "I needed to hear that right now."

Thought so.

"One question, though."

Shoot.

"If your powers of perception are so fantastic, why'd it take you so long to realize it was her?"

The gleaming wraith shifted in the air a bit. *Honest truth?*

"Sure."

I know this sounds a little wrong coming from me, but . . . well, I always figured Stealth was white under the mask.

St. George laughed.

You know, probably some uber-blonde like Tricia Helfer or Rebecca Romjin. I wasn't expecting Zoe Saldana's hotter, older sister. It kind of threw me, that's all.

"I think I thought that for a while, too," said St. George, "and then it just didn't matter what she looked like."

A voice crackled over his headset. Zzzap's head tilted, watching the radio signals buzz through the air. "Hey, boss," said the voice. "It's Makana over at the East Gate. You on?"

He turned in the air and tapped his mic. "Go for St. George."

"That you and Zzzap up there on the tower?"

The gleaming wraith waved to the east and let off a pulse of light. "Yeah, it's us," said St. George. "What's up?"

"We've got kind of a thick patch of exes over here, heading up to the Corner. We're not cleared for shots, but I was wondering if you'd want to come thin them out a bit?"

"We'll be right over," said St. George. He looked over at his friend. "Want to go throw some zombies around?"

Mindless violence against the undead? said Zzzap. *Count me in.*

The two of them shot into the sky, heading east.

Acknowledgments

Three books in, and people are still interested in a handful of superheroes I made up in fifth grade. This is a source of constant amazement to me. My thanks to you for reading this far, and hopefully past this.

Of course, I couldn't've made it this far on my own, and for this book I owe a collection of thanks to a number of people . . .

David found the Ex-Heroes series a new home at Broadway Books, and in doing so he made sure you're all going to be seeing a fourth book somewhere not far down the road, and possibly one more after that as well.

Matthew talked with me a lot about religion, faith, and the Bible. I'm not a very religious person myself, but I also didn't want to be writing thin parodies of religious people. Any mistakes or offenses on this front are entirely mine.

Sam and Sara helped me make sure Maddy didn't sound too much like a guy in his forties writing about a girl in her teens. Also, once again, thanks to John (aka Professor Tansey of the Otterbein University Department of Chemistry), who traded a lot of e-mails about nanotechnology with me and made sure I wasn't writing about little robots that looked like mechanical insects or spaceships. Corpse Girl owes a debt to all three of them.

Laura, Thom, and Carrie all talked to me a bit about tattoos. Meredith told me lots about removing them.

Claudia and Mindy helped expand my vocabulary where Spanish profanity was concerned.

John, Larry, and CD all read early versions of this book and helped make sure no one else had to see most of those early mistakes and stumbles.

Julian at Broadway Books forced me to stay on my toes and made sure that—even though we were dipping into magic—things still followed logical rules and reasons.

Last but by no means least, many thanks, as always, to my lovely lady, Colleen, who listens calmly while I insist this latest project isn't going to work, reminds me that's what I say every time, and then tells me to get back to work. With love.

—P.C.

Los Angeles, April 11, 2013

About the Author

Peter Clines grew up in the Stephen King fallout zone of Maine and started writing science fiction and fantasy stories at the age of eight, fueled by a steady diet of comic books and Saturday morning cartoons.

He made his first writing sale at age seventeen, and the first screenplay he wrote got him an open door to pitch story ideas at *Star Trek: Deep Space Nine* and *Voyager*. After working in the film and television industries for almost fifteen years, he moved on to write articles and reviews for *Cinema Blend* and *Creative Screenwriting Magazine*, where he interviewed dozens of Hollywood's biggest screenwriters and stars, including Kevin Smith, Shane Black, George Romero, Susannah Grant, Frank Darabont, Seth Rogen, Sylvester Stallone, Akiva Goldsman, Alex Kurtzman & Roberto Orci, and Will Forte.

He is the author of the Ex-Heroes series—*Ex-Heroes, Ex-Patriots,* and *Ex-Communication*—the acclaimed *14,* the mashup novel *The Eerie Adventures of the Lycanthrope Robinson Crusoe, The Junkie Quatrain,* numerous short stories, and countless film articles. He currently lives and writes somewhere in Southern California.

If anyone knows exactly where, he would appreciate a few hints.

Also by Peter Clines

"*The Avengers* meets *The Walking Dead* with a large order of epic served on the side . . . I loved it!"

—Ernest Cline, *New York Times* bestselling author of *Ready Player One*